THE ESSENCE OF SHADE

DEBORAH JEAN MILLER

Opal Stone Press

The Essence of Shade

deborahjeanmiller.com

First Edition

Cover design & book layout by Emilie Hendryx of E.A. Hendryx Creative

Copyediting by Debra Viguie

Author photo by Marisa Miller, Focal Point Studio

ISBN: 978-0-9980489-0-1 (Paperback edition)

ISBN: 978-0-9980489-1-8 (eBook edition)

Plymouth, Michigan

For my family.

The best and most beautiful things in this world cannot be seen or even heard, but must be felt with the heart.

— HELEN KELLER

A NOTE FROM THE AUTHOR

I've often been asked about how the plot for my book was formed; but it wasn't really a conscious effort. It seems it has forever been a whisper in my mind. It tip-toed into my head one day about 15 years ago and never left.

I always knew the beginning, the middle, and the end, but had no idea what went in between. So, I sat down one day and wrote. And wrote. And couldn't stop. In fact, I found myself caught in a time machine, trying to make it back to present day where the story would finally end.

This is a work of fiction portraying the errs we as humans make throughout our lives. And how the finger of God can take our tangled mess and weave a masterpiece. It's about a woman's journey, her struggles with faith, and grace that leads her home.

Now that it's all said and done, I'm grateful for my journey and for that gentle whisper in my mind.

CHAPTER ONE

Be careful not to forget the covenant of the Lord your God that he made with you; do not make for yourselves an idol in the form of anything the Lord your God has forbidden.

— DEUTERONOMY 4:23

Year 1996

Before her world imploded, Shade slept, her back nestled into Stan's chest. A snort inches from her ear jerked her from sleep. She rolled over and gazed at the man lying next to her. He slept, his mouth relaxed. Cupping her hand on his cheek, her eyes lingered. He didn't stir. She lay motionless, savoring the cool summer breeze wafting in through the open window as the flimsy horizontal blinds rapped against the pane.

As darkness surrendered to dawn, she tiptoed into the kitchen and skimmed the recipe she'd chosen for the Holy Grace Baked Goods Auction. In a life filled with simple pleasures, today was her favorite day of the year.

Inside the cramped kitchen of her modest home in rural Michigan, Shade admired her latest culinary creation—raspberry and white chocolate cheesecake with a shortbread crust. After placing the cake on a decorative platter, she added a dusting of confectioners' sugar.

Stanley's looming presence cast a shadow in the room. He embraced her from behind and nuzzled her neck with his clean-shaven chin. A whiff of menthol from the Aqua Velva after-shave filled her nostrils, leaving her woozy.

"My wife is the best darned baker in Emmet County. Everyone knows my Shady's donation will bring in the highest bid, just like last year's peaches and cream pie." His fingers tugged on her apron strings, and he slipped her smock over her shoulders.

"Darling," she said, "I've already showered. We need to leave in thirty minutes."

Stan's lips puckered in that special way of his. "This will only take ten. You know what the Bible says about honoring your man's needs."

Ten minutes turned out to be five, at best. After showering again, she gathered her thick chestnut brown hair into a traditional bun. As she dabbed a hint of gloss on her lips, Stan squeezed into the bathroom behind her, frowning.

"Why are you putting that stuff on? It makes you look older."

"It's only tinted lip gloss. You know me better than that."

After patting him on the back, she retreated to the bedroom to change. Dolefully, she removed the new dress from the closet. Stan had purchased the button-down, short-sleeved frock at Kmart while shopping for WD-40. He claimed he'd spotted it on a seventy percent-off rack, and it screamed "Shady" to him as he wandered by the flashing blue strobe light. Embellished with a brown and gold pineapple print, the polyester material sagged from her shoulders in generous folds, dipping well below her knees.

Biting her lower lip, she assessed her image in the mirror. She couldn't hurt his feelings, but she wished he would allow her to buy more fashionable clothing and wear a touch of makeup. At thirty-five, she had the face and figure of a woman in her twenties, but her garments added layers of frump.

Since their first day of marriage, Stan insisted on choosing her wardrobe—right down to her underwear. While her clothes looked like garage sale cast-offs, her undergarments—well those were another story. When the monthly Frederick's of Hollywood catalog arrived, he pored over every page circling a selection of risqué bras and panties before phoning in his order. And Shade appreciated having something new to wear—something that brought pleasure to Stan.

After donning her thick-lens eyeglasses, which magnified her ocean-blue eyes to the size of the frame, she packed up her cheesecake.

"I'll pull out the car and meet you in front," he said.

As they drove along the country road that led to Holy Grace, Stan broke the silence. "Have you heard from Addy?"

"I called and left a message asking if we could take Tyler to the picnic. I never heard back. You know how she feels about church-related events. She's afraid we're brainwashing our grandchild. She thinks we're on the lunatic fringe of Christianity."

"What's that supposed to mean? She's just ungrateful. And who is she to talk—living with that drug-addict thug, Jaime? And *we're* the lunatics?"

Slumping in her seat, Shade reflected on Addy's wayward lifestyle. Every day she prayed for Addy and Tyler, but nothing changed. When Addy had brought Tyler over a few weeks before, she appeared disheveled and lethargic. The tank top she tried to wear kept slipping off her frail, bony shoulder. Her once flawless complexion was now pale and drawn, her eyes lifeless and sunken. Plastered against her head, her jet-black hair looked like it had gone for a dip in Crisco. And there was that strange odor emanating from her body. Burnt plastic?

Despite her anxiety, Shade reveled in the time she got to spend with her grandson, though. The adorable two-year-old had stolen her heart.

"Why don't you let him live here with us until you get your life straightened out?" Shade had asked when Addy came to pick up Tyler.

"We're not having this conversation again. What makes you think you can raise him any better than I can? He has a home, and Jaime loves him. Yeah, I'm not the ideal daughter you hoped for, but I'm not a bad mother." She threw up her arms. "Just mind your own business and be grateful you get to see him at all." In a flurry, Addy scooped up Tyler and stormed out the door.

"Bye-bye, Gamma," Tyler said, waving.

Shade drew in her lips and followed them to the car. "Thanks for bringing him over today," she said, handing Addy a paper bag. "We made cookies. These are for you."

"Thanks." Addy snatched the bag out of Shade's hand and drove off without another word.

Shade never shared the unpleasant details of Addy's behavior with Stan. He got too worked up when it came to their daughter.

Their Ford Probe rolled into the parking lot, as church members ambled about, setting up the auction table. Blanche Buford, the church gossip, made a beeline to Shade and Stan. Shade tried to make a quick escape.

"Shade," said Blanche, eyeing her from head to toe. "Don't you look delightful today. Let me guess. You made a pineapple-upside-down cake for the auction this year."

Shade's face burned hot as she looked down, pushing her

eyeglasses against the bridge of her nose. Oblivious to the back-handed compliment, Stan swelled with pride.

"Actually, I made a cheesecake this year. Speaking of which, I'd better get this over to the auction table." She hurried off before the next round of insults could devour her dignity.

"Hey you two," Pastor Dave called. "I've been looking for you. Stan, do you mind leading us in prayer after the auction? I'd like our church elders to have a more prominent role in the summer picnic."

"I'd be happy to," Stan replied.

While Shade arranged her dessert on the auction table, Mary Crosby came over and gave her a hug.

"It's so good to see you," Mary said.

"And you, too," said Shade, smiling. Despite their thirty-year age difference, Mary was her dearest friend. Being in Mary's presence brought her comfort, like warm apple pie on a chilly fall day. Sunlight danced over Mary's cheerful face, igniting her auburn hair and illuminating her mismatched eyes; one pale green, the other dark brown.

"And your cheesecake looks delicious. You know all the women are intimidated by your baking skills."

"Well, they shouldn't be," said Shade as redness crept across her cheeks. "There are so many talented bakers in our church."

"But not like you. Baking is your special gift."

As if she were about to launch into a Broadway melody, Blanche swaggered to the front of the crowd and gripped the microphone. "Attention everyone. It's my great pleasure to lead the auction bidding today. But first, I'd like to thank our bakers. The money raised will go to our mission team in Haiti. So, let's give a hearty round of applause to all our Betty Crocker wannabes."

When her cheesecake came up for bid, Shade's stomach coiled

as waves of anxiety ripped through her body. Chewing her bottom lip, she tried blending into the crowd. Stan came to her side, his thick arm wrapped around her waist. Her tension eased.

"I bid thirty dollars," said one woman.

"Forty dollars," came the next bid.

Other bids followed until the final offer came in at a record-breaking sixty-three dollars.

Stan swept her off the ground, smothering her face with kisses. "Honey, you outdid yourself this year. I told you everyone knows you're the best baker in town."

Her hand flew to her mouth. She couldn't imagine anyone paying that much for her cheesecake. A swell of pride crept in if only for a second.

Pastor Dave nodded to Stan.

Stan stepped in front of the large crowd and bowed his head. "Dear Lord. We are so grateful for this blessed family of believers who've gathered today to enjoy fellowship and to raise money for a worthy cause."

With a surge in her heart, Shade was held captive by the sound of her husband's baritone voice reverberating through the crowd.

"And we thank the hands that prepared the baked goods for the auction today and for those who brought a dish to pass for our..." Stan paused, all the color draining from his contorted face. Then he stumbled onto the baked goods auction table, knocking Blanche Buford's triple-chocolate-mousse torte onto the lawn.

Stan's large form lay lifeless on the grass amid a cluster of smashed fruit pies and overturned layer cakes. His white, short-sleeved shirt bloomed with blobs of blueberry and strawberry filling. A lone cherry stuck to his vanilla-white forehead, like the topping on an ice-cream sundae.

Pandemonium arose as the crowd rushed to help. "Someone call an ambulance!"

At the age of fifty-six, Stanley Lane departed this world. Her beloved husband, the man she idolized and had never spent a night apart from, slipped away forever, enveloping Shade in a dreadful darkness that seeped into her pores. There were no other emotions. Once again, abandoned, she descended into the emptiness she had become all too familiar with as a young, lost child.

CHAPTER TWO

My frame was not hidden from you when I was made in the secret place, when I was woven together in the depths of the earth. Your eyes saw my unformed body; all the days ordained for me were written in your book before one of them came to be.

— PSALM 139:15-16

Year 1960

Amanda retreated to her bedroom, the August heat pressing her. Dampness hung in the air as she struggled to breathe. Her oversized cotton blouse clung to her damp skin in the dilapidated house she shared with her parents on a dusty Michigan road.

It was Friday. They often arrived home late after a night of drinking at the Yankee Clipper Lounge. The typical argument would erupt, provoking flying dishes and overturned furniture, her father stumbling down the rickety steps and spending the night in the rusted-out Chrysler Imperial. The same ole' story, the spool rewound.

Life for Amanda held no glimmer of hope. At fourteen, she gave herself to any interested male, young or old, hoping one day a man would whisk her away from the hell she was living in. But the 'knight in shining armor' didn't come—only a seed left in her belly eight months before. When her periods stopped, she contemplated telling her mom, but she knew her dad would beat her. So, she masked her bulging abdomen under loose-fitting clothes and spent most of her time alone in her room.

Amanda formulated a plan. Give birth in secret, wrap the baby up and place the child in a conspicuous location. She crafted a carrying handle from a leather belt and secured it to the sides of a wooden box left in an abandoned garage. Using hay gathered from a nearby field, she stuffed the box and covered the straw with old pillowcases.

At the local library, she came across a book, 'Giving Birth at Home.' She read it several times and knew what had to be done on that looming day.

After giving birth, she would run away and start a new life. And with any luck, a normal, loving family would adopt her baby.

Amanda lay motionless on her bed, the liquid voice of Roy Orbison's "Only the Lonely" broke through the quiet of her room. Without warning, a gush of water surged, soaking her underwear. Her head jerked, her eyes grew wide. *It's too soon. Not yet. Please God, don't let my parents come home now.*

They never checked on her. Her plan might succeed if she could silence her cries. As the contractions intensified, she stuffed a rag in her mouth. The searing, hot pain of birth crowning—the 'ring of fire'—ripped her. A baby girl lay between her legs, taking air into its lungs for the first time, crying.

Using scissors, she cut the umbilical cord and tied it off with a shoelace. In a blur, she cleaned up the evidence, wrapped the infant in pillowcases and placed her in the wooden box. Her parents were still out. With tears wetting her face, her body racked in pain, she stepped into the night toward the spot she had chosen to leave her newborn child.

She gazed at her one last time, reaching inside the box. The baby's tiny hand grasped her finger, clinging to her mother. "Fly away my little angel, to a fairy-tale land of happy-ever-after." She bent and kissed her forehead, her lips brushing the slime still clinging to her daughter's body. Guilt stung like a viper, as salty drops fell from her chin.

Carol went for a walk with her golden retriever. The morning sun blazed hot. Goldie ran ahead. She called to her, but Goldie wouldn't budge. Something in the large Oak tree piqued her interest. *Probably a squirrel.* Carol walked over and spotted a wooden box with a leather strap. It hung several feet from the ground on a limb in the crook of the tree. Faint crying came from inside. A baby. Its mouth open in a feeble cry, wrapped in dirty pillowcases. Flushed from the heat, the infant whimpered, struggling for air. Carol removed the box and raced home before calling the police. Officers rushed the baby to the hospital and called in child protective services.

Sucked into foster care, the newborn was given the name Shade Doe. "If it hadn't been for the shade of that old Oak tree, she wouldn't have survived," the social worker declared.

And so, Shade entered this world. Unwanted. Branded with a badge of shame. A throwaway. Human garbage. She would spend her early years living in several foster homes, a tumbleweed bouncing from one barren dust bowl to the next.

At the age of ten, she moved in with Millie and John Rodriguez —her third family. They were the family she craved. She had found her place in the world, thriving in school and at home. Evenings were spent reading the Bible together and discussing the virtues of living a Christian life.

As Shade grew older, she blossomed into a striking young lady and at fifteen, Matthew Caldwell took notice. While walking the hallway of Stonewood Middle School, Shade glanced around, referring to her class curriculum.

"What room are you looking for?"

"Room 256. History."

"Follow me. I'm in the same class," he said, smiling. "By the way, I'm Matthew."

"I'm Shade," she said, her eyes cast down.

"Interesting name, but I bet you've heard that before."

Matthew and Shade soon became close friends, often studying together and meeting at the local diner after Matthew's football practice.

"So, you planning to go to college?" asked Matthew, stabbing a french fry into a puddle of ketchup.

"Not sure, but I hope so. I live with a foster family. They said they would help with college if I kept my grades up. I don't know what area I wanna study, but I'd love to start my own business."

"My dad's hoping I can get into the University of Michigan on a football scholarship. I plan to study engineering."

Over the weeks, Matthew and Shade became inseparable.

"We need to talk," said Matthew, reaching for her hand at the diner. "I have feelings for you—feelings I've never had for anyone else. He leaned in, his expression softening. "I can borrow my dad's car on Friday. *Clueless* is playing at the show. Do you wanna go?"

"I'd love to."

They went on their first date. After the show, Matthew drove to his favorite spot down a wooded dirt road. He cut the engine and turned, pulling her into him.

Their first kiss sparked warm feelings throughout her body as he caressed her face, holding her in his arms. But his kisses became more aggressive, his hands groping underneath her sweater.

She drew back, pushing him away. "What are you doing?"

"I thought we meant something to each other. Guess I'm wrong."

"If that's all you're looking for, then take me home."

Matthew drew back and started the car. They drove home in silence. When they reached her house, she glanced over at him. "Please don't be angry."

He looked ahead, his chin jutting forward. "I gotta go."

She opened the door and stepped out as he peeled away, the taillights growing smaller, disappearing into the night. She stood sobbing, watching him drive out of her life.

Over the next several days, she moped around the house, her energetic smile turned to stone. She tried calling him, but he avoided her. In desperation, Shade approached him at school.

"I made a mistake. I care about you. Please, give me another chance. I want us to be together."

In November 1975, she missed her first period. She waited another month before telling Matthew.

"How do I know it's mine?" he asked. "How do I know you're not trying to trap me?"

With nowhere to turn, she went to Millie and John.

"We don't want you to have an abortion," said John. "We've contacted a Christian home for unwed mothers. You can live there. After the baby comes, you can put it up for adoption, and we'll talk about next steps."

"So…so I can't live here anymore? You don't want me?"

Shade looked at Millie, hoping to hear words of encouragement, but the pain etched on her face told her what she didn't want to hear.

She never saw or heard from Matthew again. His father moved the family to California, and Shade moved into the shelter for unwed mothers.

Once again, alone and insecure, she withdrew into herself. An outcast with no place to call home. No roots to anchor her to this world.

Mabel Johnson felt led by the Lord to mentor young, pregnant girls, so she started Mabel's House. The young women lived there until their babies arrived, but many had no place to go. Mabel gave in, allowing them to remain until they got their lives straightened out.

Shade kept to herself, often alone, staring off into emptiness. Wandering the hall one day, she stopped in front of a framed needlepoint and read the words of the poem:

"My life is but a weaving
Between my God and me.
I cannot choose the colors
He weaveth steadily.
Oft' times He weaveth sorrow;
And I in foolish pride
Forget He sees the upper
And I the underside.
Not 'til the loom is silent
And the shuttles cease to fly
Will God unroll the canvas
And reveal the reason why.
The dark threads are as needful
In the weaver's skillful hand

As the threads of gold and silver
In the pattern He has planned"

Mabel came up beside her, her arm around Shade's waist. "Some say this poem was written by a woman named Corrie ten Boom. Others say the author is unknown. I'm not really sure, but I enjoyed it so much I made a needlepoint and had it framed. It speaks about God weaving our lives like a tapestry. We only see the underside, a tangled mess of thread with no clear design. But from above, God sees a glorious, finished work of art, skillfully woven together."

Mabel turned and peered deep into Shade's eyes. "Honey, God often takes a bad situation and turns it into a blessing. I know you're frightened, but trust in the Lord. A favorite verse of mine is Jeremiah 29:11-13. Why don't you look it up?"

Alone in her room, Shade opened her Bible to the verse; "For I know the plans I have for you," declares the Lord, "plans to prosper you and not to harm you, plans to give you hope and a future. Then you will call on me and come and pray to me, and I will listen to you. You will seek me and find me when you seek me with all your heart."

Drawing her finger over the words, tears trickled down. She had been searching for solace, desperate and lonely. She had not expected her soul to be so hungry. Her eyes hung on a single word. *When. When* I seek, I will find. Closing her eyes, she meditated on the verse. A heavy weight lifted. Her pillar of shame crumbled. She wasn't alone. God drew her close, loving her, and she sensed His presence for the first time in her life. She belonged in this world, and God had a plan for her.

Mabel continued to guide Shade in her faith, and Shade drew nearer to God.

While attending Sunday church services with Mabel, Shade noticed a man watching her. An older man.

He approached her during coffee hour. "I'm Stanley Lane. Did you enjoy the service?"

"Yeah, I did," she said, stammering. "I'm Shade Doe. I've only been here a few times."

"I've been happy with this church. When you're a single man, the church becomes your home."

Over the next few months Stanley continued to seek her out after Sunday service.

"When is your baby due?" he asked.

"In three months. I live at a home for unwed mothers." His compassionate smile eased her anxiety.

During their frequent talks, she learned a great deal about Stanley. He owned his own home and managed a used car dealership in town. Born and raised in Michigan, he had no siblings, and both his parents had passed away by the time he turned eighteen. He had been on his own since, and at thirty-five, he had never married.

Stan stood over six-feet tall, lean and brawny. Losing ground to his expansive forehead, thin strands of hair formed a swirly pattern and moved like a cardboard flap when the wind caught hold. His razor-sharp nose jutted an awkward distance from his peculiar face, which sat perched atop his neck like a character on a PEZ dispenser. No, not a handsome man. But the more time she spent with him, the better looking he became—to her. He carried himself with a flair of confidence. She found herself drawn into his world.

One Sunday he asked her to go out for coffee. She talked it over with Mabel. She gave her blessing, but with caution. "I'm not sure what his intentions are, but I don't want to see you get hurt. He's quite a bit older than you. You'll be bringing new life into this world in a few months. Stay focused on your baby and pray for guidance."

Over the next month the two spent hours chatting over coffee after Sunday service. Despite their age difference they had a lot in common and shared a deep faith in God. Stanley revealed his goal to one day marry and start a family. He hadn't met the woman of his dreams, and time continued to tick away.

"Shade," he said, clearing his throat and repositioning a strand of hair. "I know this seems sudden, but I'm attracted to you. Yes, there's a twenty-year age difference, but I want to spend more time with you. In fact, the rest of my days with you—taking care of you. I've been searching for the right woman, and I feel God has placed you in my life. I know this seems hasty, but I want to marry you after the baby is born. I'll adopt the child and raise it like my own. Don't answer me now. I want you to pray about it." He reached for her hand. "I'm in love with you Shade. I want you to be my wife."

Her eyes glistened. Her smile frozen. *Could it be God's plan? This gift of a man sent to rescue my baby and me? To give me the family I never had?*

When Shade approached Mabel about Stan's proposal, Mabel sat silent, considering her words before responding. "I don't want to dampen your spirits, but we need to pray about this—for God's guidance. You know nothing about him. This is a big decision. I want you to make the right choice."

She lay in bed, her heart on fire. God had given her a gift, Stanley, and she couldn't be happier. A family. Her family.

Shade informed Mabel she had decided to marry Stan.

"Honey, I'm not sure this is the path God wants for you. You're still a child, and he's a grown man." Mabel placed her hands on Shade's shoulders, her eyes searching Shade's face. "Did you pray for guidance?"

"I know this is what God wants for me. It's what I've been hoping for. A family of my own."

In July 1976, Shade gave birth to a daughter and named her Adeline. When Shade turned sixteen, they were wed in a small ceremony.

Stanley accepted a job managing a car dealership in Emmet County, Michigan. It would be a new start for them. He sold his home and purchased a small house on Birch Street. True to his word, he adopted Adeline.

Shade settled into her new role as wife and mother. She spent her days honing her culinary skills, wanting her beloved Stanley to come home to a delicious meal after a long day at work. Everything she wanted in life came true, and she aspired for nothing more.

CHAPTER THREE

He will wipe every tear from their eyes. There will be no more death or mourning or crying or pain, for the old order of things has passed away.

— REVELATION 21:4

Year 1996

No one knows what a day might bring. Shade woke that morning, happily married and content. She went to bed, a widow. At thirty-five, she had no sense of self. Her identity hinged on the man she married twenty years ago. A part of her perished.

When evening came, Shade gathered the strength to call Addy. "Something terrible happened," she said, emotion gripping her.

"What's wrong? Are you okay? Mom—talk to me."

"It's your father. We—we were at the picnic. He collapsed. He's gone. A heart attack. Oh Addy, how will I live without him?"

"I'm on my way over."

Addy let herself in and found her mother sitting on the edge of her bed stroking a framed photo taken on their wedding day. Addy sat beside her.

"Mom, I'm here." Addy pulled her into her arms.

Shade sat weeping, clutching the frame against her chest. But no tears fell from Adeline's eyes.

In the weeks following the funeral, Shade slowly emerged from the blackened bowels of despair. Growing stronger each day, she pondered life beyond her bubble. Her former world had been small. A dollhouse. Stanley controlled every aspect of her existence. He believed women belonged in the home. And she never wanted it any other way.

She never finished high school, never drove on an expressway or pumped gas, knew nothing of their financial situation, didn't go out with friends and never went shopping without Stan. She didn't even know what she didn't know.

He had kept her tucked away all these years. But she had never desired to be anything but a good wife. Stan's good wife. Even her mothering skills were lacking, but now she needed to take control. She registered for the GED test and accepted a part-time job at a bakery in the charming beach town of Edelweiss.

With bills coming in, and little to no income, she met with Gwen Foster at Emmet County Bank.

"It's good to meet you," said Gwen, smiling at the reserved woman sitting across from her. "I'll walk you through your financial standing and make sure your name appears on everything. Mr. Lane had a checking account and a savings account. You also have a mortgage with us. It looks like you're behind on payments. I would suggest you write a check today to get caught up."

Noticing the startled look on Shade's face, Gwen's tone softened. "Do you know if your husband had a life insurance policy?"

"I—I'm not sure," she replied, pushing her glasses against her nose. "How would I know?"

"You might check for a policy at home. Or you could look in

your safe deposit box here at our bank. You'll need to bring in the key."

"Thank you. I'd like to write a check for the mortgage payments. How much do I owe?"

When she heard the amount, her heart fluttered, and her hand shook as she wrote the check.

Shade left the bank, heaviness crushing down on her. How would she keep up with the bills? The income from her new job would hardly cover expenses.

She sat at the kitchen table, lowered her head into her hands, and prayed. In the evening, she found a file box in the closet and looked for an insurance policy. Nothing. However, she found a key in a small envelope labeled 'Emmet County Bank.' She would return to the bank tomorrow.

That night, she called Addy. "Do you think I can come over this week and take Tyler for the day? I got a job at a bakery. I wanted to spend time with him before starting."

"What? You've gotten a job? And you're driving the car all by yourself? How does it feel to be free, doing things normal women do?"

She sighed. "Your father always treated me well. He only wanted to make things easier for me."

"No, he wanted to control you. It wasn't about you. It was about *him*. He had you right where he wanted you. Now look at you. You're like a little, lost puppy trying to find her way in the big, scary world."

"Please don't talk like that," said Shade. "Can I pick up Tyler this week?"

"Fine. How about Thursday? Jaime and I need to get out and have a little fun for a change. Maybe he can spend the night."

"That'd be great. I'll pick him up around ten. Thanks, honey."

At the bank the next day, Gwen Foster handed Shade the metal box and took her into a private room. Alone, Shade shuffled through the contents of the box.

Within the stack of paperwork, she found the deed to their house—in both their names—the title to the car, the registration for his hunting rifle and Stanley's birth certificate. She examined the birth certificate; Stanley Lane, born in 1940 in Spring Hill, Ohio. Mother's name: Hazel Lane. Father's name: Henry Lane. *That's odd. He never mentioned living in Ohio.* "Born and raised in Michigan," is what he'd said. Dismissing the thought, she went through the other documents.

At the bottom of the pile she discovered a brown envelope labeled "American Guardian Life." It appeared to be a life insurance policy with her name listed as the beneficiary. As she stared at the amount, her body melted like warm wax. She re-read the policy. Five-hundred-thousand dollars. With trembling hands, she placed the envelope in her purse and left the bank.

Two days later, she entered the nondescript building of American Guardian Life. An agent ushered her to a seat.

"Hello Mrs. Lane. Stanley came to see me about five years ago. He wanted to make sure you were taken care of if anything happened to him. He worried about your age difference. I see you brought the death certificate," said the agent, reviewing the document. "Everything looks to be in order. I'll have our auditors do a review. Provided everything looks good, you'll receive a check within a few weeks."

After leaving the building, she sat in her car, her fingers pressed against her lips. For the first time since Stanley's death she felt hope. *I need to be responsible with this money. I'll pay off the mortgage, put some into checking and invest a portion for Tyler's college tuition. And I need to keep this to myself. I don't want Addy asking for money to support her bad habits.*

On Thursday, Shade pulled up to the farmhouse Addy shared with Jaime. The mottled gray house appeared to have been dropped from the sky by a tornado and struggled to stand erect. An old beater car sat off to the side, along with a broken-down tractor leaning askew on the gravel driveway. A rusted pole barn in back showed signs of smoke damage.

She climbed the warped, wooden steps leading to the front door and called through the screen, "Addy, it's Mom."

Tyler ran to the door and screamed, "Gamma."

Addy ambled to the door as though her limbs were too heavy to carry her; the previous day's makeup caked around her eyes. She handed Shade a brown paper bag. "There's a change of underwear and some clothes. You can bring him back tomorrow afternoon. We'll be out late. I'd like to sleep in."

Shade flinched, her cold eyes boring into her. "Thanks." She took Tyler's hand and steered him down the steps and into her car. She noticed Jaime tinkering with the tractor. "Hey, buddy," he yelled. "Have a good time."

"Bye, Jaime. Sleep at Gamma."

With Tyler settled in back, she slid into the driver's seat, her mind trying to process the scene she'd just left. *How did my adorable grandson end up with such a sweet demeanor?* Addy seemed so indifferent to him, yet happiness filled his soul.

"Tyler, when we get to Grandma's house I'll make lunch, then we can go to the park. How does that sound?"

"Park," he squealed, clapping his hands.

After settling Tyler in bed that night, she pulled out a book of children's Bible stories, the one she used to read to Addy. His eyes grew heavy, and before long, he fell asleep. She gazed at him for some time, stroking his hair.

She reflected on the depth of her love for Tyler. She didn't remember feeling this much affection for Addy at his age. Her thoughts turned to Addy and Tyler's living conditions. How could they live in that house? And how did they earn money? Addy never worked a day in her life, and Jaime always seemed to be home. Was it possible they were on government assistance? She thought about giving them money, but something told her not to. She prayed God would watch over Tyler and Addy. If only Stanley were alive to help her carry this burden.

The phone rang early the next morning.

"It's Mary. Just checking in and wondering if you'd like to get together? I'll be at church this morning with my granddaughter, Leah. Thought I'd take her over to the playground. Maybe we could go to lunch after?"

"I have Tyler today. Why don't we meet you at church?"

Shade pulled into the parking lot. Her heart warmed at the sight of her good friend.

"Tyler, this is Leah," said Shade.

"Wee-uh, pwetty," said Tyler, waddling over and grabbing her auburn hair. He planted a wet, open-mouth kiss on her lips.

Leah squealed, jumping up and down. They toddled off, holding hands.

"Well, it looks like they hit it off," said Mary. "You look great. How've you been?"

"Much better. I'm feeling more confident each day. I got a job at Bonnie's Bakery in Edelweiss. I start next week. And I'm working on my GED."

"I'm so proud of you. You've lived a sheltered life. I'm happy to see you're becoming more independent."

Shade looked off, searching for words. "Before Clive passed away, did you feel independent in your marriage? Stan always told me that a good Christian woman's role was to take care of her husband and the house. And honestly, I wanted nothing else."

Mary sighed, her lips curling inward. "I always felt independent. Clive allowed me the freedom to be my own person. We had a relationship built on respect for one another."

Shade stared at the ground, shuffling her feet. "You know, it never bothered me—being dependent. But now I feel cheated."

"Maybe Stan didn't want you to worry. It was his way of being the man of the house," Mary said, patting her arm.

A mass of ringlets poked through the back door. "Hey you two," said Blanche. "I was practicing for choir and thought I heard voices. Shade, honey, I've been thinking about calling you. What do you say I take you out for the day? We can do a little shopping and pampering. My treat. It'll help lift your spirits. How does that sound?"

She pushed her glasses against her nose, looking over at Mary.

Mary smiled and whispered, "She wants to do this for you. She means well."

"Thank you, Blanche. I'd like that," said Shade, half-smiling. "How sweet of you to offer."

After getting Tyler dressed, Shade packed his few belongings into the paper sack. "Are you ready to go home?"

"Sleep at Gamma? Again?" he asked.

His words stung her heart. "No, honey. Not tonight. You have to go home. But I'm sure your mommy will be excited to see you."

"Home. Jaime."

When she pulled up to the farmhouse, Jaime stood nearby talking to a guy with straggly long hair and tattoos running down both arms. His protruding belly peeked through random holes in his grease-stained muscle shirt.

Lifting Tyler from the car seat, she gave him a hug. "Give Grandma a kiss goodbye."

Tyler wrapped his arms around her neck and kissed her face. "Get down now." He squirmed out of her arms and ran across the lawn toward Jaime.

"Hey buddy. We missed you." Jaime swooped Tyler up into the air and twirled him around, while the other guy guffawed, open-mouthed, backslapping Jaime and swigging down a beer. The man sneered at her, baring brown-pitted teeth that looked like a Samba line of ants were dancing across his choppers.

Darting to the front steps, Shade shouted through the screen, "It's Mom—with Tyler."

Addy shuffled to the door. "Hey. Come in. You want something? Beer? Pop?"

"No, thanks."

Shade looked around. Dirty dishes lay stacked on the kitchen counter, clothing strewn across the furniture. Shade jumped when a pair of boxer shorts came alive.

"Those shorts are moving."

"Relax. It's Flipper. Jaime bought Tyler a hamster. He doesn't like his cage."

"I don't think it's safe for wild animals to be running loose with Tyler around. What if it has rabies?"

"It's not a coyote. It's a hamster, okay?" Addy walked to the door and held it open. "Too bad you can't stay."

On the drive home, she obsessed over Tyler. Her mind went to Stan. *If only he were alive. Maybe we could figure something out together.*

On Saturday, Blanche rolled into Shade's driveway in a red

metallic Fleetwood Cadillac. Shade peered out the front window, taking in Blanche's outfit. She wore a chic, pink pantsuit with clear, plastic sling-back sandals dusted with lavender and gold glitter flakes. Her blonde hair rested high atop her head in a mass of loose curls, cascading down the nape of her neck.

She opened the door, and in swept Blanche. "Your place is so cozy, honey," said Blanche, her head snapping, causing her ringlets to dance. "I'm sure you've been thinking about redecorating now that Stan's gone. But first things first. We're gonna do a number on you today, and it's all on me. I've scheduled an appointment to get your hair and makeup done, and then we'll grab lunch and go off on a little shopping spree. Doesn't that sound like fun, honey?"

"It sounds wonderful," she replied, smiling. "You didn't have to do this, but I'm grateful."

As they drove, Shade's posture softened as she thought about the day ahead. She had never had her hair done in a salon. She'd always cut her own hair, and Stan trimmed the back. Since she wasn't allowed to wear makeup, she didn't know what to buy or how to apply it.

Entering the salon, Blanche introduced Shade to Flavio. "Flavio is gonna transform you, honey, so put your seatbelt on."

Flavio sat Shade in the chair and removed the pins from her bun. Her voluminous hair fell past her shoulders. He ran his fingers through her mane, tousling it this way and that, walking around her, eyeing her from every angle.

"Well, it looks like I've got my work cut out for me. The good news is you have a flawless complexion and a great head of hair. The bad news…I'll have to pull out my Weed Wacker to cut through your coif."

Blanche and Flavio burst into laughter. Shade looked down, her face aflame.

"Oh, honey, we're just teasing," said Blanche, squeezing her hand. "You're gonna be stunning by the time he's done. They don't call him the Miracle Worker for nothing."

Flavio went to work shaping her chestnut brown hair into a flattering layered cut falling to her shoulders. He applied subtle highlights to "add interest," according to Flavio. Twirling the brush through her hair, he shaped it into a contemporary style. Shade's eyes popped wide.

"How do you like it?" asked Flavio.

"I'm speechless," she replied, turning her head from side-to-side, studying her reflection. "I can't believe it's me."

"Well, we're just getting started my friend. Why don't you take off those Coke-bottle goggles, and I'll do your makeup?" When she removed her glasses, Flavio let out a shriek. "I can't believe you've kept those beautiful azure eyes hidden beneath those magnifiers. Stunning. Absolutely stunning."

Flavio plucked her eyebrows and applied a light foundation and a dusting of blush to her cheekbones. He brushed a light taupe shadow on her eyelids, added a smudge of eyeliner, a hint of pale pink lipstick and finished with several coats of black mascara.

Shade stared in disbelief, her smile widening into a brilliant grin. "I can't get over how different I look. Thank you so much."

Strolling to the Cadillac, Blanche locked her arm through Shade's. "Let's grab lunch, and then we'll go shopping. Sound okay, honey?"

"It sounds terrific. I feel like a princess, and I'm having the best time."

"Well, I'm glad you're enjoying yourself. You deserve it. I want you to call my eye doctor and ask him about getting you fitted with contact lenses. I think it'll make a difference."

"It would be nice to get rid of these heavy glasses."

They went into several stores. Blanche purchased new tops and pants, shoes, purses, and a handful of skirts and blouses for Shade. Exhausted, they called it a day.

On the ride home, she thanked Blanche again. "Why did you do all this for me?"

"Well, honey, I see you at church, and I was always a little sad for you. No offense. You're such a sweet thing, but you're like a little mouse, the way you followed that man around." She patted her hand. "I'm blessed to be comfortable financially, and I wanted to do something nice for you. It's gonna be hard trying to make it in this crazy world. I think it'll be easier for you if you fit in a little better. And with starting a new job next week why not start fresh with a new look?"

"I don't know what to say. I'm overwhelmed by your generosity."

After they parked in the driveway, she embraced Blanche. Watching her pull away, deep gratitude and love surrounded Shade. *Every person has a story. We judge people too quickly without ever knowing anything about them.* She prayed God would open her eyes and help her see the inner beauty in others.

On Sunday morning, Shade arrived at church. Pastor Dave walked over to greet her. "I almost didn't recognize you. You look so—so different. But in a good way. How are you doing?"

"I'm doing well, thank you."

"Our church has been praying for you."

"I don't know what I would have done without the support of Holy Grace."

Shade spotted Blanche walking toward her. Instead of running the other way, she threw open her arms and welcomed her embrace.

"Honey, I can't believe how beautiful you look. Now remember, head high and walk tall. You're a new woman. A woman of essence."

"Let me look at you," said Mary, taking Shade's hands and holding her at arms-length. "You look stunning. Once you get settled in your job, I'd like to have you and Blanche over for dinner."

"I'd love that. Let me know what I can bring."

"A dessert, of course. After all, it's your calling."

Shade eased into life, a single woman, becoming more confident each day. Nothing could fill the void in her heart, but she knew with time and prayer things would continue to improve.

CHAPTER FOUR

I can do all this through him who gives me strength.

— PHILIPPIANS 4:13

Ready to conquer the world, Shade sprang out of bed and headed toward the shower. Her first day of work—ever. Fear and doubt found their way back, binding her. *There is nothing to fear but fear itself,* she chanted, but she couldn't hush its ugly voice.

After dressing and eating a light breakfast, she left her house at 6 a.m., allowing plenty of time for any unanticipated delays. Upon reaching the end of her street, the low fuel indicator light illuminated. She'd been driving on the same tank of gas since Stan's passing.

Pulling up to the pump, she glanced around the car interior looking for a mechanism to open the fuel tank door. She found the lever and spent another ten minutes trying to figure out what to do until a young woman came to her rescue. Thanking the woman, she jumped back into her car and hurried off. *Oh God, please don't let me be late.*

Nearing the expressway, her vision tunneled, and her palms dripped with sweat. She eased onto the entrance ramp and came to a complete stop at the end with her left blinker on. Cars sped by on the left in a blur, and no one stopped to let her in. Drivers lined up behind her, horns tooting. With her eyes squeezed shut she pressed her foot hard on the accelerator, and the Ford Probe lurched forward onto the expressway. Quivering, she joined the mass of racing vehicles. The sound of brakes screamed out behind her, and the violent bang of metal pierced her ears. Glancing in the rearview mirror, she witnessed several cars taking on a new shape. A delivery truck overturned, its contents tumbling onto the road. She drove on, praying no one was hurt.

Ten minutes late, she arrived at Bonnie's Bakery, breathless and soaked in her own perspiration. Rushing through the front door, she stumbled and knocked over a small display table, sending 'day old bread at day old prices' flying. Bonnie stood with hands on her hips, rolling her eyes.

"Oh, I'm so sorry. And I'm sorry I'm late. I promise it won't happen again."

"Well, I hope this isn't a sign of things to come. After you pick up the mess you made, you can go over there and grab an apron, and I'll show you the ropes," said Bonnie, giving her a once-over. "I almost didn't recognize you. You don't look like the same person I interviewed."

"I wanted to make a good impression so I had a makeover."

"Well, I'd rather you work on your punctuality and balance."

Bonnie took her into the back room and gave her her first task. "This is an industrial mixer. And here is the recipe for my lemon and blueberry muffins. The ingredients are along that wall and in the refrigerator. Will you be okay if I leave you alone? I need to get out front and assist my other employee, Sally. It'll get busy soon."

"Oh, yes. I can handle this. I'm on it."

The Beast stood atop four metal claws, grimacing. She'd never met an industrial mixer, and the massive contraption sent her heart into overdrive. She considered fleeing through the back door, but her gut told her to stay. Buck it up.

Steadying her nerves, she blew out a succession of short pants before dropping sticks of butter into the stainless-steel bowl. She located the lever and set it to the lowest speed. While the butter was creaming, she added sugar and eggs, buttermilk, vanilla, and lemon zest. Off to the side, she mixed the flour, baking powder and salt, and carried the gigantic bowl over to the mixer. While adding the flour mixture to the butter mixture, her sleeve snagged the control lever. The motor whirred to high, and the entire bowl flipped. Flour sprayed, and the room became a winter whiteout, dusting her face and clothes. She whirled, scanning for towels, when in walked Bonnie.

"Well, I see you're getting to know your way around the kitchen."

Sally appeared and threw her hand to her mouth; a small gasp escaped. She rolled up her sleeves and went to work helping Shade wipe down the room.

At the end of the day, Shade approached Bonnie. "I don't blame you if you want to get rid of me. I thought I could do a good job, but I see I've created more problems."

"Hey, don't worry. We'll both look back one day and have a good laugh. Now go home, get some rest, and let's start fresh tomorrow. And be here at 7 a.m. Sharp."

"I promise I won't disappoint you."

Sally walked with Shade to the parking lot and gave her hand a squeeze. "I doubt every day will be as exciting as today. Thanks for making it so memorable. I think we're gonna work well together, you and I. Bonnie is a tough boss, but she has a heart of gold. As long as you're giving a hundred percent she'll have your back. I'll see you Wednesday."

"Thank you. And thanks for helping me today. I'm looking forward to working with you."

On the drive home, she reflected on the day. She liked Sally, and she sensed the two of them would get along. Sally couldn't be over twenty-one. A cute girl. Tall with long curly blond hair and soft brown eyes. She seemed mature for her age. Despite the rough start, gladness filled Shade's heart.

Shade kicked off her shoes and called Addy to arrange a day to pick up Tyler. Exhausted, she sat in front of the TV with a bowl of Corn Flakes and turned on the local news.

"This morning, traffic was tied up on the interstate expressway for two miles after a car merged into oncoming traffic at a high rate of speed, causing a massive pile-up."

Her mouth fell open. Milk dribbled on her chin.

"No one was injured, but several vehicles, including a meat delivery truck, incurred extensive damage. Adding to an already chaotic situation, what appeared to be a hindquarter of beef splattered across the expressway. Crows swooped down and began feeding on the meat." The anchors openly grinned. *"One witness said it reminded her of a scene from The Birds. The witness went on to say she saw a woman barreling into traffic and suspected she may have been drinking or on drugs. Police have little information on the perpetrator, and witnesses couldn't identify the make or model of the car. Anyone with information is asked to call the Emmet County police."*

The sports anchor reached inside his breast pocket. "Let me find out where my mother-in-law was today."

She dropped her head in her hands, trying to erase the lingering image. She pressed the power button on the remote and went to bed. Stan's robe hung on the closet door, waiting for him. Her mind churned. The awful accident. Whirring mixers. Pumping gas. *Stan. Oh, Stan.* Tears clouded her eyes. She missed him. His body next to hers. His arms holding her secure. *Will this emptiness ever fade—this feeling of loneliness?*

The dust stirred when she drove down the driveway to the farmhouse. Addy sat on the front porch smoking a cigarette. Tyler played out front, entertaining himself.

"Is that you Mom?" Addy asked, flicking her cigarette over the side of the porch. "What in the hell happened? You look twenty years younger." She stood, eyeing her. "I'm shocked. You know, you're actually quite attractive, but you wouldn't have known it hidden beneath that Amish costume Stan made you wear. It's good to see you're dressing like a normal person."

"Whoa, Mrs. Lane, I didn't recognize you," said Jaime, stepping onto the porch. "I came over to meet the foxy lady talking to Addy. Wow, what a mind-blower."

A hot blush pulsed. "I thought it might be a nice change for me."

"Hell, yeah," said Jaime. "For sure. Now that you're single, maybe I can fix you up with one of my bros."

Tyler waddled over and wrapped his arms around Shade's legs. Grateful for the interruption, she bent and picked him up.

His palms cupped her face. "Gamma. Sleep at Gamma?"

"Not tonight, honey. Grandma has to work tomorrow, but we'll spend the day together."

Shade never tired of spending time with Tyler. She loved watching the little O's his mouth formed when he experienced something new in his tiny world. "Whas sat?" he asked repeatedly, as she drove to her house. Her heart pained for his well-being. She wished he could stay with her, away from the dysfunctional environment he lived in. She prayed things would change.

"It's so good to see you," said Mary, greeting Shade at her door the following evening. "You've been so busy, I wasn't sure you could come."

The three ladies were finally getting together for the promised dinner. Shade had been looking forward to spending time with her friends.

"I wouldn't have missed it for the world. I hope you like mocha pecan pie."

"It sounds delicious. Blanche is here helping me set the table."

"It looks like you got contact lenses," said Blanche. "Aren't you the prettiest thing these days? How about a glass of wine? I brought red and white. What do you prefer?"

"Gosh, I don't drink wine much." In fact, she had never tasted wine. "But why not? Maybe white?"

"You got it." Blanche poured a generous glass of Sauvignon Blanc. They sat sipping their wine and chatting while Mary prepared dinner.

"Can we help?" asked Shade.

"Definitely not. I want you to enjoy yourselves."

"Tell us about your new job and what you've been doing," said Blanche.

"Well, I love my job, and the location is great. I'm working three days a week, but that might change. Bonnie, the owner, opened the bakery fifteen years ago, and sales have increased each year. It's busy, so time flies." She took a gulp of wine, enjoying the taste. "And, I got my GED and scored in the top ten percent of test takers. I'm planning to take computer classes soon. And I've been spending time with Tyler. Life's been a real blessing."

The wine oozed into her, and she felt her body release. She had always kept her guard up, but tonight she felt comfortable sharing her life with her friends. "I'm worried about Adeline and Tyler. Addy lives with a guy, not the father of Tyler, who's not a good influence on either of them. I don't think he works, but they get by—somehow. The environment isn't good for my grandson, and I don't know what to do. I've asked Addy to let me take him for a while, but she's opposed. I feel helpless and wish Stan were here to help me through this." Her eyes teared up. "Oh, I'm sorry. I didn't mean to be a downer tonight."

Blanche gave her a hug. "Honey, that's what friends are for. To share our highs and lows with and to build up each other. Here, let me pour you another glass of wine."

Mary finished in the kitchen and set a platter of Chicken Piccata on the table, along with bowls containing buttered red skin potatoes, garlic green beans, and a tossed salad. They bowed their heads, and Mary said grace.

"Mary, you've outdone yourself," said Blanche. "Everything looks delicious."

After finishing their meal, Blanche turned to Shade. "I don't think I ever heard how you and Stanley met. You must have gotten married young to be a grandmother at thirty-six."

She had never discussed this topic with anyone. When she was around others, Stan was glued at her side. But tonight, she told them everything. Her years in foster care, the home for unwed mothers, and how Stanley offered her the family she never had.

"Stan was my gift from God. He adopted Addy and raised her as if she were his own. Stan is—or was—the love of my life. I miss him every day."

Mary and Blanche wrapped Shade in their arms.

"Thanks for telling your story," said Mary. "I always thought Stanley was Addy's biological father. It must have been hard for you being so young and pregnant. At what age did you tell Addy about Stan?"

"She found out when she left home. She got pregnant and moved in with Tyler's dad, Scott. She needed her birth certificate. I wanted to tell her sooner, but Stan wanted to wait."

"She must have been shocked," said Blanche, shaking her head. "That's quite a life you've lived, honey. And you've nothing to be ashamed about. We don't all get the same opportunities in this world."

"Well, enough about me. Why don't I cut the pie?" Shade got up from her chair and weaved into the kitchen.

"You go sit, and I'll slice the pie," said Mary. "How about some coffee?"

"So, what secret tales do you two have?" asked Shade, as they were eating pie and sipping coffee. "I can't be the only one with a checkered past."

"I'll go," said Blanche. "At eighteen, I left home for New York to become a Broadway star. I auditioned for the Rockettes but didn't make it. They said I upstaged the other girls. Can you believe it? Feeling defeated—and starving—I walked to a café and ordered water and waited for the breadbasket. When the bread arrived, I took a napkin and wrapped it up and started to leave. The waiter stopped me, demanding I order something. A handsome man sitting at a table walked over and told the waiter he would take care of my bill. And that's how I met my Harry. He was ten years my senior and a partner at a large law firm in Michigan. Over the next few months, he came to New York more often and one day proposed. And I accepted. It's been a comfortable marriage, but we're different. I'm outgoing, and he's a homebody. I enjoy church, and he thinks it's nonsense. But, he's been good to me. We never had children. We tried, but it didn't work out. So, it's just been me and my Harry." She sat back in her chair. "Well Mary, it's time for you to reveal your secrets."

Mary leaned forward, her hands clasped on the table. "My story is one of redemption. Clive and I met when we were in high school. We got married right after graduating and had our daughter Carly a year later. We were young and didn't have time to work on our marriage. Struggling to make ends meet, bills piled up, and Clive started going to the bar after work, coming home drunk. Before long, our parents intervened. They threatened to take Carly away so Clive joined Alcoholics Anonymous.

By the grace of God, he met a man who told him he attended Holy Grace Baptist church and thought it would be an excellent church for a young family like ours. Over time, this man led us to Christ, and we haven't looked back. The man's name was Mark. When we attended Holy Grace, we asked about a man named Mark, but no one ever heard of him, and we never saw him again. Call it what you like, but we felt certain he was an angel sent by God. Every day I thank God for putting us on the right path. I miss Clive, but I know I'll see him again, and I have Carly and my granddaughter, Leah. I've lived a blessed life."

A crooked smile grew across Shade's face. "I don't think I can drive home," she said, her head listing from side to side.

"Oh my," said Mary. "You can stay here tonight. Blanche, can you help me get her to bed? Thankfully, she doesn't work tomorrow."

They escorted her to the bedroom, removed her shoes and tucked her in. Her eyes narrowed, struggling to focus. "Stanley, when are you coming home?" she mumbled, before passing out.

Shade awoke, her head heavier than she remembered. She heard noise coming from the kitchen and thought back to the night before. She pulled herself out of bed.

"Good morning," said Mary. "You look so much better."

"Oh, I hope I didn't embarrass myself. I can't remember when I've had that much fun, but I think I'll pay for it."

"You didn't embarrass yourself. I enjoyed learning more about your past. You've always been so guarded. I feel closer to you now. And I won't ever judge you."

She gave Mary a hug. "Thanks so much for everything. If God had granted me a mother I'd want someone just like you." She kissed Mary on the cheek. "I better be on my way."

"How about some coffee? I can make you breakfast."

"You've done enough. I've got too much to do today. I love you."

Returning home, she put on a pot of coffee and made a poached egg. After showering, she called Addy.

"I'd like to pick up Tyler this week," said Shade when Addy answered the phone. "Maybe the three of us could spend the day together. I could make lunch, and maybe we could all go shopping."

"I'd rather you two spend the day together so I can spend time alone," she said, slurring her words. "Funny, you seem concerned about spending time with Tyler, but you never seemed to wanna spend time with me when I was young. Why is that? Is it because you're all alone now without Mr. Control Freak dictating your every move?"

"I don't want to argue. I'm just trying to be a good grandmother to Tyler."

"What about being a good mother to me? Why weren't you ever concerned about me? You were only concerned about *him*."

"What's gotten in to you? Why are you trying to start an argument? You know both your father and I cared deeply about you."

"Oh? Did you ever pay attention to what really went on? Those times Stan took me with him on Saturdays—didn't you ever wonder why we stayed away so long? Why you never went with us? Or what about those nights he insisted on reading me bedtime stories with the door shut? He told you it was our special time alone. Just me and Daddy."

The words struck her like a wrecking ball. Her legs turned to Jell-O. She slid down the wall melting into the floor.

"Why—why are you saying those things?" she said, lips quivering. "Your father would never, ever do anything like that. He was a good Christian man."

"He's not my father, and he was not a good Christian man. He was a child molester, Mother. A predator. It's about time you faced reality. You did nothing about it." The line went dead.

She couldn't digest it. She sat on the floor in a heap, the phone slipping out of her hand. Her heart staged a stampede in her chest. She went numb. Paralyzed. She remained catatonic for what seemed like hours before she found the energy to stand.

CHAPTER FIVE

Watch out for false prophets. They come to you in sheep's clothing, but inwardly they are ferocious wolves.

— MATTHEW 7:15

Shade pulled herself up from the floor, steadying her gait. She made her way to the bathroom, sinking to her knees on the cold tile. Clutching the porcelain bowl, she retched up clear liquid. Her throat burned from bile, a salty mix of tears stained her face. Darkness folded, choking her heart.

It can't be true. She's lying. I would have known. She's trying to hurt me, or she's high. Delusional. And she's jealous of my affection for Tyler.

Unable to sleep, she lay in bed. Thinking. Trying to make sense of Addy's words. She prayed, asking God for guidance. She would call Addy next week. Give her time to come to her senses.

The next morning Shade drove to work, trying to bury Addy's haunting words.

"Good morning," said Bonnie. "It's gonna be busy today. We have a corporate order for twenty-five coffee cakes, and they want them by 8 a.m. tomorrow. Do you think you can handle it alone?"

"I'll get right on it."

"Is everything okay?" asked Bonnie, noticing the change in her demeanor.

"I'm fine," she replied. "A restless night, but I'll be okay. I'll get on those coffee cakes right away."

Shade busied herself in the prep area, working in silence, lost in thought. Sally came into the kitchen.

"Morning Shade. Why don't you let me help? It's slow out front."

"I'm good."

"You okay? You seem quiet."

"I'm fine. A little tired, that's all."

She finished baking the coffee cakes, packaged them in boxes, and cleaned the kitchen. "I guess I'll head out now, unless you need anything else," said Shade, half smiling.

"Go ahead," said Bonnie. "You've done enough for one day. Are you sure everything's okay?"

"I'm sure. I'll see you Monday." She turned away, her eyes glossy.

On Sunday morning she pulled into the Holy Grace parking lot. She spotted Mary, and they settled into the pew. Blanche performed a solo, one of Shade's favorite hymns. Her voice filled the small church. Shade struggled to contain her emotions. Funny, she never felt Blanche could sing. She sounded like a tortured bird. But today God comforted her through the words of the hymn.

"Let's open our Bibles and turn to 1 John 4:1," said Pastor

Dave. "Dear friends, do not believe every spirit, but test the spirits to see whether they are from God, because many false prophets have gone out into the world," he said, closing the Bible. "People aren't always what they seem. They may talk like Christians, attend church and even work in church leadership. Many of us sense something is wrong, but we look the other way, not wanting to believe the ugliness of the world. It's too painful. The Holy Spirit has given us a discerning heart, and if we continue to trust in Christ, seeking His guidance, He will lead us into all truth."

Shade's mind sparked. *Is this message for me? I've asked for guidance for Addy, but is God telling me something?* She didn't pay attention to the rest of the sermon. Something inside her was prodding. Her mind kept drifting back to the Bible verse.

When the sermon concluded, Mary asked if she wanted to go out for breakfast.

"No, I'll pass. I'm not feeling well." She gave Mary a hug and left.

Inside the quiet stillness of her home, she sat at the kitchen table and prayed for a spirit of discernment and the wisdom to recognize the truth. The aroma of fresh coffee filled the small kitchen. She sat nursing a cup, lost in reflection. Addy's haunting words were lurking. She tried pushing them from her mind, but something nudged.

On Monday she left work early and drove to Emmet County Bank to revisit the contents of the safe deposit box. After Stan died, she went through everything, but something kept prompting her. *Look closer,* a small voice told her. She pulled out his birth certificate and put it in her purse.

Back at home, she reviewed the document. 'Place of Birth—Spring Hill, Ohio.' She recalled one of her first meetings with Stan and remembered him telling her he lived in Michigan his entire life. Born and raised. Why lie about his place of birth? And then she noticed something she had overlooked. 'Number of children born and living to this mother and father (including this child)—two.' Stan said he was an only child. A slow shock radiated through her body. He had a brother or sister.

She stared at the birth certificate, her palms greasy with sweat. With two days off the following week she could make the drive to Ohio. It would be the farthest trip she'd ever driven, but she needed to understand if there was more to Stan than she realized.

She packed an overnight bag and examined the TripTik from AAA; the route marked to the Holiday Inn in Spring Hill, Ohio.

At 5 a.m. she got up and made a small lunch for the five-hour trip. She considered alerting someone but decided against it. She didn't want to explain the purpose of her trip.

An hour into the drive her pent-up anxiety faded, leaving her with a sense of renewal and self-discovery. The cloudless fall day illuminated the reds and golds of the autumn leaves—God's fingerprints everywhere in the world. She flipped through the stations looking for a song to complement her carefree mood. Whitney Houston's "I Will Always Love You" blared from the speakers, a favorite song.

She was only somewhat familiar with the lyrics, but that didn't stop her from snapping out the words, or some words, at the top of her lungs. The shrill of inhaled helium filled the air. With the windows open and the warm breeze blowing through her hair, she basked in her newfound freedom.

A man on a motorcycle kept pace beside her, tossing a glance. A spark of sunlight bounced off his blinding white teeth, causing her to squint. She gulped in a blast of air and rolled up the window, staring straight ahead. Clutching the steering wheel, she slowed the car. *What if he's one of those Hells Angels, trying to lure me off the road to rape me?* When he slowed, she sped up, and he kept pace. She pressed her foot to the pedal and shot forward. With her heart racing and sweat clinging to her body she pulled off at the next rest area.

Vacationing families filled the parking spaces. Safe. She found a spot next to a trash container and pulled in. A small child sat crying after having dropped his ice cream cone. Poor little guy. He was about Tyler's age. The mother scooped up the cone from the pavement and tossed it into the trash, causing the little toddler to wail.

She found a vacant picnic table and unwrapped her chicken salad sandwich. A handsome man in a black leather jacket approached.

"Hi. My name's Calvin. The guy on the motorcycle."

"Oh" she stuttered, fumbling with her sandwich and dispensing globs of chicken onto the table. "I'm Shade. Nice to meet you."

"Mind if I sit?"

"Sure. I mean—I guess."

"Where you headed? Beautiful day for a drive."

"Ohio. Look, I don't mean to be rude, but I should get going."

"Aren't you gonna eat your sandwich? You just sat down."

"Um—er—right. My sandwich. I didn't realize the time. I'm running late."

"Well, I wanted to introduce myself and thought maybe you'd like to hang sometime."

"Hang what?"

"You know, hang out."

Intense heat burned her cheeks; she worried her hair would catch on fire. No one had made a pass at her since she'd met Stan, and she wasn't sure how to react.

"I—I'm flattered, but I'm married." She feigned a smile, gathered her lunch and stood up, her legs catching between the bench and the table, causing her to stagger. She freed herself, straightening her blouse.

"Well, I'm married too. If you change your mind, here's my number," he said, handing her a card.

"Thank you." Shade took the card and hurried back to her parking spot, her legs moving faster than she expected. She tripped, flailing hands waving wildly in the air and sprawled headlong into the trash can. The container tipped, scattering garbage everywhere. She recovered and sprang into a perpendicular position with melted double-dip chocolate ice cream dripping from her new hair design. She raced to her car and sped out of the rest area, gravel spraying from her tires. In her rearview mirror she spotted Calvin sprinting her way, blurred in a cloud of dust. *What an idiot I am.* Despite her antics, a flame of flattery flickered. Calvin was, without question, a good-looking man. And interested. A newfound confidence settled. She continued on her road trip, dabbing ice cream from her hair.

Welcome to Ohio. A sharp tug of nausea ripped through her gut as she read the sign. She feared what she might learn.

After settling in her room at the Holiday Inn, she went downstairs to the front desk and asked for directions to the Vital Statistics Office and the Public Library.

Stan claimed both his parents passed away by the time he turned eighteen. Arriving at Vital Statistics, she requested the birth and death certificates of his parents, Hazel and Henry Lane. The clerk provided a copy of both documents.

Settled in her car, she examined the paperwork:

Henry Lane of Spring Hill, Ohio, born in 1918, passed away in 1976; Hazel Lane of Spring Hill, Ohio, born in 1920, passed away in 1994.

Her heart galloped as she sat staring at the documents. His

father died the year she married Stan. His mother passed away two years ago. Visions shuffled through her mind like an animated flipbook. *Why did you lie Stan? What other secrets are you hiding?*

She kept digging. At the Public Library, she found the obituary archives and located his parent's records:

Henry Lane, July 31, 1976. Beloved husband of Hazel Lane. Loving father of Caroline (Lane) Baskin and Stanley Lane.

Hazel Lane, March 30, 1994. Beloved wife of the late Henry Lane. Loving mother of Caroline (Lane) Baskin and Stanley Lane.

The hairs on her arms stood tall. Stan had a sister? Caroline? Stan must have been younger. The relentless thudding of her heart vibrated in her ears. It was too much information for one day. She needed a good meal and some rest.

After washing up at the hotel, she went for a bite to eat. She had never eaten in a restaurant alone. A first. She ordered the daily special and picked at her food.

Thoughts exploded. *Maybe his parents did something horrible to him, and he ran away. But why not tell me? And why didn't he talk about his sister?*

Back at the hotel, in bed and exhausted, she pulled out her Bible and opened to the daily reading—Psalm 61:2. "From the ends of the earth I call to you, I call as my heart grows faint; lead me to the rock that is higher than I." She drifted off to sleep meditating on the Rock that doesn't move. Her Savior.

She got up early, showered, and then packed her overnight bag for the drive home. At the checkout desk, she asked for a copy of the White Pages, hoping to find the address for Hazel Lane or Caroline Baskin. Nothing appeared for Caroline, however, she found a listing for Hazel Lane in Spring Hill. She jotted down the address, 682 Cardwell, and asked the hotel clerk for directions.

The modest houses stood clustered together on the narrow tree-lined street. She spotted the address. The house appeared vacant—a 'For Sale by Owner' sign leaned askew in the overgrown grass.

She walked up the short driveway and rang the doorbell. No answer. Cupping her hands around her eyes, she peered into the front window. Empty. Deprived of all furnishings. She walked around to the side and raised the gate latch leading to the fenced-in yard.

"Hello. Can I help you?" said a voice from the other side of the fence.

"Hi. My name is Shade. I was looking for Hazel Lane, but I see the house is vacant?"

"Did you know Hazel?"

"She's a friend of the family. I was in town and thought I'd stop by."

"Well, Hazel passed away a few years ago. Such a shame. We were neighbors for twenty-two years. She lived here over fifty years."

"I'm sorry to hear that. I see the house is for sale by owner. Who's selling the house?"

"Her daughter, Caroline. She took it hard when her mother passed and didn't have the heart to put the house up for sale until now. I see her occasionally. I can tell her you were here if you'd like. Do you know Caroline?"

"No, I never met Caroline but would appreciate it if you gave her my phone number. I live in Michigan. I'm heading home today."

"I'd be happy to," she said, taking the scrap of paper from Shade.

"Thanks. Well, I better get going. It was nice talking to you."

She opened the car door. The woman called out.

"I didn't get your last name?"

Shade waved goodbye, jumped in her car and drove away.

One last thing to do. Return to the library and search the newspaper archives to see if she could find anything related to Stanley Lane.

At the computer terminal, she searched on 'Stanley Lane' and '682 Cardwell' with a date range of 1940-1976. Several results appeared. A birth announcement for Stanley and the obituaries for Henry and Hazel Lane. And a news article, dated October 12, 1956:

Teen Charged with Sexual Assault Gets Time in Juvenile Detention Center–*Spring Hill, Ohio–Police arrested a sixteen-year-old male for the sexual assault of a nine-year-old female. The victim was at the home of the accused at 682 Cardwell while the accused's older sister babysat. The victim later revealed the assault to her parents, who contacted the police. The accused was convicted in juvenile court and sentenced to two years in the juvenile detention center. A hearing will be held when the perpetrator reaches the age of eighteen to determine if further incarceration will be imposed.*

Shade collapsed in her seat, struggling to breathe. A thickness formed in the back of her throat, choking her. As she was gasping for air, a library assistant rushed over.

"Do you need me to call an ambulance, Miss?"

"No. I—I'll be okay," said Shade, panting. Gasp. "Just need air."

The assistant helped her outside. Her bones felt like they were out of joint. She sat on the concrete step.

"Wait here, and I'll get some water." When the woman returned, Shade had gone.

The five-hour drive home was a blur. Images of Stan molesting the young girl and Stan molesting Addy exploded in her mind like popcorn. Devastation turned to anger and anger to extreme hatred for the man she once loved. The man she slept with and idolized. A child molester. Her thoughts crushed down. *For twenty years, he pulled my strings and watched me dance. Why God? Why did you let me marry a monster? Why didn't you stop me?*

She pulled into her driveway, bitter bile rising in her throat. The thud-thud-thud of her heart tormented her. After opening the door, she paused in the foyer, staring ahead. A den of horrors. Everything appeared distorted. Soiled. Defiled.

The overnight bag slipped from her grip and onto the floor. She wandered down the hall toward Stan's office. At the computer terminal, she pressed the power button. The screeching static sound of the modem searched for intelligence. A heightened level of fear shrouded her. The hum brought back memories of Stan "working" in this room. She didn't want to know more. She needed to know more.

The screen lit up. She discovered his AOL account. Scrolling through his emails, she noticed nothing unusual. Employee names from the car dealership, a few advertisements. Stop. Lolita? She clicked on it. The sender appeared to be a teenager using an alias. The message was sexual. X-rated. Her skin tightened. Excessive saliva formed in her mouth. She moved on to his online file folders and opened one. Inside were photos of nude or scantily clad teens in various poses. Her blood churned. A battle raged inside. Her brain darted from fact to fact. *Oh God, no. Make it stop.*

With nostrils flaring, she stormed down the hall into their bedroom, tossing his possessions into trash bags. Clothes.

Toiletries. His watch. The gold chain with a cross. Anything she could find belonging to him. She bagged it up and chucked it into the trash container.

Back in his office, she noticed a binder—Elder Notes, Holy Grace Baptist. Garbage. She found his Bible and with a deep guttural cry, hurled it at the wall. *You are nothing but a fraud, Stan. I hate you!*

Each step fueled her rage as she tore through the house. In the bedroom, her head snapped from side to side, searching. The bed. She grabbed hold of the queen-size mattress and dragged it from the room, bashing over tables, knocking pictures from the wall. She crashed through the front door, dragging the mattress to the curb. Her neighbor stood on his porch; his mouth slung open. He offered a tentative wave.

Back inside, she flung photos, jewelry—anything reminding her of Stan—into trash bags. Mission accomplished.

She sat in the kitchen, gasping for air. Tears puddled on the table into small ponds, the rims of her eyes red and raw. A glint of light bounced off her ring finger. The simple wedding band, now a dog collar. She stood, sending the kitchen chair flying across the linoleum and ran to the front door like a cheetah. Out on the lawn, she screwed herself into a pitcher's windup and heaved the wedding band at the blackened sky.

Floating through the fog, she emerged in her bedroom. Little relief. Her mind trailed back in time. Searching. Dissecting memories of their life together. The missed signs. Addy's bedroom door. Saturdays with Stan.

Shame folded over her. The pain would still be there in the morning, taunting her. She pulled herself into a fetal position atop the knobby box spring and locked her thoughts away, drifting to the happy place she'd so often gone to as a frightened little child.

CHAPTER SIX

And the God of all grace, who called you to his eternal glory in Christ, after you have suffered a little while, will himself restore you and make you strong, firm and steadfast.

— 1 PETER 5:10

I'll get through this. I'll make a new life for myself. Start fresh. Focus on raising Tyler. And make use of the insurance money—the only good thing left from him.

Stan. A living paradox. A pendulum. Swinging from lightness into dark. A man of God. A pedophile. No one must know. She would bury his ugly past with him.

Shade had one burning question. The time had come.

On the second ring, Addy answered. "Hi, Addy. It's Mom."

"Hey, look, I'm sorry I laid that on you the other day, but it's time you stopped living a lie."

"I—I've been so blind," said Shade, grief surging with every gasp. "I'm so sorry. Why didn't you tell me? I would have taken you and left him."

"He threatened me. Said I would end up in foster care. But it's in the past. It's time to move forward."

"I wish you would have come to me." Shade blew her nose into a tissue. "Addy—I need to ask you a question. Tyler. Is he...?"

"Tyler is Scott's son. Without a doubt. I left home long after that slime ball laid his filthy hands on me."

She heaved a sigh. "I don't know how to ever apologize to you. I could tell you I'm sorry forever, but it'll never be enough." She sobbed. Raw emotion.

Addy waited until the crying stopped. "When do you wanna pick up Tyler?" she asked in a calm voice. "It's been over a week. He keeps asking for his Gamma."

"How's Friday?" she asked, wiping her eyes. "I can keep him overnight."

"Sure. And don't beat yourself up, Mom. It's over."

She returned to work the following day, determined to shut down the misery nipping at her heels.

"Hope you had a nice couple of days off," said Bonnie. "We missed you. Sally and I were pretty busy."

"I'm glad to be back. What do you need me to do?"

"I have the recipes in the kitchen laid out. Why don't you get started on those?"

Shade worked efficiently, humming to herself, ticking off each of her tasks. When visions of Stan darkened her thoughts, she went to the happy place in her mind, focusing on Tyler or work. She would not let this beat her.

She cleaned up the kitchen prep area and set up for the next day. Before leaving, Shade approached Bonnie. "Do you have a minute?"

"What's up?"

"I've been thinking. Have you ever considered adding cheesecakes to the menu? You could promote three to four different flavors each week and sell them by the slice. I've made several cheesecakes for the church, and they're always the first thing to go. I could help with the recipes."

"That's an interesting idea. Let's talk tomorrow when you get in." Bonnie touched Shade's arm. "I wanna tell you how happy I am to see you in better spirits. I worried about you last week. Not sure what was going on, and I don't expect you to tell me, but please know I'm always here if you need to talk."

"Thanks Bonnie. See you tomorrow."

After arriving home, she prepared a small salad and settled at the kitchen table. She looked around at the dated interior of her home. The place could use a fresh paint job to liven it up. And some new furniture—void of plastic covers. Things needed to change.

The phone interrupted her decorating thoughts.

"Hi. Shade? This is Caroline Baskin, Hazel Lane's daughter. You left your number with my neighbor on Cardwell Street. She said you were a family friend."

"Caroline," Shade stammered. "Thanks for calling me back. When I mentioned I was a family friend, I was referring to your brother, Stanley Lane."

"Stanley?"

Shade heard a gasp. An awkward silence lingered. When Caroline spoke, her voice seemed small. Cautious.

"Stanley left home at eighteen, and neither I nor my parents ever saw him again. How do you know Stanley?"

"I am, or was, Stanley's wife. We married in 1976. Stanley passed away a few months ago of a heart attack."

"Oh," Caroline uttered, seeming impervious to the death of her brother. "How did you two meet?"

"I lived in a home for unwed mothers. In Michigan. We met at church. After my baby arrived, we got married, and he adopted my daughter, Adeline. We were married for twenty years."

"What did he tell you about his family?"

"He said he was an only child, and both parents died when he was eighteen."

"So, you know he lied."

"Yes," said Shade, her voice trembling. "After Stanley died, I learned he wasn't the man I thought I knew."

Shade revealed all she had learned about Stanley, including Addy's abuse and the article she came across regarding the sexual assault.

Caroline remained quiet, clearly gathering her thoughts before speaking. "It must have been quite a shock. Do you want to know about the assault?"

"Yes, please."

"Well, from an early age, maybe fourteen, Stanley exhibited an attraction to young girls. There were complaints around the neighborhood. Inappropriate touching. Kissing. Things like that. My parents got him counseling, and he seemed to improve, until that day when I was babysitting. The girl was nine, and Stanley was sixteen. My parents were out with the young girl's parents. I put her to bed in my bedroom and watched TV in the living room. Stan was doing homework in the basement. I fell asleep on the couch and awoke to the sound of whimpering. When I went to check on her, I saw Stanley walking out of my bedroom, and I asked what he was doing. He told me he heard crying and went to see if she was okay. I believed him. When I asked Jackie—that was her name—if she was okay, she said she'd had a nightmare. She was shaking and sobbing. It wasn't until the next day, when the police came to our home and took Stanley away, that I learned what happened. He got convicted in juvenile court and served two years. It broke my family. Our friends avoided us and treated us like criminals. My parents were good, upstanding people. They raised him the best they could. But there was something about him that wasn't right. It was as if he had no conscience. I think that's why he got a vasectomy at such a young age. He either didn't want to bring another person into the world carrying his genes, or he wanted to continue his shameful lifestyle and not worry about unwanted pregnancies. Anyway, when his two-year sentence ended, he tried moving back home, but my parents told him he would have to find someplace else to live. That's the last we saw of him."

Shade listened, the seal of confirmation stamped on her brain. "It sounds like your parents did all they could to help him."

"Yes, they did. I'm sorry he deceived you. I hope you can move forward and find the strength to put this behind you."

"It'll take time, but I have to move on. Thank you for sharing this information, and I'm sorry for any pain I've caused you," said Shade. "I should let you go. Goodbye."

"Goodbye, Shade. If you ever want to talk, feel free to call."

"Thank you," she said, placing the phone on the cradle.

She sat motionless, replaying their conversation. *When I think I've heard it all, more junk gets tossed on the pile. All those years spent trying to conceive, and he knew all along it would never happen.*

Drained of all emotion, her mind rested. She had a life ahead of her and a grandson who needed her. Things would change. For the better.

"Let's talk about your cheesecake idea," said Bonnie, when Shade arrived at the bakery the next morning.

"Well, I've made cheesecakes for years and have several recipes that might go over well. We could start with four different types; white chocolate, chocolate and sour cream, Oreo cookie, and sea salt caramel. And I have a delicious crust recipe. It tastes like buttered shortbread. It could be our signature pastry. We could make signs for the front window and offer samples to our customers. And for anyone interested in purchasing a whole cheesecake, we could offer two sizes; a six-inch and a ten-inch."

"It's a great idea," said Bonnie. "I'm impressed by how well you've thought this through. I say let's go for it. Why don't you shop for the ingredients and equipment? Can we pull this together by next week?"

"Absolutely. Thanks for being open to my idea."

"And thank you for taking such an interest in the business."

The cheesecake idea proved to be a success, and orders for whole cheesecakes were in demand. Bonnie purchased a few tables and chairs, staggering them throughout the bakery. Customers and tourists dropped in throughout the day for slices of heaven.

Shade grew to love the business and set a goal for herself—to one day open her own bakery, but in another town away from Bonnie so as not to compete. If things worked out, perhaps she could lure Addy and Tyler away from Jaime, and Addy might take over the bakery one day.

After work on Friday, she drove to Addy's to pick up Tyler. She hadn't seen her face-to-face since the revelation about Stan. Her stomach tumbled.

No one answered her knock on the door. She went around back and found Tyler and Jaime sitting in an old beat-up car, listening to the radio. Jaime sang along to "Big Bang Baby", his fingers drumming the dashboard, while Tyler sat next to him clapping his hands and rocking back and forth to the music. Spotting Shade, Tyler jumped out of the car and ran toward her.

"Gamma. Gamma."

Shade swept Tyler into her arms and gave him a hug, planting kisses over his dirty face. “Oh, I missed you so much. Are you going to stay with Grandma tonight?”

“Sleep at Gamma.”

Jaime emerged from the car. “Good to see you, Mrs. Lane. So, you’re gonna take my little buddy away for the night?” he said, ruffling Tyler’s hair. “Hey buddy, give me a hug.”

Tyler wiggled away from Shade and grabbed Jaime around the legs and squeezed tight. “Bye-bye.”

“I knocked on the door,” said Shade, “but Addy didn’t answer. Is she home?”

“Yeah. Just go in.”

She took Tyler’s hand and led him into the house. Sprawled out on the sofa lay Addy, half asleep. The house reeked of stale cigarettes and that other odd smell. Burnt plastic. Cigarette butts overflowed in the ashtray, beer cans lay strewn across the table and counter, and a strange looking glass pipe sat smoldering on a coffee table.

Shade approached and gave her a gentle nudge. “Addy, are you awake? I came to pick up Tyler.”

Addy shot up from the sofa like a missile, running fingers through her slippery hair. “Hey. Sorry, I must have fallen asleep.” She reached for a cigarette, her hands shaking, her jaw clenched. “Jaime put Tyler’s things in that paper bag over there. Can you bring him back late tomorrow? Like after six?”

“Sure. Are you all right? You look a little out of it.”

“Yeah. I’m fine. Just a rough night. Come say goodbye, Tyler.”

Addy reached for him, but he scurried away, giggling, and ran out the front door. Addy stared vacantly after him and collapsed on the sofa. A cloud of dust dispersed into the air.

Driving back to her place, her mind settled on Addy. *She has to be on drugs. She doesn't seem at all concerned about Tyler. And that place. It's filthy and not fit for a two-year-old.*

The tiny passenger in the backseat disrupted her thoughts. "Whass sat...whass sat, Gamma?" he said, pointing out the car window.

"Hey little guy. We're almost at Grandma's."

Tyler ran through the front door ahead of Shade, shooting in and out of each room. She gazed upon his grubby little body and his dirty, worn clothes. A heavy pull tugged at her heart.

"Tyler. Come over here. Grandma will give you a bath, then I'll make lunch. And later, we'll go shopping for new clothes."

She lowered Tyler in the bubble-filled bathtub, scrubbing him down. The bathwater turned murky from the grime that fell away. His little body looked so thin. She could see his ribcage pushing through his chest. Her heart hurt. Tyler sat in the tub, splashing and playing with a rubber duck, water sloshing over the side. When she tried lifting him out, he wailed and pushed her away until she bribed him with food.

He devoured his lunch, and she wondered when he had last eaten. Shade doubted Addy had ever taken him to the doctor for a check-up. She made a note to schedule an appointment.

They spent the next two days together. She bought him new outfits, shoes, a jacket, and pajamas. At night, she read stories from Addy's children's books. When Tyler grabbed for the Bible stories, she placed it back on the shelf. "No. Grandma's gonna read 'Peter Rabbit' tonight.'"

The clock ticked, moving the inevitable forward. Time to take Tyler home. An ominous cloud of gloom descended. She placed the outfits she had purchased inside his new overnight bag, along with the cookies they had made and some containers of fruits and vegetables.

When she pulled up to the farmhouse, Addy stood on the porch, a cigarette burning between her fingers. Tyler ran out back, searching for Jaime.

"Do you have time to talk?" asked Shade.

"Yeah, c'mon in."

"I'm concerned about you. And I'm concerned about Tyler."

Addy flailed her hand in the air. "Don't start again."

"No, we will start again," said Shade, surprised by her tone. "This place isn't fit for a dog. Tyler looks like he's malnourished. He's filthy, and you act like you're high on something. You don't even seem to care about him. It seems like he's closer to Jaime than to you. And where do you two get your money? You're both always home. Does anyone work around here?"

"How dare you talk about caring. If you cared about me, maybe you would have noticed what was going on under your roof. Instead, you turned a blind eye and settled into your little Ozzie and Harriet fantasy world. Well, at least I don't put on an act, pretending to be what I'm not. Take a good look, Mom," she said, throwing her arms wide. "It's Addy—the dysfunctional screw-up you helped create." Addy dropped into a chair and lit a cigarette, her hands shaking. "Go home. Just go home. We'll talk."

Jaime came around to the front door with Tyler and spotted Shade walking to her car. "Hey, what's up? Everything good?"

Ignoring him, she kneeled and held Tyler, kissing him goodbye. Tyler gazed into her eyes, wiping the wetness from her cheeks with his tiny fingers. "Gamma cwy?"

"Grandma is fine. I'll see you soon, honey. I love you."

As she drove away, she couldn't still her trembling body. She pulled over to the side of the road and wept, her forehead resting on the steering wheel. *What am I going to do? You don't care, God. If you did, this wouldn't be happening. Where are you? Do you even exist?*

Shade stepped inside her front door to the sound of a ringing phone.

"It's Mary. Just checking in. I haven't seen you at church and was worried. Is everything okay?"

"That's sweet of you to ask, but everything's fine. I've been busy working and spending time with Tyler."

"Blanche and I were wondering if you could go to lunch next week. We'd love to catch up."

"I'd love to see you both. Why don't you come here and I'll make lunch? How's Wednesday?"

"Sounds wonderful. I'll let Blanche know."

Equipped with her home's dimensions, she met with a decorator at Wilson's Furniture store the following day. Kallie asked about her style. Shade decided she had none. Kallie offered to follow her home to get a better feel of the space.

"It's a charming house, but I see what you mean about style. It's lacking."

Kallie walked through the house, scribbling notes. Back at the furniture store, they selected a sofa, side chairs and tables, accessories, two bedroom sets and a kitchen table. Kallie recommended a painter and gave her the colors for each room.

On Wednesday, she got up early to prepare lunch for Mary and Blanche. After assembling the Chicken Artichoke Spinach Pie, she made a salad with mandarin oranges, slivered almonds and goat cheese. For dessert, she chose something light. Fruit salad with Limoncello and a topping of Greek yogurt, lemon curd, honey and vanilla.

Excitement swept in when Blanche's Cadillac pulled into the driveway.

"Oh, honey," said Blanche. "Look what you've done with this place. It looks fabulous. I love the new furniture and the new paint colors. I can't get over the transformation."

Mary squeezed Shade's hand. "It looks like you've been keeping your mind occupied. It's like a new house."

"Thank you. I love the way it turned out," said Shade.

"It smells delicious in here," said Mary. "I can't wait to see what Chef Lane prepared."

They sat at the table. Shade picked up her fork when Mary asked to say grace.

"Sure," said Shade, placing her fork aside.

While the other two bowed their heads, Shade stared ahead in defiance to God who had forsaken her.

"The meal was delicious," said Blanche. "Honey, you're so talented."

"You're too kind," said Shade, smiling. Her mood turned pensive. "Remember when I told you about my concerns for Addy and Tyler? Well, nothing seems to get better. In fact, it's getting worse. Blanche, I know Harry is an attorney. Does he work on custody lawsuits? I'm not sure this is the path I want to take, but I'd like to keep that option open."

"Oh, honey. I'm sorry to hear that. Let me talk to Harry tonight. It's not his specialty, but maybe you two can chat, and he can point you in the right direction."

"I've been praying for you, and for Addy and Tyler," said Mary, taking Shade's hand. "Sometimes it seems like God isn't listening, but be patient."

She squeezed Mary's hand. Mary meant well, but a wedge had been driven between her and God, and she wasn't sure it would ever be removed.

"Oh, Shade," said Mary, as they were preparing to leave. "I forgot to mention that Holy Grace is starting a ministry to help support the unwed mothers in our community. I thought you might join, based on your experience. You'd be a blessing to the group."

"I don't think so. Not with my job and spending time with Tyler. But thanks for asking."

"I'll talk to Harry about Tyler," said Blanche, as she walked to her car. "Thanks again for the wonderful meal."

Shade watched her two friends drive away. She felt guilty declining Mary's offer, but it would require her to be involved with Holy Grace, and she wasn't interested. She had moved on.

Before retiring to bed, she added tasks to her "to do" list: contact Harry Buford, doctor's appointment for Tyler, Calvin—the motorcycle guy?

CHAPTER SEVEN

Now faith is confidence in what we hope for and assurance about what we do not see.

— HEBREWS 11:1

Shade scheduled a doctor's appointment with a pediatrician, Lois Blake. She didn't consult Addy beforehand. Based on their last confrontation, this wouldn't go over well. But she pressed on, her focus on Tyler.

Her stomach shifted as she dialed Addy's number.

"Hey, Mom," she answered, her voice drowsy.

"Look, I'm sorry about the argument, and I'm sure we both said things we didn't mean, but can we put this behind us and move on? For Tyler's sake?"

"Whatever you want."

"Good. I'd like to pick him up this week. I'm thinking Thursday. Early. Will that work?"

"Yeah, sounds good."

She struggled to soften the blow, but the words tumbled out.

"I'm taking Tyler in for a physical. I'll pay for everything. I just think he needs to be checked out."

"Excuse me? You mean you wanna be sure he's not half-starved or addicted to drugs?"

"I want him to be healthy, that's all. I'm sure you want the same thing."

"Fine, but I'm going with you." The phone went dead.

Addy and Tyler were waiting on the porch when Shade arrived. Addy's hair was washed and pulled back in a ponytail. She even wore a hint of make-up. Clad in a pair of conservative, black slacks and a simple white blouse, she looked beautiful.

"Gamma," Tyler squealed and ran out to greet her. She lifted him, kissing his face, before settling him into his car seat. Addy climbed in the front, staring ahead.

An uneasy silence hung in the air while Tyler jabbered non-stop in the backseat. Shade tried starting a conversation, but Addy replied with clipped, one-word answers.

"What brings you in today?" asked Dr. Blake.

Addy spoke up. "I'd like for my son, Tyler, to get a complete physical. And to get him up-to-date on his vaccines. I've been negligent, due to my financial situation, but my mother has graciously volunteered to pay the bill," she said, flashing a forced smile at Shade.

Shade's eyes grew wide, agitated by Addy's uncharacteristic behavior.

"I'm glad you came in today, but keep in mind there are ways of paying through public assistance," said Dr. Blake. "It's best not to wait. How old is Tyler?"

"He was two in September," Addy responded, casting a warm gaze at her son. "He's such a bundle of joy. I'm so blessed."

Shade's head whirled. She shot Addy an irritated glance. *What's gotten into her? She never talks like that.*

Tyler ran around the examination room in his diaper, touching everything within reach. Dr. Blake coaxed him over. "Would you like to sit on the big table for me?"

"Tay-bow ... big," Tyler responded, throwing his arms into the air.

Dr. Blake set Tyler on the table, listening to his heart and checking his ears and nose. His cheerful disposition went south when the nurse came in with a syringe, bearing down on him. He let out a piercing scream, stretching his arms toward Shade.

"Gamma. Want Gamma."

Addy went over to Tyler, brushing Shade aside, wrapping her arms around him and stroking his head. "It's okay, honey. Mama's here."

Tyler pushed her away and continued reaching for Shade. "No. Want Gamma."

"Everything looks good," said Dr. Blake. "He's underweight, though. I recommend placing him on a diet of nutritious foods with plenty of fruits and vegetables. Other than that, he has a clean bill of health. I'd like to see him in a month to recheck his weight."

"Thank you so much." Addy glanced at Shade, feigning a smile.

The drive to Addy's was a repeat of the drive in. When they arrived at the house, Jaime stood by the pole barn talking to two guys. One had a shaved head with a large hoop earring dangling from his ear. The other, clad from neck to foot in black leather; a silver-studded dog collar clasped his throat. Addy pulled Tyler from the car seat.

"I'm sorry you can't stay," said Addy. "Tyler, tell Grandma good-bye."

"Bye, Gamma." He hugged her and ran toward Jaime.

Shade caught a whiff of that odd smell again, wafting through the air from the direction of the pole barn. Jaime waved. She responded with a limp gesture.

Settling into her car, she drove off, her shoulders drooping. *At least he got a clean bill of health. But what about Addy? She deserved an Academy Award for that performance.*

Exhausted, Shade tossed her coat aside and sat in the living room. The doorbell startled her. She tiptoed to the front window and pulled the curtain aside, peeking. Darn. Pastor Dave and his wife, Jessica. *Maybe they didn't see me.* She dropped to the floor and slithered across the carpet—an army crawl—when his voice called out.

"Shade? It's Pastor Dave. Are you in there?"

She sighed and stood up, opening the door. "What a nice surprise. Please, come in."

"Sorry for popping in on you, but we were in the area and thought we'd stop by."

"I love what you've done to your place," said Jessica. "You've been busy. I'm sure it helps keep your mind off of Stanley."

"So, speaking of Stanley, how are you doing?" said Pastor Dave. "We haven't seen you in church. Is everything okay? Our prayer warriors continually pray for you."

"That's nice to hear. Would you like coffee? I can make a fresh pot?"

"No. We aren't staying. We just wanted to check in."

"Well, I'm doing good. I've been busy working and babysitting Tyler. By the time Sunday rolls around, I'm drained."

"That's understandable," said Jessica. "But we miss you. You're like family, and it pains us to not see your smiling face on Sunday."

"How's Tyler?" asked Pastor Dave. "We started a new Sunday school class for toddlers. Why don't you bring him next week?"

"Sunday won't work. I have plans."

"Maybe another time. Jessica, why don't we pray for Shade before we leave?" Dave and Jessica locked hands with Shade, bowing their heads.

"Heavenly Father. We lift up our dear sister in Christ today as she journeys through life without her beloved Stan. We ask that you move the Spirit more boldly in Shade. Give her a heart of discernment and the strength and courage to follow you, even when it's hard. Amen."

Her lips pressed tight. They were good people but ignorant to Stan's monstrous ways. Had they known God allowed this to happen, maybe they would understand why she pulled away.

Later that week, Harry greeted Shade in his office. "Blanche told me a lot about you," he said, taking her hands. "I'd like to offer my condolences. I'm sure it's hard being alone. So, what brings you in today?"

"Thank you. I'm here to talk about my grandson, Tyler. My daughter, Adeline, is a single mother, and she and Tyler live with a guy named Jaime. I believe Adeline and Jaime are on drugs, and I think they're selling drugs. The house is unfit for my grandson, and Adeline is an unfit mother. I'd like to understand what my options are for gaining custody of my grandson."

"Well, I have little experience with custody suits, but I can put you in contact with someone who does. I do know it's difficult to win custody but not impossible. There are things the court looks at. You'll need to prove she's an unfit mother. Perhaps, get child protective services to check in on him. Maybe a note from the child's pediatrician. Also, there needs to be documentation of abuse or neglect. The key here is documentation. Something in writing, like a police report or protective services report. If Adeline is a drug addict, it would be a compelling argument. Have you spoken to Adeline about this?"

"Yes, but she shuts me down."

"Prepare for a long battle. One to two years. I'd suggest you put in a call, anonymously, to child protective services and issue a complaint. When you get more documentation, call me. I'll put you in touch with a good attorney who specializes in custody lawsuits."

Leaving Harry's office, she fixated on the menacing thoughts plaguing her. It wouldn't be easy. If Addy got suspicious, she might leave the state, and she would never see Tyler again.

She longed for things to be different between her and Addy. Her thoughts turned to the smart, popular girl she once was—until Stan destroyed her. Grief pooled in her soul, as she considered her own shortcomings. Her ignorance. Never paying attention to the signs. Worshipping Stan while sacrificing her daughter. A lamb to the slaughter.

One last task. She fingered the card Calvin had given her at the rest area. Picturing him in his worn, black leather jacket sent prickles through her body. *But, he's a married man. Oh, but a little tryst wouldn't hurt anything.* She stared at the card for several minutes, her stomach pitching. Should she, or shouldn't she?

She jerked at the sound of his voice on the other end of the line. She considered hanging up but reclaimed her courage.

"Hi. This is Shade. Not sure you remember me, but you gave me your card at a rest area in Michigan. You were on your motorcycle."

"Well, hello. I'm glad you called."

Now what? Do I ask him out? "So, how've you been? How's the wife?" She let out a gasp. *What a ridiculous comment.* She contemplated ending the call. Again.

"I see you have a sense of humor. I like that. You're not just a brainless beauty."

Her face flushed at the backhanded compliment. "So, why did you give me your number?"

"Why did you call?"

"To be honest, I don't know."

"Well, why don't we meet sometime, and we can figure it out. What are you doing this Saturday?"

"Let me look at my calendar." She let a few seconds pass. "Oh, I'm free on Saturday. Looks like you hit the jackpot."

He laughed. "Why don't we meet around seven in the bar at the Hyatt Inn over in Fairmont? Are you familiar with the place?"

"No, but I can ask my husband," she said, smirking. "He might know."

"Funny. See ya then."

Hair up? Hair down? Black dress? Red dress? She spent over an hour primping, and re-primping. She blew her hair dry and let it fall over her shoulders. After applying makeup, she put on the casual, clingy black dress, slipped on a pair of high heels and looked in the mirror, remarking to her decked out self, "Knock 'em dead, Shade." She grabbed her clutch bag and sashayed out the front door.

Emotions swirled during the thirty-minute drive to the Hyatt Inn. Excitement turned to panic. *What if he wants to sleep with me? How naïve of me to assume we'd meet in a hotel, both of us married—or so he thinks—and just chat.* Something told her to turn back. She ignored her conscience and pulled into the parking lot.

The cocktail bar was packed with lively patrons. Calvin sat at a high-top table against the wall, drinking a beer and checking himself out in a mirror.

A large potted fern in the lobby provided the perfect smoke-screen. She stood behind it, observing. *Should I go through with this?* She had to admit he was gorgeous.

Coming around from behind the plant, she sauntered toward him. Her head high. Her stride seductive. An attractive woman walked past his table. He handed her his card and uttered something to her. The woman turned and tossed her cocktail in his face, causing a colorful paper umbrella to plunge into his hair and stick.

Shade gulped. She stepped back behind the fern, watching. While blotting his face with a napkin, oblivious to the umbrella garnish in his hair, a large, muscular man approached and grabbed him by the collar, hurling him against the bar and sending bottles crashing to the floor. Calvin tried to recapture his dignity before Mr. Universe delivered a blow to his face, knocking him unconscious.

Driving home in her little black dress, she reflected on the evening. *I'm trying to get custody of my grandson, and I'm acting like the town whore. What am I thinking?*

Once inside her cozy little house, she slipped on her pajamas. *Be more careful. And responsible. Duly noted.*

CHAPTER EIGHT

When tempted, no one should say, "God is tempting me." For God cannot be tempted by evil, nor does he tempt anyone; but each person is tempted when they are dragged away by their own evil desire and enticed.

— JAMES 1:13-14

Year 1997

The dove gray skies gave way to spring as the lifeless landscape exploded into a dazzling array of colors. Rejuvenated, Shade labored in her yard, digging her fingers into the moist soil, dropping in the small herb and vegetable plants she purchased at the nursery.

Business at the bakery thrived, and Shade picked up additional hours to help handle the workload. Bonnie had given her a pay increase and more responsibilities; keeping the books, taking inventory and ordering supplies. The business ran like a well-oiled machine.

Shade continued her efforts to gain custody of Tyler, placing several anonymous calls into child protective services. But each time she inquired, she received the same answer. "We found no evidence of abuse or neglect in the home."

Addy called the following week, asking if Tyler could stay overnight. Jaime had something planned for the two of them—for Addy's birthday. Any opportunity to spend time with Tyler was a godsend.

At three-years-old, Tyler developed into a typical 'rough and tumble' little boy. He loved getting dirty, picking at insects and playing with Matchbox cars. And he loved helping Shade around the house with her chores. His sweet disposition continued to baffle Shade. Living in that home, and under those conditions, it made little sense.

After an active day together, she dressed Tyler in his pajamas. He heaved himself up on his new toddler bed, bouncing around until he wore himself out.

"Sweet dreams my little one," she said, kissing his forehead. "No more reading tonight." She tucked the covers around him. "Do you like sleeping at Grandmas?"

"Yeah. Sleep with Jaime, too. Jaime read."

Her throat squeezed shut, her heart clobbered against her chest. "Do you sleep with Momma and Jaime?"

"Sleep with Jaime. Man-to-man."

"But—do you sleep in your own bed too?"

"No. Jaime. We sleep."

"Do you sleep in the big bed? Where your momma sometimes sleeps?"

"No. Jaime. Sleep with Jaime. Man-to-man."

Her fingers stroked his hair until his eyelids fluttered. Sleep seized him. She went into the kitchen and sat at the table. *It's happening again. My family is cursed. And what does Addy think? Or is she too spaced out to notice?* She needed to think. She would reflect on it tomorrow, with a clearer head.

Sunlight streamed through the bedroom window, rousing her from sleep. Her conversation with Tyler came rushing back.

The sound of little feet padding down the hall distracted her. Tyler appeared in the doorway, hands on hips. "Get up Gamma." He hauled himself up on the bed and jumped around. "Get up. Get up." Laughing, she pulled him down, snuggling him and planting kisses over his face.

"Would you like pancakes for breakfast? Maybe you can help Grandma in the kitchen."

"Yeah. I help Gamma."

Hours ticked away. The snake of despair slithered in. She would soon leave to take Tyler home. How could she look at Jaime? And what would she say to Addy? Addy had to know, but then again, she hadn't known about Addy and Stan.

On the drive to Addy's, she decided she would call her the next day. Based on her reaction, she'd determine what to do. She didn't want to jump to conclusions, but she also didn't want to repeat the same mistakes she'd made in the past—viewing life through a painted veil.

The time came to make the dreaded call. Her stomach wanted out, tumbling and pounding.

"Do you have time to talk?" asked Shade when Addy answered the phone.

"Yeah, sure. What's up?"

"I don't know how to say this, but please listen before you get angry. When Tyler was here yesterday, he said something that troubled me. He told me he sleeps with Jaime—man-to-man. I asked if he slept with both of you, and he said no. Just Jaime. He kept saying 'man-to-man.' Is there something going on? Were you aware of this?"'

An unsettling silence lingered before Addy responded. "After what I've been through, don't you think I would know better than anyone, including you, if something horrible was going on? Jaime loves Tyler. They're buddies. Give it a break, and stop trying to swoop in and rescue Tyler so you can feel good about yourself. I'm done with this ludicrous conversation. And don't ever bring it up again or you'll never see Tyler." Click.

Shade paced the kitchen floor, chewing at her lip. She needed to develop a plan. To continue seeing Tyler, she would make amends with Addy and somehow increase Tyler's overnight visits. In the meantime, she would get the name of a child custody attorney from Harry. But she had to be careful. Once Addy found out, she'd stop her visits with Tyler, unless she could petition the court for visitation rights. So much to figure out.

Work became her outlet during the day, but sleep evaded her. Images of Jaime abusing Tyler forced their way in. *Things will work out,* she told herself. She had to stay positive. Think good thoughts.

A week after the difficult conversation, the phone rang. "Hey, Mrs. Lane. It's Jaime."

"Jaime? Is everything okay?"

"Yeah, but we're at Emmet County hospital. Addy fell off the porch and broke her arm. They wanna keep her overnight. She wanted me to ask if you could take Tyler for the night."

"Yes. Absolutely. I'm on my way."

Shade ran down the hospital corridor and spotted Jaime and Tyler.

"Gamma," screamed Tyler, running down the hall toward Shade. "Mama tipped over and broke herself."

After hugging Tyler, she turned to Jaime. "Where is she? Is she okay?"

"They're putting a cast on her arm. They said they wanna keep her overnight for observation. I don't understand why."

"I'll try to find the doctor." Shade headed toward the information desk and spoke to a nurse, who paged Dr. Brown.

"Hello," said Dr. Brown. "Are you related to Adeline Lane?"

"Yes. I'm her mother. Will she be okay?"

"Yes. She has a fractured ulna. We're putting a cast on it now. We want to keep her overnight to monitor her vitals. We have reason to believe she's addicted to street drugs. We're running some tests."

Shade's face turned ashen, her eyes like saucers. "What kind of street drugs?"

"I don't want to say until we get the test results. We'll discuss next steps then."

Shade found Jaime and Tyler sitting next to Addy's hospital bed. She was propped up, sporting a cast partially covering her left hand and running up to her elbow.

"Hey, Mom," said Addy, her words tripping over her tongue. "Guess I took a little tumble off the porch."

Shade went to her, leaning and kissing her forehead. "How are you feeling?'

"Swell," she said, with a skewed smile. "Can you take Tyler tonight? Jaime wanted to take him home, but I want Jaime to stay here with me for a while."

"Sure. Did they say how long you'll be in a cast?" asked Shade.

"Six weeks," said Addy. "But Jaime will take care of me."

"What about Tyler? Maybe I can take him until you get the cast off."

"No need, Mrs. Lane," said Jaime. "I can take care of them both."

Shade looked at Tyler curled up in Jaime's lap, sleeping. "He's exhausted," said Shade, reaching for Tyler. "I should get him home and into bed. I'll bring him back in the morning. Early." She leaned to kiss Addy. "You get some sleep, honey. I'll see you tomorrow."

Tyler crawled into bed, his little eyelids struggling to stay open. After reading a bedtime story, she tucked him in.

Shade lay awake, blaming herself for Addy's troubles. She couldn't let the same thing happen to Tyler. She vowed to keep him safe. Her mind churned, desperate for answers—for a plan. *Maybe I can persuade Addy to live with me for six weeks. Get them both away from Jaime. I can help her get off the drugs and take care of Tyler. But what if she doesn't agree? Jaime will have more control over Tyler. If he's abusing Tyler, things could worsen. Think, Shade, think. I need a plan.* The minutes dragged into hours as she stared at the ceiling. Two a.m.

The knock at the door caused her to jolt. She looked at the clock. Five a.m. Slipping on her robe and slippers, she peered through the curtains. Two men stood on the porch. One looked like a police officer. She opened the door slightly, her heart twanging hard.

"Mrs. Lane?" said the man, peering in, brandishing a silver badge. "I'm Detective Kent Monroe, and this is Officer Bob Thornton. May we come in?"

"Yes—yes, come in," said Shade, her face pallid. "Has something happened?"

"Do you have a daughter named Adeline Lane?" asked Kent.

"Yes. Why? Is she in trouble?" Sweat bathed her skin, the thump, thump, thump of her heart slammed against her chest.

"I'm sorry to tell you this, but your daughter is dead. We found her at 3765 Needmore Road. We presume she lived there. We're trying to understand what happened, but it looks like she had been murdered. Along with a guy, Jaime Holder.

Shade sucked in a spurt of air and dropped to the floor, her legs unable to support her. Her chin shuddered, rattling her teeth. She couldn't speak. The two men helped her up and moved her to the sofa.

"She—She's in the hospital. I don't understand."

"We're investigating, ma'am. Did your daughter have enemies?"

"No. I—I don't know. She didn't say."

"Do you know if Jaime had any enemies?"

"I—I don't know. She's supposed to be in the hospital. Overnight. Are you sure it's her?"

Tyler appeared in the hallway, balled fists rubbing sleepy eyes. He climbed onto Shade's lap, snuggling into her neck and sucking his thumb.

Holding him tight, she rocked Tyler from side to side. "It's okay, honey."

"Is this your son, ma'am?"

"This is my grandson—Adeline's son. How did this happen?"

"They were shot."

She gasped, pulling Tyler closer.

"Did your daughter mention any plans for the night?"

"She wasn't supposed to be home."

"Were you aware of any drug activity at the house?"

"I—I wasn't sure."

"We've been watching the house. We believe they were cooking methamphetamine and selling it."

Her breath seized. She had suspected, but hearing it validated her suspicions. She recalled the odd smell. Too numb to speak, she swayed Tyler back and forth, clutching him like a rag doll.

Kent continued, choosing his words delicately. "We suspect it may have been a drug deal gone bad. We must ask you to come in and identify the body. Is there anyone available to take care of your grandson?"

"Body?" she cried, her body racked with grief. "Oh, Addy, Addy. Why? Why were you home? My beautiful Addy."

"Gamma's sad?" said Tyler, dabbing her eyes with his tiny hand.

Kent asked again about calling someone. She gave him Mary's number.

Mary arrived with Pastor Dave. She rushed toward Shade, embracing her and Tyler. Fear crept over Tyler's face, accompanied by hiccupping sobs.

Pastor Dave wrapped his arms around them, bowing his head and said a silent prayer. "I'll go with you to the morgue. Why don't you get dressed? Mary can stay with Tyler."

The coroner escorted her into the frigid, stark room. Fluorescent lights buzzed overhead. The repulsive odor of death jarred her senses. Resting atop a shiny metal table lay the covered body. Pastor Dave stood at her side, bracing her. The coroner peeled back a corner of the white sheet, revealing Adeline's handsome, undamaged face. She looked so cold. Frozen. Grief exploded in Shade's mind like a grenade. She squeezed her eyes shut and nodded as the tears escaped in a steady stream.

"She looked so peaceful," said Shade, on the drive home. "I

don't understand. She was at the hospital. Overnight. And now she's gone—forever. Do you think she's in heaven?"

"I can't answer that," said Pastor Dave. "Only God knew Adeline's heart." He patted her hand. "I remember her as a young child. She always had a thousand questions. Always searching for truth. A beautiful girl. But you need to focus on Tyler. You have a big responsibility ahead of you—raising him alone. Keep God at your side, and He'll walk you through."

"Tyler, Grandma wants to talk to you so listen carefully," said Shade, sitting outside on the cushioned glider. She stroked his hair, her arm around him. "You're going to live with me. You're not going back home. This is your home now. Your mama and Jaime went away forever, and they're not coming back. And they want you to stay with me."

"Jaime sleep? I go home?" said Tyler. Little pools formed in his crystal blue eyes.

Her heart turned to liquid. "No, my darling. You're gonna stay with me. Forever. You'll sleep here every night."

Tyler's uncertainty faded. "Sleep at Gamma's? Forever?" he said, clapping his hands and bouncing in his seat.

She pulled him onto her lap and held onto him before he squirmed free. "I wanna get down," said Tyler. And off he went, running through the yard, chasing a butterfly.

Emotion seeped. She reflected on the good times with Addy, before Stan ruined her. Such promise. Such beauty. She could have done something with her life, but it wasn't meant to be. Gone forever. No turning back.

Detective Kent Monroe reviewed the Lane/Holder case file on his desk. He had been observing the farmhouse for months, waiting for more evidence of drug activity before making arrests. He did a background check on both Adeline and Jaime. Adeline's record came back clean. Jaime had earlier arrests for drunk driving and drug possession. He also did a check on a previous renter. Scott Bailey. The guy caught himself on fire in the pole barn while lighting a meth pipe. He later expired. Scott had a long arrest record. Armed robbery, assault with a deadly weapon, driving under the influence, and drug trafficking. Kent made a note to look into Scott's former acquaintances. He also needed to talk to the mother of Adeline again, Shade Lane, about the night of the murder. She mentioned Adeline was supposed to be staying overnight at the hospital. What happened? Why was she home? Kent wanted to know more about their friends.

Kent interviewed the mother of Jaime Holder, a nice woman by the name of Donna. She seemed pretty choked up. Said she hadn't seen Jaime in a few weeks. He usually came by once a week and called at least twice a week. They spoke on Saturday morning. Everything seemed fine. He told her he would come over Sunday and take her to dinner. She seldom visited his place, but when she did she noticed nothing unusual, other than the messy condition of the home.

Adeline died of a single gunshot wound to the chest. Jaime had two gunshot wounds; one to the face and one to the chest. It appeared they had been caught unaware. Jaime may have been sleeping or passed out on the sofa. Based on the position of Adeline's body, she may have stepped in front of Jaime, taking the first bullet intended for him. There were no shell-casings at the scene. Odd. Meth pipes burned next to the victims' bodies.

A neighbor called 911 after hearing gunshots around three a.m. The caller didn't see vehicles on or near the property at the time of the assault. Said caller lived approximately one-thousand feet from the farmhouse. It was difficult to view the property from his vantage point.

Kent contacted Shade and asked her to come in for a follow-up interview.

"Mrs. Lane," said Kent, "I apologize for calling you in so soon, but I don't want to stall the investigation. You mentioned Adeline was supposed to be staying overnight in the hospital. I contacted the hospital and was told a nurse found the bed empty when she went to check on her. It appears she took off with Jaime without checking out."

"I don't understand. She would still be alive if she had stayed in the hospital." Shade lowered her head, tears puddling in her lap.

"I know this is hard, but can you tell me anything about the people you saw at the house in the past?"

"Only a few," said Shade, clasping her damp hands. "A guy named O.D. He used to live there when Scott was alive. Do you know about Scott?"

"Yes. He had quite a long record. We're also looking into his acquaintances."

Shade slumped in her seat. "I'm not sure you knew, but Scott was my grandson's biological father. After he died in an accident, O.D. moved out and Jaime and Addy became an item."

She described anyone she had seen at the house while Kent took notes. She explained that Addy didn't share her personal life with Shade. Their relationship was strained.

Kent wrapped up the interview. "Well, thanks for coming by. You're free to go."

"I'd like to go to the house to get my daughter's belongings. Do you know when that would be possible?"

"I'm sorry ma'am," he replied. "It's a crime scene. We can't allow anyone onto the premises, but I'll let you know when we're through. Here's my card. I want you to call me if there's anything else you remember, no matter how trivial you think it is. We'll do everything we can to find your daughter's murderer."

"Thank you," said Shade, standing to leave. "Can I call you periodically—for an update?"

"Feel free." Kent shook her hand and showed her out.

Kent felt sorry for the attractive woman. She didn't look old enough to have a grandchild. And she appeared to be single.

He read through his notes again and studied the crime scene sketch. They had a few suspects they were trailing. The ones that showed up at the house while they were casing the place. Sure smelled like a drug deal gone bad. He'd be surprised if this wasn't solved within a week. Drug dealers were notoriously sloppy when it came to leaving clues.

CHAPTER NINE

I remember the devotion of your youth, how as a bride you loved me and followed me through the wilderness, through a land not sown.

— JEREMIAH 2:2

Addy had nothing decent to wear for her funeral. Blanche volunteered to go shopping with Shade, and they selected a simple turquoise dress. The color reminded Shade of Addy's eyes.

It would be an open casket. Addy's face had been unscathed by the gunshot blast, and the funeral director assured Shade the gaping hole in her torso would be unnoticeable.

The service would take place at Holy Grace Baptist church with Pastor Dave presiding. Addy would be laid to rest in the same cemetery where Stanley was buried almost one year ago.

"I see you've chosen the farthest plot away from Stanley's grave," said Pastor Dave. "Don't you want Adeline buried beside Stan?"

She looked away. "Addy was always on the run, so I thought she'd prefer a plot closer to a busy road. I think she'd be happy with my decision."

"Whatever you think," he said, clearly baffled by her reasoning.

The day turned grey and foggy, mimicking Shade's mood. Mary and Blanche escorted her to the church while Sally babysat Tyler.

Shade succumbed to the enormity of her grief—liquid dripping between her fingers, saturating her black crepe dress. She would never look upon Addy's face again. Never have the opportunity to mend their broken relationship. Guilt gripped her hollow heart.

The pastor's eulogy escaped her. The mute button pressed. His lips moved, but the words she heard were those that played over and over in her head. *You failed her.*

The luncheon afterward overflowed with friends who came to offer support.

"Shade, do you remember me?" said a soft voice.

She immediately recognized the elderly black woman with the soothing smile. "Oh, Mabel," Shade cried, throwing her arms around her. "I've thought about calling you so many times. Thank you for coming today. Are you still running Mabel's House?"

"Why, yes, I am. But I'm not sure how much longer. I'm eighty-two now and slowing down a little." Her kind smile morphed into sorrow. "I came to tell you how sorry I am. I read about it in the newspaper. My heart aches for you. Tell me, do you have any other children? And are you still married to Stanley?"

"No, to both questions. Adeline was my only child, and Stanley passed away a year ago. Adeline was a single mother so I'll have custody of my grandson, Tyler. So, I guess you could say I have another child. He's my little golden nugget buried in this heartache."

"You poor dear. So much for one person to go through."

"When things settle down let's go to lunch. I'd like you to meet Tyler."

"I would love that, dear. Here's my number. Call me when you're ready." Mabel hugged her and left.

"Honey, who was that woman you were talking to?" asked Blanche.

"Remember when I told you about the home for unwed mothers? Well, that was Mabel, the woman who ran the home. Such a kind woman. I'll never forget her." She stared off, sadness creeping into her eyes.

"Are you doing okay?" asked Mary. "Just tell us when you're ready to leave."

"Soon. I'd like to get home to Tyler."

As she headed toward the restroom, a woman in her late forties approached. "Shade Lane?" she said, extending her hand. "I'm Donna Holder, Jaime's mom."

Shade tried masking the stunned expression on her face. She offered her hand. "It's nice to meet you, Donna. How good of you to come."

"I wanted to be here for you. I adored Addy and your grandson, Tyler. Jaime used to bring them over to my house at least once a week."

Shade's posture stiffened. Addy and Tyler spent time with this woman. As a family.

"Jaime loved that little boy, as if he was his own son," said Donna. "He was hoping he and Addy could get clean one day and marry. But it was hard for them both—you know, the drugs. I don't know about Addy's past, but Jaime had a troubled life."

"I'd like to hear more about Jaime, if you don't mind. I never got to know him."

"He was a good son. His father left us when Jaime was five. I had two sons. Jaime and Jacob. Their dad was an alcoholic. He'd only see them twice a year, so Jaime took on a fatherly role with little Jacob. Whenever Jacob felt frightened, Jaime tried to make things better. I'd often find Jaime in bed with Jacob in the morning with a protective arm wrapped around his little brother.

Jaime used to say to him, 'We'll always be here for each other—man-to-man.'"

The words slapped Shade in the face. She buried her surprise, and Donna continued.

"When Jaime was seven and Jacob five, their father picked them up for a rare overnight visit. The boys wanted to go, and I thought it would be good for them. Turns out, their dad left them alone and got drunk. When he returned, Jacob started crying. In a drunken rage, his father struck him. Jacob fell and hit his head. He died." Tears appeared, her face etched with pain. "Jaime was such a loving kid. But that tragic event changed him. He was never the same. He felt responsible. And then he got into drugs. I thought things might change when he met Addy, but they both had their struggles. The last time I spoke to Jaime, he talked about his 'little buddy', Tyler, and how much Tyler reminded him of Jacob." Donna pulled a tissue from her purse, dabbing her eyes.

Shade's loathing for Jaime slipped away. Witnessing the pain of Donna's agony burned a hole in her heart. Shade reached out and took Donna into her arms. They clung to each other, weeping.

"If you ever want to talk, here's my number," said Donna. "I'd love to see Tyler again."

"Thank you for sharing your story with me," said Shade, taking the number.

Shade stood unmoving, overcome with sadness as she watched Donna walk away. This poor woman had nothing left in the world. And she had Tyler, her little diamond, radiant and shining.

Inside the restroom stall, Shade leaned back against the cold metal partition—her chest heaving—her breaths coming in short gasps. Panic rose like a tide pulling her under. *Focus, Shade. Deep breaths. Remember the happy place. The place where you used to go.*

After several minutes, her mind steadied. She stood over the bathroom sink splashing cool water over her face before emerging into the crowd. |

"Honey, will you be okay?" asked Blanche, on the drive home.

"I'll be fine. Tyler will lift my spirits."

When they dropped her off, Mary took Shade's face in her hands, staring deeply, as though peering inside her soul. "You can't do this without Him. Don't push God away. It's the only way you'll get through this." She held her tight and kissed her cheek before letting go.

"Thank you for everything. I need time to think through things. I love you both."

Stepping inside her front door, she found Sally on the floor with Tyler. Every plastic bowl and wooden spoon she owned lay scattered across the carpet.

"Gamma's home," screamed Tyler, tossing aside his "toys." He ran toward her. She lifted him into her arms, kissing his face.

"Me and Sally dance. Moonwalk."

"You did?" said Shade, smiling at Sally.

"Yeah, I taught him how to do the moonwalk to the song, 'Billie Jean,'" said Sally. "It's hilarious. Hey Tyler, let's show your grandma the dance you learned? I'll put on the song."

When the beat blared, Sally and Tyler positioned themselves on the linoleum floor in the kitchen, standing side-by-side like toy soldiers.

"One-two-three," said Sally. With one foot in front of the other, they raised their back foot onto their toes, and pushed off, sliding the front foot backwards. "Now the other foot."

Shade threw her head back, consumed with laughter. And the more she laughed, the more animated Tyler became.

Sally smiled, stroking her arm. "I'm sorry for the mess. How did everything go today?"

"I was so touched by all the people that came. There must have been over a hundred."

"I'm glad it went well," said Sally, picking up the clutter. "Well, if you don't need me I'll get going."

"We'll be fine. Thanks for watching Tyler. I really appreciate it."

"Not a problem. Bye, Tyler."

Tyler ran over and grabbed Sally's legs. "Let's dance."

"I have to go," said Sally, grinning. "He's such a good boy. If you ever need someone to babysit, just call me. I'll see you at the bakery in a few weeks."

In bed that night, Shade reflected on the people who stood by her today. Her mind traveled to Donna. She replayed their conversation. The Jaime Donna described differed from the man she knew, or thought she knew. Did he truly love Tyler like a son, or was there something more sinister going on?

Guilt spread through her brain like a ravenous cancer. Addy's silhouette lingered behind her eyelids. She pulled the pillow over her face, trying to erase the harrowing memories, longing for sleep.

The white nightgown filled the darkened room, billowing as though caught in a gentle breeze. Addy glowed, her face smiling, her body levitating over the bed. Her arms reached for Shade. And then the blast came—cracking into the air. Addy's eyes popped wide, filled with terror. She screamed, her arms locked in a defensive position, her body propelled backward against the ceiling. The crimson speck on her white gown swelled. Addy's body drifted down. Down. The gore of the red, flowing blood covering Shade.

"Go back!" Shade tried to scream, but her voice was trapped in her throat. She awoke. Her body bathed in a cold sweat. Sheets twisted around her limbs. She sat up, struggling to still her thrashing heart. Her mind straining to discern fantasy from reality.

She got out of bed and walked down the hall into Tyler's room.

She sat on the bed, watching him sleep, gazing at his peaceful face. Tears gushed down.

A few weeks after the funeral, Shade took Tyler to child psychologist, Margaret Mills. After speaking to them both, Margaret asked Shade to leave the room so she could evaluate Tyler. Shade sat in the waiting room, trying to distract her mind, flipping through magazines. Too nervous to focus, she went outside for a walk. Thoughts raced. What if Jaime abused him? Then what? More tests? And how would his new environment influence him? He seemed normal, but would there be a delayed response?

Margaret and Tyler emerged to find Shade pacing. Tyler ran to her jabbering about the games he played—coloring, building blocks, and dolls.

"He's a great little boy. And very smart. I'll type up a report and call you in a few days so we can review everything. I'd suggest getting a sitter when you come back. Do you have any questions?"

"I was hoping to know something today. Should I be worried?"

"Don't be worried. We'll talk once I have everything prepared. It's typical procedure." Margaret crouched and patted Tyler on the head. "It was nice meeting you, Tyler. Did you have fun today?"

"Yeah!" Tyler said, bouncing up and down.

Shade arrived at Margaret's office for the follow-up meeting. Despite Margaret's reassurance, her stomach shifted.

Margaret handed Shade the report. "I'm pleased to tell you Tyler appears to be an extremely well-adjusted boy. Regarding his new living arrangements, he expressed sadness about his losses, but it's a normal reaction. He exhibits great affection for you,

Shade. He seems perfectly content to live with you going forward."

She heaved a sigh of relief. Her posture softened.

"Regarding Tyler's relationship with Jaime, I found no evidence Tyler had been abused. In fact, Jaime seemed to be the more responsible, nurturing influence. Perhaps more so than his own mother. He was a father figure to Tyler. Your daughter and Tyler may have had some bonding issues. You and I didn't talk much about Adeline, but there may have been something preventing her from fulfilling her maternal role. Perhaps Jaime tried to compensate."

Shade swallowed hard, trying to tame the lump forming in her throat. "Yes, Adeline had problems, but I'd rather not go into it unless it's necessary."

"It may be important, but we can talk about that later. Tyler is a special little boy, and I think he'll adjust well in your care. Raise him as you would your own child, but it's also important to talk about his mother and Jaime. If he asks questions, keep reaffirming the fact they're gone. And let Tyler take the lead on these discussions. It's essential for him you keep their memory alive. You may see oppositional behavior and some developmental regression. Let's keep an eye on it and see how things go. Do you have questions?"

"I don't have any questions—at least now. I'm just so relieved. Thank you."

"Call me any time." Margaret rose and shook Shade's hand.

On the drive home, a wave of elation washed over her, anguish sliding in behind. A briny mix poured from her eyes, bathing her face. She pulled into a nearby parking lot, searching for a tissue. Spotting a dirty rag underneath her seat, she wiped her face and blew her nose. When she thought she had pulled herself together, raw emotion came crashing in. Her breathing rapid and shallow. Her heart racing faster. Too fast. The world around her spun. Everything blurred.

With her head in her hands, she pleaded with God. *Please help me. I turned away from You. But I was wrong. About everything. About Jaime. His hurt. His pain. I tried playing judge. I've made such a mess of things. Oh, dear God, please forgive me. Don't turn your face from me. I abandoned you, but I want to come back home. Help me raise Tyler to be a good man. To get him settled in life and on his way in this world. I want to make things right and be the mother I should have been to Addy. Grant me that much time, God. Please. Then I'll do what needs to be done, but just help me raise Tyler.*

She sat in her car for over an hour, praying and wrestling with God, until an eerie peace washed over her. Her breathing became measured, her heart settled into its normal rhythm. Her body filled with uncanny calm. A restrained sea, flattened. In that moment, she felt His presence. God heard her. He was with her. Right here. Right now. And He took hold of her soul and led her back. A lost sheep found.

CHAPTER TEN

And God is able to bless you abundantly, so that in all things at all times, having all that you need, you will abound in every good work.

— 2 CORINTHIANS 9:8

Year 1999

Detective Kent Monroe fingered the Lane/Holder file. It had become a permanent fixture on his desk the last two years. With no new leads the case had gone cold, and he took on other assignments. Immediately after the murders, he felt confident they would solve the case, but each lead led to a dead end. He wasn't able to bring closure to the grieving mothers.

Kent appeared at Shade's front door holding a box. "Good evening, Mrs. Lane," he said, when she opened the door. "I'm sorry to pop in on you, but I wanted to drop off your daughter's belongings."

"Come in, Kent. What a nice surprise. Would you like coffee?"

"Sure. I'm sorry it took so long to get these to you. I brought everything I could without compromising the investigation. I found one item hidden under a mattress. Looks like a scrapbook. I wanted to be sure you got it."

"Thank you," said Shade, her eyebrows elevating. "I didn't realize she kept a scrapbook." She poured two cups of coffee. They moved into the living room.

"So, how are you doing? And how is Tyler doing?"

"Good. Tyler has adjusted to his new home here with me. He'll be five this September. He starts kindergarten in the fall."

"That's great. I'm happy to hear things are working out for you both." Kent paused as he stared into his coffee. "I want you to know how sorry I am we haven't been able to break this case. But I'll continue to do everything I can to help find the killer or killers. I'm on another assignment, but it doesn't mean I can't pick it back up again when things slow down, or if we receive new leads."

"I know you've done all you can, and I appreciate it. Do you still feel the murders were drug related?"

"Yes, I do. I just don't have enough concrete evidence." He glanced at the toys scattered around. "It must be hard raising your grandson alone. Assuming you are alone?"

Kent hoped it didn't sound like a come-on. He was rusty. He'd been divorced for five years, and work kept him busy, leaving him little time for a relationship.

She smiled. "Yes, I'm alone. My husband passed away three years ago. It's just the two of us."

"I'm sorry," Kent replied. "You've had a lot of grief in your life."

"Yes," she said, staring into her coffee. "But I don't dwell on it. I have a grandson to raise now."

"He's lucky to have you. Well, thanks for the coffee. I better get going. I wanted to make sure I brought you the scrapbook."

Kent stood and moved to the front door. Shade followed to see him out.

He opened the door and turned back, catching her off guard,

causing her to stumble backwards to avoid burying her head in his chest. Kent reached out and took hold of her arm.

"You okay?"

"Yes," she laughed, "I'm fine." Her face burned crimson.

"Hey, I was wondering if you'd like to go out for dinner sometime?"

"Oh," Shade stammered, jarred by the unexpected invitation. "Let me think about it. I don't like leaving Tyler in the evening after working all day."

Kent smiled. "I'm sorry. I shouldn't have been so forward. I guess I'm a little out of practice with women. If you change your mind, though, call me. Whatever you decide, it won't affect my commitment to solving this case."

After Kent left, she thought about accepting his invitation. She felt attracted to him, but she couldn't allow anyone to get too close. She had to stay guarded and focused on raising Tyler.

She turned to face the box he had brought her. It smelled musty. Burnt plastic mingled with cigarette smoke. She pulled out toys and clothes. So few belongings. As though Addy barely existed. Shade removed the scrapbook from the bottom of the pile and sat at the kitchen table.

Turning the pages, she stopped at several photos and other mementos laid out under the heading, "My Beautiful Family." Her eyebrows gathered as her fingers touched her parted lips. Photos of Shade and Addy graced the pages—Addy as a toddler and up through her early teens. There were hand-written notes under several photos; *The prettiest Mom in the world, Me and Mom having a special day together—just the two of us, Mom making cookies—the world's best baker.* Liquid burned in her eyes. She recalled their good years together. Still an open wound.

Turning to a section dedicated to Tyler, she found photos, locks of his hair glued to the pages, a cellophane bag with his first fingernail and toenail clippings, and a section entitled, "Five Things I Love About You," with blue cut-out hearts pasted across the page. A single sentence was written within each; *I Love Your Smile, I Love the Way You Smell, I Love Watching You Chase Butterflies, I Love Hearing You Say Gamma, I Love Watching You Sleep—Curled Up in Jaime's Arms.*

Shade brushed her fingers over the scrapbook, as though stroking her daughter's face. Emptiness weighed in. She wondered if she ever knew Addy. Concealed beneath her hard-hearted exterior lived a woman who silently loved. Memories she kept tucked away. As though not worthy of anything good.

"Oh Addy," she cried, "if only things had worked out differently. If only I could have been stronger—your protector. If only you hadn't left the hospital that night." She swallowed deep, trying to dilute the pain.

She wrapped the scrapbook in a piece of felt cloth and tucked it away for Tyler. When he was mature enough to appreciate it, she would give it to him.

Mary's car pulled into the driveway. After Shade received custody of Tyler, Mary had volunteered to babysit so Shade could return to work. The arrangement worked out perfectly. Mary looked after her granddaughter, Leah, so Tyler had a steady playmate.

"Hi, Grandma," said Tyler, hopping out of the car and running into the house. "Guess what? Leah has a dog. Can I have a dog, Grandma? Please, Grandma."

Mary followed Tyler into the house, smirking. "Leah's parents bought her a puppy. A Golden Retriever. I volunteered to take care of the dog when I babysit Leah. I should have warned you."

Shade smiled and bent to kiss Tyler. "I missed you today."

"Grandma, I want a dog. I really *need* a dog."

"Tyler, we'll talk about this later."

"What time later?"

"When I say it's time. But not now."

After dinner, she got Tyler ready for bed. His Mediterranean blue eyes followed her every move, awaiting the talk. When she had tucked him in, she pulled out the children's Bible stories book and read Tyler's favorite story, Noah's Ark. "I will make it rain forty days and forty nights. There will be a great flood, but you and your family, and all the animals will be safe in the ark."

"Grandma, did dogs go in the ark?"

"Maybe."

"I think dogs went into the ark. If God wanted dogs in the ark, he probably wants a dog in our house. Don't you think, Grandma?"

She sighed, closing the book. "Honey, a dog is a lot of responsibility. I work all day and you're with Mary. Soon you'll be starting kindergarten. It's not good to leave a dog alone."

"But I can take it to Mary's. Like Leah does. And I'll take the dog to school."

"Dogs aren't allowed in school. And we can't ask Mary to watch another dog." She sighed. "It's not a good time." She pulled the covers over him, kissing his forehead. Tyler stared up at her, droplets brimming in his eyes.

The city of Edelweiss thrived. New restaurants, specialty shops, and bed and breakfasts sprouted up along the bustling streets of the small beach town. About a mile from Lake Michigan, summer tourists packed the downtown area, while winter brought in respectable numbers of snow enthusiasts. Business at Bonnie's Bakery continued to swell.

Shade presented new ideas to Bonnie to help grow the business. Besides baked goods, they now offered an array of soups, using recipes from Shade's vast collection. The most popular soups on the menu were Chorizo and White Bean, Wild Mushroom with Madeira Wine, and Midwest Cream of Chicken.

Bonnie started to show signs of slowing down. At the end of an especially hectic day, she pulled Shade aside. "Do you have a few minutes?"

"Sure. What's up?"

"I've been giving this a lot of thought lately, so hear me out. There are so many things I want to do in life. Travel, plant a garden, or just do nothing at all. I've spent over fifteen years tied to this bakery. It's time for me to retire. And you're the ideal candidate to take over. You know this business inside and out, and you've done such a great job—coming up with new ideas and increasing sales. I could sell the bakery to you and stay on as a consultant until you're comfortable running things on your own. I'd make it worth your while. We could work out a payment plan. Maybe even waive payments for a few years until you're established. It'd be a new opportunity for you. Why don't you mull it over and let's talk next week? If you agree, I'd like to make this happen soon."

"You caught me by surprise," said Shade. "It sounds like a wonderful opportunity, but I want to pray about it. It's a big responsibility. Is everything okay with you?"

"Yes. I'm fine, so don't worry. I'm just ready for the next phase of my life."

On the drive to Mary's, the conversation with Bonnie consumed her. The prospect of owning a business thrilled her, but they would have to work out the details. She didn't want to get in over her head, and she wanted to be sure she preserved enough money for Tyler's education.

Mary greeted Shade at the door. Tyler ran to meet her, the puppy chasing his heels. "Grandma. Look, it's Willow." Shade bent to pet the puppy. Willow jumped on her, urinating on her shoes.

"Is this what they call a golden shower?" Shade asked.

"Willow!" said Mary. "Leah, can you get a towel so we can clean her shoes? I'm so sorry."

"Bad, Willow," said Leah, shaking her finger at Willow's nose.

Tyler joined in, exemplifying the behavior of a responsible pet owner. "Bad, bad, Willow. God doesn't like it when you pee on people. Grandma, can we stay longer? Leah and me wanna play."

Mary insisted she stay for coffee. They sat at the kitchen table, and Shade revealed her conversation with Bonnie.

"So, what are you thinking? Do you want to own the bakery?"

"It's a great opportunity. I understand everything about running the business. The only caveat is the location. It's a perfect area, but I'd want to live closer. Coincidently, I've been planning to move somewhere with a better school system for Tyler, and I know Edelweiss is rated high. I'm sure I could find a decent home there."

"It sounds wonderful, but it's a big step."

After praying, Shade felt led to take over the bakery, and Bonnie was thrilled. They signed the paperwork, working through Bonnie's attorney, and Shade agreed to keep the current employees, now totaling five. She decided to make Sally supervisor, if she accepted.

The timing couldn't be better. School would start in a month, allowing her ample time to get Tyler settled and enrolled.

"Tyler, I want to talk to you about some big changes," said Shade.

"Are we getting a dog?" asked Tyler, his face beaming.

"No. But we're going to move to a new house. Away from here. And you're going to start school near the new house. Doesn't that sound exciting?"

Tyler frowned. "What about Mary? And Leah? And Willow?"

"Mary will still pick you up from school each day."

"What if Jaime comes back and can't find us?" asked Tyler, whimpering.

Her breath caught. It had been awhile since Tyler had mentioned his past. "Honey, do you remember when I told you your mom and Jaime wouldn't be coming back, and they wanted you to live with me?"

"Yeah. Does that mean they won't try to find us?"

"Yes, honey, they won't try to find us."

"But don't they want to see us?"

She struggled to stop the swell rising in her throat. "Oh, honey, of course they want to see us. But they can't. Jaime and your mom went to sleep and they won't wake up again."

"Well, alright. If they're not coming back, then let's move."

Bonnie turned the bakery over to Shade and stayed on in an advisory role. Shade listed her house with a realtor. She held off looking for a new place until her house sold. In the meantime, Bonnie invited Shade to move in with her until she found something in Edelweiss and suggested she bring Tyler over to look around before accepting.

They made their way down the winding tree-lined driveway leading to Bonnie's home. She liked the natural setting. Surrounded by birch and pine trees, the gray and white Craftsman style cottage rested on a small bluff overlooking Lake

Michigan. Bonnie stepped out onto the large wrap-around porch to greet them.

"Did you have a hard time finding me?"

"No, not at all. It's gorgeous here."

Tyler bolted out of the car and ran around the property. "Wow. The water is so big."

"Well, come in and I'll give you the tour. This was my parents' home. I inherited it after they passed."

Entering the front door, floor to ceiling windows greeted them, flaunting the magnificence of Lake Michigan. A large stone fireplace stood in the main living area, surrounded by weathered hickory plank flooring. The home had 1,800 square-feet of living space with three bedrooms and two baths. The kitchen was a professional cook's dream, outfitted with high-end appliances, plenty of counter space and a large kitchen island. Out back, the deck spanned the entire length of the house. Steps descended from the deck to the white sand beach.

"This is beautiful. I love the cottage feel of your home."

"I love it, Grandma. Are we going to live here?"

"Just for a while. Until we find our own house."

"You can stay as long as you like," said Bonnie. "I welcome the company. It's quiet here, so the change will be good."

"Do you ever get lonely out here?"

"I did until I got a puppy. I put him out back so he wouldn't jump on you. His name is Scone, after the first bakery sale I ever made. He's a golden Labrador. Would you like to meet him?"

Tyler let out a squeal, bouncing on his toes. "Puppy. We got a puppy."

"Honey, Scone is Bonnie's puppy, not ours."

Bonnie brought Scone over to meet Tyler and Shade. Tyler sat on the ground coaxing the trembling puppy in a gentle voice.

"Hi, Scone. My name is Tyler Lane. I've been praying for someone like you. Come, Scone." The puppy went to Tyler, lapping at his face.

"When are we moving, Grandma?"

"When we sell our house." Shade looked at Bonnie. "It looks like this will be perfect for us. My only concern is prying Tyler away from Scone when it's time to move."

"Don't worry. Tyler can come by and visit Scone whenever he likes."

Shade's house sold for the asking price within the first week. She put Sally in charge of the bakery while she took time off to move. She sold a handful of belongings—filing cabinets, Stan's hunting equipment, and a few framed pieces of artwork. The other furnishings went into storage until she purchased a home.

Before disconnecting her phone, she called Detective Kent.

"Shade. Good to hear from you. How are you doing?"

"I'm doing well. I'm calling to tell you I'll be moving, and I wanted to give you my contact information in case there were any new developments. I'm buying a bakery over in Edelweiss, so I'm moving closer to the shop."

"That's good to know. Congratulations. For a minute there, I thought you were calling to take me up on that dinner date."

She laughed. "About that offer—I was flattered, but I'm not ready to date again. My focus needs to be on Tyler."

"I understand. But if you change your mind, the offer stands. Regarding the investigation, I have no new leads, but I'll let you know if anything changes. Good luck, and stay in touch."

"Thanks, and if you're in the area stop in at the bakery. I'll buy you a coffee and a muffin. We don't sell donuts."

"Funny. Take care of yourself."

CHAPTER ELEVEN

You, Lord, keep my lamp burning; my God turns my darkness into light.

— PSALM 18:28

Bonnie looked forward to her retirement years and celebrated by treating herself to a ten-day Mediterranean cruise, targeted toward mature, single adults. The itinerary included stops in Italy, France, Spain, and Portugal. She couldn't wait to tell Shade.

Since Tyler and Shade had moved in, the cottage bustled with energy—something foreign to her. She could sit for hours watching Tyler and Scone running through the yard, or listening to Shade read Bible stories to Tyler while he interrupted with one amusing question after another. She dreaded the day they would move away.

Shade enrolled Tyler in kindergarten at Edelweiss Elementary School. She worked out a schedule with Mary. She would drop him off in the morning, and Mary would pick him up and take him to her house, where he'd play with Leah and Willow until she got off work.

Under her management, Shade renamed the business to Shady Lane's Bakery and Café. She hired a creative designer to develop a new brand image and an interior designer to revamp the floor space and redesign the storefront.

Whimsical and airy tones enhanced the café interior, complementing the beach town feel of the neighborhood. New lighting added visual interest, fresh paint covered the walls, and the entrance area was reconfigured to enrich the customer's first impression.

Sally proved to be a competent supervisor, allowing Shade to focus on new product development and marketing the business within the community. Together they made a dynamic team.

She found a new church—First Church of Edelweiss—a thriving non-denominational church with several young families. Tyler loved attending Sunday school, and Shade admired their outreach events. The pieces of her life were falling into place.

With the remodel of the bakery complete, she contacted a realtor and focused her time searching for a new house. She would miss Bonnie, but she didn't want to overstay her welcome. Since moving in, the two of them developed a strong bond, like mother and daughter. And Bonnie had grown to adore Tyler.

"My realtor has a few properties for me to look at today," said Shade, as Bonnie sat nursing a mug of coffee.

"That's great. Are you taking Tyler?"

"Yes. Hopefully, he'll be patient."

"Why don't you leave him with me? It won't be any bother. Besides, he can spend the day with Scone. You should see that dog when Tyler leaves for school. He lays at the front door whimpering and looking out the window. Last night Scone wasn't in my bedroom, so I went looking for him. I found him with Tyler, the two of them cuddled up in his bed."

Tyler ran through the cottage, playing fetch with Scone, while Bonnie sat and read in front of the fireplace.

"What are you reading?" asked Tyler.

"It's a book my mother gave me when I was young. 'Anne of Green Gables.'"

"My grandma reads Bible stories at night. If I get my book, can you read to me?"

"I'd love to, honey. Bring it over."

Tyler handed Bonnie the book and sat at her feet. "Can you read the Christmas Story?"

"Sure," she said, donning her reading glasses.

"Do you think Jesus wears glasses?"

"Probably not. I bet he has perfect eyesight."

"Me too. Did you know God's real name is Howard?"

"No. I didn't."

"Yeah. A boy in Sunday school told me. It's in the Lord's Prayer," he declared. "Our Father who does art in heaven, Howard be his name."

Bonnie grinned, patting him on the head. She had never spent much time around children and found herself fascinated by Tyler's innocence and sense of wonder.

When Shade returned home, Tyler was asleep on the floor next to Bonnie. "Looks like you wore him out," she whispered. "How was he?"

"Like a little angel. Did you find anything?"

"Perhaps. I almost put in a bid but decided to look around a little more."

"Come sit, and tell me."

Shade removed her coat. "It's a cute house, with a lot of character. About 1,500 square feet with a large fenced-in yard in a well-maintained neighborhood. I'd like to get Tyler a dog, so this would be perfect. I'll need to make improvements, but not right away."

"It sounds nice. I'll miss you two when you move. It's been nice having you here."

"Well, I'm sure we'll still see each other. Do you have family nearby?"

"I was an only child, so no family to speak of. Just a cousin, Francis. Haven't seen her in years. She calls once a year. To check if I'm still alive." Bonnie shook her head and let out a sigh. "Hey, you'll never guess what I did. I booked a European cruise." She handed Shade the brochure. "I leave in two weeks, so you'll have the house to yourself."

"I'm so excited for you. A cruise sounds wonderful."

"I can't wait. Do you mind if I leave Scone here with you? I could take him to a kennel, but Tyler would be devastated."

"Without question. You've done so much for us. It's the least we could do."

The idyllic towns and villages of Western Europe captivated Bonnie's heart. On the first day of the cruise, she met another single woman, Labushka from Yugoslavia, and they became inseparable traveling companions. Labushka was a professional photographer and gave Bonnie several tips for scoring that perfect photo. With cameras dangling from their necks, they'd meet on the ship each day to begin their trek through the bustling streets and alleyways.

On the last day of the cruise they set out, negotiating the hidden side roads of Lisbon, Portugal, in search of that elusive National Geographic shot. They stopped at a trendy outdoor café for lunch with a view overlooking terracotta rooftops and chalk-white church domes. In celebration of their last day, they ordered a bottle of wine from the Lisboa region, a full-bodied Arruda. For their entrée, they feasted on Bacalhau à brás, a shredded codfish with fried potato, onion and scrambled eggs topped with a sprinkle of black olives and chopped parsley. While they savored their lunch and sipped wine, Labushka outlined their plan for the day.

"Ve must hurry vhile sun shines perfectly," said Labushka, pushing her chair away from the table and knocking it over backwards—with her in it.

"Labushka," screamed Bonnie, shocked at the sight of her friend's shape lying on the ground, camera straps tangled around her neck. "Are you alright?"

"Oosh. Maybe much too much vine," laughed Labushka, struggling to right herself, brushing pebbles from her embroidered linen skirt and matching woolen knee socks. "I'm good. Ve must hurry," she said, gathering her equipment and walking briskly down the road, Bonnie at her heels trying to keep pace.

They spotted an old gothic church and pulled out their cameras. Labushka directed Bonnie to a location near the entrance of the ancient town, down a charming cobblestone passageway. "Bon-a," shouted Labushka, "you look to lens—vhile valking. Keep shooting—vhile valking. I tell you to stop."

Bonnie walked forward, staring into the wide-angle lens, adjusting the outer ring until the image came into focus. She heard Labushka scream—in Slovenian. "Ustaviti!"

"What?" Bonnie responded, still peering through the lens. Simulating a slow-motion scene, her heel caught the edge of immovable metal. The manhole cover rested alongside the gaping hole. And Bonnie, in an instant, plunged fifteen feet. Head first. Into the dark abyss.

Labushka would later lament, "One time I see her head. Next time I see her feet. Oh, Bon-a," she cried, "I so sorry."

The phone rang, stirring Shade from sleep.

"Hello," said a heavily accented voice. "I'm calling on behalf of Bonnie Langley. You were listed as an emergency contact. Are you a relative?"

"No, I'm a friend. Who's calling?"

"This is Constable Sousa, from Lisbon, Portugal. I'm saddened to inform you Bonnie had an unfortunate accident. In an open manhole. We will prepare to send the body back. My condolences, Madame. I'll be in touch soon."

She sat stunned, holding the phone to her ear, listening to dead silence. This must be a sick joke. But it wasn't. Bonnie had retired. Literally. "Oh, Bonnie," Shade cried. "It isn't fair."

The following morning, Shade rummaged through Bonnie's desk and found the number of her estate attorney, David Cunningham. "Hello David. My name is Shade Lane. I'm a good friend of Bonnie Langley." Her voice quivered as she spoke. "She fell into a manhole," she sobbed.

"She what? Is she okay? I met with Bonnie right before she left. She told me about her European cruise."

"She's dead," Shade hiccupped. "It's so tragic. I wanted to get a hold of her relatives, but the only person I'm aware of is a cousin named Francis."

"Yes, Francis Cabot. Her only living relative. Did you say a manhole?"

"Yes, a manhole."

"How unfortunate. Can you meet today? I could drive to the cottage."

"Yes. I'd like to get in contact with Francis as soon as possible."

David arrived at the cottage toting a briefcase. After settling at the kitchen table, he pulled out Bonnie's estate plan and slid it across to Shade.

"This may come as a shock," he said, removing his glasses, "but you are the sole beneficiary of Bonnie's estate."

She stared at David, her eyebrows furrowed. "What? Me?"

"Yes. Bonnie met with me before the cruise. She wanted to change her trust before she left in case anything happened. Bonnie wasn't comfortable leaving everything to her cousin, Francis. They hadn't seen each other in years. She talked a lot about you, Shade. And about Tyler. Said you two were the closest thing she had to family, and nothing would make her happier than to know you were both taken care of after she's gone."

Shade dropped her head in her hands and wept. David sat, waiting for her to come to terms with the news.

He patted the estate plan. "Everything is spelled out for you in this binder. You are the named Successor Trustee and Power of Attorney. You should have no problem accessing Bonnie's assets and transferring them into your name. Please call me if you have questions."

Everything Bonnie owned now belonged to Shade, including Scone. Aside from the house and the bakery business, Bonnie left over $960,000 in savings and mutual funds.

Shade worked with David Cunningham to create a Trust in her name, naming Tyler the Successor Trustee.

Overcome with gratefulness, she thought back to her unprivileged childhood, the horror of Stan's secret life, Addy's murder, the stain of her guilt. And now this. Why me, God? I'm not worthy.

CHAPTER TWELVE

You have stolen my heart, my sister, my bride; you have stolen my heart with one glance of your eyes, with one jewel of your necklace.

— SONG OF SONGS 4:9

Year 2000

Tyler discovered a new love besides Scone. Baseball. Edelweiss Elementary sponsored a baseball camp, and Tyler begged Shade to enroll. At six-years-old, he understood the mechanics of the game and could name every player on the Detroit Tigers team.

Baseball camp took place after school, and parents were encouraged to practice with their youngsters at home. She worried about the time commitment until Mary offered to help.

Enthralled with the game, Tyler had an eye for the ball, whether hurling toward his bat or running to catch a fly ball in the outfield. When Shade got off work, they played catch on the beach, or she pitched while Tyler practiced hitting—and Scone practiced retrieving.

Shade wondered if Tyler inherited his athletic ability from his father. She didn't know much about Scott other than what Addy had mentioned—his passion for weight lifting. She considered Addy's father, Matthew, and his athleticism. Matthew dreamed of getting into the University of Michigan on a football scholarship. Were sports in Tyler's genes?

When the baseball team played their first official game, Mary, Leah, and Willow met at Shade's house, and they drove to the game together. Tyler managed two base hits, one stolen base and an outfield catch that brought the crowd to their feet.

"I'm so proud of you," said Shade, after the game. "All that practice is paying off."

"Thanks. We're a good team," he declared, before running off to join his teammates.

"You've got one talented son," said the man, offering his hand. "I don't think we've met. I'm Brent Meyers, Tyler's coach."

"It's nice to meet you. I'm Tyler's grandmother, Shade. I've heard a lot about you."

"Well, I hope it's all good," said Brent, trying to mask his surprise. "Everyone is meeting at Dairy Cone for ice cream. I hope to see you there."

"We wouldn't miss it."

"I met Tyler's coach, Brent," Shade said to Mary on the drive to Dairy Cone. "He seems like a nice guy."

"Yes, he's good with those boys. I watch him during practice. He's so patient, but he's also firm. The boys have a lot of respect for him. And he never singles a player out, whether good or bad. It's all about teamwork."

"That explains it," said Shade, lowering her voice. "When I congratulated Tyler, he was quick to point out it wasn't about him. It was about the team."

Mary laughed. "I guess he's paying attention."

Arriving at Dairy Cone, Shade studied Brent as he corralled the raucous boys into an orderly group. She was amused at his ability to handle the chaos.

While they sat eating ice cream, she gazed openly at Brent. She liked the way he looked and how he handled himself. His skin tanned and slightly weathered. His eyes were the color of sapphire and warmed when he smiled, causing faint wrinkles to form at the corners. He had a nice build. Well-toned and tall. He looked to be in his early forties. Her eyes traveled to his left hand. No ring. Mary awakened her from her dreamy state.

"I heard Brent used to be a Major League Baseball scout but changed careers when he got married. It required too much travel, and he didn't want to be away from his family. Now he's the Athletic Director for Edelweiss Schools, and he coaches baseball camp in his spare time."

"Well, we're lucky to have him," Shade responded, hiding her disappointment.

Brent approached their table while making the rounds. "Great game today," he said, tousling Tyler's hair. "You played like you wanted to win." He extended his hand to Mary. "I'm not sure we've met, but I've seen you at practice. I'm Brent Meyers."

"I'm Mary, Shade's friend, and this is Leah, my granddaughter."

"Nice to meet you both. Do you like baseball, Leah?"

"Yes," said Leah. "I like watching Tyler. We play catch together."

"That's great. Tyler, have you been practicing at home—like we talked about?"

"Yes. Me and Grandma practice. She pitches while I bat, and we play catch."

Shade laughed. "Well, I try to play, but I'm not very good."

"Well, keep it up. Every bit helps. It was nice meeting everyone. I'd better get back to my mingling duties." His eyes landed on Shade. "Will I be seeing you at camp this week? Maybe I can give you a few pointers on things to practice with Tyler."

That week, Shade called Mary to tell her she would take Tyler to baseball camp. On the drive, Tyler babbled on and on about baseball, and Brent, and his future aspirations.

"Grandma, do you know what I wanna be when I grow up?"

"Let me guess. A baseball player?"

"How did you guess?"

"I had a good idea. But you might change your mind. Sometimes God has other plans for us."

"I think God wants me to be a baseball player. And sometimes, but not all the time, I think God wants me to marry Leah. Because she plays baseball with me. And we could practice together. Will you ever get married, Grandma?"

"I have you. And that's all I need."

"But if I marry Leah, you'll be alone."

"I'll never be alone. God will be with me. Always."

"If you got married, would the man be my grandpa or my dad?"

"He'd be your grandpa. But let's not talk about that. I'm not getting married."

"Guess what, Grandma? I love you."

"Guess what, Tyler? I love you, too."

Tyler bolted from the car and ran toward Brent. "Hey, Brent. I'm here."

Brent straightened and stopped what he was doing. "Hi, Tyler," he said, smiling, looking around. He saw her and waved.

Shade strode over, her legs drawing his eyes. She wore a loose-fitting casual skirt with a simple white T-shirt and running shoes.

"Hi, Brent. I came for my pointers. Remember?"

"I do," he said, smiling. "Can you stick around after practice?"

She took a seat while Brent walked the boys through their warm-up exercises.

"Okay, boys," Brent shouted. "What's the most important thing you can bring to the team today? Remember, we talked about this last week."

"Attitude," they shouted.

"That's right. If you don't have a good attitude, you won't work hard, and you won't be excited to play."

Brent went to work, teaching the boys how to keep the ball in front of them when fielding. He paid special attention to the less athletic kids, administering one-on-one instructions, never losing patience.

When they were done practicing, Brent walked over to her. Tyler stood beside him, talking about the game and asking questions, while Brent thoughtfully answered.

"Are you ready for your pointers?" Brent asked Shade.

"Ready as I'll ever be."

He took her out onto the field, demonstrating batting techniques for Tyler to practice.

"As much as you can, let him practice swinging the bat while you throw the ball. Watch his hands. He needs to keep his hands at chest level, never dropping to the stomach. If he does, it will cut down on his reaction time to the pitch. Here," he said, handing her the ball. "Why don't you throw and watch how I swing."

She tossed the ball to Brent. A rush of wind caught hold causing her to grapple with her skirt. It sailed airborne. Brent, distracted by the scene, failed to duck. The ball zeroed in at his left temple, smacking him on the side of the head.

"Grandma," Tyler screamed. "You hurt him."

"I'm so sorry." She ran to him, fingering the spot on his head where the ball struck. "Are you okay?"

"Don't worry. I'm fine," said Brent. He shook his head, as though trying to shake the intimate moment away.

When they finished, Tyler ran ahead to the car. Brent walked with Shade.

"I've coached a lot of kids, but Tyler is different. His skills at such a young age are rare. If this is something he wants, it's important that you continue to feed his drive."

"He's obsessed with baseball. And I'll do everything I can to help him."

"I'm glad to hear that. I used to be a baseball scout for the MLB. I know what they look for, and I'd be willing to mentor him."

A wave of suspicion swept over her. *Be cautious.* "A baseball scout?" she asked. "Is that like the Boy Scouts but focused on baseball—for adults?"

He grinned. "No. I represented Major League Baseball teams and evaluated athletes to determine if they were talented enough to be in the Majors."

"Sounds exciting. What do you do now?"

"I'm the Athletic Director for Edelweiss Schools. I love working with young kids. I guess it's in my blood. What about you? Where do you work?"

"I'm the owner of Shady Lane's Bakery and Café. It used to be Bonnie's Bakery, but I recently took it over."

"I've heard of Bonnie's Bakery but haven't been there in a while. It must keep you busy."

"Yes, it does," said Shade.

On the drive home, Tyler talked baseball while Shade thought about Brent. He was good with Tyler, but she had to be careful. Vigilant. She wondered if he was married. At least that's what Mary thought.

"Grandma, do you like Brent? I like him a lot."

"I like him a lot, too," said Shade. "He seems like a nice man."

The flashing light on the answering machine caught her attention when she walked in the door. "Hello, Shade. It's Mabel Johnson. We talked about getting together. Maybe we could meet for lunch. Please call me."

"It's so good to see you, Mabel," said Shade, arriving at the restaurant the next day. "I'm glad you called. How have you been?"

"I'm doing good. Just having a few health issues, but nothing concerning. These bodies weren't meant to last forever. I turned Mabel's House over to a lovely woman, Patsy, but I still help occasionally."

"It's good to keep busy. I wanted to bring Tyler, but he's in school. So much has happened since we spoke."

Shade told Mabel about Bonnie's accident and all she had inherited, including the bakery, and about Tyler's progress and his passion for baseball.

"How sad for Bonnie," said Mabel, shaking her head. "What a horrible way to die. But it sounds like you've been blessed, dear."

"Yes, I have," said Shade. "Mabel, I need to ask you something. Something that's always eating at me. Do you remember when Stanley asked me to marry him—when I was living at your home?"

"I sure do, honey. Like it was yesterday."

"You told me we needed to pray before I accepted—to be sure it was God's plan. But I never waited for an answer, or a sign. I was so overcome with joy, I accepted, convinced it was what God wanted for me. But looking back, I wonder if it was only what I wanted. When you prayed for me, did you get an answer?"

"You know, God gives us signs. Thoughts he puts in our heads, or a feeling something isn't right. That was the answer I received.

A feeling something wasn't right, but I didn't understand why. Do you feel you didn't make the right decision by marrying Stanley?"

She looked off before answering. "He wasn't the man I thought he was, and I wonder why God didn't intervene."

"Maybe God did intervene, and you weren't listening. You don't have to give me the details, honey. What's done is done. That's the path you chose, and you can't turn back. As you go forward, raising Tyler, remember to look for signs or a subtle nudging at your heart. It may be God's way of speaking to you. Pay attention and try to make right choices."

"I don't feel I've made right choices in life," said Shade, pulling in her tears. "I know God is forgiving, but as much as I try to believe, I still feel stained. Unforgiven."

"Stop punishing yourself. No matter how much remorse we carry or how far-off God seems, He is still with us, leading us out of our mess and into His blessing."

Shade reached for Mabel's hand. "You've always been such an inspiration. You'll never know how much you've impacted my life. Thank you."

Driving home, she considered Mabel's words. They brought her comfort. Hope. She felt blessed seeing her again, and she thanked God for the beautiful woman He wove into her life.

Her joyfulness quickly shifted south. The prince of darkness took hold, shrouding her soul like an unforgiving spirit, haunting her all over again. He was always there, ready to pounce. To strip away anything good.

She pushed the negative feelings away. She had gotten good at hiding her pain—wearing a mask. Her defense mechanism, the byproduct of her dysfunctional life, kept her sane. *Fix your eye on the goal,* she chanted.

CHAPTER THIRTEEN

One person gives freely, yet gains even more; another withholds unduly, but comes to poverty. A generous person will prosper; whoever refreshes others will be refreshed.

— PROVERBS 11:24-25

Shady Lane's Bakery and Café continued to flourish. Shade marketed the business by sponsoring community events, offering reward points to regular customers and hosting cooking classes at the bakery.

With the Christmas season approaching, orders for cheesecakes were on the rise. She expanded the lunch menu beyond soups, by offering unique sandwiches; Eggplant with Fontina & Caramelized Onions and Prosciutto & Fig Panini were the top sellers. She also added a variety of salads; Balsamic Roasted Beet Salad, Grilled Chicken Orzo, and Creamy Pesto Tortellini. Aside from the dine-in lunch crowd, corporate orders continued to increase. Word had spread throughout Edelweiss.

At twenty-three, Sally proved to be a capable businesswoman and supervisor, and Shade often bounced ideas off of her. "I'd like to do something for my employees for the holiday and thought about a small gathering at my place," said Shade, during their morning meeting. "If our single employees brought a guest, and married employees brought their families, how many people would that be?"

"Let's see. There would be me and Chad. That's my new boyfriend. Liz and Ellen plus their families, Ben and Holly and their guests. You'd be looking at twelve, not including you and Tyler. A small party is an excellent idea."

"So, Chad, huh? How long have you been seeing him?"

"About six months. I'm sure you'll like him. He's a police officer in Edelweiss."

"As long as he makes you happy, then I'll like him."

When the day of the Christmas party approached, Shade's insides tightened like a twisted rope. *What if no one talks, and they stand around staring at each other? And what if no one comes?*

But her worries were unfounded. The guests arrived, and the cottage swelled with merrymakers dressed in their finest garb.

"Shade, meet my friend Chad," said Sally. Chad extended his hand.

"It's nice to meet you, Chad. Sally tells me you're a police officer. How long have you been on the force?"

"About two years. Edelweiss is a great community. And safe. In fact, so safe we get a little bored."

Sally gazed up at Chad, his arm wrapped around her shoulders. "Hey, where's Tyler?"

"Sally," Tyler squealed, running toward her, Scone chasing after him. "Look. I have a dog now."

"That's so cool. Hey, do I get a Christmas hug?" asked Sally, bending and embracing him.

The guests mingled, helping themselves to a menu of heavy

appetizers; beef tenderloin served on biscuits, shrimp cocktail, bacon-wrapped scallops, chicken fingers for the children, a mashed potato bar with an assortment of toppings, and dessert parfaits served in tiny cocktail glasses.

As the evening wore on, Tyler glanced at Sally, a querying look on his face. She smiled and nodded. They went over to the CD player and dropped in the *Thriller* CD, queuing up "Billie Jean." They stood side-by-side, bouncing their heads to the beat, before launching into a rendition of the moonwalk, sliding along the wood plank floor, gliding on air. Before long, the entire group of partygoers joined in.

Later that evening, Shade walked around and handed each employee an envelope. She whispered to Sally, "I'll give you your envelope in the morning."

"I'd like to thank each of you for your hard work this past year and for contributing to the success of the business," said Shade, addressing her employees. "I couldn't do it without you, and I'm hoping this gift will help make your holiday season a little brighter." When the employees opened their envelopes, gasps filled the room as they took in the amount. One-thousand dollars.

After the guests left, she scooped up Tyler, passed out with Scone underneath the Christmas tree, and carried him to bed.

"Why were people crying tonight?" asked Tyler, after getting tucked in. "Didn't they like their gift?"

She smiled. "I hope they did. Maybe they were crying because they were happy."

"What did you give them?"

"I gave them money. God has blessed us with so much. We need to be generous and share with others."

"Can I have money so I can share with others?"

"What would you do?"

"I'd buy a gift for Leah. And Mary. And Brent."

"That's nice of you. Maybe we can go shopping tomorrow. Do you still see Brent now that baseball camp is over?"

"Yeah. I see him in the hall at school, and he always talks to me."

"Do you ever see him when you're alone. Just the two of you?" She felt deceptive asking the question, but she needed to protect Tyler.

"No. Just in the hall. I told him you liked him a lot."

Her eyes grew wide. "Why did you tell him that?"

"Remember in the car? I told you I liked him a lot, and you said I like him a lot, too."

"Yes, I remember," Shade smiled. "Now, let's get you to sleep. I love you," she said, kissing him on the forehead. "Don't forget your prayers."

"I love you, too."

She stressed over Tyler's comment. *Watch what you say. So embarrassing. Here he is, a married man, and he's probably thinking he's got a grandmother hitting on him.* She let out a long sigh. *Let it go. There are more important things to worry about.*

"Shade, I can't thank you enough for the gift," said Sally, embracing her. "It was too generous. Five-thousand dollars? You have no idea how much I appreciate it. And it will help pay for our wedding."

"Your wedding?"

Sally extended her left hand and flashed a diamond ring. "He asked me last night."

"Oh, Sally, I'm so happy for you. That's great news."

"We decided on a destination wedding. In Hawaii, next October. Neither of us has a big family. We'll be lucky to have fifty people, total. And I'd like for you and Tyler to come."

"I'd be honored. I've hardly been out of the state, let alone across the Pacific. October will give us plenty of time to figure out who'll manage the bakery. Oh Sally, this is such great news."

Shade took Tyler Christmas shopping with the money he had earned doing chores. "Do you know what you want to buy everyone?" asked Shade, on the drive to the mall.

"Yes. I've thought a lot about it. I'm gonna get Scone a baseball, Leah a baseball mitt, Mary a Detroit Tigers T-shirt, and Brent a jockstrap."

Her eyebrows came together. She tried containing herself, turning away so Tyler couldn't see her unrepressed smile. When she tried to speak, her words came out in an unusual, high-pitched tone. "What made you decide to buy Brent a jockstrap?"

"I saw it in a magazine at school that showed a bunch of baseball uniforms and stuff. I asked a teacher what it was. Mr. Phelps said it was for men. To help them stay in place. Brent's always saying batters need to stay in place at home plate, so I thought he might like something like that."

Her shoulders shook, before she exploded into raucous laughter, wetness tickling her face.

"Grandma, what's wrong with you?"

"Oh honey, I was thinking how much I love you," she said, choking on her words.

"You're weird."

"Well, that's a thoughtful gift," she said, after gathering herself. "Maybe you'll find something else when we get to the store in case they don't have one."

Tyler purchased all the gifts on his list, except the jockstrap. Shade convinced him that since they didn't know Brent's size, a Detroit Tigers coffee mug would be a better gift. And Tyler agreed.

Shade pulled into the parking lot at First Church of Edelweiss. After dropping Tyler off at Sunday school, she approached the information desk to review the list of volunteer opportunities. One event captured her interest—women's prison ministry. She thought about Addy and her struggle with drugs. She may have ended up in prison had she lived. An ache formed in her throat as she considered Addy's ruined life and the broken lives of the incarcerated women.

"Hi. Can I help you?" asked the woman at the desk.

"Yes, can you tell me about the prison ministry?" Shade asked.

"Sure. A group of women meet at Emmet County Correctional twice a month. The volunteers get involved by leading small group Bible discussions, and they offer one-on-one mentorship to help prepare the women for life outside prison. If you're interested, call this number and speak to Diane Gallows."

"Thank you. It sounds interesting." Shade took the number. Walking to the sanctuary, she thought about serving in prison ministry. *Can I do this? Can I make a difference in someone's life?*

Shade slid into the pew, her mind focused on serving. She pulled out her Bible and turned to the verse that came to mind about the needs of the less fortunate. Matthew 25:36. "I needed clothes and you clothed me, I was sick and you looked after me, I was in prison and you came to visit me." She felt a gentle nudging.

The passage of time caught her unaware. The sermon drew to a close.

"I'd like to end today with a quote from Augustine of Hippo," said Pastor Ralph. "He lived sixteen-hundred-years ago, and his restless heart led him to pursue a life of immorality, until one day he was driven to a verse in the Bible. Romans 13:13-14. In Augustine's autobiography, *Confessions*, he wrote, 'You have made us for yourself, O Lord, and our hearts are restless until they find their rest in you.' We are all seeking meaning in life, yet we don't know what it is we're searching for. And we are restless until we find it. This longing can be quieted, but it can never be entirely silenced. If your heart is restless today, know that true rest can only be found in Christ.'"

Shade sat, meditating on the quote. Her thoughts were interrupted when the Sunday school children came into the sanctuary. Tyler slid in next to her.

"Grandma, guess what?"

"Shh, Tyler. You need to be quiet."

"Why?" whispered Tyler, looking around. "Because I'll wake everyone up? I wanted to tell you I saw Brent in the hall."

Pastor Ralph closed the service with a blessing, and the parishioners rushed the exit. Shade typically lingered after the service, but not today. She didn't want to bump into Brent. Grabbing Tyler's hand, she jockeyed for the next open space in the crowd, darting this way and that—a fluttering hummingbird. The sea of people parted and she dashed forward, Tyler's feet struggling to keep up with his head.

"Grandma. Why are you walking so fast?"

"So we can get home and eat breakfast. I'm starving."

"I saw Brent in the hall at church," Tyler repeated on the drive home. "He asked about you."

"Oh? Did you meet his family?"

"I only saw him. I like Brent—a lot."

She smiled. "Hey, when we get home you need to finish your Christmas list, and I need to call Mary and Blanche and invite them over for Christmas dinner."

On Christmas day, Harry and Blanche, Mary and her daughter and son-in-law, Carly and Steve, and Leah and Willow were invited for dinner at the cottage.

Blanche and Harry arrived first, bearing Champagne and gifts.

Blanche wore red-sequined palazzo pants with a shimmering gold blouse. Christmas lights were strung throughout her hair, powered by a hidden battery pack, causing her blonde up-do to twinkle. Harry wore a conservative navy-blue blazer, khaki pants and a permanent grin.

"Oh, honey," exclaimed Blanche, whooshing in through the front door, planting kisses on Shade's cheeks. "This place is amazing. And you look beautiful. I love the black velvet pants with the white satin top. You look like a runway model."

Shade laughed, realizing how much she missed Blanche. "Merry Christmas. I love the festive outfit. And the lights in your hair—brilliant. Harry, you're one lucky guy."

"It's good seeing you again," said Harry. "I've learned over the years to expect the unexpected when it comes to Blanche's wardrobe. I just go along for the ride."

"Well, look at you, Tyler," said Blanche. "You've grown since the last time I saw you." Blanche bent to give him a kiss, leaving a large red lip imprint on his cheek.

"You've grown too," said Tyler, smiling and wiping his face. "I like your hair design."

The Christmas menu included lobster bisque, beef prime rib with horseradish sauce, grilled asparagus, scalloped potatoes with Boursin cheese, and red Oak Leaf salad, followed by the traditional French yule log cake, Bûche de Noël.

After the meal, Leah and Tyler played outside with the dogs, while the adults chatted by the fireplace.

"Thank you for the exceptional meal and for inviting us over," said Carly.

"That's all Leah has talked about for the last few days," said Steve. "Spending Christmas with Tyler."

"And that's all Blanche and I have talked about. Eating dinner at Shade's house," said Mary.

After the guests had left, she sat with Tyler in front of the fireplace reading the Christmas story. Tyler dozed. She gazed at him, her heart bubbled over with thankfulness. The camaraderie of good friends, her beloved grandson and her lovely home. All undeserved.

Her mind shifted to Addy. The brightness inside her gave way to something dark. Guilt. It was always there, casting its shadow on her life, slowly crushing her. *Oh, Addy, you'll never experience the remarkable child Tyler has become.* Tears snuck down her face. The night of Addy's murder. Kent appearing at her door. Addy's lifeless body at the morgue. The funeral.

A splendid evening shattered. The shame of being an unwanted foster child, an unwed mother and the horror of Stan. Her idol. She sank like a stone. *Oh, dear God. Forgive me. Please help me make a better life for Tyler. Help me settle him on the right path and break this cycle of misery. That is my prayer.*

CHAPTER FOURTEEN

For here we do not have an enduring city, but we are looking for the city that is to come.

— HEBREWS 13:14

Year 2001

"Kent, what a surprise," said Shade, coming around the counter, balancing a tray of soup and sandwiches. Her gut tightened, wondering if he had any updates on the murder investigation. "So, did you come in for that free muffin and coffee?"

"I was in the area and thought I'd take you up on the offer," said Kent, smiling. "Looks like business is booming."

"Business is good. Do you have time for lunch? I can get someone to cover for me."

"That'd be great. I'm starving."

She took a seat at a table with Kent and pulled out the menu. "Would you like a recommendation?"

"Sure."

She waved Liz over. "We'd like two chicken breast sandwiches with caramelized onions and garlic aioli, and two bowls of corn and crab bisque."

"So, how is everything?" asked Kent.

"Good. Tyler's still obsessed with baseball, and we love living in Edelweiss. And I signed up to volunteer in women's prison ministry. I start this week. What about you? Any updates on the investigation? We haven't spoken in a few months."

"Excuse me," said Liz, placing their soup and sandwiches on the table. "Can I get you anything else?"

"Thanks, Liz," said Shade. "I think we're set."

"I'm doing good, and no updates," said Kent, plunging his spoon into the steaming hot, creamy bisque. "Things are slowing down at the station so I should be able to pick the case up again. By the way, the soup is delicious," he said, wiping his mouth and placing his napkin on the table. "I have a question regarding the night of the murder. You mentioned a guy named O.D. who used to live with Adeline and Jaime. You said you didn't know much about him, but did Adeline ever mention why he moved?"

"No, she said he left after Scott died. Why?"

"Just looking at all possibilities. If you think of anything Adeline might have said about O.D., please call me."

She sighed. "I will. Have you spoken to Donna, Jaime's mother? She may know more about O.D."

"We've stayed in touch. She didn't know much about him." He shifted subjects. "So, what made you decide to volunteer in prison ministry?"

"It seems like a good fit for me. I often think about Addy and Jaime's life choices and how the drugs controlled them. They could have easily ended up in prison." She looked down at her folded hands on the table. "I can't save Addy. It's too late. But maybe I can bring hope to another lost soul."

"I admire your commitment. In my job, I deal with broken lives every day. It's nice to know there are people that are trying to make a difference."

They lingered over lunch. Conversation was easy. Unhindered.

"Well, I better get back before they send out an APB," said Kent, standing. "Thanks for lunch and take care of yourself. If you ever change your mind about that dinner, the offer still stands."

"Thank you," said Shade, smiling and extending her hand. "I'll do that. And thanks for stopping in. Here," she said, handing him a bakery box, tied in twine. "I put a few slices of cheesecake in there for you, and some Caramel Apple Pie bars. You're welcome back anytime."

While walking back to the kitchen, Shade spotted a woman sitting at a table in the corner. She looked to be in her mid-fifties —an Audrey Hepburn classic beauty. She had seen her in the bakery before, always alone. Her striking blue eyes followed Shade wherever she went. Shade smiled at her. The woman returned a smile before turning back to her newspaper. She didn't understand why, but something about the woman flustered her. Probably her imagination.

Pulling into Emmet County Correctional, Shade ran into Diane Gallows who headed up the weekly ministry.

"Shade, we're happy to have you on board. Are you nervous?"

"Yes, but also excited. I read through the material. I didn't realize the degree of their sentences. Several are in for life."

"And many of them never receive visitors. It's a lonely life, but thank God for volunteers like you."

They entered the complex. The air inside was different. Cold. Stale. The clang of metal echoed off the walls. A guard stopped Shade. "What's in the box, ma'am," he said, glaring.

"Baked goods for the women. I brought a box for the guards, too," said Shade, smiling.

He gave her a once over and inspected the box. "Okay. And thanks."

They passed through security and were escorted down a hall. No colors. No light. Just spaces of empty white. A suffocating feeling gripped Shade as she questioned her decision to join this ministry.

"Are you okay?" asked Diane, as they neared the chapel.

"Just a little nervous," said Shade, trying to still her trembling body.

"It's normal. I felt the same way my first time. It gets easier."

They joined the other volunteers in the chapel. A door opened and the prisoners filed in one-by-one. Young. Old. Black. White. A melting pot of storied lives.

When the chaplain completed the sermon, the women separated into groups of five, two volunteers leading each group.

Diane encouraged Shade to lead the group while she observed. Shade's heart drummed in her chest as she asked the women to open their Bibles. "Acts 15:11," she read, her hands shaking. 'We believe it is through the grace of our Lord Jesus that we are saved, just as they are.' Does anyone want to discuss what that means to you, personally?"'

"Well," said the young, slender woman staring at her feet. "I think it means that no matter where we are, or what we've done, Jesus will forgive those who've received Him."

"Yes," said Shade. "We all sin. And some sin is greater. But sin is sin in God's eyes."

"Thank you for sharing, Meghan," said Diane.

Shade felt her anxiety fade as she focused on the women's hungry hearts. She wondered about their circumstances. What brought them to this place? Did they come from dysfunctional families? Were they foster children like herself? And how is it some could claw their way out of the trenches while others remained stuck in the mire? She contemplated her own life and the many blessings she had received. All undeserved. Life was unfair.

Shade drove home from the prison, secure in her decision to serve.

"Did you two have a good night?" asked Shade, when she entered the cottage.

"Yes, we did," said Mary. "We took Scone for a walk down the beach, all the way to Lakeside Shores."

"Wow," said Shade. "That's almost two miles."

"And guess what, Grandma? We saw Brent walking his dog. He has a black Labrador. His name is Coach. And he pointed to his house. He lives near the beach."

Mary laughed. "Yes, we ran into Brent. He mentioned baseball camp would start soon and he would call you this week."

"Can I join again?" asked Tyler.

"I don't see why not," said Shade, hugging him.

"How did it go at the prison?" asked Mary.

She sighed. "I think I'm going to love serving in this ministry. The women are so eager to hear the Word and to learn. It brought me such pleasure, knowing I might help change someone's life."

"It sounds like a perfect fit for you. I'm happy you found you're calling. Well, I better get going."

Shade was in the kitchen preparing dinner the following night when the phone rang. "Tyler, can you answer that?" She heard Tyler carrying on a conversation and giggling. She peeked around the corner.

"It's Brent," said Tyler. "He wants to talk to you."

Her heart cranked up a notch. "Hi, Brent. Sounds like you and Tyler were deep in conversation."

"He's a talker," said Brent. "Hey, I'm calling to see if you want to enroll Tyler in baseball camp this year. It starts after school lets out and it goes through the summer."

"It sounds great. Baseball is all he's talked about since camp ended. He's been practicing all winter. He's obsessed. Given your experience, do boys his age become so consumed with a sport like Tyler is with baseball?"

"To a degree, yes, but it's usually a fad. Tyler seems more driven than most. He has this innate sense of concentration that's quite unique. He may lose interest, but then again, this could be something he continues to pursue. Do you think you'll be able to attend the orientation for the adults? I'd like you to be there."

"Yes, I'll be there. I'll see you in a few weeks."

Two weeks later, Shade dropped Tyler off at Mary's before driving to Edelweiss Schools. Determined not to miss orientation, she arrived just as Brent was addressing the crowd. She found an open spot in the bleachers and took a seat.

"My goal for baseball camp is to instill a love of the game in these youngsters," said Brent, addressing the adults. "It's not about winning and losing, it's about how they play the game. Are they coachable, respectful, mentally tough, team players? These are attributes to teach at home, so please, work with your kids to make sure they bring their game face with them every day they show up at practice."

Shade focused. He had a smooth delivery. The way he enunciated each word. The way he used his hands to express himself. And that smile. So endearing. He wasn't showy. He simply laid out the facts.

"Hi, are you Tyler's mother?" asked a woman, interrupting her thoughts.

"I'm his grandmother. Do you know Tyler?"

"My son, Cody, was in camp last year with Tyler."

"Ah, yes, I know Cody. I'm Shade Lane."

"I'm Victoria. So, what do you think of the coach? Brent?"

"He's good with the kids, and Tyler loves him. He's so patient. And a great motivator."

"Agreed. And not bad looking," said Victoria, smiling. "He's been a positive influence on Cody. I'm single. Divorced. And Cody doesn't see much of his father. I feel like Brent fills that void. Are you married?"

"I'm a widow. Tyler lost both of his parents, so it's just the two of us."

"I'm so sorry. Tyler is such a good kid."

"Thank you. I appreciate hearing that."

"Hey, Shade, do you have a minute?" asked Brent, when orientation ended.

"Sure," said Shade.

Victoria approached Shade as she walked toward Brent. "Hey, if you want to get together so the boys can play, let me know. Cody doesn't have many friends, and I don't know any single women. It might be nice to hook up."

They exchanged phone numbers. Victoria seemed pleasant. And it would be nice for Tyler to have more playmates and for Shade to have a friend her age. Victoria had an interesting look. Tall and shapely, with large, dark brown eyes and faint freckles dotting her tanned face. Her strawberry-blonde hair was pulled tightly into a ponytail, causing her eyebrows to reach farther into her hairline than they should have. She looked more attractive when she smiled and less so when she didn't. She wore no makeup, and her blonde eyelashes stood out in stark contrast to her dark eyes, giving the impression of two lonely black dots on a blank canvas. Shade liked her bubbly personality and the ease with which she spoke. She made a note to call her.

"I enjoyed your talk today," said Shade, standing next to Brent. "Thanks for reminding us of our role. So, what's up?"

"I've been thinking about Tyler and was wondering if I could spend one day a week practicing with him. Maybe on the weekend. He told me he doesn't have a father or a grandfather to practice with. I hope this doesn't hurt your feelings," Brent paused, smiling, "but he also told me you try really hard to help him, but you're not that good."

Why is he trying to spend time alone with Tyler? She laughed. A nervous laugh. "Well, he wasn't lying. In fact, I'm terrible. I know Tyler would love spending time with you, but I don't want you to give up your weekends."

"It's not a problem. How about Sundays? Maybe an hour of practice. I could pick him up, or we could meet at a park. I'm in Lakeside Shores. There's a park nearby."

"I know where that is. You live close to me. Why don't we meet there?"

"Sounds good. Hey, I saw Tyler one Sunday at the First Church in Edelweiss. I tried catching up with you after service, but you were rushing toward the parking lot. It looked like you were in a hurry."

Her face burned red. "I must have been running late. Tyler told me he saw you. Do you attend often?"

"Not as much as I should. How about noon on Sunday?"

"See you then. And thank you. Tyler will be thrilled."

Upon learning he would practice with Brent, Tyler had talked about it all week. After church, they got ready for practice. Tyler insisted on dressing in his baseball uniform while Shade pondered her outfit. The weather forecast predicted low eighties and sunny skies. After putting on a pair of white shorts, a black scoop T-shirt and sandals, she pulled her hair up into a messy bun. Knowing they'd be hungry, she packed a cooler with bottled water, sandwiches and cookies from the bakery, along with reading material to occupy her time.

When they arrived at the park with Scone, Brent was there with his dog, Coach, tossing a Frisbee.

"Good morning," said Brent, trotting over to greet them.

She noticed his eyes glancing at her legs. She wondered if she should have chosen something less revealing.

"Hey, Tyler. Are you ready to practice?" he asked, ruffling his hair.

"I'm ready," said Tyler, leaping around the park and doing a cartwheel, powerless to contain his enthusiasm.

"It's all he talked about last night," said Shade, laughing.

"Well, why don't we get started before you wear yourself out?" said Brent, grinning at Tyler. "I hope you're not bored. You may want to sit over there where there's shade. It might get hot out here."

"Don't worry about me. I'll be fine," replied Shade, donning her sunglasses and spreading a blanket on the grass. "I brought something to read. I'm looking forward to basking in the sun after being indoors all week."

Shade hadn't felt this relaxed in a long time, stretched out on the blanket, the gentle breeze caressing her skin. She flipped through the prison ministry material, but she couldn't concentrate. Her eyes kept traveling to Brent and Tyler. She wondered why he never talked about a wife or child, and she questioned why he would sacrifice his Sundays for Tyler.

She studied him. His patient way with Tyler. His athleticism, clear when he fielded a ball or demonstrated hitting techniques. She closed her eyes and thanked God for the gorgeous day and for placing Brent in their lives.

"Grandma. Grandma. Wake up. I'm hungry."

She squinted, shaken from her siesta, and found Tyler and

Brent standing over her. She wiped the small dribble of drool puddled at the corner of her mouth.

"I must have fallen asleep," she said, trying to gather her composure.

"Tyler tells me you brought lunch. I think we worked up an appetite," said Brent, amused at her dormant state. "Uh, you have a twig in your hair," he said, reaching to pull it free.

"Oh," said Shade, running her fingers through her hair. "Yes, I brought lunch," she said, sitting up and unpacking the cooler. She pulled out paper plates and gave them a sandwich.

Brent took a bite. "Wow. This is a great sandwich. Seriously. What is this?"

"Prosciutto and fig panini with goat cheese and arugula. It's one of our signature sandwiches."

"It's my favorite," said Tyler. "My grandma is the best cook in the world."

"I don't even like goat cheese," remarked Brent, "but I guess I'm converted."

"Can we have cookies now?" asked Tyler.

She handed them a cookie. Brent bit into it, paused and stared at the morsel.

"Okay, what is this? This is one great cookie," said Brent.

"It's mocha pecan shortbread. From the bakery."

"It's delicious." He stood. "Hey Tyler. Let's get back to practice. We have some time before we wrap up for the day."

Shade watched the two of them sprint off. She delved back into her reading.

After twenty minutes, Brent and Tyler returned, announcing they were through for the day.

"Grandma. You look like Bozo the Clown. Your nose is red."

She removed her sunglasses and touched her nose. It felt like a hot coal.

"Grandma, you look like you have white sunglasses on."

"Oh boy," said Brent, cringing. "You got too much sun. Does it hurt?"

"I didn't feel it until you said something, but I guess it is a little tender." Shade found the bottle of sunscreen she had packed but forgot to put on. She applied it to her face.

"Here, let me," said Brent. "The top of your back and neck is burnt." He squirted a glob of lotion into his hands and smeared it on her upper back and neck.

Her breath caught as she fought back the unwanted emotion. He seemed oblivious to her reaction.

"I better get home before I do more damage," said Shade, packing up their things. Brent and Tyler gathered the cooler, the blanket and the dogs and loaded them into the car.

"I can't thank you enough."

"My pleasure. I'll see you next Sunday?"

"Absolutely."

She prepared Tyler for bed before going into the bathroom to take a cold shower. She looked in the mirror and gasped. Her nose appeared to be twice its normal size and white circles tattooed her eyes. Her torso and upper thighs were lily white while her appendages looked as though she had been turning on a rotisserie. *Good grief. He must have done everything in his power to contain his amusement. I look ridiculous.*

"I'm sorry you got burned today," said Tyler, when Shade kissed him goodnight. "You look funny."

"I know. Never let me forget to put on my sunscreen. And that goes for you, too."

"I like Brent. He taught me a lot today. I wish he could be my dad."

Regret washed over her like a cold wave. She cupped his cheek with her hand. "Well, think about how much time you get to spend with him. Baseball camp and now Sundays. Now get to sleep my little baseball-star. I love you."

"Goodnight Bozo. I love you, too."

The phone began to ring. She answered to the comforting sound of Brent's voice.

"Hey. I'm calling to see if you're okay. You got pretty toasted today."

"Thanks for checking in. I think I'll live, but I'll never again forget my sunscreen."

"Yeah, be careful. I also wanted to thank you for lunch today. And to tell you how impressed I was with Tyler's progress. He's a good kid. I hope all of this practice pays off for him someday, regardless of where he ends up."

"Me, too. And thanks again for the special day. It meant a lot to Tyler, and to me."

"Well, call if you need anything. And take two aspirin. It'll ease the pain. Good night."

She lay in bed, Brent's eyes loitering behind her eyelids. She thought about how good he was with Tyler. But today, she noticed something more profound. A poignant smile that crossed his lips when he studied Tyler's moves. Or when Tyler behaved like a fun-loving kid. He had a vulnerability that piqued her curiosity, and she wanted to know more. Despite her attraction, she cautioned herself—remain focused on Tyler—and her goal. She couldn't allow anyone to get too close, or she might end up in another situation like before. God gave her a second chance, and she wouldn't do anything to mess it up.

CHAPTER FIFTEEN

Set your minds on things above, not on earthly things.

— COLOSSIANS 3:2

"Hi, Tyler. Wanna play catch?" asked Cody, bounding down the steps wearing a baseball cap and glove.

"Yeah. I brought my glove and bat," said Tyler.

"Glad you could make it," said Victoria, holding the door open to her tastefully decorated, modest home.

Victoria looked different from the woman Shade knew from baseball practice. She wore a casual short skirt with flip-flops. Her hair hung around her shoulders and her eyes no longer appeared as black dots, likely enhanced by a few swipes of mascara.

"Thanks for inviting us," said Shade. "I brought you a cheesecake."

"Thank you. Cheesecake is my favorite."

"You have a lovely home. How long have you lived here?"

"Five years. I kept the house after my divorce. How about something to drink? Beer, a whiskey sour, soda?"

"I'll take a soda."

Victoria handed her a Coke and grabbed a beer for herself. They moved to the screened-in porch out back. "So, how long have you lived in Edelweiss?" asked Victoria.

"Less than a year. I love it here, and the school is perfect for Tyler."

"That's why Jack and I bought a house in Edelweiss. For the schools. Jack's my ex-husband. So, do you work?"

"Yes. I'm the owner of Shady Lane's Bakery & Café in town. Are you familiar with it?"

"I sure am. It used to be Bonnie's Bakery. Right?"

"Yeah. When Bonnie retired, I took it over. How about you?"

"I'm a police officer in Edelweiss."

"That's impressive. Do you know an officer named Chad? He's the fiancé of one of my employees, Sally."

"Yeah, I know Chad. Great guy."

"How long have you been divorced?"

"Two years. I joined the police force after the divorce. I'm still adjusting to being a single mom and working too many hours. It's been hard on Cody. He wants to see his dad more often, but he travels for work. How long have you been a widow?"

"My husband passed away in 1996."

"I'm sorry. And Tyler's parents?"

"My daughter, Adeline, died in 1997, and Tyler's dad passed a few years before that," said Shade, uncomfortable talking about her past. "Is Cody a baseball fanatic? Tyler's obsessed with the game."

"Yeah, I guess he is," said Victoria, clearly mindful of Shade's evasiveness. "I think his coach, Brent, helped stimulate his passion. So, what's Brent's story? Do you know if he's married? He sure is interesting to look at," she said, grinning wide.

Shade smiled. "I'm not sure, but he's good with the boys."

Cody and Tyler ran to the back porch. "We're starving."

"Well, I guess I should start the grill. I hope you're okay with burgers. Sure you don't want something stronger to drink?" asked Victoria, grabbing another beer.

"I'm fine, but thanks. Let me help."

After eating, the boys retreated to the backyard for another round of catch. Shade learned more about Victoria during her third beer—more than she cared to know. She and Jack divorced when Victoria learned he had a girlfriend in another state. She got suspicious when his travels extended into the weekends, so she hired a private investigator. Victoria, on the other hand, hadn't slept with a man since her divorce. And it wasn't for lack of trying. There just weren't any good opportunities. But, she was on the hunt, looking to rein in a wild stallion.

Victoria continued to talk, and Shade continued to listen.

"So, what about you?" asked Victoria. "Are you seeing anyone?"

"No. My life is too busy. I'm enjoying running the bakery and raising Tyler."

"Hey, maybe we can get a sitter sometime and go out trolling. Put a spark of excitement into our lives."

"I'll give it some thought," said Shade, laughing, but she knew she wouldn't. Dusk flirted with the sky. "Well, it's getting late. Thanks for dinner. Will you be at practice this week?"

"I'll be there."

Early the next morning, Shade and Sally arrived at the bakery to fill a corporate lunch order for fifty people. Corporate orders had seen a boost, based on Shade's marketing efforts. She gained traction after an article appeared in the Edelweiss Gazette, commending her efforts organizing food donations to local homeless shelters.

"Chad and I picked a wedding date," said Sally. "October 27th. We're so excited. Invitations go out this week, but I wanted to give you a heads-up. We found a gorgeous resort on Maui. We're getting married on the beach."

"It sounds wonderful. I'm so excited for you both. I'll make reservations."

"We've held a block of rooms at the resort. I'm hoping you and Tyler stay there. And Shade, I have a favor to ask. I'd like Tyler to be our ring bearer, if it's okay with you."

"Oh, Sally," said Shade, overcome with delight. "It's fine with me, and I'm sure Tyler will be thrilled. I'll talk to him tonight. Do you think Liz will be okay running the bakery while we're gone?"

"She's doing great. No worries. How long do you think you'll stay in Maui?"

"Maybe a week. I'd like to go sightseeing. I've never taken a vacation, except for a deer hunting trip with Stan in the Upper Peninsula, if you call that a vacation."

"I'm so happy you two are coming. It means a lot to us."

"I wouldn't miss it for the world."

Two more corporate lunch orders came in for the following day, causing Shade and Sally to work longer than expected. She would have to miss baseball camp. Again. Thankfully, Mary volunteered to take Tyler.

"How was practice?" asked Shade, while getting Tyler ready for bed that night.

"Brent made us pitch and aim for a bull's eye. It's like a dot in the center. Then he would make the bull's eye smaller so it would be harder to hit. Guess what? I think I wanna be a pitcher. I liked throwing at the bull's eye."

"It sounds like fun. Was Victoria there with Cody?"

"Yeah. And guess what? She kept laughing with Brent after practice ended."

"Well, maybe he said something funny."

"Nah. He was talking and she kept laughing, like she was pretending laughing. Like this." He let out an exaggerated cackle, pitching his head from side to side like an oscillating fan. "And then she kept rubbing his arm."

"Let's not talk about Victoria. It's not nice. Hey, I have good news. We're going to Sally's wedding, and we're going to fly on an airplane. And Sally wants you to be the ring bearer. It means you'll have a part in the wedding."

"Wow. We're going on an airplane? When?"

"In a few months, but we'll talk more when it gets closer. Now go to sleep. Love you."

She dressed for bed, her thoughts on Victoria. What did Brent think of her? Jealously rattled her consciousness. She suppressed her emotions and focused on something more meaningful. This week's study for the prison ministry.

A few nights later, Shade entered the chapel of Emmet County Correctional. The women's faces beamed, as the chaplain spoke about God's forgiveness. Shade spotted Meghan sitting alone in the back of the chapel. She recalled the story Meghan had shared with the group last week. Shade ached for her, sadness reaching deep into her heart.

At eighteen, Meghan Barnes had been convicted of first-degree murder and sentenced to twenty years. On that fateful night two years ago, she decided to rid the world of Jackson Davis. She'd tolerated his beatings, convinced she deserved it. But when he went after her two-year-old son, she snapped. While he lay snoring, passed out in a drunken stupor, she took his loaded handgun and shot him three times. When the police arrived, she was still pointing the smoking gun at Jackson's lifeless body, fearing he would pounce at any minute.

Meghan's life was a mess, and she saw no way out. Had she

been thinking logically, she would have realized her parents would have done everything possible to rescue her and Ethan from her self-imposed hell. Instead, she would spend the next twenty years locked away for a decision she made while under the influence of Jackson and cocaine. Her parents were awarded custody of Ethan. He would be twenty-two by the time she got out.

Shade walked over to Meghan and took a seat next to her.

"Hi Meghan. Did you enjoy Bible study?"

"Yeah, I guess."

"Anything you want to pray about?"

"Nah. I'm good."

"Have you had any visitors this week?"

"My dad. Mom stayed home with Ethan. She doesn't wanna bring him here. Says it's not good for him."

"I'm sorry," said Shade. "Hey, I heard you're taking GED courses. I went for my GED when I was thirty-six. I didn't graduate from high school like I had planned. But I'm so glad I got my diploma. It'll help you when you get out."

"If I ever get out," said Meghan, shuffling her feet and staring down.

"I know it seems far off, but it's best to be prepared when that day comes."

"How would you know? Have you ever been in prison?"

She paused. "Not with metal bars. Just my personal prison. I struggle every day, but I try to focus on my blessings. We all have baggage. Some heavier than others. But we can't dwell on what we can't change. We can only look forward."

Meghan looked off, staring vacantly.

"I'll keep you in my prayers, Meghan. See you next week."

Shade drove home, her thoughts centered on Meghan. She reminded her of Addy. That same tough demeanor. She thought about the parallels in their lives. Meghan's son, Ethan. Raised by his grandparents, just two years younger than Tyler. She said a silent prayer for them.

Lying in bed that night, she tossed and turned. Images of Meghan's shattered life occupied her brain, until sleep seized. And then it came. The white nightgown billowing. Addy's body levitating. The blast. The blood.

She awakened to the sound of her scream, soaked in perspiration. Her heart staggering.

Tyler appeared in the doorway. "Are you okay, Grandma? I heard you screaming again."

"I'm fine honey. Go back to bed. I just had a bad dream."

The next morning, Shade arrived at the park with Tyler and Scone, exhausted from lack of sleep. Brent walked over to greet them.

"Hey, Tyler," said Brent, mussing his hair. "You ready to practice pitching today?"

"Yeah. I wanna throw faster than Iron Man. Did you know he has supersonic speed? That's five times faster than sound. Watch this." Tyler grabbed a stone from the ground and hurled it at a tree. It ricocheted off a thick branch, ripped through a patch of leaves, and evoked a high-pitched chattering. A squirrel somersaulted to the ground.

"Oh, no," Tyler screamed, running over to the dazed squirrel walking sideways. "I hope he's okay."

"You need to be careful, Tyler," said Shade. "You could hurt someone."

"Did you bring your sunscreen?" Brent asked Shade.

"I don't leave home without it," she said, with a wry smile.

Brent smiled, his eyes lingering. He turned his attention to Tyler. "C'mon buddy, let's get started."

Shade settled on a blanket, pulling out her reading material. She glanced over to the parking lot. Victoria was sprinting her way while Cody ran out to Brent and Tyler.

"Hey, Shade. Fancy meeting you here. I heard Brent was offering Sunday baseball practice and thought Cody might like to join. Hope you don't mind if we crash your party."

"Not at all," Shade lied, irritated by the disruption—and by Victoria's outfit. She had poured herself into a pair of miniature shorts and a halter-top, insufficient to cover her abundant breasts.

"Hi, Brent," said Victoria, waving. "Cody was pumped about practice today."

Brent waved back, disappointed by the added responsibility. He looked forward to spending time alone with Tyler and Shade, but Cody was a good kid, and he felt sorry for him. He would make the best of it.

"What are you reading?" Victoria asked, plopping down next to Shade.

"Material for the prison ministry. A group of us meet there every two weeks."

"So, my job is to get them off the streets, and your job is to rehabilitate them. Right?"

"We try to help them, so I guess you could say that."

Victoria and Shade continued to exchange small talk.

"Well, I'm gonna do a little workout," said Victoria. She removed her flip-flops and put on a pair of running shoes before trotting over to the field, her breasts leaping skyward with each stride.

Shade couldn't concentrate on her reading. Her eyes tracked Victoria. While Brent instructed the boys, Victoria stood in his direct line of sight, bending and stretching like an Olympic gymnast warming up for a floor routine.

And then things took a turn. Victoria ran in place, her feet pounding the ground like a frenetic warlord, until she worked up enough momentum to thrust her body forward into a frenzied dash across the park. Nearing a large maple tree, she hurled her body into a front aerial flip, snagging her halter-top on a jutting tree limb. She landed. Two-footed. Topless. Without a pause, she retrieved her top from the limb and re-clothed herself. Brent feigned ignorance, and the boys appeared too consumed with practice to observe the astonishing calisthenics.

Victoria sprinted over to Shade, planting her butt on the blanket. "Whoa. Did you see that? Talk about being embarrassed. I hope Brent didn't see me."

"Oh, I'm sure he did. Did they teach you that in police academy?"

Victoria howled with laughter. "The flip or the strip?"

"I think we're done for the day," said Brent, returning with the boys. "Good practice today," he said, glancing over at Shade, grinning.

Victoria shot up from the blanket and stood near Brent, rubbing his arm. "Thank you so much for working with Cody. I'll see you next Sunday."

"Looking forward to it." He spoke to Victoria, but his eyes hung on Shade.

She wondered how Victoria knew about Sunday practice. Had he invited her? And her behavior. Tactless. She couldn't wait to see what she had planned for next week. Maybe an equestrian event. Lady Godiva style.

"Hey, Grandma, did you see me pitch today? Brent said I did good. He said I'm ready for the big leagues."

"I did see you pitch. You looked like a professional. Do you still want to be a pitcher?" Shade asked, while preparing dinner.

"Yeah, and Cody wants to be a catcher. Grandma, do you like Victoria?"

"Yes," said Shade, stretching the truth. "Don't you?"

"I don't know. She acts weird. I saw her boobies today."

Her eyebrows puckered. "Well, that was an accident. You shouldn't have seen that."

"Why not? I hope Leah doesn't get boobies that big when she gets older. I might not wanna marry her."

"Come on, buddy. Let's eat dinner and stop talking about Victoria."

After putting Tyler to bed, she sat on the back porch, enjoying the sound of the waves rolling into shore. She thought about Blanche and Mary. She hadn't spent much time with them and decided to invite them over for a picnic.

Brent. Victoria. She didn't like this feeling, wondering what he thought of her. But she couldn't suppress her emotions. *It's not about me,* she told herself. *It's about Tyler. Focus on Tyler. His future. Let it go.*

CHAPTER SIXTEEN

The Lord will keep you from all harm—he will watch over your life; the Lord will watch over your coming and going both now and forevermore.

— PSALM 121:7-8

Summer was drifting away. The demands of the bakery caused Shade to miss several baseball games, however, she made it a point to show up every Sunday for practice, along with Victoria and Cody. She didn't know if Brent had feelings for Victoria, but she willed herself to stop thinking about it. It was none of her concern.

Potato salad. Check. Beverages on ice. Check. Pork tenderloins marinating. Check. She wiped down the kitchen and went to her room to change.

"Tyler, did you clean your bedroom? Company will be here soon."

"I'm finishing now," he said, throwing himself on the floor and using his arm as a broom to sweep everything under the bed. Scone joined in, his nose maneuvering a rolling baseball bat into the closet.

Blanche arrived at the cottage. "Oh, honey," she said, adorned in rhinestone studded sunglasses, an oversized straw hat garnished with yellow daisies and a red ribbon trailing down the back of her sleeveless, floral print smock. "It's been too long and don't you look like a bronzed beauty."

"It's good to see you," said Shade, hugging Blanche. "Mary and Leah are on the beach. What can I get you? White wine, lemonade or soda?"

"I'll have lemonade," said Blanche, letting herself out back and strolling over to join the others. Tyler and Leah were busy building a sand castle, while Mary watched from her lawn chair, inhaling the scenery.

"Oh, this is heaven," said Mary. "Leah couldn't wait to spend the day with Tyler, and I couldn't wait to spend the day with my two beautiful friends."

"And you, too," Blanche responded. "My, how Leah and Tyler have grown. It looks like they're still the best of buddies. How old are they now?"

"Tyler will be seven in September," Shade replied. "And Leah will be seven in December. They're inseparable."

"Honey, so tell me what's going on in your life, besides Tyler and the bakery," said Blanche. "Are you dating anyone?"

"No. A man would complicate my life, and I don't need that. Besides, I'm fixated on our upcoming trip to Hawaii. We leave in a month."

"I'm jealous," Mary sighed. "I've never been to Hawaii."

"Don't you ever think about having a man in your life?" Blanche asked. "You're still young."

Mary interjected. "Someone like Tyler's coach, Brent. Too bad he's married, or at least we think he's married. He's so good with the boys. Maybe he has a single brother."

"Okay, ladies," said Shade. "I'm happy the way things are. Who's hungry?"

After devouring grilled honey-ginger pork tenderloins, corn on the cob, potato salad, and fresh tomatoes with basil, they went for a walk on the beach. Shade put on a turquoise, sheer lace tunic over her bathing suit.

Leah and Tyler ran ahead with Willow and Scone, the ladies lagging behind. She could see Tyler talking to someone with a dog. Brent. She waved, as he came toward them.

"Hello ladies," said Brent, his eyes hanging on Shade. "Beautiful day, isn't it? Thought I'd take Coach for a walk."

"Good to see you, Brent," said Shade. "You know Mary and Leah, but this is my friend, Blanche. Blanche, this is Brent, Tyler's baseball coach."

"So, you're Brent," said Blanche. "I've heard about you. And it's all good."

"Hey, Brent," Tyler interrupted. "Want some dessert? We're walking now so we can eat more food when we get back. Grandma made peach pie and homemade ice cream."

"Thank you, but I don't want to intrude," said Brent, clearly amused at Tyler's unfettered invitation.

"It's no problem," Blanche piped in. "You'd be doing me a favor. It would be less for me to stuff into my big mouth."

Brent looked at Shade, raising his eyebrows.

"Please, join us. If you're not busy."

"Well, I guess I could stop over. Do you mind if I bring Coach?"

"What's one more dog?" asked Shade, laughing.

Shade gave Brent a tour of the cottage while the others retreated to the back porch. She felt exposed standing near him in her beach outfit. She sensed his eyes. Not lingering. Just a slight caress here and there.

"You have a beautiful home," said Brent.

"Thank you. We love it here," she said, walking into the kitchen. "How long have you lived in your home?"

"About six years. It's a great area."

"And what about family?"

"Most of my family lives out of state, except my nephew. Hey, can I help with anything?" he said, shifting the subject.

"Would you mind taking this tray out to the porch?"

"Sure," said Brent. "It would make me feel useful after crashing your party."

"You're always welcome," said Shade.

Blanche plopped her floral print rear-end in a chair. "Brent," she said, patting the seat next to her. "Come sit and tell me about yourself."

Brent smiled and sat down. "Well, I'm the Athletic Director for Edelweiss Schools. I live a few miles down the beach, close to where we met today. I've lived there about six years."

Tyler and Leah ran over, pulling Brent's hand.

"Brent, can you play Frisbee with me and Leah? Please, Brent?"

"Well, looks like I'm being called away," said Brent, rising from his chair and joining them on the beach.

Blanche looked at Mary and Shade, grinning. "Darn. I was hoping to get the scoop on that handsome fellow. Honey, your mission, should you choose to accept it, is to find out if he's married. And if not, you must do everything in your power to lasso that chap."

Mary and Shade laughed at Blanche's candor. "I'm thinking he's single," said Shade. "He told me he has family out of state, so I assume he lives alone."

The ladies chatted while Brent entertained Leah and Tyler on the beach. Shade studied Brent. He seemed genuinely content playing with the kids. And Tyler clearly enjoyed having him around.

After about thirty minutes, Brent climbed the steps from the beach. "Well, I better head back. It's past Coach's bedtime. Thanks for inviting me, and nice meeting you Blanche."

After everyone left, Shade sat alone in the living room, thinking. It was odd how Brent changed the subject when she asked about family. Maybe he was divorced and didn't want to talk about it. But what did it matter? Enough of these endless mind games.

A month had passed, and the trip to Hawaii was fast approaching. Arriving at the bakery, she found Sally and Liz deep in conversation.

"Good morning, ladies," said Shade. "I see you two are using Sally's last day wisely. Do you think you'll be comfortable, Liz, while we're away?"

"I'll be fine. And I know I can call either one of you if something urgent comes up."

"Yes, but call me first," said Shade. "Sally will be preoccupied. Sally, I can't believe this is it. When you get back, you'll be a married woman. How many people are coming to the wedding?"

"It looks like forty-five. Everyone is staying at the resort. Don't forget your bathing suits."

"We won't. Tyler and I are thrilled, although, I think he's more excited about the plane ride."

"I'm so envious," said Liz. "Have a wonderful time, and don't worry about the bakery."

"Tyler, can you come in here?" asked Shade from her bedroom as she packed for the trip. "I want you to look through your suitcase and see if there's anything else you want to bring. Remember, only clothes. No toys."

He pulled out his Detroit Tigers baseball cap and his baseball glove. "How about these?"

"You can take your cap but not your glove."

"But, you said I could bring clothes. A glove is clothes. I wear it on my hand."

"You won't have a ball, honey, so you don't need a glove."

Tyler walked over to her suitcase, inspecting its contents. "What's this?"

"It's my curling iron. For my hair."

"Do you *wear* it in your hair?"

"Okay, you can bring your glove," Shade recanted. "But that's it. Hey, did you remind Brent we wouldn't be at the park this Sunday for practice? I told him a while ago, but I hope he didn't forget."

"I told him we were going on a plane. He said he's going away, too, and he would see us when we got back."

"Okay, good. Let's not forget to pack your homework."

"When is Mary coming to pick up Scone?"

"When she picks us up to take us to the airport."

"Grandma, we're going on the plane!" said Tyler, as their section was called. "Why is your face white?"

"I'm a little nervous, that's all. I've never been on a plane. Just like you."

"Don't worry, Grandma. Remember? We prayed with Mary for a safe trip."

"That's right," said Shade, grateful for the reminder. "God will watch over us."

Squeezing their way down the narrow aisle, they located their seats. A drowning helplessness washed over her. In contrast, Tyler's eyes grew large, fascinated by the experience.

"Flight attendants, please prepare for takeoff."

The enormous plane roared down the runway. She sat rigid, biting her lip. Eyes pinched tight. Fingernails digging into Tyler's arm.

"Faster, faster," screamed Tyler. "Oh, wow. Look Grandma, the clouds are below us."

Shade released her eyelids and glanced out the window, awestruck by the blanket of fluffy white clouds shrouding the huge metal tube. Terror gave way to tranquility.

"See, Grandma," said Tyler, patting her hand. "Everything will be okay. I'll take care of you."

"I love you, Tyler." She leaned over and kissed the top of his head. "Thanks for taking care of me."

The chauffeur waited in baggage claim, holding a sign, *Shade & Tyler Lane*. When they approached, he placed a flower lei around each of their necks. "Aloha. Welcome to Hawaii. I'll have you at the resort in Wailea in twenty minutes."

"I don't wear necklaces, sir," said Tyler, removing the lei from his neck and handing it back.

"Tyler, he's welcoming us to his state," said Shade.

"In Hawaii, that's how we greet people arriving on our island. Both men and women," said the chauffeur, smiling. "You'll hurt my feelings if you don't wear it."

She retrieved the lei and placed it around Tyler's neck.

"Thank you, sir," said Tyler. "It's real pretty."

"Oh, Tyler," Shade sighed, gazing out the open car window a couple of minutes later. "Isn't everything beautiful? Can you smell the flowers and the salt in the air from the ocean?"

"Wow, Grandma. The ocean looks like Lake Michigan."

When Shade opened the door to their room, the incandescent expanse of the Pacific greeted them. Majestic mountains surrounded the resort. Palm trees rose like tropical goddesses, their wispy fronds fanning the sky. She had never seen such lush greenery, colorful flowers spilling out from everywhere.

"Tyler, look. We have a private balcony."

"Can we go swimming now?"

"Sure," she said. "Oh, look. Sally and Chad gave us a gift basket and an itinerary. Let's see, there's a barbecue by the pool tonight. Beachwear recommended. Okay, buddy, let's put our swimsuits on and go down to the beach before the barbecue."

Shade dressed in one of the new swimsuits she had purchased. She chose the blush pink, two-piece suit with matching cover-up and pinned her hair back into a chignon. After getting Tyler dressed in his baseball-themed swim trunks and baseball cap, they headed to the beach.

"Shade," said Sally, waving. She and Chad headed toward them, arms open wide. "When did you get in?"

"About an hour ago. I can't believe how beautiful it is."

"Isn't it gorgeous? Hey, Tyler, are you ready to be in our wedding? You'll have to go to rehearsal tomorrow."

"Grandma says I carry the ring on a pillow. It seems kinda strange."

"Yeah, I agree," said Chad, laughing. "But it'll be over before you know it."

"Have all the guests arrived?" asked Shade.

"Pretty much," Sally responded. "I'm expecting the rest to show up for the barbecue tonight, so you'll be able to meet everyone. We have the whole pool area reserved."

"Hi, Mom," said Chad to the woman approaching them. "This is my mom, Mindy. Mom, this is Shade and her grandson, Tyler. Sally works for Shade at the bakery."

"Nice to meet you Shade and Tyler," said Mindy, extending her hand. "Sally speaks highly of you. We're so glad you could make it."

"Nice to meet you, too. Do you live in Michigan?" asked Shade.

"No. Chad's father, Kevin, and I live in Wisconsin. Most of our family lives there except for my brother and Chad, who live in Michigan. How long are you staying?"

"We'll be here for a week. We thought we'd hit the beach before the barbecue tonight. Tyler has been dying to swim in the ocean."

"I don't blame him. Well, it was nice meeting you. See you at the barbecue."

Sally and Chad left to get things settled. Shade and Tyler spent the next hour frolicking in the ocean, struggling to stand erect against the crashing waves of the Pacific. After wearing themselves out, she toweled herself off and retreated to one of the hotel cabanas while Tyler played nearby in the sand.

"Hey, buddy. It looks like Sally and Chad are waiting for everyone by the pool. Let's head up there."

"Shade," said Sally. "How was the beach?"

"Wonderful. I almost fell asleep in the cabana."

"Excuse me," said Chad. "I spotted my uncle. He must have just gotten in."

"Hello again," said Mindy, walking over to join them. "Shade, this is my husband, Kevin. Kevin, this is Tyler and Shade. Hey Tyler, would you like to meet my granddaughter, Hanna? She's about your age. I can take you over to her. She's in the pool."

"Yeah," said Tyler, glancing at Shade for her approval.

"Sure," said Shade.

"Oh, look Kevin," said Mindy, "my brother's here."

Mindy took Tyler by the hand to greet her brother before taking him to meet Hanna. Shade heard Tyler shriek.

"Brent," yelled Tyler, waving wildly and turning around. "Look Grandma. It's Brent."

CHAPTER SEVENTEEN

Children are a heritage from the Lord, offspring a reward from him.

— PSALM 127:3

Brent's smile widened, as Tyler raced toward him, his sister, Mindy, following. He embraced Mindy before looking at Tyler. "Well, this is a surprise," he said, tousling Tyler's hair. "Are you here with your grandmother?"

"Yeah. She's over there," said Tyler, pointing to Shade standing beside Sally.

"Hey, Sally," yelled Chad, waving her over. "Come and meet my Uncle Brent,"

Sally looked at Shade. "Do you know Brent?"

"Yes. He's Tyler's baseball coach. What a shock," said Shade, grappling with the connection.

Sally and Shade walked over to the group.

"Sal, this is my Uncle Brent, my mom's brother. Brent, meet my soon-to-be-wife, Sally. It sounds like you already know Shade and Tyler."

Brent smiled at Sally and cupped her hand in his. "It's a pleasure to meet you, Sally. I've heard so much about you." He turned to Shade with a whimsical smile, taking her hand. "Shade, what a nice surprise. How do you know Chad and Sally?"

"Sally works at the bakery. I've known her for five years. It's so good seeing you, Brent."

"It's a small world," said Mindy. "Brent, did you get settled in your room? I see you didn't get the memo about beachwear."

"No," replied Brent. "I came right to the pool."

Mindy took Tyler's hand to introduce him to Hanna, while Chad and Sally went off to greet their guests, leaving Shade standing with Brent.

He was still wearing a surprised look on his face. "I'm glad to see you and Tyler here. When did you get in? And how long are you staying?"

"We got in this afternoon. We'll be here for a week. And you?"

"Six days. Is it just the two of you?" he asked.

"Yep, just me and my buddy, Tyler," said Shade, grinning. "And you?" she asked, hoping he was with someone so she wouldn't have to fantasize all week.

"Just me. Hey, I'm going to change. Can I buy you a drink later —from the open bar?"

"I'd like that," said Shade, smiling.

Sally found Shade by the pool. "Hey, Brent's not a bad looking guy. How well do you know him?"

"I see him at Tyler's baseball camp, when I can make it, and on Sundays for practice. He's great with Tyler. What a shock—seeing him here."

"Chad told me all about him. Do you know about the accident? It's so sad."

"No. What accident?"

"His wife and two-year-old son were broadsided. A guy ran a red light. They were both killed. And his wife was five-months pregnant. Chad said it took Brent a few years before he acted like himself again."

"Oh," Shade choked, trying to blink back the rising swell in her eyes. "How horrible. I had no idea. When did this happen?"

"About five years ago. They had just moved into their house. Chad thinks the world of his Uncle Brent. The family is always trying to set him up with someone, but he keeps to himself. Sorry, Shade," said Sally, rubbing her arm. "Didn't mean to upset you. Oh, darn. Chad is waving me over. I'm sure he wants to introduce me to someone else. Let's catch up later."

Shade walked to the pool, her upbeat mood dampened.

"Have a seat, Shade," said Mindy, patting the edge of the pool. "I'm so glad Hanna found someone her age. So, do you know my brother well?"

"Just through Tyler. Tyler adores him. It was such a surprise seeing him. I didn't realize he was related to Chad."

Kevin walked over and kissed Mindy on the forehead. "There you are, sweetheart. I've been looking for you. Shade, do you mind if I pull my wife away?"

"Not at all. I'll look after the kids."

She sat at the edge of the pool watching Tyler and Hanna, her legs dangling in the water.

"Look, Grandma. I have a new friend. Hanna. She's the flower girl."

Shade smiled and waved to Hanna, her mind trailing. She recalled the day she noticed Brent studying Tyler. Could he have been thinking about his son? He would have been Tyler's age. And his wife and unborn child—all taken away from him. She tasted the salty stain on her lips before she realized she was crying.

"There you are," said Brent, waving to Tyler in the pool. "I see you have a new friend, Hanna."

"Can you come in the pool with us?" asked Tyler.

"Please Uncle Brent," said Hanna.

"In a minute."

Shade wiped her face. Brent sat next to her, smiling as he

watched the two youngsters splashing in the pool. She wanted to take him in her arms. To tell him how sorry she was.

"So, first time in Hawaii?" asked Brent.

"First time leaving Michigan, except for a short trip to Ohio. And the first time on a plane. I've lived a sheltered life. How about you?"

"I've been here a few times. There's so much to see and do on Maui. Hey, since we'll be here after the wedding, maybe I can show you and Tyler around."

"I'd like that. And Tyler would be thrilled. Hey, where's that drink you promised me?"

"How about a Mai Tai? It's the quintessential drink of the islands. Be right back."

After finishing their cocktails, Brent left to greet family members. Shade and Tyler strolled over to the buffet area. Silver chafing dishes and plates overflowed with shredded kalua pork, shoyu glazed chicken, lomi-lomi salmon, honey-roasted sweet potatoes with coconut flakes, poi, and guava cake.

"Grandma. Can I go in the pool again?" Tyler asked, after they had finished eating.

"Sure. I'll join you," she said, removing her cover-up and lowering herself into the tepid water. "Are you having a good time, buddy?"

"Yeah. And I'm happy Brent is here. Aren't you?"

"Yes, I'm happy, too."

Shade heard a splash and turned to see Brent's toned arms cutting through the water toward them. His eyes brushed over her exposed skin. She wished she'd chosen the one-piece suit.

"Who taught you to swim, Tyler?" asked Brent. "I was watching you earlier. You look comfortable in the water."

"Grandma taught me. She said I had to learn since we live on the lake."

"That's good. Hey, it looks like we've got the pool to ourselves."

As dusk settled, they emerged from the pool. "Oh, look how beautiful," said Shade, staring off into the horizon. The sun dipped into the ocean, illuminating the sky in a fiery orange-red, silhouetting wispy palm trees against the backdrop.

"Maui is one of my favorite places," said Brent. "And the beaches are phenomenal."

"I could sleep out here," said Shade, sighing. She looked at Tyler, his eyelids struggling to open. "Speaking of sleep, I think the time difference is catching up with us. Tyler, are you ready to hit the sack?"

"Can we sleep outside, Grandma? In the cabana?"

"Not tonight, honey. Will we see you tomorrow at dinner?" she asked Brent. "I understand we're going to a luau."

"I'll be there. It should be fun. Hey, buddy. I'll see you tomorrow. Go get some sleep."

After saying goodnight to Sally and Chad, Shade and Tyler went back to their room. They barely made it inside the door before dropping on their beds and falling asleep.

Shade stepped onto the balcony the next morning with a cup of Kona coffee, digesting the quiet solitude. She opened her Bible to the daily reading when the phone rang.

"Good morning," said Sally, in a cheerful voice. "A few ladies are going out today for lunch and a spa treatment. I'd love for you to join us. Chad is going deep-sea fishing with the guys, and he suggested taking Tyler. He'd have a blast."

"Oh, gosh, Sally. It sounds like fun, but I'm not comfortable leaving Tyler."

"Chad said he'd take good care of him. And Brent will be there. I'm sure he'll be fine. I really want you to come with the ladies."

"Let me talk to Tyler. Can I call you back?" Her mind spun. She wasn't comfortable leaving Tyler. *Maybe I'm being too over-protective.*

As she was waking Tyler, the phone rang again.

"Good morning," said Brent. "How was your first night in Hawaii?"

"I slept like a rock. Tyler is still half asleep. How about you?"

"I slept well—when I got to bed. I ended up staying at the party until after midnight. Hey, Chad is taking the guys deep-sea fishing. We wanted to take Tyler so the ladies could spend the day together. What do you think?"

She heaved a sigh. "To be honest, I'm uneasy leaving him. I haven't said anything to Tyler yet. He just woke up."

"I promise I'll take excellent care of him. I won't let him out of my sight."

After a long pause, she caved. "Well, I guess. Provided Tyler wants to go. Let me talk to him, and I'll call you back."

"Why don't you put him on the phone, and I'll talk to him?"

She handed the phone to Tyler. His face beamed. "Yeah. When are we leaving?" Tyler gave the phone to Shade.

"Sounds like he's in," said Brent. "I'll come to your room in an hour to pick him up."

They took their time getting ready. When Brent finally knocked on the door, Tyler ran to answer it. "Hi Brent. I'm ready to go fishing."

She walked over with a small bag and warmed at the sight of Brent standing in the doorway. "I'm not sure what he'll need, but I have his baseball cap, some sunscreen, and a few snacks. Here's some money."

"I got this," said Brent. Sensing her worry, he touched her arm. "Hey, don't be anxious. Here's my cell number if you want to call. I won't let anything happen to my star pitcher."

Her heart skipped, as Brent took Tyler's hand, steering him out the door. She said a silent prayer for their safety. And for God to give her peace.

The small group converged on the dock, prepared for the "males only" fishing expedition. Brent was amused at Tyler's thirst for knowledge, as he relayed the basics of deep-sea fishing. He'd forgotten how much joy a young child could bring. He thought about Luke and yearned for his son's presence.

"Fishing requires a lot of patience," said Brent, strapping on Tyler's life jacket. "You need to look for signs in the water. If you see a pod of dolphins, it may mean yellowfin tuna are feeding close by. That's when we pay attention to our fishing rod in the rod holder. Hey, let's put your sunscreen on."

"Hey, Uncle Brent, how about a beer?" asked Chad, as the boat trolled through the deep blue Pacific. "Tyler, would you like water or pop?"

"How about two waters," Brent replied.

Tyler sat patiently, peppering Brent with one question after another while monitoring the line. "Brent. Our rod is bending."

"Whoa. Looks like we got a bite." The line whirred on the spool as Brent reeled in the combative fish cutting back and forth across the water.

"It's a yellowfin," said Brent. "You can tell by the two dorsal fins and the bright yellow small fins along the spine."

"Can I reel it in?" asked Tyler.

"Here, put your hand over mine and help me turn the spool. See how I keep my knees bent against the side of the boat. It helps me brace myself so I can stay in place."

"Like a jockstrap? Wouldn't that help you stay in place?"

Brent's eyebrows furrowed. "That's not for fishing, buddy. It's more for sports. Like baseball."

"Yeah. I saw it in a catalog, and Mr. Phelps, at school, said it helps men stay in place. I wanted to get you one for Christmas, but my grandma said we didn't know your size."

Brent's lips curled upward. His attention was soon diverted to the aggressive pull on the line. After an hour of reeling, the fish swam to the surface, allowing the captain to gaff the catch and bring it aboard.

"Looks like you got about an eighty-pound yellowfin," said the captain.

"Can I take the fish home to show Grandma?"

"We'll ask the captain to take a picture, but we will give the fish to him."

On the ride back to shore, Tyler fell asleep leaning into Brent's side, Brent's arm wrapped around him.

"Hope everyone is ready for the luau tonight," said Chad.

"Yeah, maybe I can meet a pretty lady to bring to the wedding," said Chad's best man, Wayne, swigging his fourth beer. "Too bad me and the old lady split or else I'd have a date."

"Well, you won't be the only single guy there," said Brent.

"I thought you were with Tyler's grandmother, Shade," said Wayne. "Now there's a pretty lady. What's the story there? She seems too young to be a grandmother."

"Hey, stay away from Shade," said Chad. "That's Sally's boss. She's too good for you."

Brent felt uncomfortable as her name was tossed around like a volleyball. He felt protective of her—and Tyler. He changed the subject.

When the boat pulled into the dock, the captain snapped a photo of Tyler and Brent with their catch and presented them with a 5 x 7. When they reached the lobby of the hotel, Brent called Shade's room. She answered on the first ring.

"Hey. Thought I'd call before I brought Tyler back up, safe and sound."

"Thanks, Brent. See you in a few."

She threw open the door, visibly trying to contain her relief.

"Grandma. We caught a huge fish today. A tuna fish. Look, here's a picture of us. I wanted to bring it back, but Brent said we should give it to the boatman."

"Wow, buddy," said Shade, planting a kiss on the top of his head. "Did you have fun?"

"Yeah. We went on a boat ride, way out in the ocean. And we saw dolphins."

"I'm jealous," said Shade. Tyler ran out to the balcony. "Thank you for taking him today. I hope he didn't infringe on your guy time."

"Not in the least. In fact, I had more fun with him than the guys. Well, I'll let you get settled. The luau starts in a few hours. How are you getting there?"

"I think there's a shuttle."

"You're welcome to ride with me. I have a rental car."

"I wanna go with Brent," said Tyler, running back into the room.

Brent looked at her with raised eyebrows. "Well? Pick you up at six?"

"Perfect. Thanks again."

After Brent left, Shade took Tyler to the beach for the rehearsal. Sally and Chad were looking at different locations with the reverend as the wedding party awaited instructions. When Shade and Tyler approached, Wayne walked over and introduced himself while Tyler ran over to greet Hanna.

"Hi. I don't think we've met. I'm Wayne, Chad's best man. I met your grandson today on the fishing boat. Great kid."

"Nice to meet you. And thank you. I'm Shade. I work with Sally."

"So, is there a mister Shade?" Wayne asked, eyeing her up and down.

"No," said Shade, half smiling. "How do you know Chad?"

"We've been friends since we were kids. We're like brothers."

"Everyone, can I have your attention?" called the reverend. "Let's get started so we can make it to the luau on time."

When practice ended, Wayne offered to drive her to the luau. She politely declined.

Shade got Tyler dressed and then showered and changed. She adjusted the spaghetti straps of the delicate floral print sundress, hoping the scoop neckline wasn't too revealing. Her skin against the billowy white fabric of the dress made her tan appear more prominent. After blow-drying her hair, she let it hang loose, the soft, sun bleached curls framing her face. While applying mascara, she heard a knock on the door.

"Tyler, can you get that while I finish up? It's probably Brent."

"Hi, Brent. Grandma's fixing herself up."

She could hear Brent asking Tyler about the rehearsal, and Tyler asking Brent if he brought a baseball.

While he waited for her to get ready, Brent stepped out onto the balcony with Tyler. His eyes drifted to the Bible laying open on the table.

She walked onto the lanai, apologizing for running behind, struggling to strap on her sandals.

"Wow, doesn't my grandma look pretty tonight?" Tyler asked Brent.

"Yes, she does," said Brent, his eyes on Shade, unwavering.

"Thank you," said Shade, her face glowing hot. "You two don't look so bad yourselves."

After dining on traditional Hawaiian cuisine, the entertainment began. The storytelling hula dancers swayed to the rhythm of the island music, urging guests to join them. Tyler sprang from his seat and grabbed his dancing partner, Sally, by the hand. Up on stage, they performed their version of the dance. Tyler's exaggerated hip action stole the show. Shade leaned into Brent, shoulder to shoulder, both weary from laughter.

"Can I get you a drink?" asked Brent, after Tyler's second curtain call.

"Sure," said Shade, dabbing her eyes. "I'll have a Mai Tai. I'm going to run to the restroom. I'll be right back."

"Hey there. Having a good time?" asked Wayne, as he came up alongside her, his bloodshot eyes leering at her. "I saw your grandkid dancing. What a ham."

"Yes. He's not shy," said Shade, tossing a forced smile. "Lovely evening, isn't it?"

"Yeah. And it just got lovelier when you walked by. Can I get you a drink?"

"Thank you, but Brent is getting me one."

"So, are you and Brent a thing?"

"We're friends."

"Good. Because I'd like to know you better. Great dress. Very sexy." He slid his finger across her shoulder and underneath the spaghetti strap.

"Excuse me," she said, jerking back.

"See you later," Wayne yelled, watching her walk away.

Returning from the restroom, she spotted Brent and stood next to him.

"Everything okay?" asked Brent, handing her a drink. "You seem tense."

"I'm fine. Did I miss anything?"

"Well, the fire-knife dance is next. I'd try to keep Tyler off the stage."

She laughed, taking a hearty gulp of her drink. Sally and Chad joined them.

"You two having fun?" asked Chad, squeezing Brent's shoulder.

Sally grabbed Shade's arm. "Hey, walk with me to the restroom."

"I see you drove here with Brent," said Sally, as they were touching up their make-up. "Is there something going on? Anything you want to share? You make a nice couple."

Shade laughed. "No. Nothing. Hey, tomorrow's the big day. Are you excited? Nervous?"

"Both. I can finally relax after the wedding. It'll be nice spending a week alone with Chad." Sally embraced her. "Oh, Shade. It means so much having you and Tyler here. Let's go get a drink."

They walked into the crowd with their cocktails. The lights dimmed as the fire-dancers took the stage. Sally wrapped her arm around Chad, leaning into him, and Shade stood beside Brent. The alcohol toyed with her balance. The sensation of his strong arm around her waist warmed her skin. Turning toward him, her lips curved upwards in a soft smile, she came face-to-face with Wayne—standing between them—one arm around Shade and the other around Brent. Her head snapped back like a detonated rubber band.

"Hey you two. Looks like you're having a good time," said Wayne, tightening his grip around Shade's side and pulling her closer.

"Yeah, it's a nice party," said Brent.

A sudden force pulled Wayne's arm downward off her waist.

"Take your hand off my grandmother," said Tyler.

"Hey, sorry kid," said Wayne, holding both hands in the air as though under arrest. "A little possessive, aren't you kid?"

"His name is Tyler," said Shade, glaring at Wayne.

"Are you okay?" Brent asked Shade on the drive back to the resort. "Did Wayne upset you?"

"It's nothing. I'm just a little tired."

Brent escorted them to their room. "Well, I'll see you both tomorrow at the wedding."

"Hey, Brent, why don't you spend the night in our room?" asked Tyler.

"Brent has his own room to sleep in, honey," said Shade, smiling at Brent.

"Well, I'd love to, but it might be too crowded."

Shade gazed at Brent, thanking him for the ride. She wanted to invite him in for a drink, but she'd had enough.

"You gonna be okay?" asked Brent, noticeably concerned. "I'm in room 304 if you need anything."

"Thanks, but I'll be okay. See you tomorrow."

Back in his room, Brent poured a glass of wine and went onto the lanai, gazing at the ocean. Shade was pulling him under. He stared at the water, breathing in the Pacific air. Hawaii. Where he'd spent his honeymoon. Vivid memories of their time together, so many years ago. He wondered if he'd ever recapture what he'd lost? And did he want to? The harder you love, the harder you fall. He wasn't sure he could handle it again.

CHAPTER EIGHTEEN

When I am afraid, I put my trust in you.

— PSALM 56:3

Tyler crawled out of bed, his balled fists rubbing sleepy eyes. He ambled to the lanai, expecting to see his grandmother. Back inside, he found her tangled in the sheets, arms and legs splayed. Sleeping. He gazed at her, smiled and kissed her forehead. He tiptoed around the room, but after an hour of this nonsense, he got things rolling. He picked up the phone and dialed his buddy's room, number 304.

"Hi, Brent. It's Tyler. Wanna go swimming?" Pause. "No, she's sleeping." Pause. "Okay, I'll ask her."

Tyler pulled the phone away from his mouth and hollered, "Hey, Grandma. Wake up. Can I go swimming with Brent?"

She rolled over, confused, squinting at the clock on the nightstand. 9 a.m. She sprang up as though she were late for a wedding. "Who are you talking to?"

"It's Brent. I'm asking if he wants to go swimming."

"Tyler, give me the phone please," she said, reaching for it. "Hi, Brent. I'm so sorry. I hope he didn't wake you."

"No, I was up. I don't mind taking him to the pool. I was planning to do a few laps before it gets crowded."

"Do you want me to bring him to your room?"

"No, I'll come get him. Fifteen minutes?"

Shade helped Tyler with his swimming trunks. She glanced in the mirror. Her hair had waged a battle with itself—a state of anarchy. There wasn't time to put in her contact lenses, and she didn't want to frighten him by wearing her magnifiers. She would have to fake it. She threw on a pair of shorts and a T-shirt and gargled with mouthwash. Just in time.

"Come on in."

"Good morning," said Brent, grinning at the sight of Shade. "Hey, why don't you come join us when you're ready?"

"Grandma. If you come, you should brush your hair first."

She smirked, trying to aerate the flattened side with her fingers. "Thank you for pointing that out, Tyler. I will come down. And I don't think I'll brush my hair. I like it this way," said Shade, kissing the top of Tyler's head. "I'll see you two in a few."

Stepping aside to let them out, she stumbled backwards, planting her bottom in a deep-cushioned chair, legs dangling over the side.

"Whoa. Are you okay?" asked Brent, reaching for her hand to pull her up.

A grin crept over her face, followed by unrestrained laughter. She caught Brent's alarmed expression. Her amusement intensified. She couldn't catch her breath.

Brent looked at Tyler, puzzled.

"Just ignore her," said Tyler. "She'll be okay. When she doesn't wear her glasses, she gets clumsy and trips over stuff. Then she laughs at herself—like this. Let's just go."

She wondered what Brent must have thought. Oh, well, no sense worrying now. She put on her halter style, one-piece suit. Less revealing. After combing her hair back into a ponytail, she scrubbed her face, applied a hint of lip gloss, and threw on a cover-up before heading down.

Approaching the pool, she found Brent bracing Tyler across his middle at the surface of the water, instructing him on swimming techniques. She stood back, watching. Her heart pulsed.

"Press your chest into the water, and keep the rest of your body level with the surface," said Brent. "When your hand hits the water, reach strong with your arm, just under the water, and pull the water toward you. Kick from your hips, not your knees, and keep your ankles relaxed. Floppy. Watch me do it."

Brent skimmed across the water, head down, rotating sideways as he took in a gulp of air before pushing his face back in the water.

"Now you do it, Tyler."

Tyler pushed off, his little arms reaching, stretching, pulling the water, feet flapping, face turning away from the water, breathing in air.

"You got it, buddy. Good job."

She removed her cover-up and settled into a lounge chair with her book. Tyler and Brent continued practicing.

"Hey, sexy lady. Ready for the big night tonight?" asked Wayne, glistening like a greased pig, coconut oil flooding the air. He plopped into the chair next to her.

"Ready as I'll ever be," said Shade, wearing a strained smile and returning to her book. She could feel his meandering eyes on her body. He sat forward, facing her, attempting small talk.

"Hey, Shade," said Brent. "I thought you were coming in."

"Be right there." She got up and dove into the pool.

"Tyler, show your grandma how fast you can swim."

They waded in the shallow end while Tyler reached out, his feet paddling across the water. She felt her tension ease. Brent's body brushing her bare skin. He swam to Tyler. She followed his muscular back rippling beneath the surface.

They remained in the pool, practicing laps. She hoped Wayne would get the message and leave, but no such luck.

After emerging, Brent stretched out on Shade's lounge chair, patting the chair on the other side for Shade and Tyler. Wayne glanced at him, frowning.

"So, Wayne," said Brent, "when are you heading home?"

"Tomorrow."

"Let me know if you need a ride to the airport. I can take you."

"Yeah," said Tyler. "We could even drop you off tonight. Me and Brent. You could be first in line."

"So, what do you do back home, Wayne?" asked Brent, trying to contain a smile.

"I'm the number one sales guy at the Porsche dealership in my area, and second in the nation. It's a lucrative career. Got me a five-thousand square foot house on a lake in the tony suburb of Elm Grove. I've done well for myself," he said, pushing his chest out like a gorilla. His voice notched an octave higher. "Just looking for a pretty lady to share my life with. So, what do you do, Brent?"

"Athletic Director for Edelweiss Schools. I've been in sports all my life, so it suits me. Well, I hate to run, but I've had enough sun for the day." He turned to Shade and Tyler. "You two ready to head back?"

"Yeah, we've had enough too," said Shade. "And I need to get my little ring bearer dressed for his big moment. See you at the wedding, Wayne."

"Yeah, let's get outta here," said Tyler. "It stinks like coconut."

Brent walked them to their room. "I'll see you in a few hours. Do you need an escort to the beach for the ceremony? You never know what lurks in these hallways."

She laughed. "I think we'll be okay. I have my little bodyguard with me. See you at dusk."

Shade helped Tyler dress in the outfit Sally had chosen. White linen shirt, pale pink bow tie, taupe suspenders, white and tan pinstriped shorts and flip-flops.

"Oh, Tyler," said Shade, rolling up his sleeves. "You look so handsome. Where's the pillow Sally gave you for the ring?"

"Do I have to hold the pillow? It's stupid."

"It's not your wedding. It's Sally and Chad's wedding."

Tyler walked around the room, his head snapping back and forth. "I think I lost it."

"What? It was here earlier," said Shade, searching everywhere. "Keep looking while I shower and get dressed."

"Okay, I'll find it, Grandma. Don't worry." After Shade went into the bathroom, Tyler lounged on the bed, flipping through his Junior Baseball magazine while eating a bag of potato chips.

"Did you find the pillow?" she yelled from the bathroom.

"No, Grandma. I'm still looking." He jumped off the bed and tossed the magazine and chips aside, opening and closing dresser drawers.

She blew her sun-streaked hair dry and then applied a coat of mascara and a hint of eyeliner, smudging the line with her finger for a smoky look. She rarely wore foundation but added a dab, using a damp facial sponge to blend. After dusting blush to her cheeks and applying pale pink lipstick, she removed her dress from the hanger and slid it over her shoulders. She loved the silkiness of the flowy, lightweight fabric against her skin. The aquamarine of the strapless dress enhanced her azure eyes, bringing out the deep bronze of her skin. She put on low-heeled, strappy sandals and emerged from the bathroom.

"Wow, Grandma. You look prettier than last night."

"Thank you, Tyler. Did you find the pillow?"

"No," he said, throwing his arms in the air. "I looked everywhere. I hope Sally isn't mad."

"Well, let's hope not. You ready to go, and break the news to her?"

A light breeze drifted in off the ocean, the sun dangling low in the brilliant, blue sky. White chairs stood in rows on the beach, Tiki torches mounted in the sand down the center aisle, casting a soft glow.

She took Tyler to the holding area where the wedding party waited. "Oh, Sally," said Shade, taking her hands. "You look stunning, and your dress is striking. You seem so calm. Are you nervous?"

"Not at all. Everything feels right. And you look beautiful. That's a great dress." She crouched down and gave Tyler a hug. "Hey, handsome. Are you ready for your big moment?"

"I lost my pillow," said Tyler, pushing his bottom lip out for effect. "Are you mad?"

"Oh, no, honey. Don't worry. Hanna is carrying leis down the aisle. Why don't you help her and hand them to people sitting at the end of each row?"

Shade left Tyler with Sally and went down to the beach. Brent waved her over to an open seat next to him.

Brent felt like a teenager on a first date. She had never looked more beautiful. Her jasmine scent lingered in the air. Intoxicating —like a drug. She was an enigma. Hysterically laughing and clumsy one minute, elegant and sexy the next. Her bare arm brushed his linen shirtsleeve, sending jolts throughout his body.

"You look nice tonight," she said, turning to him.

"And you look gorgeous."

"Thank you," she replied, holding his stare before looking away. "I hope Tyler does okay."

"I'm sure he'll be fine."

Tyler and Hanna sauntered along the sandy pathway, shoeless, swaying their hips to the ukulele rendition of the "Hawaiian Wedding Song", tossing leis to the guests.

"Never a dull moment with that boy," Brent whispered in her ear.

She caught a whiff of musk cologne—his sun-bleached hair tickling her cheek—teasing her emotions.

The bride and groom said their "I do's," and Shade dabbed the corners of her eyes. She couldn't be happier for Sally. The sister she never had.

The reception party was in full swing. Brent remained by Shade's side until Chad pulled him away to smoke a cigar.

"Hey, Shade," said Sally. "Let's go get some champagne. I haven't talked to you all night, and I'll be leaving early in the morning."

"What a lovely wedding," said Shade, as they stood at the bar. "I get depressed thinking about leaving."

"I'm glad you're having a good time. And what about you and Brent?" Sally asked, tilting her head and raising her eyebrows.

Shade smiled. She took a sip of champagne, her eyes looking away. "He's perfect. And if I was looking I would want someone just like him. But I'm not looking. Things are going well for me and Tyler. I don't want to upset that."

"But Brent is so good with Tyler. And what about you? Don't you want someone to share your life with?"

"It's not about me, Sally. Don't worry about me."

"Oh, Shade. I want what's best for you." Sally took her in her arms. "Chad wants to sneak away soon. If I don't see you later, I'll see you when we get home. Enjoy the rest of your vacation. I love you."

"Hey, Grandma, let's dance."

"My pleasure."

As they spun across the dance floor, Tyler's feet kept pace with the rhythm, his limbs partially liquid. He'd adapted a unique mix of moonwalking and hula dance, sending Shade into spasms of laughter. When a slow song came on, he wrapped his arms around her waist, and they swayed to the Polynesian music.

"Excuse me," said Wayne, tapping Tyler on the head. "I think it's my turn."

Tyler cocked his head, staring at Shade. Before he could get a read, Wayne had whisked her away, into the crowd. He watched from the side, Wayne's hand traveling up and down her back, his mouth to her ear. Tyler wasn't certain, but it looked like she was trying to push him away. He became furious. Looking around, he spotted Brent sitting at a table, smoking a cigar with Chad and Kevin.

"Hey, buddy," said Brent, smiling when Tyler approached.

"Can I tell you something?"

"Sure," said Brent.

Tyler stepped closer to Brent and cupped his hand over his ear, whispering.

Brent excused himself and walked away with Tyler. Nearing the dance floor, he could see Shade with Wayne. She appeared to be struggling to free herself from his grip.

"Hey, buddy," said Brent. "Why don't you go over there with Mindy and Hanna? Everything will be okay."

"Mind if I cut in?" asked Brent.

"Yeah, I do," said Wayne, slurring his words, squeezing her tighter.

Brent noted the look of panic on her face. "Hey, I don't want to create a scene at my nephew's wedding. I'm asking you nicely to let her go."

"I think the lady wants to be with me, so why don't you get lost."

Brent grabbed the back of Wayne's shirt collar with one hand and jerked Wayne's arm off Shade with his other hand, pulling his arm behind his back. "Like I said, I don't want to cause a scene, so why don't you move on?"

Wayne yanked himself free. "Hey, sorry. I didn't know you two were an item." He straightened his tie, gave Shade a once over and stumbled away.

"May I have this dance?" Brent asked, holding his open palm to her.

She fell into him. He wrapped his arm around her waist and held her hand in his, between them, pressed against his chest. The delicate bones in her hand, so fragile. Like a China doll. He held her, pulling her closer.

"Hey. It's all right," said Brent, leaning back and looking into her tear-filled eyes before pulling her close again. "He's gone. He had too much to drink. Chad's talking to him now. I don't think he'll bother you again."

Shade hiccupped as she tried to talk, but she couldn't get the words out.

"Shh. Let's dance. It's a beautiful night. Let's enjoy ourselves."

Her shoulders softened. She leaned into him, swaying to the music. She felt safe.

"You realize you blew it, don't you?" he whispered in her ear.

She leaned back and looked quizzically into his smiling eyes.

"You know, five-thousand square foot house in the tony suburb of Elm Grove. A Porsche. You could have had it all."

She laughed and inclined back into the security of his arms.

Tyler watched the whole scenario unfold, his lips curling, nostrils flaring. He spotted Wayne staggering at the edge of the pool, alone, smoking a cigar and staring into space. Tyler scanned the area, searching. He found a kiwi sitting atop a table adorned with tropical fruit. Sneaking behind a large palm tree, he positioned himself into his pitcher's stance. Target. Wind up. Rear back. Fire. Just how Brent had taught him. The kiwi left his hand at an impressive rate of speed, whacking Wayne on the back of his head and propelling him forward into the pool, cigar and all. Bullseye!

Wayne emerged from the water rubbing the back of his head, a limp cigar dangling from his lips.

Tyler leapt in the air, high-fiving the palm tree. He straightened his bow-tie and went back to enjoy the party. Out on the dance floor, he spotted them—Brent and Grandma—swaying to the music. He let out a slow sigh. Life was good.

CHAPTER NINETEEN

Do you know how God controls the clouds and makes his lightning flash? Do you know how the clouds hang poised, those wonders of him who has perfect knowledge?

— JOB 37:15-16

"Tyler, Brent will be here soon. Don't forget to grab your hat and sunscreen." She opened the small refrigerator to grab a bottled water. "Tyler, come over here, please. What's this?"

He slapped his hands on top of his head, feigning surprise, gasp and all. "Oh, wow! Now I remember. I put the ring pillow in the refrigerator so it wouldn't get stolen. I forgot. I looked everywhere for it."

"Tyler. I don't believe you," said Shade, hands on hips. "That wasn't a nice thing to do. You should be ashamed of yourself."

Tyler's eyes glossed over, as he pursed his lips and stared at Shade. "I'm sorry, Grandma."

Brent's knock disrupted the uneasy moment. "Hey, buddy, why the down face?"

"I did a bad thing, and Grandma is not happy with me."

Brent glanced at her, eyebrows raised.

"Tyler, tell Brent what you did."

"I thought the ring bearer pillow was dumb so I hid it in the refrigerator," said Tyler, looking at his feet. "I lied to Grandma and said I didn't know where it was."

Brent turned away to conceal his smile. "Well, I planned on giving you this baseball, but now I'm not sure if I should. I'll let your grandmother decide."

"I brought my glove," said Tyler, his face beaming. "Can I have the ball, Grandma?"

"You can take your glove today, but I'll decide later if you get the ball."

They set out at daybreak for the road trip to Hana, stopping along the way to buy a picnic lunch.

"It's about the journey, not the destination," said Brent. "The town of Hana itself is small with few attractions, but the ride is full of hairpin turns, ocean-side cliffs, and insanely gorgeous scenery. I think you'll love it."

Reaching the winding road, Shade and Tyler were struck by the raw, lush landscape and cascading waterfalls that appeared around every turn.

"Now this feels like real Hawaii," Shade remarked. "It takes my breath away. The zig-zag road makes me feel lightheaded."

"Some people take Dramamine before they go. I should have warned you. Do you think you'll be okay?"

"I'll be fine. Tyler, are you okay back there?"

"Yeah. Can you go faster, Brent?"

"Not unless you want to take the more scenic route—over the side of the cliff and into the ocean," said Brent. "Wait until you see the black sand beach. We'll stop and have lunch there."

Brent followed the road leading to Waianapanapa State Park.

He pulled a blanket from the trunk, along with their cooler packed with sandwiches and water.

"Here we are. Pa'iloa. The black sand beach."

"It's spectacular," said Shade, looking out at the cresting waves pounding against the jagged cliffs surrounding the beach. "It's like a postcard from God," she sighed.

They waded near shore, Brent's eye on them both. Tyler was enthralled by the size and power of the waves, repeatedly knocking him off his feet and causing him to shriek with laughter. Exhausted, they walked back to the blanket to eat lunch.

Brent studied them. Laughing together. Talking. She lay stretched next to him on the blanket. Her body, long and slender. Her calves, smooth and shapely. He considered the previous night when he held her in his arms. She seemed oblivious to the effect she had on him.

He felt a sudden urge to touch her. To kiss her. Right here. He was reminded of the classic beach scene from Kendra's favorite movie, *From Here to Eternity*. Burt Lancaster and Deborah Kerr, rolling on the beach, kissing passionately, while waves crashed over their waterlogged bodies, nearly washing them out to sea. He thought it was comical, but Kendra would let out a passionate sigh each time she watched that scene. He could picture her now, curled up on the sofa, hugging a folded pillow in her lap, a box of tissue on the table. How he loved her, despite her quirky habits.

"Hey, Brent, can we go surfing?" asked Tyler.

Brent was shaken from his thoughts. "I can give you a few lessons tomorrow, if your grandmother says it's okay."

"You've surfed before, I take it," said Shade. "Can we go somewhere calmer? Maybe you can teach me, too."

"I admire your courage." He stood. "We'd better get going. I have one more thing to show you. The Seven Sacred Pools."

The next stop on their road trip took them into a verdant valley and rainforest. They hiked the sloping path, bypassing tropical fruit trees and a bamboo forest. Each available nook exploded with flora and fauna, the shouts of insects and birds coming from every direction. The trail ended at cascading waterfalls tumbling into several plunge pools. The last pool emptied into the ocean along the Kipahula coastline. They lowered themselves in, bathing in the cool, turquoise water.

"I'm in paradise," Shade sighed, floating on her back, staring up into the cloudless blue sky. Brent's presence beside her stirred unwanted feelings. Thoughts that frightened her. She tried pushing them away.

"Anything special you want to do before I go back to Michigan?" asked Brent, as he drove back to the resort.

"I just wanna surf," said Tyler.

"Sounds good," said Brent. "Then I'd like to take you both somewhere nice for dinner. A special restaurant on the beach."

"It sounds wonderful," said Shade. "Are you sure you want to spend your last day with us?"

"There's no place I'd rather be than here with you both," he said.

The candor with which he said it caused her heart to flutter. She stared at him, studying his profile. Her body flushed warm. He wasn't looking for a response; he stated what was on his mind. And she didn't offer a reply. But Tyler did.

"You know what, Brent? There's no one else I wanna be with except you and Grandma. And I don't wanna be with that coconut man, Wayne. I'm glad he left. And I'm glad he fell in the pool with his clothes on."

"Well, thanks buddy," said Brent, smiling.

When they arrived at the resort, he walked them to their room. He wanted to embrace her, kiss her cheek, or better still, throw her on the bed.

"Well, I'll see you tomorrow," said Shade. She leaned forward and gave him a hug. A 'hey, good-seeing-you-old-pal' type hug. But he held on, his breath caressing her neck. Tyler rushed forward and wrapped his arms around Brent's legs.

"Thanks, Brent," said Tyler. "I can't wait to go surfing."

Brent smiled and ruffled his hair. "Good night, buddy. See you tomorrow."

Brent returned to his room, tormented. He searched the contents of the mini-fridge and found a small bottle of Scotch. He hadn't had Scotch in years, but he needed something to take the edge off. After pouring a glass over ice, he went out onto the balcony. He couldn't read her, but his feelings for her consumed him. She never spoke of a husband. Was she widowed? Divorced? And Tyler's parents—where were they? And why did she have custody? She was a mystery. This intriguing woman who tortured his soul. He felt the liquid dripping through his veins like an IV, tension disintegrating. He loved that little boy, like his own. Tomorrow. Their last day together. He wanted his intentions known. Out in the open. Before they returned home.

She stood in the shower, the warm water beating hard against her bare skin, washing away her unfulfilled passion. Anguish pricked her core. He was perfect. But he deserved so much more. She was stained. Her inexcusable choices had left a mark on her. CAUTION: DO NOT TOUCH. Her mission in life was raising Tyler. *Dear God, help me stay focused on my vow so I can live the life you intended for me.* Raw emotion escaped. She tilted her face toward the shower head. The water rained down. *Help me get through this last day. Then everything will fall back into place.*

The next morning, Brent took Tyler to the beach to play catch while Shade sunbathed on a lounge chair. "Have you been practicing the pointers we discussed?" asked Brent, while they were warming up.

"Yeah," Tyler replied. He came near to Brent, whispering. "I did everything you said when I threw that piece of fruit and hit Wayne in the head. When he fell in the pool."

Brent's eyebrows gathered. He spoke in a low voice. "What did you do?"

"At the wedding. After you helped Grandma get away from him. I hid by a tree and took a piece of hard fruit. And I did what you taught me. Wind up, rear back, fire. I threw it fast, and it knocked his stupid body in the pool."

Brent knelt and put his hands on Tyler's shoulders. "Listen," he said, "I won't tell your grandmother, but I don't want you to do that again. You have a fast pitch. You need to be careful and not use your special gift in a bad way. Someone could get hurt. Understand?"

Tyler's eyes welled with tears, as he looked at his toes curling in the sand. "I'm sorry, Brent. I did another bad thing. Next time I'll throw something soft. Like a muffin."

"No, not even a muffin. You should never throw anything at

anybody." Brent wrapped his arms around Tyler, patting his back. "Hey, let's get to work and get some pitches in before we go surfing. Okay?" A wry smile seized the corner of Brent's mouth when he turned away. It had taken great restraint not to high-five him and commend his resourcefulness.

After renting surfboards and wetsuits in Lahaina, Brent drove to Launiupoko Beach in West Maui.

"The waves here are long, slow and rolling. Perfect for beginners."

"So, how did you learn to surf?" asked Shade.

"In college. I went to Pepperdine University in Malibu, California and took a surf class for PE credit. I got hooked. Spent most of my free time surfing. I haven't been in a while, but it's like riding a bike. You don't forget."

"You kinda strike me as the surfer boy type," said Shade, smiling.

"Thanks, I think," he grinned. "Okay, are you two ready?" he asked, after unpacking their gear.

"Yeah," said Tyler, digging his feet in the sand, faking a surfer's stance. Arms out, one foot in front of the other, shifting back and forth.

"We need to go through a few things before we get in the water," said Brent. "Look at your surfboard. They call the line down the center the stringer. The front of the board is the nose and the back is the tail. When you're surfing and you want to stop, sit at the tail and pull the nose of the board up. Ninety percent of surfing is paddling in the water. When you're lying on your belly, keep your fingers together, and pull your hands through the water. Like swimming freestyle. When you're ready to stand up, there are four steps to remember; push up with your hands on the board, bring both knees to your hands, put your front foot on the stringer between your hands, then stand up by pushing off with your back foot. But before we get in the water, let's practice in the sand."

After practicing, Brent moved into the water. "Okay, watch me first, then we'll all get in and try it."

Shade and Tyler stood on shore while Brent demonstrated. He was fearless in the water. His tight wetsuit against his firm abs and strong shoulders played with her mind. He was confident. Never showy. Just quietly sure of himself. He had nothing to prove.

Brent paddled out, then positioned the nose of the surfboard toward the beach. He glanced behind, searching for the ideal wave. Finding one, he paddled hard as the tide raised him higher. He waited until he caught the white-water roll. Bringing his knees to his hands, he pushed up and rode the wave into shore.

Tyler watched from shore, jumping around and clapping, before running into the water. "I'm ready. Can I try it?"

Tyler was a natural. And fearless like Brent. Shade was hesitant but slowly catching on. They practiced paddling, standing and riding the waves. Shade continued to wipe out when she caught a wave. Feeling incompetent after watching her seven-year-old grandson master the technique, Brent took her aside and gave her some pointers.

"Don't get discouraged. You're doing good. It's easier for Tyler because he's shorter. Keep trying. I think you're too far forward when you're on your tummy. Try laying further back. As the wave takes you, arch your back and put more weight on your legs and thighs. And keep your feet closer together with your knees bent, arms loose, and your eyes forward."

When she conquered her first wave, she screamed out, "Look. I'm standing. Everyone, get out of my way." Brent laughed at the exhilaration on her face. Within a few hours, they were both riding waves like quasi-decent surfers.

During the ride back, Shade and Tyler couldn't stop talking about their experience.

"That was crazy fun," said Shade. "I felt so free, gliding on top of the water."

"Brent, can you take us again tomorrow?" asked Tyler.

"Honey, Brent is leaving in the morning."

"Brent, why can't you stay?" asked Tyler.

"I have to get back to work." He glanced at her. "Trust me, if I could I'd change my flight, but it isn't possible. But I'm looking forward to taking you both to dinner tonight."

CHAPTER TWENTY

Place me like a seal over your heart, like a seal on your arm; for love is as strong as death, its jealousy unyielding as the grave. It burns like blazing fire, like a mighty flame.

— SONG OF SONGS 8:6

The striking figure at the door knocked him breathless. It was written in his gaze. Her chestnut hair, streaked with threads of sun-kissed gold, hung over her bare shoulders. His eyes followed her as she gathered her purse, the flowy pale blue dress draping her body as she moved.

"Well, we're ready for our dinner date," she said, smiling. Her head turned toward the lanai, but her eyes hung on his as she called out, "Tyler, Brent is here."

"You look beautiful," said Brent, surrendering to his impulses.

"Hey, Brent. How do I look?" asked Tyler, fingering his pink bow tie and strutting around the room. "Grandma let me wear the ring bearer outfit but without the pillow."

"Whoa. You look handsome, buddy. I love the bow tie."

"And you look handsome," said Shade, her cheeks glowing.

The words fell out before she could stop them. She found her stare unwavering from his blue-sky eyes, pulling her into him. His black tailored pants hugged his taut waist and long legs. The sleeves of his white linen shirt were rolled, exposing tanned forearms and solid wrists. Her breath seized.

"What a gorgeous setting," said Shade, when the maître d escorted them to their beach-side table. The sun dipped into the ocean, splashes of orange and red bathing the sky.

"I thought you'd enjoy this place."

"Have you been here before?" asked Shade.

"Yes. They have excellent seafood. Hey, Tyler, do you like fish?"

"I eat everything. My grandma says she can make me anything, and I eat it. Maybe I'll have a tuna fish sandwich."

"I don't think they have tuna sandwiches, but since you're an adventurous eater, try something different," said Brent, tousling Tyler's hair. He turned to Shade. "How about some wine? Maybe a bottle of red? And they have a Kiddie Mai Tai on the menu for Tyler."

"Sounds like a perfect way to celebrate our last night together in Hawaii. And why don't you order dinner for us since you're more familiar? We like surprises. Don't we, Tyler?"

"Yeah. Like when we saw Brent at the pool. That was my most favorite surprise ever."

"Guess what, buddy. It was my favorite surprise, too," said Brent, winking at Shade.

Her heart pole-vaulted. The wink. The sly smile. She was falling helpless. She considered him as he studied the wine list.

"We'll have a bottle of the 1999 Chappellet Pritchard Hill Cabernet, and a Kiddie Mai Tai for the young man," said Brent.

A few minutes later, the sommelier presented the bottle to

Brent. "A fine choice, sir," he said, removing the cork and pouring a splash into Brent's glass.

"Hey, mister," said Tyler. "Is that all you're gonna give him?"

Brent laughed. "He's letting me taste it to make sure it's okay." He swirled his glass, sniffed the wine and took a sip before nodding. The sommelier retreated after filling Brent and Shade's glasses.

"Let's make a toast," said Brent. "Here's to a wonderful week together with two beautiful people. There's nowhere else I'd rather be than here with you both. Cheers."

"Thank you," said Shade, gazing into his eyes before taking a sip. "I've never had red wine before. This is exceptional," she said, trying to swirl like an aficionado, sending wine sloshing onto the white tablecloth. "Oh my," she sputtered. "I got a little carried away with the swishing thing."

"I'm glad you like it," said Brent, grinning. "Hey, Tyler, how's your Mai Tai?"

"It's exceptional," replied Tyler, sucking the straw and making loud slurping noises. "Can I get another one, please?"

"Just one more, Tyler, and that's it for the night," said Shade.

The waitress presented Tyler with crayons and paper while Brent ordered an appetizer. "We'll start with the Taster Sampler."

Conversation came easy, as they sampled Keahole Lobster, Kalua Pork Quesadilla, and Ahi Ginger Poke. She glanced at Tyler sitting across from them, looking adorable in his pink bow tie and suspenders. "Hey, honey, what are you drawing?"

"It's a surprise," said Tyler, curling his arms protectively. Head down. Tongue rolling around inside his cheek. "Okay, are you ready?" asked Tyler. He revealed his drawing of three stick figures walking hand-in-hand, the smaller of the three in the middle. Palm trees graced the background, and little hearts floated above. "This is us," said Tyler. "Grandma, Grandpa Brent, and me. Do you like it?"

She blushed, smiling at Brent.

"I love it," said Brent. "Thank you for drawing it."

"Yes, thank you, honey. It's very nice."

"It's a present for Brent," said Tyler. "You can take it home and stick it on your refrigerator."

"I'll cherish it always," said Brent, glancing at Shade. She looked uncomfortable. He reached over and squeezed her hand.

"More wine, sir?" said the sommelier, lifting the bottle from the table.

"I think we're good for now," said Brent.

Tyler gulped his second Mai Tai, while they dined on Kula broccoli with macadamia nuts, pan seared Diver Sea Scallops with ginger garlic black-bean sauce and whipped garlic mashed potatoes.

"Do you like your dinner, Tyler?" asked Shade. "Tyler, are you okay?" His eyes were loose, unfocused. He swayed in his seat.

"Yep, Gamma," he replied, with a twisted smile, before launching into unprovoked laughter.

"What's so funny?" asked Shade, disturbed.

"Everything's funny," he slurred, before his head dropped forward, landing onto his plate.

They rushed to him, lifting his head—mashed potato globs pasted to his face. He smiled crookedly, eyes askew. "I wuv you guys," he slurred, before slumping forward.

The waiter rushed to their table. "I'm so sorry. The bartender mixed up the orders. I was coming over to give you the right one. The second Mai Tai had alcohol in it."

"Are you sure only one drink had alcohol?" asked Brent.

"Yes, we're sure. Let me get the manager," the waiter replied.

"I'm so sorry about what happened," said the manager moments later. "There was a mix-up."

"That's inexcusable," said Brent, as Shade wiped Tyler's face.

"Please accept our apologies. Is there anything I can do, sir?"

"You need to be more careful," Brent said, while Shade attended to Tyler.

Brent carried Tyler to the car, Tyler's hands draped around Brent's neck.

"I'm glad you suggested we call the doctor," said Shade, on the drive home. "It was reassuring. I'll keep an eye on him."

Brent was quiet, lost in thought. He reached over and touched her knee, his hand lingered.

He carried Tyler into the hotel room. Shade sat him on the edge of the bed and undressed him while Brent supported his listing body. Tyler wore a steady smile, his head bobbing. Once in his pajamas, Shade tucked him into bed and scrutinized him, kissing his forehead and stroking his hair. "Poor little guy."

"I'm so sorry, Shade," said Brent, wounded. "I suggested the Mai Tai."

"It's not your fault. He'll be okay. I just hope he doesn't wake up with a hangover. There's nothing more we can do. Do you want to sit out on the lanai? Maybe we can finish the wine." The manager had corked their bottle and provided another, gratis.

"Sure. I'd like that." Brent poured two glasses.

They stepped out onto the balcony and settled into the lounge chairs. "I'm sure he'll be raring to go in the morning." He raised his glass. "To paradise," he said, clinking glasses. "It's been nice, being here with you both." He took a sip, then turned toward her. "We've spent a lot of time together, but I don't know much about you—your life—Tyler. I'd like to know more, if you're comfortable."

She breathed deep, caressing the stem of her wineglass. She looked into his eyes and held them for a minute before answering. "I've had a complicated life," she said, turning and staring into the night. She sipped her wine. Started and stopped. Then spoke. "I was an orphan, abandoned by my mother and left hanging in a box under a tree." She laughed nervously. "That's how I got the name, Shade. Because the shade of the tree kept me from baking in the sun."

"I lived in three foster homes. At fifteen, I fell for a guy and got pregnant. When he found out, he ran. My foster parents didn't know what to do, so they took me to a home for unwed mothers. We went to church every Sunday, and that's how I met my husband, Stanley. He was much older, but he wanted to marry me despite my condition. And he adopted my daughter, Adeline. When Addy turned sixteen, she fell in with the wrong crowd and ran away with a guy named Scott and eventually became pregnant with Tyler. Scott died in an accident when Tyler was a baby. He never knew his father," said Shade, struggling to find the right words. "Adeline hooked up with another guy, Jaime, and she and Tyler lived with him. My husband died five years ago. A heart attack. A year later, Adeline and Jaime were murdered. They never found the killer."

She swallowed hard, staring at the wineglass pressed between her fingers. There was more, but she had said enough. Too much shame. "So, that's my life. I got custody of Tyler, and now it's just the two of us. He's the only family I have."

Brent let out a long sigh as he studied her face. He felt helpless. Words escaped him. He reached over and took her hand. His thumb brushing her delicate fingers.

"Did you have a good marriage?" he asked.

"Yes, it seemed to be a good marriage." She stopped short, changing the subject. "So, tell me about you. Your life." She felt deceptive asking what she already knew. But she sensed he wanted to talk—to lay everything out in the open.

He took a swallow of wine and withdrew his hand from hers. "I was married to a beautiful woman, Kendra. We met in college. In California. We got married after we graduated. We spent our honeymoon here, in Hawaii. Her family lived in Michigan, so we moved there. I was working as a Major League Baseball scout. The position required a lot of travel, so when Kendra got pregnant, I looked for a job that would keep me close to home. That's when I became the Athletic Director for Edelweiss Schools. When our son, Luke, was born, we were thrilled." Brent hesitated, running his finger around the edge of the wineglass. He stared ahead, jaw clenching. Unclenching.

She waited, studying his profile, the muscle pulsing above his jawline. He looked exposed, and she wanted to draw nearer to him. Her heart thundered in her chest.

"When Luke turned two, Kendra got pregnant again. We were elated. She was five months along when she took Luke and drove to the supermarket. A guy ran a red light. They were broadsided. Both killed," he said, his breaths long. "That was five years ago."

She was breathing hard. Her shoulders tight. She studied his eyes, shiny with tears. "Oh, Brent, I am so sorry."

"We've had a lot of tragedy in our lives," said Brent, picking up the bottle. "Why don't we kill this wine? Things are getting gloomy out here."

"Sure," she said, brushing a tear from her face. "I'll go check on Tyler."

She returned to the lanai and found Brent leaning against the balcony rail, wineglass in hand. She grabbed her glass and joined him, their forearms touching, as they gazed into the night. He placed his glass on the table and turned, facing her. He removed the glass from her hand and set it aside. Their eyes locked. He moved closer, pulling her into him, his lips touched hers. Gently at first, then deeper. Desperate. An intense hunger unleashed. He drank from her mouth as though dying of thirst.

Her legs felt as though they could no longer hold her, her body dissolving into his. She ran her fingers through his hair, pulling him closer. He pressed her against the wall, his lips brushed her neck—her shoulder. His hands moved over her. Everywhere.

She had never felt like this. And she didn't want him to stop. Her hands pulled him closer, feeling the strength of his back. Tears coursed, as all emotion gushed out. He pulled back, his hands framing her face. He stared into her, wiping the wetness with his thumbs.

"What's wrong?" he breathed, concern in his eyes.

"I don't know," she said. "I've never …," she stopped and breathed in, biting her lip. "I don't know."

He pulled her close to him, tucking her head into the crook of his neck, his arms wrapped around her, stroking her hair. "Shade, you make me crazy. I've wanted you for so long. It feels right. Here. With you." She clung to him, tears stained his shirt.

"Hey," he said, holding her at arms-length, searching her face. "I would never do anything you didn't want. Maybe things went too fast. I'm sorry."

"Oh, Brent," she sighed, staring into him. "It's just that …."

"Hello, is anybody here?" Tyler slurred, sitting up in bed, swaying back and forth. "Can I get another Mai Tai?"

Shade and Brent drew back from one another and went to him.

"How are you feeling, honey?" asked Shade, running her fingers through his hair.

"Great," he replied, smiling. "Brent, are you sleeping over?"

"No, buddy," said Brent, smiling. "I'm leaving now. I have to get up early to catch my flight. Can I have a hug goodbye?"

Tyler flung himself at Brent, his arms wrapped around him. "I love you, Brent," he garbled, before falling over backwards. He was asleep.

A mist formed in Brent's eyes. He pulled the cover over him, tucking it around his neck, and kissed his forehead. "Well," Brent sighed, "I should leave."

She walked him to the door.

"I'll see you in Michigan," he said, as he ran his finger over her lips, his eyes holding hers. "Do you want me to pick you up from the airport?"

"No, but thank you. Mary's coming with Scone and Leah."

"Call me when you get in?"

"I will. And thank you for everything. You don't know how much I appreciate what you've done—for me and for Tyler." She reached up and took his face in her hands, pressing her lips against his—lingering.

His arms encircled her. His tongue moved between her lips. He pulled away. "I need to leave." He kissed her forehead before opening the door and walking out.

Shade leaned against the door. Undone. She could taste him, still wet on her mouth. Her chin burning from the stubble of his whiskers. She wanted him. Desperately. She needed a shower, but she didn't want to wash away his scent. Not tonight.

She pulled on her nightgown and slipped under the covers, droplets wetting her face and pillow. Her protective barrier had been shattered. *Why did I let it go this far? Dear God, I know you will not let me be tempted beyond what I can bear. Please God. Help me find a way out.* She lay awake for hours before sleep took hold.

Shade got up early and went out to the lanai with her coffee and daily reading. She prayed for a safe trip for Brent and wondered if he was thinking about her. She tried concentrating, but her mind kept traveling back to last night, longing for him to be with her.

"My head hurts," said Tyler, stepping out onto the lanai, hair disheveled, eyes squinting against the sun. He went to Shade and crawled into her lap, wrapping his arms around her neck. "Where's Brent?"

She embraced him, kissing his cheek. "I'll get you some Tylenol. Brent had to leave this morning. He went back to Michigan."

"Why didn't he say good-bye?"

"He did. In fact, he tucked you into bed and kissed you goodnight."

"I don't remember. Can Brent live with us when we get back to Michigan?"

"No, honey. He has his own home, but you can still see him."

"Grandma, I'm gonna pray Brent will come live with us and be my grandpa."

She squeezed him tight, rubbing his back. "It's good to pray. God doesn't always give us what we want, but he gives us what we need."

"Do you ever wish my mom was alive? And she could live with us?"

"Always, honey. Every day." She pulled in her emotions. "But I'm thankful I have you. You're my special gift from God. Hey, what do you want to do on our last day?"

"Can we go shopping? I wanna get a present for Leah and Mary."

"Yes. I was planning on that. Anything else?"

"Maybe go swimming?"

"You got it, buddy. Let's get a move on."

"Mind if I join you?" said Mindy, spotting Shade in a lounge chair. Kevin and Evangeline helped Hanna into the pool as Tyler swam to greet them.

"Please do," replied Shade. "When do you go home?"

"Day after tomorrow," Mindy replied. "It was such a beautiful wedding and Chad seems so happy. It sounds like you've known Sally for some time. We're happy to have her in our family."

"Sally is a wonderful person. I don't know what I would do without her."

"We haven't spent much time with her, but hopefully that will change now that they're married. We were hoping to spend more time with Brent, but it sounds like he was busy with you and Tyler. Did you have a good time together?"

She felt uneasy talking about him. Was she fishing? "Yes, we did. He's so good with Tyler, and Tyler adores him."

"He loves children, so that's not surprising," said Mindy. "Does Tyler live with you?"

"Yes. My daughter, Tyler's mother, passed away." She paused. "Adeline was a single mom, so I have custody of Tyler."

"Oh, Shade. I'm so sorry," Mindy said, touching her hand. She didn't pry. "It must have been hard for you. Do you know about Brent's family? The accident?"

"Yes, he told me," said Shade, stopping for a minute to slow the conversation. "I can't imagine what he must have gone through."

"It was unbearable. He's my baby brother, so I worry about him. He was such a free spirit when he was young. Into sports. Incredibly adventurous. Wanted to travel the world, climb mountains and jump out of airplanes. But when he met Kendra, he became more responsible. More settled. And when Luke was born, his world was complete—until that day when everything changed. He became withdrawn. Introspective. Like someone had sucked the life out of him. There wasn't anything we could do to help him. I always hoped he would meet someone, but he doesn't seem interested. He dates, but it always ends the same—one or two dates and he's done. He told me no one could replace what he'd lost."

Mindy sighed. "It's been five years since I've seen him this content. I see the old Brent coming back to life, and it makes me so happy. But I worry he could get hurt again. I guess what I'm trying to say is he seems to have feelings for you. I'm not sure what your intentions are. And it's none of my business, but please don't hurt him." Mindy rubbed Shade's arm, tears brimming in her eyes. She was visibly shaken. "I love him so much. He's such a good man."

Shade put her hand over Mindy's. She couldn't swallow. The lump in her throat fixed. "I think the world of Brent. And so does Tyler. I only want what's best for all of us. It's in God's hands."

"Hey," she smiled, still touching Shade's arm. "Would you like to join us for dinner tonight? We're eating here at the resort. We'd love to have you."

"I'd like that. Thank you." She was conflicted, but didn't want to appear impolite.

Shade was eager to get home—to settle things with Brent. She had let it go too far.

CHAPTER TWENTY-ONE

The Lord is close to the brokenhearted and saves those who are crushed in spirit.

— PSALM 34:18

Scone leapt at Tyler, licking his face, his tail spinning like a ceiling fan. "I missed you so much, Scone," said Tyler, nuzzling his face into Scone's neck.

Mary and Shade embraced before loading the luggage into the car. "Did you have a nice time?" asked Mary, when they were settled in the front seat.

Tyler yelled out from the back seat. "Brent was there, and we spent a lot of time with him."

"Oh?" said Mary, her eyebrows elevating.

"You'll never believe this, but Brent is Chad's uncle," said Shade. "When we saw him at the resort, I almost fell over in shock. We had a wonderful time. The wedding was beautiful, Hawaii is stunning, and Brent took us sightseeing. He'd been there before, so he knew where to go."

"And he taught us how to surf," said Tyler. "Leah, I'll teach you how to surf when you get a little older. And I bought you a present."

"Oh, Tyler," said Leah. "I missed you. And I took good care of Scone for you."

"Thanks," replied Tyler. "One day, I'll take you to Hawaii."

Mary and Shade exchanged looks, smirking. When they pulled up to the cottage, Shade invited them in.

Shade handed Mary a gift bag. "This is for you—from me and Tyler."

Mary removed the box and ran her hand over the rippling curl pattern of the wood. "Oh, it's beautiful. I've never seen anything like it."

"It's a Koa box. The wood comes from the Koa tree, known for some of the hardest and rarest wood in the world. The trees only grow in Hawaii."

"Thank you," said Mary, still admiring the box.

"And this is for you, Leah, from me and Grandma," said Tyler, pushing his chest out. "I picked it out. It's a red coral dolphin. It matches your red hair. You hang it on a chain around your neck, but I didn't get you a chain. You'll have to buy one for yourself."

"Thank you, Tyler," said Leah. "I'll wear it every day."

When the kids ran off to play, Mary and Shade settled at the kitchen counter sipping coffee.

"So, is he married?" asked Mary.

"He's not." Her mood turned solemn, her face tense. "His wife and son were killed in a car accident five years ago."

Mary gasped. "That poor man. I can't imagine what he's been through." She imparted a quizzical look. "What about the two of you?"

"We had a great time with Brent. He showed us around the island, and Tyler adores him, as you know." She sighed, looking down. "Oh, Mary. I can't bring anyone into my life. I made a vow to God. That I would stay focused on raising Tyler until he's on his own. I didn't do a good job raising Adeline, and I don't want to repeat the same mistakes."

"Shade, I know how much you loved Stanley, but you're young. It's okay to love again. And Tyler needs a man in his life. A father figure. Brent is perfect for you. Don't you feel God wants that for Tyler? And for you?"

She cooled at the sound of Stan's name. "I appreciate your concern, but I feel God wants my focus to remain on Tyler."

"Well, my prayers are always with you," said Mary, embracing her. "We better get going and let you unpack. Thanks for the beautiful gifts. I love you, dear."

Shade reached for the phone, her hands trembling. She felt disembodied. The tone of his voice caused her heart to lurch.

"Well, we made it home," said Shade—trying to sound upbeat. "We had dinner with Mindy and her family on the last day."

"She told me. I've been thinking about you two. Did you just get home?"

"About an hour ago. Mary and Leah stayed awhile. I'm trying to get organized now. Did you work today?"

"Yeah, but I'm off the next two days. I want to see you, Shade. I miss you. Any chance you can get someone to watch Tyler tomorrow night so we can spend time alone? Maybe go out to dinner?"

"I want to see you, too. Let me ask Mary. I'd rather not go out, if you don't mind. Why don't I come over to your house?"

"Sure. I can make dinner if you don't expect anything fancy."

"No, please don't bother. I'll eat with Tyler before I take him to Mary's. Does seven o'clock work?"

"Sounds good." He hung up. Something was off. She seemed too abrupt. Serious. Could be jet lag, but he sensed something more.

Shade unpacked and started a few loads of laundry while Tyler played outside with Scone. She picked up the pale blue dress she'd worn to dinner, pulling it to her face. His scent clung to the folds of the material. She hung it in her closet and sat on the edge of her bed. Her stomach simmered as she stared at the dress, taunting her. Memories passed like a warm ocean wave washing over her. She slid to the floor, on her knees, and prayed for strength. *I know what must be done, but I don't want to do it. God, please help me through this and take away the temptation that's crushing me.*

"Tyler, I'm going to Brent's house, and Mary will watch you tonight. I want you to be a good boy for her, okay?"

"Why can't I go? I wanna see Brent."

"Because we want to talk."

"About getting married?" said Tyler, grinning wide. "Shouldn't I be there, too?"

"No, it's grown-up talk. I'll pick you up later tonight."

She pulled into Brent's driveway, her heart thumping, her stomach pitching. He lived in a large, Country French style home. A single story, with a mix of stone and stucco and a steep, mansard roof. Several narrow windows lined the facade. She pictured him living here with his wife and son. Her heart ached.

He opened the door, his face beaming at the sight of her. She was dressed in a pair of low rise, straight-legged jeans with a white cotton shirt and black blazer. It had only been two days since he'd seen her, but it seemed longer. "It's good to see you," he said, embracing her.

"You, too," she said, returning his embrace. Her body trembled. She felt faint. Her appetite had dwindled since returning home, and the lack of nourishment was catching up with her. "What a lovely home. Do you ever get lost in here?"

He smiled. "It's too much for me. I've been thinking about selling and downsizing, but I never get around to it. Let me give you the tour," he said, taking her hand.

Exposed wood beams flanked the vaulted ceilings. A large porch ran along the back of the house with an expansive view of Lake Michigan. The master suite had a fireplace with a limestone mantel, displaying several framed photos. She walked over, studying each.

"She's beautiful," said Shade, lingering on an image of Brent and Kendra. Two lovers on a beach somewhere.

"Yes, she was," he remarked. "That picture was taken in St. John—in the Caribbean."

"And this must be Luke," said Shade, holding a photo of a toddler wearing a baseball hat and a Detroit Tigers T-shirt. "He's adorable. I can see the resemblance," she said, eyeing the photo and then Brent.

Brent turned serious, their eyes meeting. "That's what everyone said. Let me finish showing you around."

They ended the tour in the wine cellar. The temperature-controlled room housed several bottles of wine, stacked within mahogany wine racks. A rustic wood tasting table stood in the center of the room atop a travertine floor.

"Good grief. I've never seen so much wine."

"I collect wines," he said, grinning. "When I lived in California, Kendra and I used to spend weekends touring different wine regions. I seriously considered becoming a winemaker. Speaking of wine, would you like a glass?"

"Maybe a small glass." She feared the wine would weaken her resolve to be forthright, but she needed something to steady her nerves. The looming conversation weighed heavily.

They went into the kitchen. She sat on a high stool at the kitchen island across from him while he opened the bottle and poured a small amount into a glass, swirling and sniffing before taking a sip. He poured two glasses.

"Here's to Michigan," he said, clinking her glass before taking a drink. "I know it's only been a few days, but it seems longer. I missed you both."

She took a generous gulp, averting his penetrating stare. "Brent," she let out a deep sigh, her throat tightening, as though she had inhaled cotton balls. "We need to talk. About us."

"Okay. Let's talk," he said.

She could feel the weight of his penetrating stare. A significant silence stretched out. "I can't be with you. I ... I need to be alone. To focus on being a good grandmother to Tyler. He has nobody in this world but me. I can't do anything to jeopardize that."

He put his glass down, his eyes boring into her. There was no expression on his face, but she could see the muscle flexing in his jaw. He released a hard breath.

"That doesn't make sense," he said. "Are you telling me I'd be a bad influence on Tyler? You know how much I care for him. And you're right. He has nobody but you. What if something happens to you? What happens to him? Foster care? Things happen. We both know that. What is this about? Is there someone else?"

"No. No one else," she stammered. "If I were looking, you would be that person. But I'm not looking. You deserve better."

"You don't know what I deserve," he retorted, catching himself and softening his tone. "I wasn't looking either until you walked into my life. I haven't felt this way about anyone since losing Kendra." He pushed his hands through his hair and turned, looking off. "There's something you're not telling me. That night in Hawaii. You wanted me as much as I wanted you. I felt it. What is it? Does it have to do with your beliefs? Are you concerned about being intimate? Because we can work through that if you are."

"It's not that," she said, no longer able to contain her emotions. Large teardrops moved down her cheeks. Her body shook with sobs. She buried her face in her hands and wept. She couldn't look at him. The pain on his face was unbearable.

He came around to her, sitting at the stool opposite her, and pulled her hands from her face. "Look at me," he said gently, turning her toward him. "I don't know what's going on, but there's something you can't or won't talk about." He stood and pulled her head into his chest, stroking her hair. She continued to sob.

"Shade, my feelings for you, and for Tyler, are genuine. I can't stop thinking about you. You're in my thoughts constantly. But if you tell me you don't feel the same way, then I'll walk away."

She looked up at him, her eyes red and mascara smeared, trying to push the words out. "You need to walk away," she said, choking on her words.

He felt as though she had plunged a knife into his chest. "Are you telling me you don't have feelings for me? If you are, I don't believe you. You're not being honest. Why can't we talk about it?"

"Just walk away," she cried, her body shivering. "You deserve better. I'm not good for you."

"I don't understand," he said. He couldn't swallow. He walked over to the window and looked out, his back to her, hands on hips, processing. He turned to her. "If that's what you want. But don't pull Tyler away from me. He needs a man in his life, and I care too much about him. Don't let this affect my relationship with him."

Her eyes filled with shame and hurt. "There is nothing I want more than for you to be involved in Tyler's life. He adores you. He loves you," she choked, water re-pooling in her eyes. She placed her fingers over her lips and stared at Brent—at the pain she had caused.

Their eyes locked. He reached for her, drawing her into him, holding her head against his chest, her tears soaking his shirt. They held onto each other for several minutes until he pulled away, releasing a heavy sigh. "Are you okay to drive home?"

She nodded. She couldn't speak. He walked her to her car, his arm around her shoulders. She felt as though she were watching herself from afar. When they reached her car door, he took her face in his hands and kissed her gently. Fully. She didn't stop him. She clung to him, but there were no words left in her mouth. Just choking sobs. She pulled away and slid into her seat. He held the car door open, studying her.

"Shade. Why can't you trust me with the truth?" he asked, sadness etched on his face.

She didn't speak. She reached up to him and put her fingers to his lips.

He took her hand away and kissed her palm, holding it against his cheek. "I'll stay away, but only because it's what you want—not what I want," he said. "We don't get to choose who we fall in love with—it just happens."

"I know, Brent," she said, crying. "I know."

He stood in the driveway, wounded to his core, as she drove out of his life. He would never understand her torment. But he loved her. And if she ever changed her mind he would be there. He opened the front door and stepped into his tomb of silence.

Shade drove home, shattered. She needed a shower before picking up Tyler. And she needed time alone. The crying hadn't stopped since she left Brent, desolate sobbing draining her body. She thought back to when Stan died, her utter devastation. But she realized for the first time, it wasn't pain from love lost. It was fear. Fear of being alone. This felt different. She had never experienced feelings like this for a man. Yearnings waged war in her soul.

In a catatonic state, she undressed and stepped into the

shower, holding her face under the spray of the faucet. Mindy's words haunted her. "Please don't hurt him. He's such a good man." She slid down the shower wall and sat on the tile floor, pulling her knees into her chest, her forehead against her knees. The water rained down. *Oh God. Please help me. I love him so much, it hurts. Please, God, strengthen me.*

Sobs tormented her body for what seemed like hours. And then it came. That still, quiet whisper stroking her mind. *Be still....and know that I am God.* She remained curled up on the tile floor for some time, a surreal peace bathing her soul.

CHAPTER TWENTY-TWO

Jesus said, "Let the little children come to me, and do not hinder them, for the kingdom of heaven belongs to such as these."

— MATTHEW 19:14

"Grandma, I saw Brent at school today. He said we only have one more Sunday to practice until next year. He said it's gonna get too cold."

Shade arrived at the park with Tyler and Scone. The fall colors were fading on the few leaves that remained on the trees, and the crisp air caused her breath to catch.

It had been a few days since 'the talk.' Anxiety coiled in her gut when she spotted Brent tossing a Frisbee to Coach. He waved when he saw them, as though nothing had changed. Her heartbeat increased. She waved and smiled. Tyler ran out to meet him, shouting his name, like he hadn't seen him in years. She watched them embrace, gladness filling her.

"Are you ready for our last practice, buddy?" asked Brent, ruffling his hair.

"Yeah. I'm ready for baseball."

Brent went to Shade and gave her a hug. "How are you doing?" he asked.

She shrugged. "Okay, I guess. I'm sorry about the other night. I was a basket case," she said, squeezing his arm.

He smiled but remained silent.

The sound of screaming tires and spitting gravel interrupted the moment. Victoria came barreling into the parking lot. "Hey everybody," she yelled, trotting over to them. "Good to see everyone."

Brent and Shade smiled and waved. Cody ran to Tyler.

"Hi Victoria," said Brent, turning toward the boys. "Well, we better get started. This is the last practice until next year."

"Brent," said Victoria, assessing him. "You're looking quite handsome with that suntan. In fact, you all have suntans," she said, looking around. "What the hell? Did you run off to Cuba for baseball practice and forget to tell me?"

Brent smiled before trotting off, leaving Shade to contend with Victoria.

"Hey, so what's up? You guys go somewhere?"

"We went to Chad and Sally's wedding in Hawaii."

"Ah, yes. Chad is still on his honeymoon. We're shorthanded at the station. So, you went together?" she asked, nudging Shade's arm. "Hey, you holding out on me?"

Shade laughed. "Brent was there. But I didn't realize that Brent is Chad's uncle. I was shocked when he showed up at the resort where we were staying. Small world, isn't it?"

"Wow. Small, cozy world. So, are you two—you know—a thing? Hey, did you find out if he's married?"

"He's not married, and no, we are not a thing."

"Excellent. I still have a chance," she snickered. "Hey, I hate to ask, but do you mind if I run out and leave Cody here with you guys? I have a few errands to run. I won't be long."

Shade studied Brent as he coached the boys on the mechanics of pitching and catching. Her heart longed for him, but it couldn't be. Disgrace had wallpapered her soul.

While the boys continued practicing, Brent walked over to her. She was sitting alone at a picnic table. She appeared fragile. Broken. He wanted to take her in his arms and protect her from her demons.

"Hey," said Brent. "Where's your friend?"

"She had an errand to run."

He sat next to her, at ease with his hand resting atop her denim clad thigh. She put her hand over his. Their eyes met. "Brent, thank you for understanding—the other night."

"I don't understand, but I'll respect your wishes."

"Brent," she said, stopping to take a breath, "about what you said—about Tyler." She gazed down at his hand over hers. "I need to ask you something, but don't feel obligated."

"So, ask me," he said, reaching over and brushing a strand of hair from her face.

She forced a weak smile. "You were right when you said Tyler has nobody in this world but me. If something happened to me, I don't know what would happen to him. Mary might take him, but she's in her seventies. I know I'm asking a lot, and I wouldn't ask if he didn't love you so much," she stammered, "but ..."

He finished her sentence. "You want me to take him if something happens to you? Like a legal guardian?"

She swallowed deep. "Yes." After what she'd done to him, she wouldn't blame him if he refused. He looked away, staring off.

Shade studied his profile. His face. His even breaths.

He squeezed her thigh. "I was devastated the other night. Crushed is a better word. I thought I'd found the family I'd lost, but sometimes the story doesn't go the way we think it should. Shade, I wish things could be different between us, but you're offering me a part of what I'd hoped for—Tyler." He inhaled long and looked away, before turning back. "I'm humbled you would ask me. The answer is yes." He gave her a gentle peck on her cheek before resting his forehead against hers.

"I can't thank you enough," she said, embracing him. He held her tight, rubbing her back.

"Well, looky here," said Victoria, standing with her hands on her hips. "Looks like I stumbled on a scene right out of a Harlequin romance novel. I hope I'm not interrupting anything, because I can go hide behind a tree if you two need privacy."

Shade stiffened, wiping her eyes, while Brent released his embrace.

"Hey, I'd better get going," said Brent. "Make sure you two keep those boys interested in the sport over the winter. I don't want them to lose momentum." He walked over and said goodbye to Tyler and Cody before driving off.

"So, what in the world was that all about?" asked Victoria.

"Nothing I want to talk about," said Shade, her face strained. "It's personal. Hey, see you at baseball camp next year?"

"Yeah, sure."

The estate documents were modified, naming Brent legal guardian if something happened to Shade before Tyler reached his eighteenth birthday. She explained everything to Tyler as she was settling him into bed.

"Is something gonna happen to you, Grandma?"

"Tyler, only God knows what's in our future. I'm trying to protect you if something ever did happen to me. Then you would live with Brent."

"I've been praying you'll marry Brent, so he could live with us now. And I'm gonna keep praying."

"I'm glad. You should always pray."

Tyler burrowed under the covers, Scone at his feet. She kissed his forehead. "Sweet dreams, my little buddy. I love you."

"I love you, too," said Tyler. He rolled over, facing the wall.

Sleep didn't come. She tossed and turned, thinking about Tyler and his innocent yearning for Brent. She had the same yearning. Thoughts kept her awake. Tomorrow would be a busy day at the bakery, and she couldn't afford to be exhausted. She got up and rummaged through the medicine cabinet, looking for the night-time aspirin. She swallowed two and went to her closet, pulling the pale blue dress from the hanger and placing it next to her on the pillow. Tears came. Brent's scent still distinct. Lulling her to dreamland.

Tyler got out of bed around midnight and stood outside his grandmother's bedroom, listening to her muffled cries. He whimpered. His grandmother couldn't see him like this. He needed to be strong for her—like a man—but he worried. He wondered if she was sick. She didn't eat much, and she was quieter. Sad. And her comment, "if something happens to me," frightened him.

Her crying stopped. He peeked into the room and tiptoed to her bed. She was sleeping with that blue dress pushed up around her face. He crept out of the room.

"Hey, Scone," he whispered. "You need to be really quiet, okay? We're gonna go for a walk down the beach. Wait here while I put on my coat and boots. We need to talk to Brent about Grandma, okay? Be a good boy," he said, petting his head.

Something startled Shade. She sprang upright, listening. It was 2 a.m. The bed creaked as she got up and walked down the hallway to Tyler's room. Peering in, she didn't see him—or Scone. She threw the covers back. Looked under his bed. Racing through the house, she yelled his name. No answer. She canvassed every nook and cranny in the house, her heart banging hard.

The ringing phone startled her as she reached to call 911.

"Hey, it's Brent. Tyler's here."

"Oh my God, Brent," Shade said, excitedly. "I was getting ready to call 911. What is he doing there? How did he get there? I'll come get him."

"Why don't you let me bring him back? He showed up on my doorstep with Scone. He said he needed to talk. Man-to-man. Maybe I can have a little chat with him before I bring him back. Is that okay?"

"I guess—if you think so. What's going on?" said Shade, choking on her words.

"I'll be over in thirty minutes. He's fine. Don't worry."

Shade chewed on her fingernails. She thought about the comment, 'man-to-man.' Memories of Jaime flooding her mind. She didn't think Tyler remembered. And it was almost two miles to Brent's place. What was he thinking, walking on the beach in the middle of the night? She shuddered at the thought. *Thank you, dear Lord, for keeping him safe.*

Brent sat Tyler next to him on the sofa, his arm around his shoulders. "Before we talk, promise me you won't do that to your grandmother again," said Brent, firmly. "She's very upset."

Tyler looked at his hands, folded in his lap. "I promise." Scone sat at his feet, paws covering his eyes.

"Brent, first of all, thank you for being my regal guard," Tyler said, rather professionally. "Grandma told me. Then I want to tell you I've been praying you and Grandma will get married. God's thinking about it now. I don't have a dad, and I've always wanted one. Not that I don't love my grandma, but I want a man to live with us. And I'm worried about Grandma."

Brent focused, wanting to laugh and cry at the same time. He pulled him closer, his heart burning. "Tyler, I'm proud to be your legal guardian. It's like a dad that doesn't live with you," he said, looking down at him. "You know, you can see me whenever you want as long as you make sure your grandmother knows where you are. And thank you for your prayers. I'm sure God is listening. Now tell me why you're worried about your grandmother."

"I worry she might be sick and die. She said she wanted you to be the regal guard in case something happened to her. She cries when she thinks I'm not listening, and she doesn't eat much. Tonight, she was sleeping with the blue dress on her pillow. The one she wore in Hawaii. I think she's sad." Tyler paused, big teardrops rolling down his face. "I don't want her to die." Tyler slumped, short gasps racking his body.

"Hey, buddy, come here." Brent pulled Tyler onto his lap and held him close to his heart, stroking his hair and rocking him. "Your grandma wants to be sure you're taken care of if something happened. It doesn't mean something will. And sometimes grownups get sad, too. About a lot of things. Things you're too young to understand. I get sad, too. But that's okay. It's part of life."

Brent continued rocking him until Tyler's sobs subsided. He looked at him, sleeping against his chest. He wanted to keep him here all night, in his arms, but she was waiting. He scooped him up and laid him in the backseat of his car. Scone insisted on sitting in front.

Shade stood on the front porch in her robe, pacing and shivering. When they pulled up, she ran down the steps to the car. Brent signaled, his finger against his lips. She put her hand to her mouth, watching, as Brent cradled Tyler's limp body and carried him into his bedroom. Scone followed, his tail between his legs.

When they stepped out of the room, she fell into Brent's arms, weeping. "I'm so sorry. He's never done anything like this. It's so unlike him."

"Hey, there's nothing to be sorry about," he said, cradling her head against his chest.

"What did you talk about?"

"Just man stuff, but I enjoyed our chat. He's worried about you." He held her tight before pulling away. "Well, I better leave. I think we both need sleep."

"You can sleep in the spare bedroom."

"That's not a good idea. I've been known to sleepwalk. I could accidently end up in your bed," he said, grinning. He kissed her forehead and left.

"Tyler, don't ever do anything like that again," said Shade at breakfast the next morning. "Something could have happened to you last night. So, you are grounded for a week. No TV, no friends over, and no snacks after dinner."

"I'm sorry, Grandma," he said, hanging his head, studying his feet. "I won't do it again. Can I keep the snacks and give up something else? Like homework?"

"No. This isn't open for discussion." She sighed, wrapping her arms around him. "I don't know what I'd do if anything bad ever happened to you. I love you too much. So, you're being punished for an entire week. Understand?"

"Yes," he said. "I love you Grandma."

Shade arrived early at the bakery, exhausted. "Well aren't you a sight for sore eyes," said Shade, when Sally strolled in wearing a wide grin.

"Oh, Shade. We had the best time in Kauai, and married life is heavenly. But, it's good to be back. Did you have a good time during the rest of your stay?"

"It was wonderful, and Tyler had a blast," Shade responded. "We learned how to surf, thanks to Brent. I hope you're well rested because it will be busy today. Lots of corporate lunch orders to get ready. Hey, before you leave today, I wanna run something by you. Get your thoughts. I've missed having you here."

"So, here's what I'm thinking," said Shade. "In Hawaii, I got hooked on Kona coffee. I've never considered myself a coffee snob, until now. And I've been noticing the summer tourists and shoppers in town, strolling around clutching their specialty coffees. The closest coffee shop around here is two miles away; there's nothing in the downtown district. The coffee we sell at the bakery is subpar. So, I'm thinking of highlighting regional coffees each week. And maybe even espresso. What do you think?"

"Great idea," said Sally. "No offense, but I've never liked the coffee here. It's boring. That's why I never drink it. I'm somewhat of a coffee snob myself. But I'm wondering if you keep the standard coffee for those who don't want to pay extra for premium. It'll be a hassle, but you'll keep everyone happy. I say let's go for it. Oh, by the way, we're running low on vanilla extract. I'll order some, but the price is outrageous."

"Let's make our own," said Shade. "It's pretty easy. Vanilla extract has only two ingredients; vanilla beans and vodka. We can buy vanilla beans in bulk. It'll take a while to go through the extraction process, but we'll have more control over the quality.

Order a few bottles now, and I'll get a batch of our own started. Who knows, maybe we can sell it at the bakery."

"Brilliant," said Sally. "That's why you're the boss."

When Shade wrapped up for the day, she noticed the strange woman again. The one she'd seen in the bakery before. Shade smiled, as the woman was leaving.

"Did you enjoy your meal?"

"Oh, yes," the woman replied. "I always do," she said, walking out the door.

Shade made a note to engage her in conversation the next time. She didn't understand why, but she had an eerie feeling, like she knew her. But she was sure she didn't.

The phone flashed red. Two messages. Mabel was in the hospital, and Brent needed to run something by her. She called Brent.

"Hi. What's up?"

"Would you be interested in getting Tyler enrolled in Little League? The season doesn't start until next year, but we could get him set up now. If he's serious about baseball, this would be the best place for him to hone his skills."

"I'm all for it, but I worry about getting him to and from practice if things get too busy at the bakery."

"I can help, so don't worry. Hey, I saw Tyler at school today. He told me he's grounded. Good call on your part. He doesn't need to be roaming the beach at night."

"I get shivers every time I think about him out there. Alone. In the middle of the night. Thanks for your support."

"Anytime."

Mabel was resting in the coronary care unit at Emmet County

Hospital. Her face brightened when Shade approached her bedside.

"Oh, honey," she said. "It's so good to see you."

Shade took her fragile hand. "How are you feeling, Mabel?"

"I'm feeling okay. I'm ready to go home. To be with Jesus," she said, smiling. "Oh, don't look so sad, honey. Be happy for me." She patted Shade's hand. "Look, I had my friend bring something to the hospital for me. I want you to have it. It's over there on the chair."

Shade picked up the framed needlepoint of the poem about the weaver's tapestry, the one that hung on the wall at Mabel's House. She thought back to when she was fifteen, pregnant and without hope. The poem held special meaning for her. She ran her fingers over the embroidered fabric, feeling the silkiness of the woven threads as tears filled her eyes. "Oh, Mabel. You don't know how much this means to me. I'll cherish it always."

"I'm glad you like it. So, how are you doing?"

She sighed. "God's been so gracious. Tyler is such a good boy. I wanted you to meet him but didn't want to bring him here in case you weren't feeling well."

"I would have liked to have met him. And you? Have you met anyone to help raise that young man?"

"No. It wouldn't be fair to bring a man into my complicated life. A man would just take my focus off Tyler, like it did with Adeline. I can't allow that to happen again. I don't trust myself. There's so much I wish I could tell you, but I can't. Secrets that are too dark. Too ugly. Sin I can't ever seem to wash away."

"Shade, honey, even though you have regrets, your experiences in life have shaped who you are. You can't wash away your sin, only Jesus can. And He did that on the cross, so stop trying to save yourself. Just believe. It's as simple as that."

"I know, Mabel. But it never seems simple for me—to be rid of my sin. I need to keep praying." Shade squeezed her hand. "Thank you for all you've done for me over the years. You'll never know how much you've changed my life." Her eyes brimmed with tears. "You look so tired. I'd better let you go." She leaned down and kissed Mabel's cheek.

"Honey," she said, her voice weak. "The next time I see you, it'll be in paradise. Now you go on home and raise Tyler to be a good Christian man. I love you, honey."

Driving home, her thoughts centered on Mabel—a golden thread in her life's tapestry. Her rock. *Thank you, God, for weaving this extraordinary woman into my life.*

A few days later, Shade entered the prison chapel. The walls shook as the women sang, glorifying God, their hands reaching high. She took a seat in the back. A curious feeling of serenity covered her. It felt like a second home now. In here, with these women. She bowed her head in reverence.

"Can I talk to you?" asked Meghan, lingering after the group Bible study.

"Sure. We have a few minutes."

Meghan looked somber, her eyes cast down. She spoke slowly. Each word painful. "I was raised in a Christian home, but I never believed in God. I thought my parents were delusional for their beliefs. But being in here, with too much time on my hands, my thoughts often turn to God. I can't see Him, and I don't understand why He doesn't make Himself known. I struggle with this all the time. How do I know God exists?"

Shade sighed. "That's a legitimate question. I've had similar questions. So, I tried making sense of things with the mind that God gave me. A mind to reason. I thought about everything that exists around me, with the knowledge that something doesn't come from nothing. For me, that meant there has to be a higher power. The proof is all around us. Nature. Feelings. Morals. Order in the universe. I could go on and on, but think about these things and pray God reveals Himself to you. Let Him draw nearer. And I'll continue to pray for you."

Meghan sat, her face set with confusion. Shade was unsure if her words were meaningful, but it was in God's hands. She could only pray.

CHAPTER TWENTY-THREE

When you pass through the waters, I will be with you; and when you pass through the rivers, they will not sweep over you. When you walk through the fire, you will not be burned; the flames will not set you ablaze.

— ISAIAH 43:2

Year 2007

The spring rains washed in like the tide, the once dismal landscape now bathed in a dazzling palette of colors. Restless shoppers converged on the streets of downtown Edelweiss, eager to celebrate the death of winter.

As she weighed the freshly prepared dried-cherry granola, scooping spoonfuls into eight-ounce packages, Shade peered through the kitchen door and took in the small crowd gathered in the lobby.

"Donna? Is that you?" asked Shade, spotting Jaime's mother walking to a table.

"Shade. It's good to see you," said Donna, embracing her. "I was in town and thought I'd stop in."

"I'm so glad to see you. Do you mind if I join you for a bit?

"Please do," said Donna.

"So, how are you doing?" Shade asked, as they settled into their seats.

"Okay, I guess. I miss Jaime every day," said Donna, tears burning the edges of her eyes. "It's been ten years since the murders, and there are still no leads. I talk to Detective Kent often, but it's always the same...we're still working on it."

"Yes, it's frustrating," said Shade. "I spoke to Kent last month. It's just a difficult case, I guess." Shade could taste a bitter bile rising in her throat.

"Yeah, I agree." Her expression brightened. "So, how's Tyler?"

"He's doing well," Shade responded. "He turned twelve last September, and he's getting so tall. Just two inches shorter than me. He's a baseball fanatic. He wants to be a pitcher for the Majors. According to his coach, he's quite talented."

"I'm so happy. I was always fond of Tyler."

"I know you were," said Shade, patting her hand.

They continued making small talk before Shade stood. "Well, I should get back to work. If you ever want to talk, please call me. It was good seeing you again." They embraced before Shade headed toward the kitchen.

Shade's heart burned for the woman who'd lost two sons. She seemed so empty. So alone. Guilt slithered inside her mind, sinking deep. Its visits had been less frequent, but now it roared back with a vengeance. The weight of the past pressed down on Shade's shoulders. She struggled to move, her face ashen.

Sally's fingers gripped her arm. "Shade, are you okay? You don't look well."

"I just need some air," she said, walking away. "I'll be out back."

"I'll go with you." Sally walked her out the back door and

placed a chair against the building. "Here, sit. I'll check on you in a few minutes."

Shade sat, her head leaning back against the brick wall. A steady surge of tears bathed her face. She tried shutting out the pain. The emotion. *Breathe, Shade. Remember when you were a frightened little girl? How you made it stop? You went to that happy place. Just breathe and tuck the pain away.*

Sally returned ten minutes later to find Shade wiping her face with her apron. She stooped down and wrapped her arms around Shade. "What's wrong? I saw you talking to a woman."

"That was Jaime's mom, the mother of Addy's boyfriend. She has no one. Both her sons are gone. And I have Tyler." Her tears reappeared.

"You've been working too hard. Why don't you leave for the day? We can handle everything."

"No, I'll be okay. I just need to pray. I'll be in in a few minutes. Thanks, Sally."

Shade arrived home from work—emotionally spent—her thoughts on Donna. Tyler met her at the door.

"Hey, Grandma, wanna go for a five-mile run? Brent can't go. He's taking Adrianna out for her birthday."

Adrianna. More torment added to an already dismal day. The sound of her name echoed in her ears, an unsettling reminder of the ache still lingering. She was thankful Brent had found someone, but her feelings for him never faded. Adrianna was a lovely woman—and good with Tyler. And she seemed to care deeply for Brent. Shade wondered if they would marry. She wouldn't be surprised. They had been dating for a year.

She thought back to the night Brent told her he'd met someone. He spoke with sadness. Shade tried to appear upbeat, but the pain was too intense. Tears came, rolling down her cheeks. He had taken her into his arms and held her close.

"Shade, I can't keep hoping for something that'll never be. You've chosen this path."

"I know. I'm happy for you," she said, trying to believe it. "You deserve a good woman."

"I found a good woman once," he'd said. "But I've been waiting too long." He had taken her face in his hands and kissed her, slow and soft. Their lips hadn't met since the night she'd told him to walk away, and she'd forgotten how helpless she was in his arms. That yielding sensation leaving her limp, blood burning through her body. She returned his kisses until something gripped her. She pushed away. The sound of defeat emanated from his body.

"Shade," he'd said, releasing a long breath, pulling her to him, his hand cupping her head. "If only you'd let me in."

"I can't," she'd told him, touching his face and searching his eyes. "I'd be lying if I said I don't have feelings for you. Feelings I can't get rid of. But there are things about me you could never understand—that I'm not able to talk about—with anyone. You're better off without me."

Despite their last intimate encounter, they remained close. Brent continued to stay involved in Tyler's life, and she developed a friendly, but guarded relationship with Adrianna.

After warming up at the local track, Tyler and Shade set out for a five-mile run. With each stride, she felt the emotional drain of the day slipping away. At forty-six, she could easily keep pace and was in the best shape she'd ever been. She felt blessed, running alongside Tyler, for the loving relationship they continued to share and for the person he'd become.

Tyler excelled in school, took part in the church youth group, and still had eyes for Leah. But his overriding passion was baseball, and Brent continued to fuel that passion.

"Grandma. I forgot to mention, Brent wants you to call him when we get back. Something about a get-together for the All-Star Little League team."

After returning from their run, Shade called Brent. "Tyler said you wanted me to call you?"

"Yeah. I thought it would be nice to get the players and their families together at my place so everyone could meet. I'm hoping you can make it."

"That's a great idea. Can I bring anything?"

"Just your expertise. Adrianna wants to talk to you about the menu. She's thinking about having food catered from the bakery."

"Well, thank you for the business. Why don't you have her meet me at work tomorrow?"

Adrianna arrived, looking stylish in casual jeans and a navy-blue blazer. Shade greeted her as the two sat down to review menu options.

Shade had never spent time alone with her. She was a striking woman, in her late thirties, with a slender figure and a warm smile. She could understand Brent's attraction.

"Thanks for helping me," said Adrianna. "Brent's always bragging about the food here and your ability to put together the 'perfect' party menu. I'm not very good in that area, or in the kitchen period."

"I'm happy to help," said Shade, smiling. "It gets easier, the more you do it. So, how many people are you expecting?"

"Brent thinks about forty."

"Well, I would offer four different sandwiches. I'd suggest Chicken Salad Croissants, Tomato Mozzarella on flatbread, Apple and Ham Cheddar Melt, and Mini Turkey Burgers. And a few different salads. A creamy pesto pasta salad and a basic potato salad. For dessert, I can put together a tray of cookies and triple-chocolate brownies. How does that sound?"

"It sounds wonderful. You're a godsend. I was panicking until Brent calmed me. He said you're an excellent cook and hostess, and you'd know what to do."

"That was sweet of him. He's a wonderful man."

Adrianna's expression shifted. "Can I ask you something?"

"Sure."

"You and Brent. Did you—were you ever more than just friends?"

Shade went silent, looking off before responding. "We've always been good friends. Why do you ask?"

"Oh, woman's intuition I guess. The way he looks at you. Or talks about you. His relationship with Tyler. It makes me wonder."

"Have you asked Brent?"

"No. He's not one to talk about his past. He holds his cards close. Like you."

Shade half smiled, unsure how to respond. She placed her hand on Adrianna's arm. "There's nothing between Brent and me. He's like a father to Tyler, and for that, I am forever grateful. He's an important part of my life, and I care about him. But I'm happy he found you."

"I care deeply for him. I guess I was feeling insecure."

Sally spotted Adrianna and came over to the table. "Hi Adrianna. I didn't know you were coming in today. How's Brent? Chad's been talking about getting together with his favorite uncle. The four of us will have to go out soon."

"I'd love that. Shade is helping me with a party menu. I was just leaving, but let's talk this weekend."

"So, what do you think of Adrianna?" asked Sally. "Brent's been dating her for some time. I wonder if they'll ever get married."

"She's lovely. And she seems perfect for Brent."

"Chad doesn't think Brent will ever marry again. Mindy told Chad she can read her brother like a book, and she doesn't believe he's in love with Adrianna. She thinks Brent is just looking for companionship, and she's good for him. If that's true, it's too bad. I like her."

Shade's eyebrows furrowed. "I like her, too. And I'm sorry to hear that, but Mindy could be wrong."

Shade wanted Brent to be happy. To find someone to love. Maybe even start a family. But despite her reasoning, she couldn't help but feel envious. In a perfect world, she and Brent would have married and had a family of their own. But this wasn't a perfect world, and she wasn't a perfect person. Suffering was her penalty for the sins of her past. A lump rose in her throat, as she thought about what could have been and what would never be.

Shade dressed in a pair of snug fitting, white pants and a steel-grey button-down blouse. She wore her hair loose and added a touch of makeup before leaving with Tyler for Brent's.

She arrived early to help Adrianna set up the buffet table. Tyler spotted Brent out back and ran into the yard. Her heart softened. Still buddies, like father and son. She never tired of the image.

"They're good together, aren't they?" asked Adrianna, observing Shade watching them. "Brent adores Tyler. And I can see the feeling is mutual."

Brent came in and gave Shade a welcoming hug. She stiffened at his touch.

"You okay?" asked Brent, eyeing Shade.

"Yeah, I'm fine. I was racing around today so I could get here early."

"Well, we appreciate it. Adrianna said you were a huge help. Hey Tyler, why don't you help me put drinks in the cooler?"

"Thanks for coming everyone," said Brent, after the guests arrived. "I'm glad we could get together before the baseball season starts. I'm excited about the All-Star team this year, and I'm hoping we make it to the World Series. But first things first. Each player was chosen because of talent. But it's not just talent. I want everyone to come to each game with a good attitude and a willingness to learn. I expect you to keep up your grades in school, to get into a good physical routine and take care of your bodies. And most importantly, I want you to have fun. So, thanks again, and I look forward to an exciting year."

The front door slammed, and in whooshed Victoria with Cody, wearing her police uniform. "Hey, sorry we're late. Crazy day at the office. Had to rescue a burglar who got stuck in an airshaft duct while trying to break into a restaurant after hours. Found his lower body swinging over a deep fryer as he was screaming for help. Took an hour to free the moron. Anyway, we made it," she said in a winded voice. "Hey, nice spread Brent. And nice digs. Mind if I help myself?" Before he could answer, Victoria heaped sandwiches and salads onto her plate, portions of it plummeting off the side to an eagerly awaiting Coach. Cody ran off in search of Tyler.

"Sure, help yourself," said Adrianna. "We were just getting ready to eat. Thanks for taking the lead. Everyone, please, let's eat. Drinks are in the cooler."

"Hi, Shade. Good to see you," said Victoria, stuffing a sandwich into her mouth. "You look nice. Hey, who's the woman? Is that Brent's main squeeze?"

"Yes. Her name's Adrianna. She's very nice."

"I'd be nice too if I was sleeping with Brent. Adrianna, eh? Sounds like the name of a Disney princess. Hey, did you see any beer?"

"There might be some in the cooler," said Shade. "I'm glad Cody made the All-Star team. Tyler was excited. Well, we should go mingle with the other parents. Let's catch up before you leave."

After everyone had eaten, Shade took a handful of dishes into the kitchen. His hand touched the small of her back as she placed plates into the sink. Her breath caught.

"Hey, I wanted to tell you you look nice today. And to thank you for helping Adrianna," said Brent.

She smiled up at him. "It's not a problem. After all you do for Tyler, it's the least I could do."

Brent sighed. "What I do for Tyler I do because I love him. Don't think you owe me anything in return."

"Hey you two. You look pretty serious," said Adrianna. "Hope I'm not interrupting."

"Not at all," said Shade. "We were talking about Tyler."

Brent wrapped his arm around Adrianna's waist. "I was telling Shade how much we appreciate her help today."

"Yes, we do," said Adrianna, leaning into Brent. "Everything was delicious. And thank you so much for helping me set up."

Shade felt awkward. She'd never witnessed an intimate moment between them, and she felt betrayed. She turned and continued cleaning the dishes.

"Shade, why don't you go and enjoy the party?" said Adrianna. "You've done enough. Brent and I can clean up. And keep an eye on that cop lady. I don't want her arresting any of our guests."

She laughed, as she walked away, grateful to escape.

As she was looking for Victoria, a man with dark eyes and thick wavy hair approached. "Hi. My name's Roger Madison," he said, extending his hand. "My son, Lucas, is on the All-Star team."

"Nice to meet you, Roger. I'm Shade Lane. My grandson, Tyler, is also on the team."

"Ah. I've met Tyler. Nice young man. Pitcher, right? Forgive me, but you don't look old enough to have a grandson his age."

"I like to get an early start," said Shade, smiling. "And yes, Tyler is a pitcher." She caught Roger's gaze traveling to her left hand. "So, Roger, what position is Lucas playing?"

"First base. I'm looking forward to attending the games. I'm hoping work doesn't get in the way."

"What type of work do you do?"

"I'm a surgeon. Orthopedic trauma. And you?"

"I own a bakery in downtown Edelweiss. Shady Lane's Bakery and Café."

"So, you're Shady Lane. It's one of my favorite places. And what does Mr. Shady Lane do?"

"Nothing. He's dead. I'm a widow." She was startled by her abrupt response.

"There you are," said Victoria, spotting Shade.

"Please excuse me Roger. I promised to catch up with Victoria. It was nice meeting you. Maybe I'll see you at the games."

She was relieved. That dumb comment about 'Mr. Shady Lane.' Who talks like that? He was attractive, but cocky. And likely married.

"Who was that?" asked Victoria.

"Lucas Madison's father."

"Ah, yes. Not a bad catch. I hear he's divorced. Does well for himself. And he's quite handsome."

"He sounds perfect for you," said Shade, smirking.

As the guests were leaving, Roger sought Brent out. "Hey, thanks for organizing the get-together, Brent. It was nice meeting the other players and parents."

"I'm glad you could make it," said Brent. "Lucas is a solid addition to the team."

"Thanks. He's excited, and so am I. Hey, what's the story on Shade Lane? Nice looking woman. She told me her husband passed away. Do you know if she's seeing anyone?"

"You'd have to ask her," said Brent. His reaction caught him off guard, a trace of jealousy taking his voice. "Feel free to contact me with any questions," Brent added, trying to soften his tone. "And thanks for coming."

The following Wednesday, Shade passed through security at Emmet County Correctional. The more time she spent here, the more comfortable she became. A strong bond had formed with the women, especially Meghan. It thrilled her to see Meghan opening up to God's word.

"Shade. Guess what?" said Meghan, her eyes beaming. "Ethan's birthday is tomorrow, and my parents are bringing him in with a cake. They got approval from the warden. I can't believe he will be ten."

"That's wonderful. He's growing up so fast. And I'm glad your parents are bringing him in for visits now."

"Yeah. I feel like we are starting to build a bond. He's such a good kid. He's getting good grades in school, loves sports, and my parents encourage him to attend church every Sunday. I just hope he doesn't end up like me."

"Keep praying. I pray all the time for Tyler. Hey, maybe your parents can bring Ethan out to one of Tyler's games this year. Get him exposed to a new environment. What do you think?"

"That'd be great. I'll talk to them," said Meghan. She turned, a thoughtful look on her face. "I don't think I've ever thanked you for what you've done for me. In here, we're treated without the slightest trace of respect. I know I'm a murderer, but I'm also still human. You've never judged me. I only feel love from you. I hope to make you proud one day—that you'll witness a changed life. One you've helped change."

"You have made me proud, Meghan. You're not the same person I met over five years ago. You have changed. For the better. I see hope in you. And I'm watching you move closer to God."

"Sometimes I don't feel like I'm moving closer to God."

"Look back at your life. You're changing. Sometimes it's so subtle we don't even notice, but it's there," said Shade. The bell chimed. "Looks like I have to go. Tell Ethan I said Happy Birthday and see you next week. I'll bring a schedule of Tyler's games."

CHAPTER TWENTY-FOUR

He has shown you, O mortal, what is good. And what does the Lord require of you? To act justly and to love mercy and walk humbly with your God.

— MICAH 6:8

The baseball hurled toward Brent as Tyler's four-seam fastball slapped into his mitt.

"Good job, buddy. That's enough pitching for today."

"Can't we keep practicing?" asked Tyler. "Can you teach me how to throw a curveball?"

"Remember what we talked about. Your arm needs rest. You're only twelve—too young to throw a curveball. It puts too much stress on your arm. We need to make sure you're in good shape for the World Series. And if you want to play professional baseball, you'll need to keep your arm healthy."

"Okay. Can you show me how to spit again? Like the pros?"

"Let's not worry about spitting right now."

After dominating the challenger at the Little League regional event, Brent's team advanced to the World Series, which would take place in Williamsport, Pennsylvania. His demanding workouts and team-building exercises had paid off.

"Are you comfortable with your pitches?" asked Brent. "We need to make sure you're in top form for the World Series."

"Yeah," Tyler responded. "And I'm not nervous. Grandma always tells me to pray, so that's what I do."

"Well, it's working," said Brent, as he considered Shade's influence on Tyler's life. "Just remember, react to things you can control, like the next pitch. Don't worry about what you can't control—the last pitch. And don't get intimidated by tough hitters, no matter how big they are, or how talented they are. Stare them down. Show them you're not afraid."

"Like David and Goliath?"

"Yes, just like David and Goliath."

"Brent, do you think you'll ever marry Adrianna?"

Brent smiled at Tyler's brashness. He had grown accustomed to his probing questions, a byproduct of their close relationship. "I don't have plans. Why are you asking?"

"Sometimes I think you'll marry her, and you won't have time for me. I always prayed you'd marry my grandma and be my grandpa."

Brent sighed. "Hey, buddy, I'll always have time for you. No one can come between us. Remember what we talked about? I'm your legal guardian. I'm like your dad, but I don't live with you."

Tyler's face lit up, as he wrapped his arms around Brent. "I love you."

"I love you, too, buddy," said Brent, holding him tight. "You know I'll always be here for you."

"Are you set with your travel plans?" asked Brent, when Shade answered the phone.

"Yeah. It looks like I'll arrive a few hours after you. It will feel strange not having Tyler with me."

"I'll take good care of him."

"I know you will. You always do. Is Adrianna coming?"

"No. It's just me and the boys. Hey, once you get settled, why don't you come over to the facility, and I can show you around?"

After checking into her room, Shade studied the schedule. There were sixteen teams split into two brackets; eight International and eight from the United States. During the first five days, teams played one another within their bracket. Two winners within each bracket would advance to the Championship Game, and the International and U.S. winner of the Championship Game would advance to the World Series.

She went down to the lobby to catch the next shuttle.

"Hey lady," said a familiar voice. "Fancy meeting you here. Are you settled in your room?"

"Hi Victoria. Yes. I was getting ready to go to the International complex to meet Brent and Tyler. There's a shuttle leaving in twenty minutes."

"Let me run up and get my purse. I'll go with you."

"Grandma," said Tyler, running with Cody toward Victoria and Shade. "Isn't this place great? We get to sleep in a dormitory with Brent and the whole team."

"Wow. It sounds like fun," said Shade, hugging him.

"Your dad and Prudence can't make it today," Victoria told Cody. "Hey, don't look so down. They'll be here soon."

Brent joined them. He gave Shade a warm embrace and shook Victoria's hand before giving them a tour of the facility.

"Our schedule is full. We won't get to spend much time together, but we'll see you at the games," said Brent. "How are the rooms at the hotel?"

"Spacious and nice," said Shade. "The hotel is close to a lot of restaurants and shops."

"And cool looking bars," Victoria added. "I saw Roger Madison in the lobby of our hotel. Maybe we can get a bunch of parents together and go bar hopping."

"Sounds like I'll be missing out on all the fun," said Brent, with a cocky grin. "Well, I should get going. I need to get the team together. I'll see you both at the game tomorrow." Brent wrapped his arm around Shade and gave her a peck on the cheek. "Have a good night, you two."

"No kisses for me, Brent?" Victoria purred.

Brent smiled and spoke over his shoulder as he walked away. "Later. Behave yourselves."

"You guys are something else," said Victoria. "You claim there's nothing going on, but you sure don't act like it."

"As I've said before, we're just dear friends."

"Yeah. Got it."

Brent's team made it through the elimination rounds. They would square off against the Southeast Region in the U.S. Championship semi-finals. The winner of that game would play the International Champions in the grand finale—the World Series.

The night before the semi-finals, Shade went alone to visit Tyler at the International complex.

Tyler ran to meet her. "Grandma, we made it through."

"I know, honey. I'm so happy for the team. I'm not staying long. I know you have to get to bed early. Are you nervous?"

"No. Whatever happens is meant to be."

She kissed the top of his head. She was proud of Tyler's maturity and confidence, so much of it due to Brent's influence.

She spotted Brent walking toward her, his eyes lit with excitement.

"Hey, what a great game today. The boys played their hearts out." He looked around. "Where's Victoria?"

"Shopping. I wanted to stop by before tomorrow. To congratulate you and Tyler." Her eyes hung on his. "Brent, I'm so proud of you."

Cody and Lucas ran over and pulled Tyler away. The three of them sat at a nearby table.

Brent turned to her, his eyes seemed to be searching inside her soul. His face grew tense.

"Is there something going on between you and Roger?" he asked.

Her head tilted, her brows gathered. "No. Nothing. Why do you ask?"

"I've seen him sitting with you every day," he said, studying her. "I was curious."

"He's not my type." She wanted to tell him there would never be anyone but him, but she sucked in her words.

"I'm sorry. I shouldn't have pried. I want you and Tyler to be safe, and happy, that's all." He embraced her. His arms holding her tighter than usual.

Tyler approached them. "Grandma, don't forget to pray for us tomorrow."

"You know I'll be praying, buddy. You've made it this far, and I'm so proud of you. Just do your best. I love you, and I'll see you tomorrow."

On the ride back to the hotel, she thought about Brent's

demeanor. The way he held her, the look in his eyes. Something seemed to be bothering him. His comment about Roger felt odd. Was he jealous, or was he really concerned for their well-being? She prayed it was the latter.

Arriving at the stadium the following day, Shade nabbed a seat away from Roger and Victoria and reveled in the solitude. Her stomach rose and fell, as she sat biting her fingernails. Tyler and Cody were warming up on the field, Tyler's face set and determined as he reached back and fired warm-up balls into Cody's mitt.

"Ladies and Gentlemen," said the announcer. "Welcome to the Little League U.S. Championship semi-finals. Great Lakes versus Southeast. Please stand for the National Anthem."

Tyler took the mound and assumed his pitching stance. He thought about Brent's last words. "Don't throw too hard. I know you have a seventy-five-mile per hour fastball, but you sometimes lose control. You need to be in command. Mix it up. Throw to different parts of the plate. Up. Down. In. Out. Keep them off balance."

Tyler said a quick prayer, took a deep breath and kicked his left leg high, delivering the first pitch down the middle for a strike. A rush of confidence swept over him. He let the second pitch fly with all the power he could muster. The ball soared past the batter's face, causing Cody to leap upward to prevent it from reaching the bleachers. The next three pitches were out of the strike zone, and the batter didn't chase. A walk. With a batter on first, Cody went out to the mound to talk to Tyler.

"Hey. You're overthrowing. Slow it down. Like the first pitch. Remember what Brent said."

Tyler took several deep breaths and focused on Brent's words. He threw the next pitch—a perfect pitch—right at the corner of the strike zone. Brent signaled to Tyler from the dugout to pay attention to the runner's lead at first base. Tyler assumed his pitching stance then spun around and fired the ball to Lucas at first before the runner could make it back. "Out!" the umpire yelled.

He struck out the next two batters and returned to the dugout, adrenaline pumping through his veins. "Good job, buddy," said Brent, patting him on the back. "You settled down. How are you feeling?"

"I feel good."

"Okay. Watch your control. Work the plate and don't be afraid to use the changeup pitch. You're doing good."

Brent's team scored a home run in the bottom of the first inning off the bat of Lucas. Tyler pitched the next four innings like an ace, allowing only one hit and striking out seven.

"How is your arm feeling?" asked Brent, after the fifth inning. "I can send you back out for the final inning, but your pitch count is at seventy. If you reach eighty-five pitches, or if I think you're getting tired, I'm gonna take you out. We can't be too careful with a one-to-nothing lead."

"Let me pitch, Brent. Let me have the ball."

Tyler took the mound at the top of the sixth inning and struck out the first batter on six straight pitches. The next batter had a pop-up for the second out. He calculated his pitch count at eighty. The final batter came to the plate and hit a long fly ball to center field. Tyler watched in trepidation, as his teammate's feet left the ground at the warning track, snatching the ball out of mid-air. The crowd exploded. The Great Lakes Edelweiss team had won the U.S. Championship title, advancing them to the World Series.

Tyler searched the stadium and locked eyes with Shade. Only then did his game face transform. He managed a wide smile, tipping his hat to her before hugging his teammates and running toward Brent.

Brent's team took the traditional victory lap around the stadium holding the United States World Series Championship banner. The news media congregated on the field, snapping team photos and clamoring for an interview with Brent.

"Think we can get a one-on-one interview with Tyler Lane?" the reporter asked Brent. "That kid threw quite a game."

"Sure. We'll meet you in the Media Room in about thirty minutes."

Shade stood, looking on, as dampness coated her cheeks. Victoria came from behind, embracing her. Roger weaseled in between them for a group hug.

After the game, Shade took the shuttle to the International Complex. It would be an early night for the team. Tomorrow was the big day, and Brent wanted everyone to get a good night's rest.

Tyler's face lit up when he saw her. He ran and gave her a hug. "Grandma, we won the U.S. Championship. And the news guy interviewed me with Brent."

"I'm so proud of you, Tyler," she said, throwing her arms around him. "You pitched a great game today."

Shade turned and embraced Brent. A lingering embrace. "All of your hard work has paid off. You must be so proud today. They couldn't have done it without you."

"They're a great team," he said, pulling away. "It was an unbelievable win. I couldn't be happier."

His eyes hung on her. She sensed he wanted to say something. She held his gaze in a curious stare. Silence.

"Well, I'd better get the boys settled. I want to give them a talk about tomorrow. Unfortunately, Tyler can't pitch, but he'll play right field. So, what are you up to tonight?"

"Victoria organized a celebration party at one of the local bars in town. I guess all the parents are going."

Brent leaned in and kissed her cheek, his hand lingering on the small of her back. "Have fun tonight. And be careful."

Back at the hotel, she reflected on Brent's mood again. What was it? The way he studied her face. So serious. Reflective. Maybe he was thinking about the game tomorrow.

The Golden Oldie bar swarmed with celebratory parents. Clanging beer mugs and raucous laughter penetrated the thin walls of the well-worn tavern, classic tunes blaring from the jukebox.

"Shade, over here," yelled Victoria, waving from across the room, beer sloshing over the rim of her glass.

Shade pushed her way through the crowd, flinching when she saw Victoria up close. She wore a skin-tight, leopard print spandex skirt with a thin black tank top exposing the curves of her bra-less breasts.

"I pictured a quiet venue with proper wine sipping clientele and classical music piped in," said Shade. "This is like something right out of *Animal House*."

"Yeah, isn't it great? Hey, how do I look?" asked Victoria, spinning around in her stilettos. "Jack's here with Prudence. I'm hoping to upstage that hoity-toity snob with her Prada handbag. I never understood what Jack saw in her."

"Well," said Shade, grappling for words. "You certainly are making a statement. I'm sure she'll take notice."

"Hey, Roger," Victoria yelled. "Over here." She turned and whispered in Shade's ear. "I think he's got a thing for me, but he might have to hold back. His ex is here."

Shade grinned and excused herself after Roger approached. She ordered a Chardonnay and strolled the venue, mingling with the other parents. She planned to nurse one glass of wine and get back to the hotel at a decent hour.

"Can I buy you a drink?" asked Roger, his hand resting on her back.

"Thank you, but no. One's enough for me."

"You look nice tonight," he said, his eyes surfing her. "Wild place. Would you be interested in going somewhere a little quieter?"

"No, thank you. I don't plan on staying long. I'd like to get to bed early tonight."

Shade heard Victoria's voice roar, as the sound of "Shake Your Tail Feather" rocked the tavern.

"Oh my God!" Victoria shouted. "This is my favorite song. Everybody, let's dance," she said, throwing her arms up and sashaying about. The crowd converged on the dance floor, a contortion of pulsating bodies and awkward movements. Victoria egged them on, singing into her beer bottle, testing the capacity of her lungs.

To Shade's astonishment, Victoria leaped onto a Formica-topped table, performing the Watusi. A crowd gathered around, clapping and shaking their tail feathers.

"Okay, everybody, do the twist," shouted Victoria. She crunched low, shimmying from side to side, head thrown back, mouth agape. While rotating her body, she hoisted one leg high, causing the table to teeter. Victoria's arms flailed, grabbing at air in a desperate attempt to catch her balance. It was too late. She plunged. A chair flew, as she crashed onto the floor—her legs splayed in a mangled heap. Like a leopard caught in a snare. Roger rushed over to inspect the damage. Victoria winced in pain.

"Oh boy, this doesn't look good," said Roger. "We'd better call 911."

They released Victoria from the hospital sporting a cast on her right foot, stopping below the knee. A fractured tibia. Shade and Roger remained with her, arriving at the hotel after midnight. Shade stayed with Victoria after Roger left.

"So, I think you made quite an impression on Prudence," said Shade, grinning.

Victoria discharged a long sigh. "I'm such an ass. Cody will be so embarrassed."

Shade had never known Victoria to cry, but huge teardrops meandered down her face. "Hey," said Shade, putting her arms around her shoulders. "We all make stupid mistakes. Don't beat yourself up over it. Tomorrow's another day so hold your head high and make the best of it."

"It's just that I'm always making stupid mistakes. Always trying to be the center of attention." She grabbed a tissue and honked into it. "I was born a mistake. At least that's what my parents told me. They never wanted me. It seems like I've spent my entire life trying to get someone to notice me, but no one ever does." Her chin dropped to her chest. She was clearly still drunk. "And I'm not a good mother. I'm a train wreck. Now look at me. I'll be out of work for months, and Jack has been no help in the parenting department."

"Hey, things will work out." Shade cupped Victoria's cheek with her hand. "And I can help with Cody. Don't worry about anything. I'll come get you tomorrow, and we'll go to the game together."

"Thanks, Shade. You're so sensible. I wish I were more like you."

"Things aren't always what they seem, Victoria. Everyone has issues, including me. Now get some rest. I'll see you in the morning."

Roger and Shade escorted Victoria to the game. She hobbled to her seat on crutches. Shade went to the dugout before the game to see Tyler and Brent.

"I'm praying for you, buddy. What position are you playing today?"

"Right field. Is Victoria going to be okay? I heard she broke her leg."

"Yes, she'll be okay."

Brent spotted Shade and walked over as Tyler ran onto the field. "Hey, I heard about Victoria. Were you there?"

"Yeah. Roger and I stayed with her at the hospital until after midnight. Long night."

"Cody is pretty upset. I think he's embarrassed. It must have been quite a party. What time did you get back to your room?"

"About 2 a.m. I planned on getting to bed early, but it didn't work out that way."

The loud speaker cracked and screeched, announcing the start of the World Series. "I'd better get going," said Brent. "Wish us luck."

"I'll do better than that. I'll pray."

Brent smiled and returned to the dugout, gathering the boys for a pep talk.

Great Lakes Edelweiss was up against Japan in the World Series. Brent wished Tyler could pitch, but he was out of the rotation.

Japan hammered the Edelweiss team. The final score was 12-5. Tyler managed two fantastic plays in the outfield and got a double. Cody hit a home run and a double and threw out a runner trying to steal second base. But it wasn't enough. The World Series championship went to the International team.

"Boys, there's nothing to be ashamed about," said Brent, after the loss. "You're still champions. You won the U.S. title, and I'm so proud of all of you. Do you realize how many teams make it this far? Not many, so hold your heads high. Great teamwork."

CHAPTER TWENTY-FIVE

Love does not delight in evil but rejoices with the truth. It always protects, always trusts, always hopes, always perseveres.

— 1 CORINTHIANS 13:6-7

The front page of the Edelweiss Gazette ran a story on the Little League U.S. Champions, much of it dedicated to Brent's management style and Tyler's pitching prowess. Tyler was unfazed by the media hype; he had learned from Brent to disregard fleeting accolades.

The town of Edelweiss organized a parade in honor of the returning champions. A huge banner hung over Main Street, and Shady Lane's Bakery and Café held a private party.

Sally organized the event in Shade's absence. Bowls of popcorn, peanuts, and Cracker Jacks were scattered throughout the bakery, along with cupcakes decorated in white frosting and topped with piped red icing to simulate a baseball thread pattern. Orange and white streamers and balloons hung throughout the space.

"Hey, thanks for doing this," said Brent, while Shade refilled the food trays.

"It wasn't me," said Shade. "Sally did everything. I don't know what I'd do without her. Hey, I saw your sister, Mindy. How nice of her to come. Where's Adrianna?"

"She's not here. Do you need help?"

"No, thank you. Enjoy the party. This is for you and the boys. You're not allowed to help."

"Hey, Shade," said Roger, interrupting their conversation. "Nice party. How's it going, Brent? Great write-up in the Gazette."

"Thanks. Lucas played his heart out. Do you plan on enrolling him next year?"

"I hope so. He's been begging me to play. He loved the whole experience. Hey, Shade, do you have any more sandwiches? The tray is empty."

"I'll grab some from the kitchen. Be right out."

"I'll help you," said Roger, following her.

Brent's eyes tracked the two of them before Mindy approached. "Everything okay?"

"Yeah, I'm good," said Brent, wrapping his arm around Mindy and kissing her forehead. "Thanks for flying out to be here for me."

"Wouldn't have missed it for the world. And it's an excuse for me to spend time with Sally and Chad. Where's Adrianna? I haven't seen her."

"We're not together anymore," said Brent, looking away. "She wants more than I can offer. It's not fair to her."

"When did this happen?"

"When I got back from Pennsylvania. I did some soul searching while I was out there. It's for the best."

Mindy sighed and rubbed his back. "Oh, Brent, I was hoping she was the one. I hate seeing you alone."

"Hey, don't worry," Brent said, embracing her. "I'm a big boy. I can take care of myself."

"Is there someone else?"

Brent looked away, staring at nothing. He sighed before answering. "I don't love Adrianna."

"That's not what I asked."

"You ask too many questions. You're supposed to be celebrating with me, not grilling me about my love life."

"Got it. Let's find Chad and get something to eat."

Roger held the tray while Shade stacked sandwiches. "Hey, would you like to go out sometime? I know this great little Italian restaurant."

"Thank you, but no," said Shade, arranging the sandwiches. "I'm not interested in dating, but I'm flattered you would ask. I'd better get these out there. Do you mind carrying the tray?"

"Sure. Let me know if you ever change your mind," he said, as they returned to the party.

"Hey, Victoria," said Shade, spotting her sitting alone with her foot propped up on a chair. "How's the leg?"

"Better than my ego. Cody barely speaks to me these days. I almost didn't come."

"You deserve to be here as much as anyone. Hey, don't look so down. Cody will get over it. Give it time."

Blanche swaggered over, sporting an orange and white glitter baseball cap nestled high atop her beehive updo. An oversized white plastic ball with a shimmering red thread pattern dangled from each ear.

"You must be Victoria," said Blanche, extending her hand.

"And you must be Blanche," said Victoria, grinning.

"I heard about your accident," Blanche said, shaking her head. "You know, I once broke my leg at a friend's Halloween party. I went as a Flapper Girl. I was doing the Charleston in the kitchen when I lost my footing and fell over backwards down the basement stairs."

Victoria howled with laughter. "Blanche, you're my kinda woman." She patted the chair. "Have a seat."

Roger appeared and sat at the table with Victoria and Blanche. "Hey, Watusi Lady. Good seeing you again."

"Well, have no fear, the orthopedist is here," Victoria said. "How are things on the cutting floor?"

Shade felt comfortable excusing herself. She spotted Ethan with his grandparents. They had been regular attendees at Tyler's games after Shade mentioned it to Meghan.

"Hey, Tyler, why don't you go talk to Ethan," said Shade. "He looks lost."

"Sure, Grandma." He turned and walked toward him. "Hey, Ethan. Wanna meet the guys on my team? I'll introduce you, but first I want you to meet my girlfriend, Leah."

"You have a girlfriend?" asked Ethan.

"Yeah. We're gonna get married. She's the love of my life."

Shade smiled, watching Tyler with Ethan. He had such a heart for others, especially those less fortunate.

When the last guests were leaving, Roger found Shade chatting with Brent, Mary, and Blanche.

"Hey, Shade," said Roger. "Lucas wants to have a sleepover tonight. Cody is coming, and Lucas was hoping Tyler could make it. Are you okay with that before Lucas asks him?"

"I guess that would be okay. I think he'd like spending time with his team. I can drop him off and pick him up in the morning."

"Great. I can bring him back tomorrow around noon," said Roger. "I'll be out that way."

"Sounds good. Thank you."

"Hey, why don't you let me take Tyler over to the cottage to get his things, and then I'll drop him off at Roger's?" Brent suggested.

"It looks like you'll be busy cleaning. I'll come back afterwards. Sounds like Sally and Chad want to talk to you, me, and Mindy."

"Oh, Brent, that would be great," said Shade.

Brent returned to the bakery as Sally and Shade were finishing up. He found Shade in the parking lot, struggling to load a box of decorations into her trunk.

"It doesn't look like that will fit," said Brent. "Let me put it in my car and I'll drop it off at your place."

"Thanks. Did everything go okay with Tyler?"

"Yeah. I dropped him off at the mansion. The butler met him at the door holding a red velvet smoking jacket and asked Tyler to put it on."

"You're kidding, right?"

Brent smiled and escorted her into the bakery. Chad, Sally and Mindy were standing at the counter, sporting enormous grins.

Chad wrapped his arm around Sally and spoke. "Hey, you two. Mom already knows, but we wanted to share our good news with you both. Sally and I are going to be parents."

"Oh, Sally," said Shade, embracing her while Mindy stood by wiping her eyes. "I'm so happy for you both. This is wonderful news."

Brent gave Chad a hug. "When's the due date?"

"Mid-April," said Sally. "We're so excited. We've been trying for five years."

"You must be exhausted," said Brent, smacking Chad on the back.

"How do you think I stay so trim?" said Chad. "Hey, I brought champagne for the occasion." He popped the cork and poured the bubbly into glasses. "Sally will settle for sparkling water."

Brent proposed a toast. "To two beautiful people. You'll make wonderful parents, and we couldn't be happier for you both. Congratulations."

Brent followed Shade home and helped her unload the boxes. "That's the last one," he said, pulling out his car keys.

"How about a glass of wine?" asked Shade. "I could use one myself."

"Sure," said Brent. He sat at the kitchen counter and watched her struggle to open the bottle. "Here, let me help."

"Let's sit on the deck," said Shade, carrying two glasses. "It's a beautiful night. Can you grab the bottle?" she asked, opening the sliding door. "I know I said this already, but I'm so proud of you, Brent. What you accomplished for the team was amazing. You have a special gift with kids, and I'm so thankful you're sharing that gift with Tyler. Here's to you." She raised her glass.

"Thank you," said Brent, gazing out over Lake Michigan. The sun hung low, ready to disappear into the water. "The boys were amazing. And Tyler's pitching—outstanding. He's a gifted young man. I think he has a real shot to go all the way."

"I know it's what he wants, and I'm all for it. I want him to be happy with whatever path he chooses."

"Me too. By the way, this wine is excellent," said Brent, picking up the bottle and studying the label. "2001 Casanova di Neri Brunello di Montalcino Tenuta Nuova. Where did you get it?"

"Roger gave it to me. I asked him about some good red wines. I guess he's quite the connoisseur. You two have something in common."

"That's about all we have in common." Brent's eyes were dark, empty pools. "So, what's the story between you and Roger?"

"Story? There's no story. You asked me that before, and I told you nothing was going on?"

"Has he come on to you?"

"Brent, why are we talking about Roger?" said Shade, her eyes narrowing. "And why are you concerned?"

"I'm concerned because I care for you, and I've respected your wishes all these years. It would destroy me if you found someone else. Don't do that to me."

Shade shook her head. "I'm confused. What about Adrianna? You've been with her for a year."

"It's over. I can't give her what she wants. I don't love her."

"So, is that what this is about? Now that you're single you want to talk about us?"

She stood and went inside. Her hands were shaking, her heart thrashing. She had never had a cross word with Brent in all the years she'd known him. She wanted to take back what she'd said.

Brent followed her inside and placed his glass heavily on the counter. "That was a low blow. The only reason I was with her is because I couldn't have you. Because you don't want us."

"That's not true. You know how much I care for you, but I can't be with you. Or anyone. We talked about this. I would ruin your life."

Brent grabbed her arm and spun her, pulling her to his chest. She flinched, surprised at the force. She tried pushing away.

"I'm tired of wanting you," he said, his face inches from hers. "I'm tired of this game. Of not knowing what's going on inside your head. I can't stop wanting you."

He pushed her up against the wall and kissed her. Hard. His hand behind her head, pulling her toward him, forcing his mouth over her clenched lips.

She struggled to free herself, every muscle in her body tense. "Brent, you're scaring me. Get away from me!"

He was possessed. Intent on having her. He ripped her blouse open. Buttons scattered across the room. Her fists pounded his back.

Suddenly, he stopped and pulled back, as though awakened from a trance. "Oh my God, Shade. I'm so sorry," he said, backing away, running his fingers through his hair. His breathing came in hot gasps. He reached for her, but she pushed him away, grasping at her blouse.

"Get out!"

"Shade, I don't know what happened," he said, tears blurring her image. "Please, forgive me. I would never hurt you."

She pulled her blouse together and turned away, heaving with sobs. "I think you should leave."

He placed his hands on her arms and buried his face in the back of her hair. "Shade, something came over me. I've never done anything like this. It'll never happen again. Please forgive me."

She remained standing with her back to him. It pained her to think of the torment she had caused him.

"Brent," she said, softly. "Please go."

He dropped his hands, arms hanging limp. "I can't get you out of my head. No matter how hard I try. I don't think I ever will."

She stood silent, staring at the wall, unable to look him in the eyes. She could hear keys jangle, his footsteps walking toward the door. The door opening. Closing. Tears trampled down her cheeks. She fell to her knees. *Why, God? Please remove this thorn. This love that can never be. Help me God. And help Brent. Help him find someone to love. He's such a good man. He deserves someone. Please God, please help us both.*

Stripping off her clothes, she stood before the mirror. Her lips swollen from his demanding kisses. She traced the large red marks on her upper arms. Thought about his tumultuous passion. His loss of control. She understood. She had been there once—when love choked her soul, hurling her into the troughs of insanity.

After a sleepless night, she drove to the First Church of Edelweiss for Sunday morning service. Tyler wouldn't be home until noon.

Solitude. She entered the sanctuary and stopped. Brent. He sat alone, his head hung. She thought about leaving, but her body moved toward him. She slid into the pew, settling next to him. He looked at her, but she said nothing. Her eyes sauntered with his as she moved her hand to his thigh. He breathed deep, placing his hand over hers, squeezing it tight. No words.

"Mark Twain said it this way," said Pastor Ralph. "'Forgiveness is the fragrance that the violet sheds on the heel that has crushed it.' We must be more like Jesus and offer forgiveness to those who have harmed us. You'll never feel free unless you forgive."

At the end of the service, Brent sat motionless. Wounded.

"Hey," said Shade. "Why don't you come over, and I'll fix you breakfast? You can be there when Roger drops off Tyler."

His lips curved upward into a strained smile. "I'm so..."

"Shh," whispered Shade, placing her fingers to his lips. "Don't say it. I'd like you to be there when Tyler gets home." Her eyes locked on his. "And to answer your question, Roger did ask me out, but I told him I wasn't interested."

He searched her face. "I guess I have a jealous bone. I didn't know it existed until I met you." He looked down. "Maybe it's too soon—me coming over. Maybe I should stay away for a while."

"I want you there, Brent. I know you would never hurt me —intentionally."

He exhaled heavily, his eyes boring into her. He wrapped his arm around her. "All right. I promise I'll behave."

"I know you will."

Brent sat at the kitchen counter, watching her crack eggs into a bowl. "How about a Mediterranean omelet with whole wheat toast?"

"Sounds good," Brent replied, sipping his coffee.

The conversation flowed, as though nothing had changed. After eating, Brent's mood turned pensive.

"I'm glad you invited me over because we need to have a serious talk. About us," he said. "Will it always be like this between us? Platonic lovers and nothing more? Because if it is, I can't continue to be around you. It's too difficult."

She peered into his eyes, questioning his comment. "About last night. I'm not upset. I understand your frustration, but can't we go back to the way things were?"

"To this game we play? Pretending nothing is there between us when we both know there is? No, Shade. I lost control last night, and it scares me to think about what could have happened. I can't go on like this. Not knowing the secrets that haunt you. Not understanding why you can't trust me enough to let me in." He paused, rubbing the back of his neck. "I've been doing a lot of thinking, and after last night it's clear to me we both need to move on. I've been offered a temporary job in California—with the possibility of full time. I'm considering taking it. It would be one to two years—to help set up an athletic program for a new school near Montecito. I've been talking to my superintendent. If it doesn't work out, I can come back. It'll be good for me. For us. I'll rent my house until I figure out what I'm doing." He took her hands into his, searching her face. "Shade, if I thought there was ever a chance for us I'd stay, but I don't think there is."

She stared at him, pools forming in her eyes. "But what about Tyler? He loves you so much, and you're like a father to him."

"I love him too, but I can't do this anymore. If anything ever happened to you, of course, I would take him. I'm still his legal guardian."

"Please don't go," she said.

He cupped her face. "Shade, don't you understand? I love you. I've never stopped loving you. I tried moving on with Adrianna. Tried forgetting about us. But it didn't work. When I'm with you, my feelings for you overpower me. Even now, sitting here next to you, it's difficult. I need to let go. I need to be away from you."

The front door swung open. Tyler rushed Brent, embracing him. "Brent, what are you doing here?"

"Your grandmother made me breakfast. Did you have fun last night?"

"Yeah," said Tyler. "We watched movies in this room with a big movie screen. And we had pizza for dinner and ice cream."

"Hey," said Roger, standing in the foyer, looking at Shade and Brent. "I think the boys had a good time. How about you two? Did you have a good time?"

"Yeah, we did," said Brent, standing. "I was just leaving." He gave Shade a hug. "Thanks for breakfast. We'll talk soon." He turned to Tyler. "I got two tickets to a Detroit Tigers game next weekend. Would you like to go?"

"Can I, Grandma?" Tyler asked, bending to pet Scone.

Her eyes glistened. "Of course, you can go. Roger, thanks for bringing him home."

"Well, I guess we better let you and Tyler get settled," said Brent, holding the door open for Roger. "See you soon."

Brent handed in his resignation and rented his house to a family moving from Florida. Sally and Chad adopted Coach. All loose ends were tied up except for Tyler.

"Hey, buddy, did you enjoy the game?" asked Brent, on the drive home.

"Yeah. The whole time I pictured me out there on the mound pitching. And about you and Grandma watching me in the stands. I hope I can play for the Detroit Tigers."

"Just keep working hard. As long as you apply yourself, you have a great shot at making the big leagues someday."

They drove in silence. "Why are you quiet, Brent? Did I do something wrong?"

"No, buddy. You did nothing wrong. But I need to talk to you about something. Something that will be hard for both of us." Dread crept over him like a menacing shadow. "I'm going to be moving to California—for a new job. It's a good opportunity. I'll be leaving in a few weeks."

Tyler stared, empty, at Brent. "So, you won't be living here anymore? Or coaching me?" Tears cut rivulets down his face. "You said you would always be here for me. Like a dad. That nothing would ever come between us. Dads don't leave. Why are you leaving?"

"Tyler, nothing will ever come between us. We'll just live farther apart, but you can always call me whenever you want to talk. I'm still your legal guardian. That won't change."

"It's not the same. I thought you loved me. How could you leave?" he said, sobbing. "I don't want you to go. Please don't go."

Brent pulled the car over at the next rest area and turned. "Listen, Tyler. I will always love you, no matter how far apart we are. I love my sister Mindy, and she lives in another state. Distance won't change my feelings for you. And I'll come back. And I want you to come out and visit me."

"You lied. You said you would always be here for me. California is not here." Tyler unbuckled his seat belt and jumped out of the car, running across the parking lot to an open field. Brent chased him, grabbing him before he reached a wooded area.

"Let me go," shouted Tyler, beating Brent with his fists. "I hate you."

Brent held him tight as Tyler struggled. "Tyler, I know you don't hate me. Don't say things you don't mean."

Tyler went limp. He buried his head in Brent's chest, sobs racking his body. "I always prayed you would marry my grandma. But God didn't listen. Now you're leaving. I don't want you to move. Please stay here with us," he pleaded.

A choking knot formed in his throat, as he held onto Tyler, stroking his hair and back until the sobbing subsided. "Life will be full of changes for you. If you want to become a Major League baseball player, you'll move away, and you'll leave your grandmother. But you'll still see each other. And you'll still love each other."

"I won't ever leave her. I'll take her with me."

"When you get older, you'll understand. You'll see things differently. This is something I need to do. But we will always be close. No matter how far away I am."

They clung to one another for a long time. "Hey, come on, buddy. Let's get back in the car."

Hand in hand, they walked back to the parking lot. Tyler didn't speak the entire drive home.

"Hey, do you want to stop for ice cream?" asked Brent.

"No," Tyler replied. "I just wanna go home."

Her stomach roiled, images of Tyler's reaction flashing through her mind. When they pulled into the driveway, Shade stood, nipping at her lower lip. Tyler jumped out of the car and ran into his bedroom. The door slammed. Brent came in wearing a troubled look.

"Well, I see it didn't go well," said Shade, hugging herself, her nails jabbing her arms.

"Not at all." He pushed his fingers through his hair and let out a long sigh. "It was gut wrenching. I feel like I ripped his heart right out of his chest."

She dropped her face into her hands and wept. "He loves you so much. Why do you have to leave?"

Brent pulled her hands away. "You can stop this, Shade. But you won't." He turned. "I have to go. It's been a rough day."

Over the next few weeks, a familiar stone of lava settled in the pit of her stomach. She pondered her life without him. Tyler's life without the man he idolized. Darkness settled upon her soul.

The night before he left, she prepared a quiet dinner for him. The air was heavy with gloom.

"Everything was delicious," said Brent, breaking the silence. "Thank you. I should get going. Tyler, come here and give me a hug."

Large tears welled in Tyler's eyes. He shuffled over and fell limp into Brent's arms. Brent gave him a lingering embrace then held him out at arm's length. "Tyler, I love you very much. I want you to call me whenever you want to talk or if you ever need anything. And we'll see each other when I'm in town. Or when you come out to visit." The lump in Brent's throat felt like gristle, choking him.

Tyler nodded, unable to speak. He turned and walked away, Scone at his side. He entered his bedroom and quietly closed the door.

Brent could see her lip quivering.

"Well, I guess this is it," said Brent. He took Shade in his arms and held her, feeling her body tremble as she clung to him. He pulled back and raised her chin with his finger and bent and kissed her—a long, compassionate kiss. She didn't stop him. "I love you, Shade," he said, his eyes glossed. He ingested the image of her face and stroked her cheek before walking away.

She couldn't speak. Tears like rain on a darkened window pane spilled down her cheeks. He opened the door and stepped out of her life. "I love you, Brent," she whispered. "You'll never know how much I love you."

He was wounded. If only she would have stopped him. Told him she loved him. He would have changed everything to be with her and Tyler forever. He thought about her demons and wondered if he would ever understand the pain that smothered her. The weight of guilt pressed on him, his thoughts turning to Tyler. His innocence. His intense desire for a father. He vowed to keep him close, no matter the distance. Despite his anguish, he felt a sense of release. He thought about his future, absent the endless yearnings for the woman he could never have.

Light peered out beneath the door of Tyler's room. She knocked before entering. He lay curled in a fetal position, tears snaking down his cheeks. She climbed into bed next to him and took him into her arms. He nestled his head against her chest.

"Tyler, I know this is hard for you, but you're strong. We'll get through this. Together. Sometimes things don't work out the way we want them to. But you can still talk to him. You can still be close."

"Did you ever want to marry Brent? Maybe he would have stayed if you married him."

Grief flooded her eyes, her face strained with guilt. "God has other plans for me. Plans that don't include Brent."

"Do the plans include me?"

"Of course. The plans are all about you—only you."

"Why can't Brent be a part of those plans? Don't you love him?"

"Yes, I love him. And I'll miss him as much as you. But God doesn't always give us what we want. He gives us what we need, even when it hurts. One day you'll understand."

CHAPTER TWENTY-SIX

Don't let anyone look down on you because you are young, but set an example for the believers in speech, in conduct, in love, in faith and in purity.

— 1 TIMOTHY 4:12

Year 2011

For the second year in a row, Tyler was the starting pitcher on the Edelweiss High School varsity team. At sixteen, his well-toned muscular body stood over six-feet tall. With angular features and turquoise eyes, his face reminded Shade of Adeline, but his form resembled his father, Scott.

True to his word, Brent remained close to Tyler during the four years he had been away, often flying him out for weekend stays. He left his temporary position in California and moved to Mesa, Arizona where he accepted a job as Director of Minor League Operations for the Oakland Athletics. He considered selling his house in Michigan but wasn't ready to break ties with his past. There were too many memories of Kendra and Luke, and Shade and Tyler.

Shade and Sally stood at the counter, discussing the following day's menu. Tyler came behind Shade, wrapping his arms around her, kissing the top of her head.

"Hey, Grams. Thought I'd stop over to see if you need help today. We finished practice early."

She turned and kissed his cheek. "You smell like sweat. Maybe you can help us clean up?"

"Sure thing, Grams."

"You're a godsend," said Sally, patting him on the back.

Shade peered out the kitchen door and noticed Tyler cleaning off tables and talking to a woman. She looked closer. It was the mysterious woman she had seen before, but it had been awhile since her last visit to the bakery. She watched the two of them talking and laughing. And then she left.

"Who was that, Tyler?"

"She didn't say her name. Asked about baseball and told me she'd seen me pitch on the varsity team. She knew who I was. Said she saw my name in the paper when we won the Championship title. Nice lady."

"Did she ask for your autograph?"

"Not exactly. Hey. Can I use the car tonight? I wanna take Leah to the show to see this movie about a mountain climber who gets trapped by a boulder in Utah."

"Sure, as long as its rated PG."

"I know the rules."

"Why don't I call Mary and ask her to bring Leah to the cottage? She and I can spend time together while you two are out."

"Fine with me. Hey, I talked to Brent today. He wants me to come out again this year. For a week. He said he'd call you."

The steady rhythm of her heart cranked up a notch. Thoughts of him plagued her every day, and she wondered if he thought about her.

Mary arrived at the cottage with Leah. At eighty-years-old, Mary's youthful image continued to astonish Shade. They embraced.

"Where's Tyler?" asked Leah.

"In the shower, making himself presentable."

Leah laughed, taking a seat with Mary at the kitchen counter. Shade had grown close to Leah over the years. She had developed into a striking and mature sixteen-year-old. Her auburn hair fell down her back like silken flames, her emerald eyes radiant against her fair complexion.

Scone nuzzled Leah's feet. "Hey, Scone," said Leah, bending and rubbing his ears. "I see you're slowing down these days."

"Mary, I hope you didn't eat," said Shade. "I thought I'd fix us a grilled Salmon salad, and I brought home cheesecake from the bakery."

"Wonderful. I'm starved. It'll be nice catching up."

Tyler emerged from his bedroom, clad in denim jeans and a simple white T-shirt that clung to his chiseled chest. Shade noticed the intimate look between him and Leah.

"I hope you don't get out of hand while we're gone," said Tyler, kissing Shade's cheek. "We'll be back by nine," he said, escorting Leah out the door.

"I wonder if they will ever have eyes for anyone else," said Mary, after they left. "Not that I want them to, but I worry. They're too young to be so attached."

"I wonder the same thing. But I leave it in God's hands."

"I think they're perfect for each other. I guess time will tell. So, how have you been?"

"I'm doing well. The bakery has exceeded my wildest dreams. And I'm still volunteering in prison ministry. Do you remember me telling you about a woman there, Meghan?"

"I do. The one with the little boy, Ethan?"

"Yes. Well, Tyler has taken Ethan under his wing, mentoring him in baseball. And Meghan is a changed woman. She's shed that rough edge, and she seems to be drawing closer to God. It's a blessing to watch God work in other peoples' lives."

"Yes, it is. Hey, have you talked to Brent?"

"On occasion. When it concerns Tyler. He seems to be doing well. It's been so long since I've seen him."

"Did he ever get married?"

"No. According to Tyler, he dates, but nothing serious. He asked Tyler to come out for a week. They're still so close, even though they're miles apart. So, how are things with you?"

"Good. I'm thinking about selling my house and buying a condo. Less maintenance. I still volunteer at Holy Grace, and I'm considering going on a missionary trip to Haiti."

"Good for you. I hope I'm as active when I get to be your age."

Later that evening, Tyler and Leah pulled into the drive and remained in the car, their silhouettes drawing close to one another.

"Oh, I hope they're careful," said Mary, peeking out the window.

"I've spoken to Tyler, and he assures me nothing will happen. Just one more thing to put on God's plate."

Shade answered the phone after Tyler retreated to his room.

"Hey, I just realized the time there," said Brent. "I hope I didn't wake you."

Her heart skipped. "No, I was awake. Mary came for dinner, and Tyler and Leah went to the show. They just got home."

"How's Mary?"

"She's great. Doesn't act or look a day over seventy."

"How are you doing? It's been a while since we talked."

"I'm good. Tyler has me on a fitness regimen, so I've been working out and trying to eat healthy. I feel better than I ever have. How about you?"

"Things are fine. Busy. But I like my job."

"I'm glad. Are you happy living out there?"

"I'm content. Arizona is nice, but I miss Michigan. Hey, the reason I called is to ask about Tyler. I'd like to fly him out for a week before school starts. There's an MLB tryout camp and a baseball pitching camp that would be great for him. MLB scouts will be there sniffing around for the latest talent. I've been talking to his coach at Edelweiss, and he's impressed with Tyler's progress."

"He would love that. He always looks forward to spending time with you. It means so much to me you've stayed involved in his life."

"He's like a son. I'll always remain involved, as long as you both want that."

"We both want that. Do you think you'll be back in Michigan soon?"

"I'm not sure, but I'll let you know. It would be good seeing you."

"You, too. It's been a long time."

Shade hung up and considered Brent's solitary life. She had hoped he would have found someone, but he seemed intent on remaining single.

"Hey, Grams. Can I borrow the car?" asked Tyler, when Shade arrived home from the bakery. "Cody and I are going to Austin's house to play pool."

"As long as you're home by nine. I assume his parents are home."

"Yeah. Don't worry. I'll behave."

Ten-thirty and no sign of Tyler. She didn't have Austin's phone number. She called Victoria.

Shade had grown close to Victoria over the years. She settled down after marrying Roger and quitting the police force. They were an unlikely pair, but there was chemistry between them.

"Hey, Victoria. It's Shade. Is Cody home yet? Tyler said he'd be home from Austin's by nine, but he's not here."

"Cody told me he was going to your place," said Victoria. "I have Austin's number. I'll call and see what's going on."

Shade paced the floor, biting her lower lip. She thought about calling Chad, but she wasn't sure what shift he was working. The phone rang.

"Hello," said Shade, breathless.

"Roger and I drove to Austin's when no one answered the phone," said Victoria. "There was a party going on. There must have been fifty kids there. I guess his parents were away. Lucas was there, too. All three of them had been drinking, and someone called the police. We got them out before the cops arrived. They're pretty wasted. We'll bring Tyler back in your car, and I'll follow Roger."

"Oh, thank God they're okay," said Shade. "And thank you for bringing him home."

Roger escorted Tyler to the front door and handed Shade her car keys. Tyler wobbled, looking at his feet. He misjudged the step into the cottage and stumbled against the wall. A framed picture crashed to the floor. Shade tried to steady him, his head rolling like a Bobblehead.

"Thank you so much, Roger," said Shade, waving to Victoria in the driveway.

"Not a problem. Thank God he didn't drive home."

She escorted Tyler, as he stumbled down the hall to his bedroom. "We'll talk in the morning—when you're sober." Shade glared at him. He didn't answer.

She let him sleep in the next day, knowing he would miss varsity practice.

Tyler emerged from his bedroom, eyes squinting and hair disheveled. "What time is it?"

"It's 9:30," said Shade. "And you missed practice, and I'm late for work."

"Why didn't you wake me? You know I have to be there at eight."

"Excuse me. Is that all you have to say? You lied to me. You could have gotten yourself or someone else killed," she said, her hands trembling. "I am so disappointed in you right now. I trusted you, and you let me down. Your car privileges are being taken away for three months. And I'm considering calling Brent and telling him you can't go to Arizona."

"But, Grandma, I already have my plane ticket."

"We're not discussing this now. I want you to think about everything. We'll talk when I get home tonight."

"Can't you drop me off at practice?"

"No. You'll have to find your own way."

She drove off, her hands tight on the wheel. Tyler had always been so sensible. *Oh, dear God, please help him learn from his mistakes, and help me make the right decision about Arizona.*

"Why are you late, and where is your grandmother?" asked Leah, when Tyler called to ask for a ride to practice.

"I'm in trouble. Cody talked me into going to a party last night, and I drank too many beers. My grandma found out, and she's taken away my car privileges. And she refused to take me to practice."

"So, Cody made you go to the party? And did he make you drink beer, too? I thought you were smarter than that. I thought you were a leader."

"Leah, can you just drive me, please? I'm late."

"No. I'm not happy with you right now. I have to go, Tyler. Goodbye."

Shade called Brent that afternoon before leaving the bakery.

"I'm disappointed to hear that," said Brent, sighing. "Maybe having him here for a week would be a good thing. If he wants to play for the big leagues, he'll need to understand the importance of character."

"I'm so upset with him," said Shade, her voice trembling. "You should have seen him this morning. He didn't even seem remorseful."

"Kids like to test the waters. I wouldn't worry unless it becomes a pattern. This may shock you, but I wasn't an angel at his age. I got caught drinking and smoking marijuana when I was fifteen."

"You, Brent? Smoking marijuana? What other secrets are you hiding?"

He laughed. "I was a curious daredevil kid, but after learning from my mistakes, I got back on track. Let's hope it's an isolated incident. And I think it'll do him good to come out here. I'll whip him into shape."

She sighed. "Maybe you're right. I wish you were closer."

"Me, too," said Brent. "I'll pick him up at the airport next week."

CHAPTER TWENTY-SEVEN

What no eye has seen, what no ear has heard, and what no human mind has conceived—the things God has prepared for those who love him.

— 1 CORINTHIANS 2:9

"So, is Leah still upset?" asked Shade, as they drove to the airport.

"Yeah," said Tyler. "She said we'd talk when I get back. Maybe she'll miss me. Grandma, thanks for letting me go to Arizona. And I'm sorry for what I did. I don't often tell you how much I love you, and I won't put you through that again."

"I love you, too, Tyler. Everyone makes mistakes. No one is perfect. Just promise you'll stay focused on doing the right thing. Being a good person. That's all I want for you."

"I promise. I'll make you proud of me."

"Hey, buddy," said Brent, embracing Tyler at the airport terminal.

"The last time I saw you, you were shorter than me. Now look at you. We're the same height."

"It's good to see you," said Tyler. "Thanks for having me out. I'm super excited about the tryout and baseball camp."

"It'll be like old times. Hey, I thought we'd drive to my condo first and get you settled and then grab something to eat. Pitching camp starts tomorrow. Maybe we can squeeze in some practice today."

"Nice condo. Do you like living in Arizona?"

"It's good. A little lonely, but I like my job—and the weather. Let's talk about you. Your grandmother told me what happened. She almost didn't let you come. What's going on?"

Tyler looked away, running his fingers through his hair. "Yeah, I made a stupid mistake."

"I won't lecture you. I think you feel bad enough. Getting into the Major Leagues is not only about being a good athlete. That's a big part, but it doesn't get you in the door. It takes self-discipline. On and off the field. Stay focused on your goals and don't get distracted by meaningless pleasure. Understand?"

"Yeah, I understand."

"Good. Enough said. Let's practice pitching."

Brent's eyes popped wide, astonished by Tyler's progress. And he was still young. Still growing. Brent estimated his pitches were close to ninety miles-per-hour as the ball smacked into his mitt, his velocity consistent and controlled.

"What do you think your best pitches are?" asked Brent. "The ones you're most comfortable with?"

"A four-seam fastball, a slider and a changeup. I'm working on my curveball."

"Have they clocked the velocity of your fastball at Edelweiss?"

"Yeah. Kyle said I'm averaging around eighty-nine to ninety-one miles per hour."

"That's impressive. And you have good control. I can tell you've been working hard. Do you think you'll be nervous with talent scouts watching you?"

"Nah. I think it'll make me more competitive."

"That's good. You have a lot of confidence. Let's wrap up for today. I'll make dinner. I'm grilling steaks. By the looks of you, I hope I bought enough. Your grandma said you eat like a horse."

Tyler's stomach was on the offensive, watching Brent flipping two enormous New York strip steaks. The smell of charcoal clung to the patio.

"How do you like your steak?" asked Brent.

"Big. And a little pink. Do you like to cook?"

"No. I can grill, make a baked potato and a salad. That's what you're getting tonight."

"Fine by me. So, do you have a woman in your life that cooks for you?"

"Nothing serious."

"Can I ask you something?" asked Tyler, when they had finished eating. "And I hope I'm not being too nosey."

"Ask away. You were never one to hold back. It'll feel like old times."

"So, what was up with you and my grandma? You always seemed close. Not like friends, but more. Especially in Hawaii. And I saw you kissing her once. You look at her the way I look at Leah. I always dreamed—well, prayed—you'd marry her, but then you were with Adrianna. And to be honest, I wasn't happy about that."

Tyler's brashness brought a smile to his face. "That's a weighty question." He focused in on Tyler. "I care deeply for your grandmother, but she isn't interested in a relationship. She's concerned with raising you. She doesn't want anything to get in the way."

"Don't you think that's weird? She's never dated anyone. Ever. It's not like she's ugly or anything. Guys hit on her all the time—like during my games—and she blows them off. I worry about her. That she'll be alone after Leah and I get married."

Brent poured himself a glass of wine. "How about a Coke? And aren't you too young to talk about marriage?"

"I'm not getting married now, but I know I'll marry Leah. Just like I know I'll be a Major League pitcher. And no Coke for me. Water's fine. So, don't you think it's weird—about my grandmother?"

"Your grandmother keeps things inside. She's not as open as you are. I'm sure she has her reasons, but I don't understand them. I wish I did."

"Is that why you moved? Because you wanted to be with her and couldn't? Because I get it. Sometimes I need to get away from Leah because I wanna be with her and I can't. She said we had to wait until we're married. And I want to wait, too, but it drives me crazy. Is that what happened to you?"

Brent laughed. He missed his conversations with Tyler—where nothing was off-limits—an open hand. "I needed a change. It was hard leaving both of you. It's still hard. But I've moved on, and things are going okay for me."

"Well, if you ask me, I think she's in love with you. When you call, she glows like a wildfire. I'm afraid she'll burn the house down. And when you moved, she wasn't herself for months. It's the craziest thing."

"Hey, let's talk about you and baseball."

"Okay. Do you have any snacks?"

"You just ate."

"That was an hour ago. I'm starving."

Brent scrutinized Tyler, whose attention remained fixated on the pitching instructor. He assessed Tyler's passion for the game—to see if he had the whole package—athleticism, coach-ability, and competitiveness. Tyler was hungry, consuming every crumb of information tossed his way.

"I hope you learned a lot this week," said Brent. "The MLB tryout camp is tomorrow, and afterwards I'll show you where I work."

"I can't wait. I did learn a lot. Things I didn't know," said Tyler. "Like doing the right exercises to keep my arm healthy. And using the weighted balls to practice pitching."

"When I asked you to come out, I wanted to see how serious you were. I'm impressed with what I'm seeing. You have the qualities scouts look for, both on and off the field. Tomorrow will be a big day. MLB scouts will be looking for talent that hasn't been discovered. If they like what they see, they'll track you and try to sign you when you graduate."

"But what about college?"

"Let's not get ahead of ourselves. We'll see what happens tomorrow."

After signing in at the MLB tryout camp, the scout hosting the event, Hunter Patton, gathered the players and went over his expectations before separating pitchers from position players.

"Okay, pitchers, listen up," shouted Hunter. "I'm only interested in guys throwing eighty-nine miles-per-hour and above, unless you're a left-hander. The average fastball speed in the Majors is around ninety so that's what I want to see. College guys throwing in the eighties won't be considered. Those under eighteen will get more leeway. You get fifteen pitches to show us your stuff. When I call your name, get out here quickly and dazzle us."

"How are you feeling?" asked Brent, waiting near the bullpen for Tyler's number to be called.

"I feel good. It's in God's hands. Like I told you, I know I'll be a Major League pitcher, even if things don't work out today."

Brent wrapped his arm around Tyler's shoulder. "I'm proud of you. I'm proud of who you are. Just do your best. That's all we can ask."

"Hey, they'll be calling your number soon," said Brent. "Start throwing in the bullpen to loosen your arm, but don't overdo it. You just wanna get slack."

"Number seventy-five."

Brent's stomach churned, as Tyler sprinted to the mound. The scout recording the pitch speed asked Tyler to begin with six fastballs. Tyler wound up and fired six straight pitches down the middle.

Brent tried to get a read on the scout's face but couldn't. From Brent's view it was the fastest he'd seen Tyler throw. The scout asked for three changeup pitches. Tyler threw three that broke perfectly. Next, he requested three breaking balls. Tyler went with the slider. The ball hooked sharply outside the strike zone, a perfect pitch. Finally, he asked Tyler to throw three pitches of his own choosing. Tyler went with a curveball. The ball hurled forward and dipped before reaching the plate. Textbook pitches.

"Thank you. Number seventy-six."

Tyler walked over to Brent. "Now what?"

"We wait until everybody is finished then they'll bring the group together to let them know if they're interested. Tyler, you were spot on. You showed more promise than many of the older guys."

"I felt comfortable. Baseball camp helped me stay focused. I'm happy with my performance, even if nothing happens."

Brent noticed a scout walking toward them. "Hi. My name is Connor. You were impressive out there, son." He asked Brent, "Are you his father?"

"No, but I'm representing him. I'm Brent Meyers, and this is Tyler Lane."

Tyler extended his hand, remembering Brent's advice—squeeze firmly and make eye contact. "Good to meet you, Connor," said Tyler.

"How old are you, Tyler?"

"Sixteen, sir. I'll be a senior in high school."

"Here's my card. I'd like to stay in touch until you graduate. You have a lot of talent. I clocked your fastball at ninety-one. That's extraordinary for a guy your age."

Brent took the card. "It was nice meeting you. We'll keep in touch."

Hunter Patton, the head scout, announced the names of the players who would be entered into the MLB tracking database, along with a scouting report. Tyler's name was called.

"Brent, they liked me!"

"What happens now?" asked Tyler, as they drove.

"They'll track you, waiting for you to graduate. If they're interested, they'll try to sign you to an MLB Minor League team. You'll have to decide if you want to try for a college baseball scholarship or sign out of high school. It's a gamble. If you forego college and you get hurt, or you don't make it to the Majors, you'll have nothing to fall back on. On the flip side, if you're successful, the years spent in the Minors would be about the time you'd spend in college. So, you'd have a jumpstart on your baseball career. It's something we need to discuss with your grandmother."

"How do I get a baseball scholarship?"

"Contact colleges now. Many don't have the resources to reach out to players. They look for players to come to them."

"My head is spinning."

"Yeah, but it's exciting. Too bad your grandma's not here. She will be so proud of you. As I am."

Tyler's expression grew serious as he considered Brent's influence on his life. "It's because of you I made it this far. The time you spent with me in Michigan—you've been more like a father than most kids have with their real father. Look at Cody. His dad hardly spends time with him. But you—you treat me like your son."

"You're like a son to me, Tyler. Did you know I had a son? Luke."

"Yes. Grandma told me. I'm sorry about what happened and how you must have felt losing him. I know God put me in your life because I needed a dad and you needed a son."

"I think you're right," said Brent, the weight of his words sitting on him. "Do you know much about your real father?"

"No. His name was Scott. Grandma met him a few times before he died in an accident. He wasn't married to my mom. I wish I could have met him. And I don't remember much of my mom, but she had this boyfriend, Jaime and I remember how much I liked spending time with him. And then there was my grandfather, but he died when I was young." Tyler looked off, pondering his unusual life. "But my grandmother certainly loves me—to raise me like I was her own son. Her whole life is dedicated to me. I wish she would—oh, never mind. You know what I wish."

"Hey," said Brent, trying to lighten the conversation. "Where do you want to eat tonight? To celebrate?"

"I'd like a gargantuan steak."

"Maybe we can find a cattle farm."

Tyler laughed. "Sounds good. Hey, I wanna call Grandma tonight, and Leah, if she'll talk to me."

Tyler handed the phone to Brent. "She wants to talk to you. I'm gonna take a shower."

"Hi, Brent. Tyler told me everything. It sounds exciting, and scary."

"Yeah, I wish you could have been here. I was so impressed with how he handled himself. He has so much potential. Everything they're looking for. If he stays on track, I'm confident he'll make it to the Major Leagues."

She sighed heavily. "He talked about possibly not going to college. I'm not sure I agree. What do you think?"

"Let's wait and see. There's a lot to consider. I'll be in Michigan in October—for two weeks. My renters are moving, and I want to look over the house—figure out if I should hang on to it or put it up for sale. We can talk then."

"It'll be good seeing you, Brent. It's been awhile."

"Yeah, it has."

"Has Tyler been behaving?"

"He's a good kid. You've done well raising him. I'll miss not having him around."

"It's quiet here. Just me and Scone."

"Well, at least you're saving money on the grocery bill."

She laughed. "Thanks for everything, Brent. I'm looking forward to seeing you."

"Is Leah still mad?" asked Brent, when Tyler emerged from the bedroom.

"No. She said she misses me, and she was pumped when I told her about the MLB tryouts. I can't wait to see her." Tyler paused long. "Hey, can I talk to you about something personal?"

"What's on your mind?"

"Well, me and Leah, we've never been together—in that way. And I want to wait until we're married. And Leah wants to wait.

But I'm not sure I can. When I'm with her, sometimes I feel like I won't be able to stop. How old were you—you know—the first time?"

Brent grinned. "Well, too young. You need to be careful, Tyler. Don't do something that'll mess up your future. If you love Leah, wait. Honor her wishes."

"I wonder when we get married," he chewed his thumbnail, "will I know what to do?"

"You'll figure it out. Trust me."

"Can I call you on my wedding night? In case I have a question?" Tyler grinned. "Kidding. Thanks for listening. Hey, I'm starving. Where's that cattle farm?"

Brent took Tyler to the Phoenix Municipal Stadium where he worked as Director of Minor League Operations. Standing behind home plate, they gazed out toward the scenic red rock formations of Papago Park, palm trees dotting the landscape.

"Wow," said Tyler. "What do you do for your job?"

"I manage baseball related matters in Arizona, Minor League Affiliates, and the Dominican Republic. Things like budgeting, facilities, staffing, merchandise, and special events."

Brent turned to say hello to the Minor League pitching coach, Buzz Ripley. "Hey, Buzz, I'd like you to meet Tyler Lane, the young man I told you about. He's visiting from Michigan. Tyler went to the MLB tryout camp yesterday."

Tyler extended his hand. "Nice to meet you, Buzz."

"How did tryout camp go?" asked Buzz.

"Well, sir, they took my name, and I got business cards from a few scouts."

"That's exciting. Would you like to see the bullpen? Maybe you can show me your stuff."

"Wow. That'd be great."

The bullpen was smaller than Tyler had imagined. "Let me find a catcher," said Buzz.

"Don't bother. I'll catch for him," said Brent, putting on a mitt, tossing one to Tyler.

"I'll show you my fastball first," said Tyler. He fingered the ball in his hand and went into his wind-up, raising his left knee high and planting his foot, as his right arm cocked and accelerated, the ball snapping into Brent's mitt. He threw ten more pitches, demonstrating his slider and changeup.

"Pretty impressive," said Buzz, raising his eyebrows and looking toward Brent. "Good arm action. How old are you?"

"Sixteen, sir."

"Well, it was nice meeting you, Tyler. I gotta run, but let's stay in contact. I like what I saw. You have a lot of potential. I'll work through Brent."

"Nice meeting you, too, sir."

Brent dropped Tyler off at the airport. "I'll be in Michigan in October. I want to talk to your grandmother about your future, but call me if you wanna talk. About anything."

"Thanks for everything," said Tyler, wrapping his arms around Brent. "I'm gonna miss you. I had a great time." They hugged before Tyler disappeared into the terminal.

Brent watched him walk away. An empty hollowness taking hold. He looked forward to spending time in Michigan, but he had mixed emotions. It had gotten easier for him over the years, being away from her and the constant cravings choking him.

Shade stopped at the Emmet County police station on her way to the airport. It had been four months since she'd touched base with

Detective Kent Monroe. She spotted him through the glass pane of his office. He waved her in.

"Shade Lane. What a nice surprise. Have a seat. What brings you here?"

"I was in the area and thought I'd stop to see if there've been any developments. But I'm sure you would have contacted me."

"I thought we had a lead, but it didn't check out. You're still a priority," said Kent. "You look good. Things going okay?"

"Things are well. The bakery business is great, and Tyler is sixteen now. You should see him. He's over six-feet tall. How about you? You look good. Very distinguished."

Kent smiled. "Still single, married to my job. Wondering if I'll ever retire."

"I know the feeling. Well, I'd better get going," said Shade, after making small talk. "I'm picking up Tyler from the airport. It was good seeing you."

"You, too. And in case you're too embarrassed to ask, I'm free for dinner through the end of the year."

"I'll keep that in mind," said Shade, laughing. "And stop at the bakery anytime. I'll buy lunch."

CHAPTER TWENTY-EIGHT

In their hearts humans plan their course, but the Lord establishes their steps.

— PROVERBS 16:9

"I'm making your favorite meal tonight. Breaded pork chops with scalloped potatoes and roasted asparagus. I know you don't like to eat too much sugar, but I also made a triple-berry pie with crumble topping."

"Thanks, Grams," said Tyler, hugging her from behind. "I missed you. It's good to be home, but I'll miss being with Brent. We had so much to talk about. No offense, Grams, but I can talk to him about things I can't talk to you about."

"Oh. Like what?"

"Man stuff. Private stuff," he said, rummaging through the refrigerator. "Hey, I'd like to see Leah, and I know I can't use the car yet. Can you take me to her house after dinner?"

"I have a surprise. Leah is coming here for dinner. She should be here any minute."

"Excellent."

Leah came through the front door, and Tyler swept her into his arms and gave her a peck on the lips. "I missed you, babe. You look beautiful."

"I missed you, too. You're so tanned," she said, gazing into his eyes, before turning to Shade and hugging her. "Can I help?"

"No. Just spend time with Tyler. I'm sure you two have a lot of catching up to do. I'll call you when dinner's ready."

Tyler took Leah's hand and led her into his bedroom. "I bought you something."

"Door open, please," Shade yelled from the kitchen.

The following week, Brent's plane touched down at Detroit Metro Airport. It felt good to be home. The trees were clothed in glistening golds and scarlets, the earthy smell of autumn lingering in the air. He missed the seasons.

He stood in the foyer. Home. The large picture window framed the grandeur of Lake Michigan, shards of sunlight sprayed against the waves. He stepped onto the deck, inhaling crisp air. Shade. He missed her. But he vowed to remain passive. This was about Tyler. Nothing more.

The corridor of Edelweiss High School appeared smaller than he remembered. The placard on the door read, Kyle Beekman, Head Coach. He knocked.

"Come in," said Kyle, shaking Brent's hand. "Good to see you. When did you get in?"

"A few days ago. It's good to be home."

"We miss you around here. They're looking for an Athletic Director. They let the last guy go. He wasn't cutting it. I'm sure they'd take you back in a heartbeat."

Brent laughed. "Well, I'm not looking. I like my job in Arizona. Hey, is Tyler around?"

"Yeah, he's practicing in the gym. Want me to get him?"

"No, not yet. Let's talk first. I was impressed with what I saw while he was in Arizona. I've received several calls from scouts. Have you seen scouts hanging around?"

"Yeah. Last week, when they were practicing on the field. I saw guys with radar guns, checking his velocity."

"Did they talk to you? Or Tyler?"

"No, they were just observing. Minding their own business. Tyler noticed them, too, but he seemed unfazed."

"So, how do you think Tyler's doing? Not just on the field, but off?"

"He's uncommon. That's the word I like to use for him. He's got this intense focus, and he soaks up everything. If I give him pointers he works at it until it's perfected. He keeps getting better."

"What about off the field? His grades—his character?"

"He gets A's and B's. Gets along with everyone. Teachers, classmates, his opponents. You remember Cody, don't you?"

"Yeah. Victoria's son. He was the catcher on the All-Star team."

"Right. You know, he and Tyler were close. Well, Cody rebelled after his mom married that doctor, Roger. He stole his mother's Mercedes and went for a joyride. Got drunk and pulled into a parking lot. Too fast. And drove over a ledge and into Lake Michigan. A witness said he sat in the car, smoking a cigarette, before trying to get out. Thankfully, he escaped through the sunroof before the current pulled the car under. He claimed he was tracking the GPS, and it guided him into the lake. Well, Tyler told him he didn't wanna have anything to do with him if he continued to act up. It changed Cody. He looks up to Tyler, as do most kids. Anyway, I see Tyler as a leader—a mentor. A good kid."

Brent thanked Kyle before leaving to find Tyler.

"Brent," said Tyler, trotting across the gym and embracing him. "When did you get home?"

"A few days ago."

Tyler frowned. "And you didn't wanna see me right away? I'm insulted."

"Just getting settled. Hey, I talked to Kyle. He has great things to say. He told me about the scouts."

"Yeah. They've been watching, like Russian spies."

"I've gotten a few calls. They're interested. I'll call your grandmother and schedule time for us to talk."

"Do you want me to be there, or do you two wanna be alone?" said Tyler, winking.

Brent grinned. "Let me talk to her alone first. Give her options before we talk to you. I want her to be informed."

"I'll give her a heads-up. She'll wanna get her hair and makeup done."

Shade wore a dusting of flour, as she shaped the dough into a circle and brushed the top with melted butter. She gathered a handful of Turbinado sugar and sprinkled it over the butter before running a floured cutter across the dough, forming eight triangles. She placed the blueberry scones on a baking sheet and put them in the oven.

Sally came into the kitchen and prepared the sandwiches.

"You okay?" asked Shade. "You seem down."

"Yeah, Drew couldn't sleep so he climbed into bed with me and Chad. Kept us up all night."

She noticed Sally wiping her eyes with the back of her hand. "Sally, what's wrong?"

Tears filled Sally's eyes and spilled down her face. "I'm pregnant. We wanted to wait because we're financially strapped. I know I should be excited, but the timing stinks. And Chad's trying to pretend like he's happy, but he's worried." Her shoulders slumped as she sobbed.

"Oh, Sally," said Shade, taking her into her arms. "This is wonderful news. A baby. The timing never seems right, but things will work out. How strapped are you?"

"We got behind on our mortgage when Drew got sick. Doctor bills piled up and Chad tried working extra shifts, but we can't get ahead."

"I don't mean to pry, but how much do you owe?"

"About ten-thousand dollars, between the mortgage and our credit card balance. And we need a new furnace. You know, police officers don't make the money they should for what they do. He puts his life on the line every day. He's trying to get promoted, but everything takes time." She wiped her eyes. "I'm sorry for dumping on you."

"Hey, you're not dumping on me. And don't worry about your situation. I know you're not a religious person, but I'll pray for you." A wide smile crept across Shade's face. "Oh, Sally, I'm so excited. You're having a baby. And Drew will have a new brother or sister."

"Thanks for being there for me," she said, carrying the tray of sandwiches out of the kitchen. "By the way, Brent's in town. He called Chad last night. He's coming over tonight for dinner. It'll be good seeing him."

"I knew he was coming home, but I wasn't sure when."

Her insides rolled at the sound of his name. She didn't realize he was in town and was disappointed he didn't call her—or Tyler.

Her thoughts turned to Sally. Such a dedicated employee and a dear friend. She would help them out, whatever way she could.

Sally came in the kitchen with someone following. "Hey, speaking of the devil."

Brent. She froze, her heart bashing her chest. She was a mess—covered in flour, her hair haphazardly piled on top of her head, no makeup.

"What a nice surprise," she said, wiping her hands on her apron. "Sally told me you got in a few days ago."

He walked over and embraced her. He looked more handsome than she remembered. Her face burned hot. Why couldn't he have ballooned out and lost his hair?

He held her out, surveying her. "You haven't changed. Except for the blast of flour in your hair and on your face."

"Hey, I'll leave you two alone," said Sally. "I have work to do. See you tonight Brent. Six-thirty?"

"Sounds good. I came to pick up a cheesecake. Remember, you said I could bring dessert."

They stood awkwardly, staring at each other. She felt like a blushing schoolgirl and struggled to find words.

"Hey," said Brent, breaking the silence. "I saw Tyler today. He gave me the third degree for not letting him know I was in town."

She laughed, fumbling with her hair. "He's been so excited about you coming home. It's all he's talked about since he got back."

Brent smiled. That smile. Little creases at the corners of his eyes. Her heart liquefied.

"I told him you and I needed to talk. Alone. I was thinking we could go somewhere neutral. Maybe out to dinner. Are you available tomorrow night?"

"Yes, I'm free after six."

"Good. I'll pick you up around seven. Does that work?"

"Perfect."

He smiled and left. Her pulse was still thrashing. *Neutral? What's that supposed to mean? Is he afraid I'll attack him if we're alone?* It had been four years since she'd seen him, and it was as though he had never left—the same lovesick sensation playing havoc with her thoughts. She inhaled deeply and went back to work, her mind on Brent.

The following night, she burst through the cottage door and ran into her bedroom. She had hoped to leave work early, but the bakery was bustling. Stripping off her clothes, she jumped into the shower. After blow-drying her hair and applying makeup, she pulled an outfit from the closet. She chose a pair of black, straight leg pants with black leather high heels. Fingering the blouses in her closet, she went with the plum-colored silk blouse with a strand of pearls. She stood in front of the mirror, turning and looking over her shoulder. Good enough. She dabbed perfume on her wrists before grabbing her clutch bag and emerging from the bedroom.

"Wow, Grams. You look nice. And you smell nice. What time will Brent be here?"

"Any minute," she said, trying to steady her nerves.

"Hey, Leah's coming over. I hope that's okay."

"Leah is welcome here anytime. You know the rules, and I trust you."

"And I hope I can trust you with Brent."

The doorbell rang, startling her. Tyler opened the door and escorted Brent in, giving him a hug. "Hey, Brent. Where are you taking Grams tonight?"

He smiled, catching sight of Shade standing in the kitchen. "I'm taking her to that little Italian restaurant on the water. What are you doing tonight?"

"Leah's coming over. We're ordering pizza."

Her heart thrashed like a caged animal. He looked striking in his pale blue shirt, opened at the collar, black wool pants hugging his long, muscular legs. He didn't have an ounce of fat on him. She wondered if he spent his free time working out.

"Well, are you ready?" Brent asked.

Shade grabbed her coat, Tyler looming over them.

"I want you both home by 9 p.m. sharp. Understand?" said Tyler.

Shade and Brent laughed. She kissed Tyler's cheek and walked out the door, Brent's hand on her back.

The maître d' escorted them to a window table overlooking Lake Michigan. The sun dipped into the calm water, an orange glow igniting the sky.

"I miss Michigan," Brent sighed, taking in the scenery. He turned and stared into her eyes. The votive candle glimmered on the table in the dimly lit restaurant, dancing off of her face. She was beautiful. He caught himself lingering and reached for the wine list.

"How about a bottle of red?"

"Please," said Shade, without hesitation. "I'm nervous tonight—being here with you."

He considered her. "To be honest, I was anxious myself. It's good seeing you, Shade. And you look great."

She felt the intensity of his gaze. "You don't look so bad yourself."

The waiter cleared his throat. "We'd like the Renato Ratti 2006 Marcenasco Barolo," said Brent.

"I've been learning more about wine," she said, swirling her glass. "I took a few regional wine tasting classes with Victoria last summer."

"That's great. Hey, speaking of Victoria, did I hear correctly? She married Roger?"

Shade laughed, her nervousness fading. "It's true. After the unfortunate Watusi episode, she changed. Became more responsible. Roger chased after her, but she held him off. She wanted to pull her life together and wasn't interested in a casual relationship. She wanted more, and he caved. They got married a few years ago. She quit her job and now spends her time shopping and hosting philanthropic events. She's a different woman." Shade sighed. "I'm happy for her."

After they had eaten, Brent leaned forward and clasped his hands atop the table.

"Let's talk about Tyler. Scouts have been calling, and I understand they've shown up at school. They're watching him—waiting for him to graduate, then they'll pounce. Try to get him to go pro before college. The Major League draft happens in June, right after he graduates. You'll need to think about options."

"If they're willing to sign him after high school, does it make sense to jump at it?"

"I think he needs to apply for a scholarship, regardless. A university with a solid baseball program like Vanderbilt, Texas Christian, or Rice. If he gets picked in the draft, he can go pro right away or wait until after college. If I wasn't so impressed with him I'd say hold off and go to college. But Tyler is different. He's ready mentally and physically. My gut is telling me he should turn pro after high school, but it shouldn't be taken lightly. He needs an airtight contract with a clause stipulating the club pay for his education if his baseball career ends. And you'd want a bigger signing bonus. Salaries in the Minors are low. Generally, high school signees have the most negotiating leverage."

"A lot to think about." She fingered the stem of her glass. "Can you come over Sunday for dinner? We can all talk together."

"I'd like that. He needs to be part of this decision, but I wanted you to have as much information as possible."

"I wish you weren't so far away. I'd be so much easier having you close."

Brent's gaze didn't break. He remained silent, reaching for the check.

His stare sent shivers through her body. She reached across the table, her hand open. "Let me pick up dinner. It's the least I can do."

Brent inserted his credit card in the leather folder and handed it to the waiter. "Everything I do for Tyler, I do because I love him. Don't think you owe me."

"Why don't you come in?" she asked, when he pulled into the driveway. "It looks like Leah is here."

"Just for a minute." Brent walked her into the cottage.

Tyler opened the door, looking at his wristwatch. "It's ten o'clock. You're late," said Tyler, smirking. "Hey Brent, come say hi to Leah."

Leah emerged from the living room. "Leah, you've grown since the last time I saw you," said Brent. "Into a beautiful, young lady."

"Thank you," Leah responded, hugging him. "Tyler raved about the time he spent with you in Arizona. How long will you be home?"

"Ten days. Hope to see you again before I leave town." Brent turned and embraced Shade and Tyler. "Well, I'd better get going. See you Sunday."

The kitchen looked like a bomb had exploded as she busied herself preparing dinner. *Why do I always pick the most difficult recipe?* She finished peeling the pearl onions before adding them to the skillet, along with the cremini mushrooms, baby carrots, and pancetta. Beef tips were simmering in Cote du Rhone wine and Cognac. She thickened the sauce for the Beef Bourguignon and added a pat of butter to make it glisten.

"Grams. What a mess. Let me clean up and you go shower. I don't want Brent to be frightened by this disaster."

"Oh, thank you, honey. That would be great."

"Everything was excellent," said Brent, after they had eaten.

"Well, it should be," said Tyler. "If you could have seen the kitchen—and her—you would have jumped back in your car and sped off." He clasped his hands on the table. "Okay you two, let's talk baseball."

Brent laid out the different options to Tyler as he sat —focusing.

"Well," said Tyler. "I'm leaning toward foregoing college if that's an option for me. But I'll still apply for a scholarship as a back-up plan. I just don't wanna spend four years in school when I can play for the MLB now."

"Okay," said Brent. "A few things you need to focus on during your last year in school. Scouts are watching. You need to shine. Every day. Both on and off the mound. Work hard. Keep your ERA low. Take care of your arm. I can't stress this enough, Tyler. You're young. Don't overdo it because you'll ruin your future. I'll talk to Kyle and make sure you're doing the proper warm-up and recovery exercises. Now it's just wait and see."

"Will he need an agent?" asked Shade.

"He should have someone represent him. I might be able to, or I have contacts who would be interested. But once he's drafted he'll need a certified MLBPA agent. They represent the Major League Players Association."

"Can you be my agent?" asked Tyler.

"I would have to get certified, which is doable. But you might want someone with more experience. Let's cross that bridge when we come to it."

Brent worked his way through the crowded hallway and found Kyle's office.

"Hey, Brent, good to see you," said Gary Murrell, the Superintendent, extending his hand. "Kyle told me you were in town. How long are you here?"

"Just a few more days. How've you been?"

"Good. Busy. Did Kyle tell you we're looking for an Athletic Director? I always said you were welcome back if things didn't work out. I still mean it. Any interest?"

Brent smiled. "I appreciate it. But I enjoy my job in Arizona."

"Well, if you change your mind call me. I'd love to talk. Hey, I gotta run, but stay in touch," he said, shaking his hand before walking away.

Kyle agreed to touch base weekly with Brent to provide updates on Tyler's progress. Brent spoke to Kyle about arm care and explained he had enlisted a physical trainer who specialized in the RAMS method; Recovery, Activation, Mobility, and Strengthening.

Brent helped Tyler fill out applications for a baseball scholarship. He wanted to make sure all loose ends were tied up before returning to Arizona. It was his last day in Michigan and he thought about his time with Shade and Tyler. He would miss them both. And he still loved her but felt more in command of his emotions.

Before listing his home for rent, Brent worked with an interior designer to make some cosmetic changes. He wasn't ready to give up his home. Maybe he would retire here. He wasn't sure why, but he couldn't let go.

Shade organized a small get-together for Brent's last day. The gathering went on into the night, conversation filling the air. Tyler stood and raised his glass in the air.

"Here's to Brent. My surrogate father and the greatest man I've ever known. I'm forever grateful to you for all you've done for me. I love you with all my heart. Safe travels, Brent."

Brent's eyes glistened, as they embraced. He couldn't speak. His heart ached for Tyler—to be nearer, now when he needed him most.

"Hey, Grams. Can I take the car and drive Leah home?" He hoped the atmosphere would prompt leniency. "Mary's leaving, and I'd like Leah to stay longer. Maybe Brent can take you home. Is that okay?"

"It's fine with me as long as Brent's okay."

"No problem," said Brent.

Brent pulled into the driveway of the cottage and walked Shade to the porch.

"Would you like to come in?" asked Shade.

"No, but thank you. I have an early flight tomorrow."

"It was good seeing you." She searched his eyes.

He inhaled sharply. "You, too." He took her in his arms, holding her longer than he intended, before pulling away. "I'll be in touch. This is a critical time for Tyler, but I'll help you through this." He took her head in his hands and pulled her to him, kissing her forehead. "I'll miss you, Shade. I always do."

She stood, watching, as he backed out of the driveway. She craved the man she'd forfeited. He was part of her soul. A single tear meandered down her cheek, as she turned and let herself into the cottage.

CHAPTER TWENTY-NINE

Because of the tender mercy of our God, by which the rising sun will come to us from heaven to shine on those living in darkness and in the shadow of death, to guide our feet into the path of peace.

— LUKE 1:78-79

Since returning to Arizona, Brent felt unsettled. Michigan was nudging. He felt responsible for Tyler, and he yearned to be close to him during his senior year of varsity baseball. He thought about the job offer from his former superintendent. It would be an easy transition but a step down from his current role. Aside from his job, nothing held him in Arizona. He was torn. A move back to Michigan would place him closer to her, and he didn't relish the thought of riding that same emotional roller coaster. But this wasn't about her. It was about Tyler. Tyler needed guidance. Someone he could trust—who had his best interests at heart.

He contacted his former superintendent to see if the position was still open. "Hey, Gary, it's Brent Meyers."

"Are you calling to tell me you want your old job back?"

Brent laughed. "I might be interested, if it's still available."

"It is still available, and it's yours if you want it. If you're serious, I can put together an offer."

"Why don't you do that? Once I see the offer, I'll decide."

"I'll have something to you in a few days. It'd be great to have you back, Brent. I'll be in touch."

Sally arrived at work to find a plain, white envelope with her name printed across the front. Shade wasn't due in for another hour. She opened the envelope and found a check inside with a handwritten note:

Dear Sally. Enclosed is your annual bonus check. I want you to know how much I appreciate your tireless work and dedication. This has been a difficult year for you and Chad, and I wanted to make your lives easier, just as you make my life easier every day. Thanks for all you do. Love, Shade.

She stared at the check, her hands trembling. Thirty-thousand dollars? It had to be a mistake.

Shade came into the kitchen and found Sally looking bewildered.

"Thank you for my bonus, but I think you made a mistake," she said, handing Shade the check.

"It's not a mistake. That's your bonus. I'm not sure if it'll be that big every year, but that's your bonus this year."

Sally's mouth hung, her eyes stretched wide. "I—I don't know what to say," she said, her voice quivering, tears crawling down her face. She wrapped her arms around Shade.

"Hey," said Shade, as they drew apart. "You deserve this, and I know you need it. And I need you. So, stop worrying about the new baby and the mortgage payments and the furnace. Things will work out."

"You don't know how much I appreciate this. And you. A huge weight has been removed. I can't wait to tell Chad.

Thank you, Shade," she said, hugging her again and wiping her tears.

"Do you ever think about owning a bakery of your own? You have a good head for business."

"I would love to, but I could never afford something like this. Besides, I like working here. It's a perfect location, and I couldn't ask for a better boss."

"Well, I'm not going to work forever. You should think about taking over my business one day. We could work something out. Who knows, maybe Chad could quit the police force and you both could run the bakery."

"Are you trying to tell me something? Are you selling the bakery?"

"Not now. But I want you to think about your future, when the time comes for me to retire."

"You scared me. The thought of not having you here when I get back from maternity leave is not a good thought."

"I just wanted to put a bug in your ear. Now, let's get to work."

Shade was thankful she had been blessed with the resources to help Sally and Chad. Tyler would be set financially, and if his baseball career took off, he'd have more than enough. She thought back to her humble beginnings. How God had moved in her life, protecting her and Tyler all these years. Answered prayers. Soon, she would honor the vow she had made.

The clang of the metal bars no longer made her jolt. She looked forward to leading the women in God's word. And she had grown close to Meghan, watching her transform from an angry, wounded woman to a woman of faith.

"Hey, Shade," said Meghan, after the study ended. "Can we talk?"

"Sure. What's up?"

"Can you give Tyler a message? I wanna thank him for what he did for Ethan."

"Thank him?"

"Ethan told me he was at Tyler's game when some older kids teased him about his mom being in prison. Being a murderer." Meghan looked down, shuffling her feet. "I guess Tyler confronted them. Told them not everyone is blessed with the perfect family. And that we don't get to choose how we grow up. And if they were smart they would back off before they created more problems for themselves. I guess he scared them away. You know, Ethan looks up to Tyler. It meant the world to him—what he did."

"Tyler didn't tell me," said Shade.

"Tyler sounds like a good kid. I hope Ethan will look up to me one day—when I get outta here. But I'm not sure he'll have anything to be proud of. I'll probably have to live with my parents until I get on my feet. And who's going to hire a convicted murderer? I'm scared of what life might look like for me."

"I'm sure it will be scary. Just keep praying. And I'll continue to do the same." The buzzer sounded. "It's time for me to leave. I'll tell Tyler you said thank you. See you in a few weeks."

The TV was blaring when Shade entered the cottage. Tyler lay sprawled on the sofa eating popcorn and watching the MLB Channel. Scone sat at his feet, scarfing up tumbling kernels which scattered across the rug.

"Hey, Grams. Brent called. He wants you to call him when you get a chance."

"Did you talk to him?"

"Yeah. We talked about my varsity team and Kyle. He said he might come out soon."

Her stomach rolled. It had only been two months, but she was looking forward to seeing him again.

"Hey, do you mind shutting off the TV? I want to talk to you."

"Sure," said Tyler. "What's up?"

"Ethan's mom, Meghan, wanted me to give you a message—to thank you for sticking up for Ethan. That was thoughtful of you, Tyler—to come to his rescue like that. She also said you told the kids we don't get to choose how we grow up. It made me wonder if you've ever been sorry about the way you grew up."

"Never, Grandma," he said, squeezing her hand. "Sure, I would have liked a dad, and I wonder about my mom, but you've been more than a mom to me. I wouldn't change a thing. I've had a good life, and I've never been ashamed of who I am. You're the most important person in my world."

Tears stung her eyes as she cupped her hand on his face. "We rarely talk about your mom. Maybe now is a good time. Is there anything you'd like to know?"

Tyler sat back. "I often wonder what she was like—her personality."

Shade sighed. "Your mom had a troubled life, but it wasn't always that way. She was a good child. Excelled in school. Popular with other kids. But when she reached her teens, she changed. That's when she started using drugs and got pregnant—with you. The drugs controlled her. She wasn't the same." She inhaled sharply and looked down. "I blame myself for her problems. We weren't close, like most mothers and daughters. I was so young when I had her. I spent too much time doting on your grandfather and not enough time being a good mother."

"You don't talk much about Grandpa. I know he's not my biological grandfather, but were you happy with him?"

"I idolized him. He married me after I had your mother. I was afraid I'd have to give her up, but he rescued me. I felt indebted to him."

"What about my real grandfather?"

Regret washed over her, thinking about Tyler's hollow ancestry. "Your real grandfather's name was Matthew Caldwell. He was sixteen, popular and athletic. Like you. I thought he loved me, but it was just a mask. When I got pregnant, he wanted nothing to do with me. His father was transferred to California, and I never saw him again."

"He sounds like a jerk." Tyler sat silently, pondering his curious life. "Do you think my mom loved me?"

"I know she did. But she had a hard time expressing her feelings. The drugs interfered with her ability to think rationally. To be a good mother. She struggled every day."

"I feel sad for her. Her life was broken, and she didn't live long enough to fix it." Tyler breathed deeply and looked off. "I wonder what my life would have looked like if she were still alive. I would probably never know Brent, and that would be sad."

"I wonder the same thing. But we'll never know," said Shade, considering the interconnectivity of life. "Hey, I've been saving something for you. Something from your mother."

She went into her bedroom closet and pulled out the scrapbook. She sat next to him and opened the book.

"When I went through this, it felt like I found my daughter. The one I once knew. And I realized, then, how much she loved you—and me." Shade swallowed, emotions clawing to escape.

They sat together, Shade leafing through each page, offering a narrative of times and places where photos were taken. They came upon the section dedicated to Tyler—photos of him as a toddler, clippings of his fingernails and toenails saved in a cellophane bag.

Tyler remained silent, lingering on each relic, taking in a world foreign to him. He came to a page titled "Five Things I Love About You."

Tyler's eyes were fixed, a deer still and perceptive. "Grandma, something just snapped into place. Like a missing piece of a jigsaw puzzle. I never thought she cared. Like I didn't matter.

But it's not true. She was just lost, trying to find her way, but it was too late for her," he said, swiping a finger beneath his eyes. "Thank you, Grandma. Now I have something tangible from her." He leaned over and wrapped his arms around Shade. "I love you."

"I love you too, honey. God gave me a second chance to raise a child, and I want to do things right this time—for you. You've made me so proud." She placed her open palm against his cheek and kissed his forehead.

Tyler retired early, clutching his treasured scrapbook. Light peeked beneath his bedroom door. She imagined him revisiting the pages. A watershed moment in his life. A hidden chapter laid bare.

"Hi, Brent," said Shade, her heart pattering. "Tyler said you called. So, you're coming out?"

"Yeah. Since I got home, I've had this relentless gnawing. This urge to be there for Tyler. To help him realize his dreams. This is his last year of high school, and critical decisions will need to be made. Edelweiss Schools has extended a generous offer as the Athletic Director. I'm moving back to Michigan in two weeks."

"Oh, Brent. That's great news. Have you told Tyler?"

"No. I wanted to tell you first." He paused. "To be honest, I struggled with this decision. Not because of Tyler, but because of you. Because of this feeling of having unfinished business with you."

She exhaled. "Is that what if feels like? Unfinished business?"

"Yes," he sighed. "It does. And we'll be spending a lot of time together. My goal is to stay focused on Tyler. On his future. This is about him, not us."

He heard her steady breathing—and he imagined her face—contrite. "Do you agree? Are you good with this? Shade?"

"Yes, I'm here," she said, her voice soft. "And I'm good with everything. Tyler will be thrilled. When will you tell him?"

"I'll call him tomorrow."

"I'll keep my lips sealed. He'll have two surprises tomorrow. I'm taking him car shopping."

"That'll be exciting. Buy him something safe, like a minivan."

"Good idea," she said, laughing. "I'll let him know it was your recommendation. Brent, I'm so happy you're moving back."

"Me too. We'll talk soon."

Her emotions were scrambled. Happy. Frightened. Unfinished business? She felt it, too. He was a part of her—carved in her soul. She wanted things to be different, but the privilege to love wasn't possible. Not for them.

"Oh no. What happened?" said Shade, when they returned from car shopping to find the kitchen floor covered in vomit. Tyler searched the house and found Scone lying under his bed.

"Scone, what's wrong, buddy?" asked Tyler, pulling him out.

Scone tried standing but couldn't steady himself. He'd been lethargic lately and his appetite had dwindled.

"Grandma. Scone doesn't look well. Maybe we should go to the vet."

Tyler carried him to the car and laid him in the back seat. He slid in next to him, stroking his head, while Shade drove.

"I'm sorry to tell you this, but Scone has bone cancer," said the vet. "He probably has a month left. He will get worse. And he'll be in a lot of pain. When you notice things progressing, I suggest you bring him in so we can put him to sleep."

What should have been a blissful day in Tyler's life turned

dark. Shade and Tyler were silent on the drive home. When they arrived at the cottage, Tyler gathered Scone in his arms and carried him up the steps.

"Grandma, I want to keep him home as long as we can, but I don't want him to suffer."

"I know, honey," said Shade. "Let's see how he does in the next few days."

The following morning, Shade found Tyler asleep on the bedroom floor, his arm slung over Scone. Scone lay still, at peace in his master's presence. When Tyler got up, Scone remained on the floor, his head lifting slightly, his eyes tracking Tyler's movements. Tyler bent down and nuzzled his face in Scone's neck. Scone didn't move.

Tyler looked at Shade, his face etched with sorrow. "Grandma, I think it's time," he said, wiping his eyes.

Tyler called Leah and the three of them drove to the vet, Tyler and Leah in the backseat cradling Scone. Once inside the veterinarian's office, they were taken to a room. The attendant placed Scone atop a table. He barely moved. They gathered around as Tyler ran his fingers through Scone's soft fur, lifting his floppy ear in his hands, feeling the weight. Silent tears spilled, unrestrained.

Tyler buried his face in Scone's neck, his fingers stroking Scone's head. Shade and Leah clung to each other, their bodies racked with sobs.

After some time, Tyler stood. "Go on home, buddy," he said, his chin trembling. "I'll look for you on the other side."

Within seconds of receiving the euthanasia medication, Scone's breathing slowed, then stopped. The vet listened for a heartbeat, nodded and left the room, allowing them time alone with Scone.

An emptiness draped Tyler's soul, lasting for several weeks. Shade worried he would never recover. But Leah was his rock. And as the weeks went by, the hole in his heart healed.

The ball left Tyler's grip, registering ninety-two mph on Kyle's radar gun. Shade sat mesmerized. She enjoyed watching him practice. Her thoughts turned to Brent. He would be home soon, and Tyler was rocked with anticipation.

Shade didn't recognize the woman until she sat beside her—the mysterious woman from the bakery.

"Hi. We've not met. I'm Amanda O'Brien," she said, extending her hand.

"Nice to meet you. I'm Shade Lane."

"I know. You own the bakery. You're Tyler's grandmother, right?"

"Yes. I've seen you at the bakery. Do you come out often to watch him practice?"

"When I have time," said Amanda. "He's quite talented."

Shade guarded her space, looking away. She seemed too straightforward and her hawkish blue eyes troubled her. She didn't look like a typical baseball fan, clad in chic grey slacks and a black cashmere sweater. Her silver hair was pulled neatly back in a fashionable chignon, and she spoke with an air of refinement.

"Do you know other players on the team?" asked Shade, avoiding her eyes.

"No, just Tyler. I used to travel a lot, but since my husband passed away, I'm trying to revive the things I used to be passionate about. Like baseball."

"Did you travel for your job?" asked Shade.

"No. I was an actress in my younger days until I married Vince. He was a businessman and wanted me to see the world with him, so I stopped working."

Slowly scraping the soil, searching for the nugget, Shade asked, "Do you have children?"

"Vince and I never had children. He never wanted a family. He only wanted us."

Shade looked at her, her eyes drawing her inward. "What type of acting did you do?"

"Mostly live theater in New York. That's how I met Vince. He was sitting in the audience, and he told me he knew I was the one." She laughed without measure, comfortable in her skin.

"Hey, Grams," yelled Tyler. "Kyle said I threw a ninety-two mile per hour fastball. I can't wait for Brent to get home so he can see what I can do." Tyler recognized the woman from the bakery and waved before trotting off.

She turned to Amanda. "This may sound strange, but I feel like I know you. I've seen you in the bakery, but I feel like we met before. Another place and time."

Amanda smiled. "It doesn't sound strange. It would be nice to get to know you better. Would you like to go for coffee?"

She hardly knew this woman, and she wanted to go for coffee? Something didn't feel right. A heavy, evening fog. "Today?"

"Yes, if you're free."

The coffee shop was located on the outskirts of downtown. As Shade drove into the parking lot, she had second thoughts. A BMW pulled up alongside. Amanda waved and smiled. Too late.

After the waitress took their orders, Amanda broke the awkward silence.

"You're probably wondering why a stranger would ask you out for coffee."

"Well, to be frank, yes."

Amanda sat quiet for a minute before speaking. "What I'm about to tell you may come as a shock."

Shade swallowed hard. She considered leaving—not wanting to hear—but she was cemented to her seat.

"In August 1960, I had a baby. A girl. I was fifteen, and my life was a mess. My parents were alcoholics, and they were too intoxicated to notice my condition. I gave birth one night while they were out. I was scared. Terrified. I wrapped the baby in blankets and placed her in a box. I hung the box on a tree. And I hoped. And I prayed."

Shade trembled. Her teeth chattering, as she clasped her hands in her lap. "And that's how I got the name. Shade. Because if not for the shade of the tree, I would have died." Her eyes bored into the woman. "You left me hanging. In a tree?" Shade's voice went higher than she expected. "What? What do you want? Why are you here?"

Amanda's blue eyes widened, searching and scared, swept with tears. "I wanted to get to know you. And Tyler. So, I hired a private detective after Vince died."

Shade's mouth dropped open. "Why now? Why didn't you try to find me when I was helpless and pregnant? When I needed you? You were married and living the good life." Anger rose from her core. Bubbling hot and violent. "You could have helped me. But you didn't. And then you watched me. Like a voyeur."

Amanda sat unmoving, bound in suffocating plastic, tears tumbling. "I wanted to help you, but Vince wouldn't let me. And I didn't want to lose Vince. I was scared. But I was wrong. I know that now. I can't go back and undo what I've done."

"None of us can," said Shade, her face stone. She pushed the chair out and stood. "Please stay away from Tyler and me."

Shade struggled to her car, as though moving against water. She came home to an empty cottage. She needed time to absorb everything. She sunk into the sofa, still shaking, mulling over the woman. The princess buried beneath Egyptian dust. Her mother. After all these years. How could she have a relationship with her now when time is fading to black.

CHAPTER THIRTY

Get rid of all bitterness, rage and anger, brawling and slander, along with every form of malice. Be kind and compassionate to one another, forgiving each other, just as in Christ God forgave you.

— EPHESIANS 4:31-32

The March winds whipped across the lake, whitecaps cresting on the rolling water. It felt good. Right. Brent was eager to get settled. He had a week before starting his job at Edelweiss Schools, and varsity baseball season would soon begin. Contentment filled him as he thought about dinner with Tyler and Shade tonight. Being with them soothed his restless spirit.

Tyler's face beamed when he saw Brent sitting at the kitchen counter, watching Shade prepare dinner. He walked over and embraced him, slapping him on the back. "You're home. For good, right?"

"As far as I know. Hey, congratulations on the Texas Christian scholarship." Brent walked over and hugged Leah. "It's good to see you, Leah. How's your grandmother?"

"She's doing well."

"Tell her I said hello." Brent turned to Tyler. "Why don't you show me your new Jeep, then we can talk about the scholarship?"

Leah went into the kitchen to help Shade. "I'm so glad Brent is back," she said, as Shade tossed the salad. "Tyler idolizes him. Can I do anything?"

"You can set the table. And yes, Tyler adores Brent. They've remained so close all these years. I'm happy he's home."

"They're good together," said Leah, returning to the kitchen. "And you did a great job raising Tyler alone, without a father. I often think about the struggles you've gone through. You must have been terrified when you got pregnant at such a young age. With no parents and no real home."

Shade thought back on her dysfunctional life, comfortable talking to Leah. "Yes, I was scared. But God has always been with me."

Leah smiled. "Tyler is a special person. His life wasn't typical, yet he's more grounded than so many others. I attribute that to you." Leah wrapped her arm around Shade's waist and leaned into her. "Thank you for raising such a remarkable man."

"Hey, where are you two," said Tyler. "We're starving."

After dinner, and a lengthy discussion about college baseball and the upcoming varsity season, Tyler drove Leah home. Brent helped Shade with the dishes before grabbing his coat.

"Can you stay awhile?" asked Shade.

"Sure." He put his coat aside.

She sat next to Brent on the sofa. "I need your opinion," she said, biting her lower lip and staring at her clasped hands. "I met my birth mother. She'd been showing up here and there for the last several years, watching me. Last week, she approached me during Tyler's practice and wanted to go for coffee. Then she told me. I stared at her in disbelief and walked out. I feel bad about the way I reacted, but she caught me off guard."

Brent's brow furrowed, as he drew in his breath. "Wow. Did you tell Tyler?"

"No. But he knows her. She's talked to him before, and they seem to get along. Part of me wants to know more about her—and about me—but part of me wants to let it go."

"It must have been hard for her—confronting you. It might be good for you to know more about your past. Maybe it would help with the things you struggle with."

"But the things I struggle with aren't connected to her."

He studied her face. "How do you know? Maybe you don't think they are, but the past always touches our lives in some way. And it would be good for Tyler to know his great-grandmother."

"But how can I forgive someone who deserted me? When I was pregnant, she was living with her wealthy husband. Why didn't she come for me?"

Brent put his glass down and stroked her hair. "I don't know, Shade. I don't know why people do the things they do. Until you walk in their shoes, you'll never understand. Haven't you ever done something terrible to someone and wanted his or her forgiveness? I know I have. I wouldn't be sitting here now if you hadn't forgiven me—that night. And I wouldn't have been here for Tyler. Everything would have changed."

She let out a long sigh. "I have," she said, her voice thick with guilt. "I'm being selfish, I guess. I don't understand her reasons, but I should be more forgiving. Thanks for listening, Brent. I feel like I can tell you anything and you'll give good advice. I'm so happy you're home."

He half smiled. "You should talk to her, when you're not so emotional, before writing her off. It might help you."

"I will. So, about the scholarship offer, do you think he should accept?"

"I do. If he gets drafted in June, he can turn it down. But this way he'll have a backup plan."

"I agree. I'll make sure we contact the university."

"Well, I'd better go. You have to work in the morning. Tell Tyler I'll be at school tomorrow if he wants to talk about TCU. I'm meeting with the superintendent. Thanks for another great dinner."

She walked him to the door and embraced him. He returned her embrace and pulled away.

Sleep was evasive. A meeting with Gary in the morning. Shade swept into his consciousness. He slammed the door. She crept back in. Still beautiful, and he was still captivated. But he felt more in control. They were friends. Nothing more. He thought about her comment—that she could tell him anything—except the one thing he wanted to know.

The ringing phone beckoned as she came through the front door lugging groceries. She raced to answer it, bags bulking before her. She'd not seen the orb—a lone baseball, skulking beyond the couch. Lurking. Her front foot rode the ball like a roller skate, forcing her into an undoable version of the splits. Groceries exploded across the floor.

She crawled to the phone, winded. "Hello?"

"Hey, it's Victoria. Were you out running?"

"No. I'm exercising. Trying out for cheerleading," she panted.

"Funny. Maybe I'll join you. Tyler and Cody would be so proud."

"Hey, I was thinking about you today. We haven't gotten together in ages."

"Well, perfect timing. I'm calling to see if you're available a week from Saturday. And also, if Shady Lane's could cater a women's benefit luncheon I'm hosting to raise money for Doctors Without Borders. If you can make it, you'll meet the snooty society women I hang with."

"I'd love to come. And yes, we can cater the event."

"Great. I'll come to the bakery tomorrow to discuss the menu."

Shade pulled herself onto the couch and assessed the damage. She might be bow-legged tomorrow, but she'd be okay.

The wrought-iron gate screamed at the hinges as Shade traversed the long asphalt entrance to Victoria's stately home. As many times as she'd been here, she was continually struck by the grandeur of the property. She thought about Victoria's life. How much it had changed. It brought a smile to her face.

"Come in," said Victoria, embracing Shade. "I can't wait for you to meet my friends. Liz and Ellen arrived an hour ago to set up the food. Everything looks delicious. Where's Sally?"

"She's on maternity leave. She had a baby girl yesterday."

"How exciting." Victoria escorted Shade into the spacious living room. A waitress balancing a tray of champagne flutes greeted them. Victoria grabbed two glasses, handing one to Shade.

"Penelope. Meet my dear friend, Shade Lane. She owns Shady Lane's bakery in downtown Edelweiss."

"Oh, it's good to meet you, dah-ling. I go there often. Charming little place," said Penelope, as she took Shade's hand. Her bauble-encrusted fingers felt dead in Shade's firm grasp.

Victoria placed her arm around Shade's waist, whispering as they walked away. "Penelope. Loaded. Just had a face-lift. Her face is stretched so tight her eyebrows became part of her hairline. Oh, there's someone else I want you to meet. Now, don't get confused.

These are not statues on loan from Madame Tussauds' wax museum. These are living people."

Shade's heartbeat bellowed in her ears, as they neared a small group of women, standing in a circle, engaged in conversation.

"Everyone, this is my dear friend, Shade Lane. Shade, this is Kitty, Aurora and Amanda."

"It's good to see you again, Shade," said Amanda, smiling bright.

"It's good to see you, too," Shade stammered.

"Do you know each other?" asked Victoria.

"Yes," said Amanda. "From the bakery."

"That's wonderful," said Victoria. "Shade, I'm going to greet the other guests. I'll seat you two at the same table."

Kitty and Aurora left, leaving Shade alone with Amanda.

"Amanda, I want to apologize for my behavior the other day," said Shade. "It was such a shock. I've been thinking about calling you. When the time felt right."

Amanda smiled, her face lit with delight. "I'm pleased to hear that. There were so many times I wanted to approach you, but I was terrified of being rejected. I decided it was time."

"I'm glad we met. You used to come to the bakery a while ago, but then you stopped. Why?"

"I was diagnosed with breast cancer. It was a long journey, but things are better."

"I'm glad to hear that. Was your husband living then?"

"No. It was hard—being alone. But I'm close to Vince's sister. I couldn't have gotten through it without her."

Shade smiled, her thoughts whirling—sand in a tornado. "There are so many things I've wondered about. Unanswered questions."

"Ask me anything. I want to be open. I owe it to you."

"My dad," said Shade, stopping for a moment. "What was he like?"

Amanda drew in her breath. "I don't know who your father

was. I was fifteen and looking for an escape from my miserable life. I thought if I got pregnant, the father of my baby would take me away, and we'd live happily ever after. So, I slept with anyone who appeared interested—and," her face morphed into sadness, "I gained a reputation as the town whore. When I found myself with child, none of my suitors laid claim to the baby." She stopped completely, eyes cast down. She held her breath at length.

Shade studied her. "I'm sorry you had an unfortunate start in life," she said, taking her hand. "As did I. But it looks like we overcame our obstacles."

"Yes," she said, dabbing her eyes. "I'd like to know more about you and Tyler."

It was slow at first, like stepping onto a thinning lake in early spring. But then the words flowed. They spent the afternoon talking, like two long-lost friends. She told Amanda about her work in the prison ministry, the bakery and Tyler's dream of becoming a professional baseball player.

"So, you never married again," said Amanda. "You're a beautiful woman. You must have met men who were interested."

"After I gained custody of Tyler, I decided it would be best if I remained single. I wanted nothing to interfere in our relationship. My focus has always been on him."

"You've raised a fine boy, and you've done well for yourself." She looked away. Shade caught the shine of tears glazing her eyes. "Shade, I'm sorry I wasn't there for you. But I look at you now and think you were better off without me."

Shade exhaled sharply. "Maybe so. Life is perplexing. I struggle with this all the time. The *ifs* and *thens*. If Adeline would have lived, how would Tyler have turned out? I don't know the answer. I just know I'm blessed."

"Would you be open to talking every now and then? But, I'll understand if you don't," said Amanda.

"I'd like that. When I asked you not to show up at the bakery, or at Tyler's games, I was wrong. You're welcome anytime."

"There's a lot of food left over," said Victoria, after the guests had left. "Most of these ladies exist on the Parakeet Diet. Bird seed and water."

Shade laughed. "Let's donate the leftovers to the food pantry."

"Perfect. Hey, how well do you know Amanda?" asked Victoria.

"You will not believe this. Maybe we should sit."

"Waiter," Victoria called out, snapping her fingers. "We'll have two champagnes, please. I have a feeling I'll need a drink by the look on your face."

"Amanda is my birth mother."

"What the...," said Victoria, her eyebrows heading north.

Shade revealed the details of their complicated lives. "She seems like a nice woman."

"Well, you come from good stock," said Victoria, swigging champagne. "Amanda is well-respected in this circle. Not only is she rich, but she's also kind. Unlike the other posh princesses. Wow. I can't believe it," she said, shaking her head. "I'm blown away."

"Hey, I gotta run. Thanks for the lovely afternoon," said Shade, embracing Victoria. "I'd appreciate it if you didn't mention this to anyone. Not until I tell Tyler."

"My lips are zipped. Hey, are you limping?"

"Yeah, a little. Cheerleading practice."

"Oh, right."

The angry wheels of the shopping cart had minds of their own as she tried steering the disobedient basket down the produce aisle.

"Hey, lady. Watch where you're going," said the familiar voice, her cart slamming into Brent's. "You look like you're in another world."

"Oh, Brent," Shade said, her eyes widening. "You'll never guess what happened. I went to a luncheon at Victoria's, and Amanda was there. We had a long talk."

"Whoa. That must have been a surprise. How do you feel?"

"Relieved. I told her to come to Tyler's games anytime. I'd like you to meet her."

"I'd love to meet her, and I'm glad you talked. Hey, I just left varsity practice. Tyler keeps getting better. This should be a good season for him."

"I hope so. He works so hard. And he wants this so badly."

"I was going to call you tonight, but now I can ask you in person. I've been invited to Kyle's wedding. It's in two weeks. I was wondering if you'd be my date. No strings attached."

"I'd love to. It sounds like fun."

The bleachers spilled over with enthusiastic fans on opening day of varsity baseball. Brent spotted several MLB scouts, radar guns locked and loaded, ready to shoot. He pulled Tyler aside before the game.

"Remember what we talked about. Power, command, control and confidence. If you throw a bad pitch, move on. Focus on the next pitch. And make sure you demonstrate your athleticism. Keep an eye on the base runners, not just the batters. Show the scouts the whole package."

"Got it." Tyler sat trancelike, fingering the ball, foot rapidly tapping the ground.

"You nervous?"

"No. I'm excited to show them my stuff."

Shade pushed her sweater over to save seats for Leah, Mary and Amanda. She was glad Amanda could come. And Tyler was thrilled to discover he had another blood relative.

Before the game, Shade took Amanda to the dugout. "Brent, I'd like you to meet Amanda."

Amanda reached both of her hands and clasped Brent's outstretched palm. "I've heard so much about you, Brent. It's nice meeting you."

"I've heard a lot about you, too," said Brent, smiling. He was struck by the startling resemblance she bore to Shade. Her smile. Her eyes. "I hope you enjoy the game."

The Edelweiss crowd was on their feet when Tyler struck out the last batter. A no-hitter. He threw seven complete innings, striking out ten and walking one. The final score was 5-0. Brent spotted two scouts heading toward the field.

"Impressive," said one scout. "We clocked his fastest pitch at ninety-three miles per hour. When does Tyler pitch next?"

"In two weeks," said Kyle. "He has practice tomorrow if you wanna come out."

"Thanks. We'll do that." He turned to Brent. "I see you're listed as Tyler's representative on the scouting report. Here's my card. Let's keep in touch."

Brent took the card. "There's been a lot of interest in him."

"Yes, we've heard. We're keeping an eye on him."

CHAPTER THIRTY-ONE

There are three things that are too amazing for me, four that I do not understand: the way of an eagle in the sky, the way of a snake on a rock, the way of a ship on the high seas, and the way of a man with a young woman.

— PROVERBS 30:18-19

The dressing room brimmed with cocktail dresses as the sales associate brought in one gown after another. Shade wanted something elegant, but simple.

Since he returned home, their relationship had transformed into something more comfortable. Good friends. If he had feelings, he kept them to himself. And she felt grateful.

"Oh, I like that one," said Shade, stepping into the satin crepe dress. The figure hugging, knee-length navy garment had a plunging cowl neckline with cap sleeves and organza covered buttons running down the back. "It's so classy. And timeless."

"It looks gorgeous on you," said the sales clerk, admiring her silhouette. "I wish I had your figure."

"Thank you," said Shade, blushing. "Do you think it's too revealing on top?"

"Not at all. It's not like your spilling out. It's just enough."

"What color shoes?"

"I'd go with silver or nude." The sales clerk returned carrying a pair of silver Jimmy Choo stilettos with glittery fabric straps crisscrossing over the toes.

"I love these," said Shade, stepping into them. "I look so tall. And they're comfortable. You've been so helpful."

The doorbell rang. "I'll get it," said Tyler, springing off the couch. "Wow, Brent. You look like James Bond."

He laughed. "How was practice today?"

"Good. The scouts were there again."

"Did they talk to you?"

"No, just sat and watched."

Shade emerged from the bedroom, her eyes fastened on Brent. He looked like a GQ model in his tailored, midnight-blue suit, stark white shirt, and silk navy tie. "Brent, I've never seen you in a suit. You look handsome," she said, smiling demurely.

"Thank you. Try to keep your hands off me tonight," he teased, his breath seizing at the sight of her. "You look good, too." He lied. She didn't look good. She looked gorgeous. He was second-guessing his decision to bring her. He walked over and gave her a hug, the sweet smell of jasmine piercing his core.

She drew back, her hand lingering on his shoulder. His eyes held her captive. "Well," she stammered. "Should we get going?"

"You two make a nice couple," said Tyler. "Color coordinated. Did you go shopping together?"

They laughed, recognizing for the first time the similarity.

"I think you're enamored with each other," said Tyler, grinning. "Do either of you need ice water?"

"Let's get out of here," said Brent. "No telling what he'll say next."

Brent held the car door open for Shade. He placed his hand on her back, guiding her along the curved walkway of the old mansion.

"Wait. Brent," she said, grabbing his arm, struggling to step forward. "My heel is caught."

Her stiletto had jammed in a metal grate. He bent, while she braced herself on his shoulders. He grabbed her ankle with one hand as he tried freeing her heel with the other.

The sensation of his palm on her bare skin sent electric jolts through her body.

"I may have to pull up hard. I hope I don't ruin your shoe."

"But these are Jimmy Choos. Please be careful."

"You got these from a guy?"

"It's a brand," said Shade, seized by the hilarity of the moment. Laughter gripped her.

"What's so funny?" he asked, looking up and laughing with her.

"How we must look," she managed to say. She dabbed her eyes with a tissue. "I'm sorry. I don't get out much."

He continued to struggle, amused by her behavior. "I think I got it," he said standing up and brushing off his pants. "Your shoes look great, but they don't look comfortable."

"Oh, Brent. It's better to look good than to feel good."

He laughed. "Your mascara is running. Try not to make a grand entrance."

The reception took place in a historic mansion, set on a bluff overlooking Lake Michigan. Swarovski crystal chandeliers dangled from spectacular domed ceilings, light dancing across dark hardwood floors.

"Do you think you could handle a glass of wine?" he asked.

He returned with two glasses of red and took her hand, leading her out the French doors and onto the stone patio.

"What a view," sighed Brent, as they gazed out, sipping their wine.

"Hey, Brent," said Gary Murrell. "Good to see you. Meet my wife, Leslie."

"Nice to meet you, and this is Shade Lane."

"Are you Tyler Lane's mother?" asked Gary.

"I'm his grandmother," Shade replied.

"Oh," said Gary, his eyebrows elevating. "Tyler is a good kid. He's making quite an impact. We're proud of him. Well, we'll see you inside. Looks like we're seated at the same table."

Brent and Shade lingered on the patio, taking in the scenery. "Are you cold?" he asked.

"A little, but it's so beautiful here."

He removed his jacket and put it around her shoulders. Their eyes met. He looked away and reached for his wineglass. "How are things with you and Amanda?"

"Good. We talk, but it feels like a forced union of sorts. Like she's trying too hard—trying to make up for lost years."

"Give it time. I was taken by the resemblance between you two. Even some of your mannerisms—the way she smiles and talks."

She looked off, pulling his jacket tighter, breathing in his cologne. "Tyler likes her, and I'm happy about that. I'm sure things will get easier. I just need to let down my guard."

"Yeah, you do," he asserted.

She struck a question mark pose. "That sounded like judgment."

He sighed. "You keep people out—so they don't get too close." His eyes cast into hers, unwavering.

She gazed down, caressing the stem of her wineglass. "Hey, do you want to head back inside? My toes are freezing."

They took their seats at the table, Gary and Leslie next to them. Brent and Gary talked sports, while Leslie and Shade talked about kids, recipes, and shopping.

Brent leaned over and whispered, his lips brushing her hair. "Are you doing okay? I hope I didn't offend you earlier."

Her emotions felt like heat billowing off a campfire. Stoked. She smiled. "No offense taken. You're right about what you said. I tend to build walls—with no doors in them. I'm working on that."

Brent drew his hand along her arm. "Maybe meeting Amanda will help."

The wine flowed, as servers distributed plated dishes of filet mignon in a burgundy wine sauce, whipped potatoes with chives, and green beans almondine. She needed food. The wine was affecting her.

She leaned into Brent with her hand on his arm. "I'm happy you moved back home. I missed you." Her body relaxed, drawn into his gaze. "Why are you looking at me like that?" she asked.

"I missed you, too," he said, placing his hand over hers.

"Excuse me sir," said the waiter, placing their meals in front of them. He continued attending the other guests at their table. As he served a woman seated across from them, the waiter's mouth fell open, a yelp escaping. His watch had snagged her bouffant updo, dragging her hairpiece and shifting it off her head. The thatch of hair looked like a dead cat dangling from the waiter's wrist.

Shade gasped, and turned her face into Brent's chest, trying to suppress her laughter. Her shoulders quivered. He tried covering her quaking by pulling her into him, his hand bracing her head.

When she gathered herself, she looked up and whispered, "Is everyone staring at me?"

"No," Brent murmured. "You can come up now. They're watching the waiter arranging the woman's hairpiece on her head."

She let out a guttural cry, standing abruptly and leaving the table.

"Excuse me," said Brent to Gary and Leslie. "I'll be right back."

He found her in the lobby, bent over with laughter, struggling to breathe. When she saw him, she grabbed his arm, her eyes like saucers.

"I'm so sorry," she blurted, dabbing her eyes, still wearing an exaggerated smile. "The more I tried to stop, the worse it got."

"You weren't alone," he said, amused by her behavior. "I could feel Leslie shaking beside me. Do you think you can control yourself so we can go back and eat?"

"I'll try," she said, still snickering.

They returned to the table to find Wig Lady digging into her filet, her adornment sitting askew atop her head. Shade and Brent slid into their seats, savoring their meal.

Gary held Brent's ear hostage, rambling on about work-related issues. Shade sensed Brent's disinterest, as he tried engaging her in conversation. But to no avail.

The band launched into a rendition of "Come Away With Me"—one of Shade's favorite songs.

"Oh, Brent," she said, interrupting their conversation. "Can we dance?"

"Please excuse me," he said to Gary. He got up and took her hand, leading her to the dance floor. "I thought you'd never ask," he whispered to her. He took her in his arms, his eyes locked on hers. "You okay?"

She smiled and nodded, hypnotized by the gentle pull of his eyes. She felt the strength of his hand against her back, his other hand cupping hers between them. His fingers curled around hers. The warmth of his breath collected on her face. She drank in the moment, feeling small and safe in his arms. She leaned her head on his shoulder, melting away into a fuzzy security—falling deeper into him—their bodies moving to the slow rhythm. She didn't want this moment to end. *If you only knew how much I love you.*

"This reminds me of Hawaii," he whispered in her ear, his hair tickling her face. "Our first dance."

"When you saved me from Wayne, the Lady's Man. It seems so long ago."

He pulled back, gazing. "You look beautiful tonight. I'm glad you came, despite your antics." He drew her close.

She smiled, settling her head on his shoulder, his lips caressing her hair.

"Shade," he whispered. "Will you ever trust me enough to share what haunts you?"

She held her breath before answering, then sighed. "Yes. One day. I will."

He inhaled deep. He wondered what it would mean for them, if anything. They continued to dance, molded into one another.

The conversation was easy and good-humored during the ride home. They climbed the steps to the cottage and turned, facing one another.

"Thanks for coming tonight," said Brent, his hands on her arms. "It felt nice. Being with you."

"Would you like to come in?"

"No, but thank you." He grew serious, measuring her. "I need to ask you something. When you open up—about your past—will that change anything between us?"

She stared into the darkness before looking at him. "Brent, nothing will change between us," she said, tears blurring her eyes. "One day you'll understand."

His arms fell limp to his side. He drew his fingers through his hair. "When I told you there were no strings attached tonight, I meant it. I've tried pushing my feelings aside, but I can't seem to let go of you. We can go back to the way things were. To the reason I came back—for Tyler. But there is one thing I know, and you will never convince me otherwise." He held her face in his hands. "I know you have feelings for me. The same feelings I have for you. I see it in your eyes. The way you look at me. The way we embrace. But I wish I understood what torments you."

She looked down—tears pooling—shame etched on her face. He leaned and kissed her forehead. She remained silent.

"I'll see you tomorrow at Tyler's game. And thanks for tonight. I had a wonderful time," he said, taking her into his arms and holding her tight, not wanting to let go.

She clung to him, buried in his sorrow. There were so many things she wanted to say, but couldn't. It wasn't time.

He poured a liberal glass of bourbon before dropping heavily onto the sofa. Defeated. There was an aching hollowness. Four years he'd tried to shed her and it was ramping up again. She was everything he wanted in a woman. And tonight, he fell back down the rabbit hole. He knew he would never find love again. Not like this. What was it that so demoralized her—burying all her shame in a box and locking it away? She said he would understand, but would he? It was time to move on. Again. The curtain closing on the final act.

He drained his glass and poured another. Staring into the amber liquid, he tossed the contents into the sink. Tyler. His reason for being here. Things happen and life goes on. He made it through the dark times of losing Kendra and Luke. And he would get through this.

She sat on the edge of her bed, leaning over and unbuckling the straps of her shoes. Tyler was sleeping. Good. She didn't want to answer questions about their evening. When she told him she was going to Kyle's wedding with Brent, his face lit up with excitement. He still yearned for them to be together.

A river ran freely down her cheeks. His love was painted across her heart, but she had no claim to him—her purpose rooted elsewhere. *Dear God, if only things could be different. So we could be together. I've never felt love like this. This endless craving for something that can never be. Like handcuffed lovers. My desire is to stay strong. Focused. Until it's time. But I'm crumbling. My thoughts are upside-down. Help me, dear Lord.*

She replayed the tender moments of their evening together. Secure in his arms, drinking him in. Mascara stained her pillow before sleep took hold.

CHAPTER THIRTY-TWO

Have I not commanded you? Be strong and courageous. Do not be afraid; do not be discouraged, for the Lord your God will be with you wherever you go.

— JOSHUA 1:9

Year 2012

The name 'Tyler Lane' was on everyone's tongue in the small town of Edelweiss. Based on his scouting report, and news of his acceptance into Texas Christian University, Baseball Times placed him on their Top 100 list of high school prospects. His pitching starts drew the largest crowds, and the number of scouts watching continued to swell.

Brent invested most of his free time in Tyler. He knew what the scouts wanted, and he made sure Tyler delivered on every level.

"I need to talk to you," said Tyler, as they were walking off the practice field.

"Why don't you come to my place?" said Brent. "I'll grill some burgers."

"Do you think you'll get another dog?" Tyler asked, as Brent fired up the grill.

"Yeah, I do. It gets pretty lonely around here."

"I wanted another dog, but Grandma said it wasn't a good idea. I thought it would keep her company after I'm gone, but she told me not to worry," he said, smearing mustard and ketchup on his bun. "So, did you two have a good time at Kyle's wedding?"

"Yes, we did. Your grandmother was in rare form that night."

Tyler smiled, scarfing down his second burger. "Anything going on between you two?" he asked, tossing a wink.

"Is that what you wanted to talk about?"

"Well, kinda. I wanna talk about me moving away. And about Leah and my grandma. I worry about Grandma. She never talks about her future. Only mine. Do you ever think about you two—you know—being more than just star-crossed lovers?"

Brent laughed. "Didn't we have this conversation in Arizona? Nothing has changed."

Tyler let out a long sigh. "I'll keep praying. The other day she asked if I would be upset if she turned over the bakery to Sally when she retires. I told her Sally deserves it. And I know I'll be okay money-wise. But I wondered why she brought it up. She's too young to retire."

Brent paused, considering Shade's comment. "Maybe she wanted to see how you felt. It doesn't mean it'll happen right now, but that's generous of her to think about Sally."

"Grandma is always generous. Every month she donates money to Mabel's House—for unwed mothers. She's done that for years, along with tithing at our church. And she started a college fund for Ethan. You know, Meghan's son from the prison. And those are only the things I know about."

"I didn't realize she was so giving."

"That doesn't surprise me. She said we shouldn't boast about what we give. Everything she has is a gift from God. And that we should always love forward. That's what I plan to do when I rake in the big bucks."

"That's noble of you. I'm glad to hear you'll be following in her footsteps. She's a remarkable lady. Now, let's discuss Leah."

"Leah—oh, how I love thee," he opined, mimicking a Shakespearean actor. "So, I know I wanna marry her, but not sure when. Do I propose before going off to wherever I go off to? She got accepted at Michigan State, so we'll be apart. I'm confused, so I thought I'd ask you."

"Well, I think you should wait. You're both young, and you haven't dated anyone else. Being apart may be a good thing. It'll either make your heart grow fonder, or you may decide she's not the right one for you. Regardless, why rush it?"

"I guess I've waited this long. What's another four years. Right? Do you think twenty-one is too old to be a virgin?"

Brent laughed. "It depends on who you ask, but I don't think there's an age limit. Marriage is a big step. It's not something to take lightly."

"Thanks, Dr. Meyers. It's been good talking this through. How much do I owe you?"

Brent shook his head. "Let's talk baseball. These scouts hanging around will want to know more about you than what you can do on the field. Don't be surprised if you find out they're asking people about your temperament. We've talked about this before, but I'm just reminding you. It'll likely happen the closer we get to the draft in June. Just food for thought."

"Got it, coach."

Fan attendance continued to swell. More people followed Edelweiss High varsity baseball than any other year on record. Tyler was at the top of his game the entire season, posting a 12-0 record, with an ERA of 0.80, and 125 strikeouts in 60 innings pitched. At Tyler's last two starts, there were close to twenty MLB scouts and executives at each game. His fastball was now sitting at ninety-five mph, at times reaching ninety-eight.

"Chances are high Tyler will be drafted in June," said Brent, as he sat with Tyler and Shade to discuss strategy. "One scout told me Tyler has one of the best high school arms he's seen. With his blue-chip velocity, I doubt he'll be passed over. We need to be prepared. I heard scouts have been talking to your acquaintances and teachers."

"Yeah," Tyler replied. "Quite a few."

"If anyone asks about your plans after school, tell them you're leaning towards signing and foregoing college."

"Is that a good move?" asked Shade.

"Yes. They're interested in his signability. They don't always like to wait until a prospect finishes college. They want them now, if they're mature enough. If they feel he'll sign out of high school his stock rises, and he'll have a better chance of getting drafted in the first round. And first round drafts usually get bigger signing bonuses. The way Tyler's pitches have been lighting up the scout's radar guns should give us more bargaining leverage."

"How do ball clubs know what I'm looking for? And what am I looking for?" asked Tyler, dizzied by all the talk.

"You're looking for a seven-figure signing bonus and a clause stating college would be paid for if your baseball career ends within a designated number of years. We'll work through the details, but that's what I'm thinking."

"Seven figures? Is that reasonable?" asked Shade.

"I've been doing research. If they're as interested as they seem, seven figures is not out of the question. There's a lot of talk surrounding Tyler, and I've seen the scouting reports. They're all positive. Some clubs have already reached out."

"If I get drafted, when would I join the ball club?"

"You'll have until mid-July to sign the contract. Once you sign, your life will change. They may want you to move right away."

Stark concern etched Tyler's face. "You'll be alone, Grandma."

Her eyes held back a glassy layer of tears. "Tyler, don't worry about me. This is what you've worked so hard for," she said, reaching over to take his hand. "I'll be okay."

"I'll have to talk to Leah," he said. "We'll be away from each other."

"Tyler, dreams don't come without sacrifices," Brent said, pragmatically. "No matter where you settle, and who you settle with, you'll spend most of your time away, on the road. You'll never be completely at home. That's the reality of the career you've chosen. Make sure it's something you want."

"I want it. Bad," said Tyler, with conviction.

On the first day of the televised draft, Brent and Leah came over to watch the proceedings. They sat huddled on the sofa, anticipation vibrating off of each other. Brent felt certain Tyler would be taken during the first round. And he was.

When Tyler Lane's name was read, excitement poured like water gushing from a broken levee. He was chosen seventh overall. A titanic smile took Tyler's face. They were yelling. Hugging. Crying. Tyler was on his way, a dream realized. Prayers answered.

The official confirmation came when the ringing phone rattled above the celebratory ruckus. Tyler took the call, adrenaline coursing through his body, hands trembling, eyes wide.

"Thank you, sir. I couldn't be happier. Tomorrow morning at ten? Sounds good."

"A representative is coming over tomorrow to go over the contract," said Tyler, sinking into the sofa, dazed.

"Brent, can you be here tomorrow?" Shade asked.

"Absolutely."

Brent negotiated a higher signing bonus that was initially offered —$5.5 million—and the ball team jumped. Tyler was now the exclusive property of a major league franchise, and he couldn't be happier.

"Hey, Brent, we got him," said Buzz, on the other end of the line. "You negotiated a sweet contract, but we feel he's worth it. There was a lot of interest in him, so we were lucky to snag him. I hear he's moving to Arizona this week."

"Yeah. He's pretty pumped. I'll be driving out with him. It'll be good seeing you."

"How's the job in Michigan? We sure miss you around here. Do you think about coming back?"

"Thanks, but I'm tired of bouncing around. But, never say never. Right?"

Tyler spent his last evening in Michigan alone with Leah. She would soon head off to Michigan State University, and he would move to Mesa, Arizona.

"Leah, I'm gonna miss you, more than you know," he said, as they sat in the Jeep parked in her driveway.

"I'll miss you too, but this isn't forever, is it Tyler?" she asked, apprehensively.

"Leah, of course not. We'll be together one day, if you'll have me. You're the only one for me. I've known it since we were kids.

When I first laid eyes on you at the playground behind Holy Grace Baptist church."

She laughed, barely recalling their first meeting so long ago. "We were toddlers. I'm not sure if I remember, or my grandmother told me, but you planted a slobbery, open mouth kiss on my lips. That's when I knew we were destined to be together," she said.

They kissed and clung to one another before Tyler let go. "I love you, Leah. I'll always love you. I'll call when I get settled."

"I love you, too. And remember, I'm flying out with my parents during spring break."

"How could I forget?"

"Grandma, we should do something special for Brent. For the time he's invested in me throughout my life. And he didn't even take a cut for negotiating my contract. I'm glad he agreed to be my agent, but I wanna do something for him now."

"I've been thinking the same thing. What about a Rolex watch? We could have it engraved."

"I don't know much about brands, but I like the watch idea. I remember him telling me about this certain brand. Phillip Nautilus. Or something like that. He said he's always wanted one but didn't want to spend that much on a watch."

Tyler and Shade studied the display of luxury watches glistening beneath the glass enclosure. "Hello. We're looking for a watch for a special person," Shade told the salesman.

"Do you carry something called a Phillip Nautilus?" asked Tyler.

"Ah. A Patek Philippe Nautilus. An exquisite choice. Follow

me," he said, inserting the key into the glass case and presenting the glimmering timepiece. "This is one of our finest watches."

"It's magnificent," said Shade.

When the salesman told them the price, Shade and Tyler's eyes froze wide, looking at each other in stunned disbelief.

"We're going to grab lunch and talk it over," Shade told the salesman.

During lunch, they reasoned Brent was deserving of the gift. After all he'd done for them both, it was a small price in comparison.

Shade flew out to Arizona. Brent and Tyler picked her up at the airport in the Jeep and drove to the apartment—Tyler's new home. The unit was small and sparsely furnished but near the stadium.

She took Tyler shopping for houseware items while Brent met with Buzz. They agreed to meet Brent at the stadium, then go out to dinner for their last night together.

"It's gonna feel lonely here," said Tyler, as Shade stood on a chair, hanging curtains.

Her stomach pitched, imagining Tyler alone in another state, still so young. She swallowed hard, trying to quell the swelling in her throat. She needed to be strong. "You won't have much time to think about it," she said, reassuringly. "And you'll make friends. It's a new start. It'll get easier as time passes."

After driving to the stadium, Brent gave them a tour. Shade could feel Tyler's anxiety give way to exhilaration, as he walked out onto the practice field and met the other players. Afterward, they enjoyed a celebratory dinner before returning to the apartment.

"Brent. We have something for you. From me and Grandma."

"Oh?" Brent responded in a weakened voice, taking the gift.

"We wanted to show our appreciation for everything you've done for us over the years," said Shade, as Brent unwrapped the package, revealing a box within.

Brent raised the sturdy top and removed a black lacquer case shrouded in felt. His eyebrows raised as he opened the lid. He removed the wristwatch and fingered the metal—the elegance and smoothness of the stainless-steel substantial in his hand. "This is too much," he said, in a low voice. He turned it over and read the inscription. 'In our hearts always—Shade & Tyler.'

"How did you know?" asked Brent, his eyes glistening. "It's stunning. And the engraving." He shook his head slowly. "I don't know what to say other than thank you."

"You told me once," Tyler responded. "You said you always wanted one."

They spent the next several hours talking—Brent repeatedly admiring his treasured gift.

"Now, you have your checkbook and an ATM card," said Shade. "Try to spend your money wisely, since the bulk of your bonus money has been invested."

"Got it, Grams. And I'm to call you when I'm broke."

"Yes," she smiled. "Well, we should get going," she said, choking back tears.

She took Tyler in her arms. They clung tightly to one another, afraid to let go.

"Oh, Grams, I'm gonna miss you so much. I love you and I promise to keep in touch."

"You'd better," said Shade, fighting to appear upbeat. "I'm so proud of you, Tyler. Not only for making it to the big leagues, but for who you are." She took his face in her hands. "Take care of yourself, honey. I love you so much. Too much, if that's possible."

Tyler walked over to Brent and threw his arms around him,

slapping him on the back. "Thank you, Brent. For everything. And take care of my grandmother."

"You know I will. I'm so happy for you. You made it, buddy," said Brent, cupping Tyler's face with his hand. "I always knew you would. Call me anytime. Whenever you need to talk. I love you, buddy."

"I love you, too, Brent," said Tyler, wiping a tear from his cheek.

As Brent pulled away from the apartment, a torrent burst from Shade's eyes, drowning her cheeks.

"Hey," said Brent, patting her thigh. "It's not like you'll never see him again. He's a phone call or a flight away."

She didn't speak. He could hear her muffled sobs as she looked out the side window, watching the world she knew fade away. Her body shuddered, as though she'd lost him forever. They drove back to the hotel in silence. He walked her to her room and tried consoling her.

"Our flight leaves early," said Brent. "Try to get some sleep."

She fell into his arms, sobbing, drained of all hope.

"Will you be all right?" he asked, taking her head in his hands. "He'll be fine, and he'll do well for himself."

She nodded and pushed her head into his chest, the strength of his arms around her, lost in his embrace. "I'll see you in the morning."

She remained subdued during the flight home, staring into nothing. Brent dropped her off at the cottage, as she climbed the steps, like a ghost in a dream. He carried her bags inside. She dropped onto the sofa and stared out the window in a catatonic state.

"Shade. What's going on? I'm worried about you," he said, sitting beside her and taking her hands. There was something in her eyes he had never seen before. A storm cloud brewing. A black hole.

She swallowed deep, pulling her hands away and clutching her chest. "I'm okay. You should go now."

He tried embracing her, but she was dead in his arms. He kissed her forehead, but she remained detached.

"I'll call you tomorrow to check on you. Do you want me to stay tonight? I could sleep in Tyler's room."

She shook her head, eyes set on blackness. Gloom.

Tyler's bed warmed her cold skin. She pulled his pillow into her face, breathing in his scent. She knew it would be hard, but she wasn't prepared for the depth of her agony.

The phone jolted her from sleep. "Hey, are you coming in?" asked Sally. "You said you'd be back today. I was worried."

"I'm sorry. I overslept. Can you handle it without me? I'm not feeling up to coming in."

"Sure. Did Tyler get settled in Arizona?"

The sound of his name made her jerk. "Yeah. Everything went well. He was so excited. Are you sure you're okay without me?"

"I'm fine. I'll call if I need anything."

When she hung up, Brent called. "Good Morning. Just checking to see if you're okay. Do you need anything?"

She could sense his concern. Hearing his voice brought her comfort. "I'm fine. I'm taking the day off. I can use the time to get things reorganized."

"It'll get easier. You're a strong woman, Shade. Time heals."

"I know. Thanks, Brent. For everything. We'll talk soon."

He didn't like the sound in her voice. Flat. Adrift. He wasn't expecting her to react this way. She'd been excited leading up to the days before Tyler moved. Supportive. But something broke. As though she had lost her purpose.

Shade sat at the kitchen counter, pulling together her thoughts, overwhelmed by the tasks ahead of her. She made a list on the yellow-lined notepad: Attorney, Amanda, bakery/Sally, Salvation Army, car, letter to Tyler, Brent.

She stared at the list. The time had come. She hung her head and prayed. *Heavenly Father. Thank you for the years you've given me. My heart bursts with thankfulness. Who am I that you've been so mindful of me? I cannot grasp the depth of your love. Always watching over me and Tyler. The people you've placed in my life. So much to be thankful for. And yet, will I ever feel clean? Forgiven? Or is this the cross I'll bear forever? Please walk with me as I close this chapter of my life. Thank you, Lord Jesus. Amen.*

CHAPTER THIRTY-THREE

My soul is weary with sorrow; strengthen me according to your word.

— PSALM 119:28

She sat across from her attorney, David Cunningham, laying out her wishes.

"So, you'd like to turn over your business to Sally McCallum, free and clear. Correct?"

"Yes. I'd also like to establish a fund to help her with operating expenses."

"Very well. I'll draft the necessary paperwork. The deed to the house will be placed in Tyler Lane's name, along with all bank accounts and financial portfolios." David removed his eyeglasses, studying her. "Can I ask, are you going somewhere?"

"Yes, and I want to be sure everything is taken care of before I leave. Thanks for your time today," said Shade, standing. "Please let me know when the documents are ready."

Amanda arrived at the restaurant clad in black linen slacks and a silk taupe sweater.

"I'm so glad you called. How is Tyler?"

"He's doing well. He's adjusted to his new life better than I expected. His coaches don't think he'll be in the Minors long. They're talking about moving him up to the Majors next year."

"That's wonderful," said Amanda, finishing her salad. "He's worked so hard. And how are you doing? Being alone?"

"Good," said Shade. Her face grew serious, staring down at her folded hands. "I want you to know how grateful I am we met, and I think you're a wonderful person. I've enjoyed our time together, learning more about you and my past. I wish we could have connected sooner, but it didn't work out that way."

Amanda sighed. "Well at least we have each other now. Shade, I don't think I'll ever get over the guilt of abandoning you. I'm so sorry."

"It's in the past. Things happen for a reason." Shade patted her hand. "About Tyler. Please remain involved in his life. The two of you get along so well, and aside from me, you're the only blood relative he has."

"Of course, I'll remain in Tyler's life. He's family, and such a wonderful, young man." She peered into Shade's eyes. "Is everything okay with you?"

"Yes. I just wanted you to know that Tyler needs you."

"And I need you both. I don't plan on disappearing again. You're stuck with me."

After a leisurely lunch, they embraced before parting. Tears slipped down Shade's face, thinking about lost opportunities. To have a relationship with her birth mother, something she always dreamed of. But it was too late.

"Sally, let's go to lunch today. Just the two of us. Why don't you wrap things up in the kitchen and let Liz take over?"

"I'd love that."

After finishing their meal, Shade pulled out a manila envelope and placed it on the table between them. "Remember when I talked about retiring?"

Sally's face paled. "But that won't be for a while. Right?"

"I've been doing a lot of thinking, and it's time for me. The bakery business has exceeded my expectations. But it's time for me to step aside and allow you to profit from something you've put your heart and soul into."

"Thank you Shade, but Chad and I are not in a position to buy the business. Things are still tight. As much as I'd love to take it over, it isn't an option."

"Bonnie left me this business when she died—free and clear. You've worked at the bakery longer than me. So, now I'm handing it over to you. Free and clear. I've set up a fund to handle operating expenses for six months. Everything is laid out in the paperwork," she said, sliding the envelope over to Sally. "You deserve this. I wouldn't have been successful without you."

"Shade," said Sally, choking on her words. "I…I don't know what to say. I'm stunned. Why are you doing this? And what about Tyler?"

"Tyler will be taken care of. He and I talked, and we agreed you should take over the business. This isn't something I've thought about lightly. It's the right thing to do. But, I want you to promise me something."

"Oh, Shade, anything," she said, wiping her eyes.

"There's a woman I meet with at the prison. Meghan Barnes. She'll be getting out in a few years. She'll have a hard time finding work. Promise me you'll give her a chance. Will you do that?"

"Of course. You've been so good to me over the years. More so than I could have ever imagined. And now this. It's too much. When do you plan to retire?"

"In two weeks. I want you and Chad to look over the paperwork," said Shade, patting the envelope. "If everything looks good, and this is what you want, go ahead and sign it."

"Two weeks? But what will you do now, with Tyler gone and no job to keep you busy?"

"I have plans," said Shade. "Don't worry about me."

The navy-blue dress dangled from the hanger. Kyle's wedding. Her time with Brent. She loved him still, and always would. Tears tumbled. She folded the dress and placed it in the box, along with her other belongings. The doorbell.

She wiped her eyes and opened the door, smiling. "Hi, Brent. Come in. What brings you this way?"

"Thought I'd come by and check on you. Everything okay?"

"Yes," she said, trying to manage the stray hairs that fell from her ponytail. Her heart burned like an insatiable fire. "Can I get you something? A glass of wine? Coffee?"

"Sure. How about a glass of wine?" he said, glancing around. His words seemed to echo off the walls. "It looks like you've been downsizing. Didn't you have more knickknacks on the tables? More pictures on the walls?"

"Yeah," she smiled, avoiding his eyes. "Just trying to get rid of the clutter." She handed him a glass. "Come. Let's sit."

He took the wine and studied her hard before taking a sip. "So, Chad told me you're retiring. Turning over the bakery to Sally."

"Yes. The timing is right," she stammered. "And it'll help them out. Hey, the watch looks good on you."

He smiled, admiring the cherished gift and running his fingers over the band. "I love the watch. You shouldn't have done that. It's the nicest present I've ever received. It means a lot to me. So, are you retiring so you can spend more time traveling? To visit Tyler?"

"There are things I need to do and now is a good time."

He wasn't buying. There was something she wasn't telling him. Dread crept in like an icy chill. He put his glass down and moved closer to her.

"Shade, what's going on? Something's not right. You turn over the bakery to Sally, the house looks empty—like you're moving. Hey, look at me. I'm worried about you."

She tried swallowing, her tongue stuck like Velcro to the roof of her mouth. She took a gulp of wine, trying to appear relaxed. "Please don't worry. We'll talk more another time, but not tonight."

His breathing deepened as he examined her face. He could see her hands trembling. He wanted to take her in his arms, to make her pain go away. "When? When will we talk?"

"Soon. Please, be patient with me. Okay?"

"I've been patient. For over ten years." He sighed heavily. "Does Tyler know about the bakery?"

"He knows I plan on turning it over to Sally, but he doesn't know when. Please don't say anything to him. He'll know soon."

His fingers stroked the side of her head as he searched her eyes. "I don't know what soon means. Does it mean I'll find out after something has happened, or are we going to talk about it? You and I? Face to face?"

"Oh, Brent," she said, pain gripping her face, her eyes glassy. "I'm sorry for all of this. Everything I've put you through. I promise. We'll talk. In a few days. I'll call you. Okay?"

His eyes gripped hers. He didn't speak. He stood and walked into the kitchen, placing his glass in the sink. The yellow-lined notepad screamed out. 'To Do.' He scrutinized the list and glanced at her, walking toward him.

"Well, I'll let you get back to whatever it was you were doing," he said.

His face bore an expression she couldn't make sense of. He loomed over her.

"Are you sure you don't wanna talk now?"

"Yes, I'm sure," she said, placing her glass on top of the notepad. "But soon."

She walked him to the door. He looked into her taunting blue eyes. He pulled her close, as though gripping wetness that was slipping away. She could sense the tension in his body. She held onto him, wrestling with her emotions. The hole in her heart growing deeper still.

"I won't do something stupid," she said, pulling away. "You'll see me in a few days."

He exhaled sharply and kissed her forehead before walking out the door.

The cardboard boxes were stacked in the foyer, filled with her clothes, shoes, jewelry, purses and anything Tyler had little use for. She loaded the boxes into her car and drove to the Salvation Army.

"Would you like a receipt, ma'am?" asked the attendant as he unloaded the trunk.

"No, thank you." She drove away, lost in reflection. Her recent lunch with Blanche and Mary. She would miss them. Two of her dearest friends, who'd been with her through so much—Stan's passing, Addy's murder, her transformation from a frightened, dependent woman. Two golden threads in her life's tapestry.

And her dinner with Victoria. So entertaining. Funny how she used to view her as the sandpaper person in her life, but now she felt a special kinship. Like sisters. A gift to the heart.

She pulled into the car dealership. "Hello. Would you be interested in buying my car?"

"Do you mean a trade-in?" asked the salesman.

"No. I don't need a car."

"It looks new," said the salesperson, walking around and examining the interior. "Low mileage. That's good. Let me talk to my manager."

The salesman returned with a fair price, and Shade accepted. "Do you think I can get a ride home?" she asked.

She sat staring at the computer screen, searching for words. It needed to be perfect, this letter to Tyler, but how God? How to put into words the immense love she had for him and why she did what she did. Who could ever understand such madness? She didn't understand herself.

Late into the night, she drafted one version after another. She settled. It was the best she could do. She penned the words to paper and neatly folded the letter, placing it into an envelope and sliding it into her overnight bag.

Her last night at home. She drifted through the cottage in a dreamy state, recalling the memories each room held. She stepped out onto the deck. The sky was dark. Moonless. Mesmerized, she stood listening to the sound of the drifting waves kissing the shore. The crisp air filled her lungs as she negotiated the wooden steps leading to the beach. Her bare toes dipped into the cool water as it moved over her skin like liquid potion. She loved this house. This lake. Her home. But it was temporary, like life itself. Tomorrow, her talk with Brent. He sounded worried when she'd called. It would be the hardest conversation of her life. A light mist fell. She tilted her face to the sky; the wind tossing her hair, tears diluted with rain.

She awoke in Tyler's bed. Reality struck. The day of reckoning. After washing and drying the sheets, she showered and put on her lone outfit—a pair of jeans, a black sweater and ballet flat shoes.

She walked through the house, checking and rechecking. Shut off the water, set the thermostat and clean out the refrigerator. She placed a change of underwear into her overnight bag, along with her Bible and photographs of Tyler and Brent. She lingered on a 5 x 7 snapshot taken of their fishing trip in Hawaii. Her lips brushed their faces, a trail of wetness dripping onto the glossy finish. She tucked the photos into her Bible.

Oh Father. Help me through my conversation with Brent. I love him so much I ache. I can't bear seeing him for the last time. But I know You are my strength and my shield. In You I will trust.

She knew this day would come—ever since that night fifteen years ago. The sweet surrender of her soul—sailing free. She laid her burden on the Lord.

The taxi idled out front. Picking up her bag, she glanced over her shoulder. Tears rained down. She locked the door and stepped into the cab.

CHAPTER THIRTY-FOUR

"Come now, let us settle the matter," says the Lord. "Though your sins are like scarlet, they shall be as white as snow; though they are red as crimson, they shall be like wool."

— ISAIAH 1:18

Brent stood inside the door and motioned her in, unsmiling, watching the cab pull away. "Where's your car?"

"I sold it," she said, avoiding his steel gaze.

He looked at the overnight bag. "Are you going somewhere?"

"It's time to talk."

His mind spun. A hamster in a wheel. He could sense something dire was about to be lobbed at him. "Let's sit. Do you want anything?"

"No," she said, settling onto the sofa. She sat perched, a small child in a corner, waiting for punishment, clammy hands clasped in her lap.

He faced her, a statue teetering on the edge of the chair. Waiting.

She tried swallowing, but her mouth was dry. Broken earth.

She heaved a sigh. "What I'm about to tell you, I—I've never shared with anyone else. Ever. Please don't say anything until I'm done," she said, running her tongue over her lips. "I—I need to get through this."

"Okay. I'm listening," he said.

She inhaled long, as though it would delay her having to speak. Her eyes cast down as she was about to peel away the layers of her shattered existence. "When I met Stan, I thought he was God's gift. A Christian man sent to rescue me from my sorry life. I was sixteen, and he was thirty-six when we married. He treated me well, but he owned me. I couldn't go anywhere alone. Wear make-up. Buy my own clothes. I totally depended on him. The way he wanted it. But, I idolized him, never forgetting how he gave me hope—for me and my newborn daughter. Addy was a good kid, until she turned fourteen. Then something snapped. She hung out with the wrong crowd. Used drugs. She left home at seventeen and moved in with Scott and got pregnant with Tyler. Other guys lived in the house, and they were all using and selling drugs. Addy got addicted to methamphetamine. When Tyler's father died in a drug accident, she hooked up with another guy. Jaime. After Stan passed away, I could do more things on my own, like spend time with Tyler. And I became concerned about his living conditions. I pleaded with Addy to let me take him until she got her life together, but she wouldn't budge. One day, we had an argument. And then she told me." She licked her lips, her mouth like baked desert clay.

Brent brought her a glass of water.

She took it, her hands shaking. She drank long and slow. Composing. "Stan began molesting Addy when she was a young teen." Her voice broke. She caught the sound of Brent's heavy sigh. "She never said a word, and I was too naive to notice. At first, I didn't believe her so I dug into his past and learned he had been incarcerated as a teen for molesting a neighbor girl. I found things on his computer. Pictures of young girls. Porn sites. I was sickened. Repulsed. Not only at him, but at myself. I tried to make things right with Addy, but she was falling deeper into drugs. One day, I was babysitting Tyler, and he kept talking about sleeping with Jaime. I thought he meant he was sleeping with the two of them, but he kept saying 'me and Jaime—man-to-man.'"

Brent raked his fingers through his hair. He could taste his breakfast in the back of his throat.

"When I confronted Addy, she told me I was crazy. She admitted they took naps but told me nothing was going on. I didn't believe her. I was obsessed, feeling as though it were happening again. I needed to save Tyler. I prayed for guidance, but God didn't answer. I was shattered. My faith was shattered. I spoke to Blanche's husband about getting custody of Tyler, but he told me it would be a long battle. I didn't have time." She hesitated. Quaking. "I would do anything to rescue Tyler. Anything."

Her shoulders slumped. Her throat bitter with bile, her shrine of guilt about to be laid bare. She put her head in her hands. Tears arrived in torrents, dripping between her fingers. Her breathing ragged, gasping.

Brent drew her into him. His arms shrouding her. He wanted her to stop. Trepidation raged in his gut.

She gathered herself and pulled away from him, staring ahead, toying with the tissue in her hand. Brick by brick, the wall came down. "Addy broke her arm," she said, as though reading a script. "She was supposed to stay overnight—in the hospital. She asked me to take Tyler. I waited until early morning—2:30. Tyler was sleeping. I loaded Stan's hunting rifle. He had taught me how to use it. I thought if Jaime was gone, Addy wouldn't be able to make it on her own. She would have to live with me. So, I drove the short distance to Addy's place. If Jaime was awake, I would leave. Turn back. But he was sleeping. I saw him through the screen door. On the sofa. Passed out. A drug pipe smoldering." She was trembling now. An Arctic wind had blown into the room. Into her soul.

"I raised the gun to shoot." She hung her head and sobbed. "Addy. Oh, Addy. Go back." Her eyes squeezed shut, her face engraved with pain. Minutes dragged before she found her voice again—a high-pitched voice. "She came out of nowhere and jumped in front of Jaime. She wasn't supposed to be there. The bullet hit her in the chest. Jaime woke up. I shot him twice. I went to her. She was gone. I picked up the shell casings. I threw them into a lake. I took a shower. I put the rifle back in the closet. I went to bed. I waited."

"Oh my God, Shade. You did what?" Brent spluttered. His breath was quick. His body was wax, melting into the sofa.

She sat numb, staring vacantly. All life had vanished from her eyes. Remnants of her tissue lay like confetti, shredded in her lap. "No one ever knew it was me," she whispered. "I took Tyler to the doctor. Later. There was no sign of sexual abuse."

She dropped her head in her hands and wept bitterly. "I tried to play God. I prayed for forgiveness. Please, take me back. I pleaded with Him. Just let me raise Tyler until he was on his own. Then I would turn myself in. And He listened. He answered my prayers. And He blessed me. So abundantly. More so than I could ever have hoped, and more than I deserved. And now I must fulfill my vow. Turn myself in." A penetrating anguish seized her, her body choked with heaving sobs.

Brent placed his forehead against the heels of his palms. His thoughts mincemeat. He walked to the kitchen and poured a glass of Scotch.

Silence lingered, the hum of the refrigerator filled the room. She stood slowly.

"Shade," he said warily. "I'm—I can't make sense of this. I need you to sit down. I have questions." He drained his glass. His face set like that of a man in denial. A man struggling with a story beyond understanding.

She sat, like a scolded child, her fists balled, resting on her knees. She didn't look at him.

"You shot them?" It was a clarifying question.

She nodded.

"And you left Tyler alone? A toddler. In the middle of the night."

"I was desperate. I had to fix everything. I didn't know what to do."

"How are you going to tell Tyler?"

"I wrote a letter. I was hoping you would give it to him."

"You're going to shatter his life in a letter? You can't be serious." He pushed his fingers through his hair.

"I—I can't look him in the face and tell him I murdered his mother and Jaime. I love him so much. I can't bear to see the horror in his eyes."

"What about the cottage? Did you sell it?"

"No. Everything's in Tyler's name," she stammered. "It's in the letter."

He exhaled sharply, looking around, as if he would find an answer somewhere. "How could you have done that? You couldn't have waited? Tried to get custody?"

She looked away. "I can't explain. I replay that night over and over in my head. It's as though it wasn't me in my body. I can't undo what I've done."

"Did you ever love me?"

She stared up at him, a look of shock. "I fell in love with you the day I met you, and I haven't stopped loving you since."

He sucked in his breath and ran his hand over his mouth and chin. "It all makes sense now. Why you never let me get close. Why there could never be a future for us."

He turned absently and walked out onto the deck. She was a murderer? The word bounced inside his brain. Murderer. Murderess. He leaned against the balcony rail, listening to the cold waves folding against his soul. What was it like that night? Her hopelessness. The fear and fury that drove her to do the unimaginable. He reflected on her faith. Her generosity. She sacrificed everything for Tyler. How could she be the same woman? The woman he loved but could never have.

He went inside, silently considering her.

Her face was shrouded in shame. "I'll call a cab. Will you give the letter to Tyler?"

"Put it on the counter by the phone."

She picked up the phone and held it to her ear, her back to him, overwhelming guilt sucking the life from her. She could hear footsteps behind her. So close. His breath on her. She froze. She felt his lean body pressed up against her, the tender touch of his hand on hers, taking the receiver and placing it in the cradle. He pushed her hair aside; the brush of his warm lips caressed her neck. Her breath caught. He turned her around, facing him.

"I'll drive you. But not today. Tomorrow. Be with me. Just one night. The way it should have always been."

She looked into his hungry eyes, his face distorted by her tears. "I love you, Brent. So, so much. But it'll make things more difficult. For us."

"Be with me." He cupped her face in his hands, searching her eyes before gently pulling her to him. Their mouths touched, long and needing. Lips, tongues, teeth. His kiss felt new. Different than before. As though he had found something that was lost. A hunger clawing to escape.

The world and all its anguish trickled away. Her body melting into his—every ounce of her flesh surrendering to him. Years of pent up passion unfurled. She ran her hands down his back, his buttocks, pulling him closer. His heart throbbed against her chest.

She knew the longing in his loins, as his grip tightened, crushing her body closer.

He took her hand and led her down the hall. Into his bedroom. She followed, without protest. He pulled her into his arms, his sapphire eyes devouring hers. "You're always on my mind, Shade. I'll never stop loving you."

Her skin felt electric. His lips brushed her eyelids. Her cheeks. His mouth eager on hers. He pulled her sweater over her head, tracing his fingers down her bare arms. Her body shuddered with anticipation. His eyes ingested her. He stared down at her unclothed body, his face desperate, his jaw clenched. She felt alive. Shameless.

"You're beautiful," he breathed, running his hands over her. Her hands moved underneath his shirt, fingers tracing his spine, the muscles in his back rippling at her touch. Unrestrained. He pulled her to his bed, their enslaved passion uncaged.

She had never known love like this. She felt complete, lying next to him, skin to skin, bound in each other's arms.

He lay facing her as she slept, her breathing steady. The moonlight crept through the window, bathing her silhouette in a soft glow. He studied her face. She looked peaceful. He thought about that night. Her murderous rage. Her infinite love for Tyler.

She awoke to his gaze. She reached over and stroked his face.

He pulled her hand to his mouth and kissed her palm. "Are you afraid?" he asked.

She paused. "I'm heartbroken I can't be with the two people I love most in the world. But, no, not afraid," she said, tracing his lips with her finger. "I feel like I've been holding my breath for fifteen years, and now I can finally breathe. And I'm thankful for the years of freedom I've had. And Tyler, his life turned out better than I had ever imagined."

He remained silent, taking her in.

"Brent. I'm so sorry for the hurt I've caused you. For leading you on. That night in Hawaii. I couldn't stop loving you, no matter how hard I tried."

His lips found hers. Gentle. Determined. He couldn't get enough of her. Her smell. The taste of her—bodies molded so perfectly together. He wanted to savor every moment.

She clung to him, as their spent bodies collapsed in contentment, her legs wrapped around his, her hands buried in his hair. He stared into her eyes, drawing in his breath. "I wish there were another way."

The sunlight poked through the window, signaling the dawn of an unwanted day. Their last together. She slept in his arms. He wondered how she could be so tranquil. She stirred and blinked up at him, kissing his mouth, her hands roaming his body, exploring every part of him. They languished in bed all morning, creating a mental scrapbook.

The hours ticked away, the inevitable drawing closer. "Can I make you breakfast?" she asked, reluctantly rising from bed.

"Sure," he said, quietly. He handed her one of his T-shirts. She slipped it over her head, as he swallowed in her raw beauty. Her hair tousled and falling loose over her shoulders. Her azure eyes captured his in gentle play.

"I've always dreamt about a day like this," she said. "Us. Together. Sleeping until noon. And then I make you breakfast. A happily married couple. Two halves of a whole." The lump in her throat swelled, as tears spilled from her eyes.

He pulled her to him, as he sat on the edge of the bed. She kissed the top of his head and held him tight.

"We'd better eat something," she said.

She prepared breakfast while he set up the coffee. The air thick with dread. She placed a plate before him at the table, then wrapped her arms around him from behind, nuzzling her face into his neck, nibbling his ear. He took her arm and pulled her onto his lap, pushing her hair from her face, holding her with his steel gaze.

"Shade, don't do this. We'll get married. Move to Arizona to be near Tyler."

"There's nothing I want more," she said, wetness seeping out the corners of her eyes. "I love you so much. My heart bleeds knowing we'll never be like this again. I'll never feel your skin against mine. Your arms wrapped around me. The warmth of your kiss. But, this is something I have to do."

She retreated to the bedroom and dressed. "I'm ready," she said, with resolve. He stood against the kitchen counter, taking her in. She walked into his space and put her head to his chest, his arms enclosing her.

The drive to the Emmet County police station was solemn. Neither spoke. His hand clutched hers as they drove. She stared at his profile, his jaw clenching, tears escaping his eyes. He parked the car and started to get out before she took his arm.

"I'm going in by myself. I don't want you to remember me that way."

"What if they won't take you?"

She smiled, struggling to stay strong. "Then I'll call you." She leaned into him and took his face in her hands, staring into his solid blue eyes. "I love you, Brent Meyers. There are no words to describe how much you mean to me. I'll love you until the day I die. But you—you need to move on. Find someone to share your life with. I wish it were me, but it's not how the story ends."

"I've tried moving on. Remember? It didn't work. You're in my soul, Shade. As long as you have breath in your body, I'll never stop loving you."

"I'm so sorry for everything," she said, stroking his hair.

He didn't answer. His suffering eyes searched her, wanting this nightmare to end.

"I know you'll watch over Tyler. Please tell him how sorry I am." She could no longer hold it, and a deluge of tears broke.

He pulled her to him; they kissed one last time. She turned away, and he grasped her arm.

"Wait. You don't have to do this. No one will know," he said, desperately.

A pained expression took her face. "God will know. It's my vow. I'm only as good as the promises I keep. I love you Brent. I always will."

She didn't look back. He watched her disappear into the police station. She was gone. Like chaff on a threshing floor, swept away by the wind. His heart would surely quit.

Shade found Kent, sitting at his desk. He smiled when he saw her standing outside his office.

"Come in. Good to see you, Shade. Sit down. Can I get you some coffee?"

"No, thank you."

"I'm sure you're wondering if I have any updates. Sadly, I have no news."

"Kent, I have something to tell you," she sighed. She breathed heavily, fighting to maintain control. "I came in to confess to the murders of Adeline Lane and Jaime Holder."

He set his coffee cup down and stared hard at her, smirking. "Ha." A strange jest. "Shade. You're joking, right?"

"I wouldn't joke about this, Kent. I'm sorry."

He studied her. "How?" He pushed his chair back. "Why? And why now?"

"I did it for Tyler. To save him from the life he was living. And now, because I've done all I can for him."

"I don't know what to...," he trailed. "Okay," he said pensively. "I need to ask you a few questions. How?"

"I shot them with my husband's hunting rifle," she said. "Addy wasn't supposed to be there. I shot her by accident."

"The shell casings?"

"I threw them in a small inland lake near the farmhouse."

"Where is the gun?"

"I sold it. When I moved. I can give you the man's name."

He shook his head slowly. "You stayed in contact with me. To throw me off?"

"No. I was anxious. Wanting to know if you were getting close. So, I could prepare for Tyler," she said, dampness consuming her face. "I'm so sorry, Kent. But I'm ready to accept the consequences."

"I think you should have a lawyer present."

"I don't want a lawyer. I don't want a trial. I want my due punishment."

The plane touched down at Phoenix Mesa Airport. Tyler stood at baggage claim. Brent embraced him, harder than usual.

"Hey," Tyler laughed. "Are you trying to break my ribs? It's good to see you."

"You, too, bud. Things going okay?"

"Yeah. I'm looking forward to working with you on my

contract. Have you talked to my grandma? I left her a few messages, but she hasn't called back."

"She's okay. I'll update you when we get back to your place tonight. We're headed to the stadium now, right?"

"Yeah. I can't wait to show you my new pitches. Buzz has invested a lot of time in me. You'll be surprised. Then we'll go to dinner and you can meet some of the other players. Sound okay with you?"

"Sounds good. Just looking forward to spending time with you."

The apartment looked the same when they arrived after dinner, small and empty. "You can take the bed, and I'll sleep on the couch," said Tyler, as Brent wheeled in his carry-on.

"Thanks, but you won't fit on the couch. I don't mind. How do you like living alone?"

"I'm never here. I hang out with the other players in my spare time."

Brent's stomach coiled, as he pulled the letter from his jacket pocket. "I have something for you. From your grandmother. Here. I'd like to leave you alone to read it. Do you mind if I take the Jeep? We can talk when I get back."

Tyler's attention became more acute. "Is she okay?"

"Let's talk when I get back."

Brent drove around Mesa and pulled into the local tavern. He ordered a beer and sat at the bar, staring blankly into the frothy head. Nausea gripped him as he pictured Tyler sitting alone, reading the letter. There was no easy way.

Half an hour later he stood outside, gathering himself before knocking on the apartment door. Tyler appeared, his eyes swollen and red. He dropped to the sofa without saying a word. Brent canvassed the small space strewn with broken dishes and overturned chairs.

"Do you feel like talking?" asked Brent.

Tyler reached for him, his body heaving with sobs. Brent held him close. He was reminded of the little boy he'd held so many times when his life seemed to be falling apart.

"I don't know what to say," said Tyler, choking on his words. "I wish she would have told me to my face."

"I haven't read your letter, but she told me everything about a week ago. I was too upset to come right away."

Tyler dropped his face in his hands. "She wrote in the letter how much she loved you. How she'd always wished we could all be together, but she had to pay for her mistakes."

Brent tried to push down the swell rising in his throat. "She loved you too much, Tyler. That was her undoing. To her, it was the only way."

"Have you seen her? Since she's been in?"

"Yes. She seems content." Brent breathed heavily. "I would have married her," he said looking down, his finger tracing his wristwatch. "I tried talking her out of turning herself in, but she made a promise to God, and she kept it. She has a strong faith. She's an extraordinary lady."

"So, how long will she be in?"

"Seven years. It was a lenient sentence. She didn't want a lawyer or a trial. The judge took into consideration her service in the community and the fact she has an otherwise spotless record. With good behavior, she could be out in five."

"God, I love her so much," Tyler said, sobbing and shaking his head. "She's everything to me. Why couldn't she have found another way?"

"I don't know. I'll never understand what drove her to do what she did. But she is so proud of you—of the man you became. Stay strong, Tyler. Live that life she wanted you to have."

Tears ran down Tyler's face. "What about you? Will you stay in Michigan? Buzz told me he wished you'd move back here. Take your old job."

"I can't. I need to stay close to her. To visit whenever I can. I'll never stop loving her."

"I'm glad you're staying. She needs you. Should I change my course? Maybe go to school in Michigan?"

"No. She wouldn't want that. She sacrificed her life for you so you could live your dream. Don't take that away from her."

They sat up until late evening, strengthening a bond that would never be broken. Two men—their lives skillfully interwoven by the finger of God.

Shade sat in the chapel of Emmet County Correctional, praising God for her many blessings. This was home now, here with so many women she had mentored over the years.

Fragments of guilt still nibbled. The anguish in Tyler's voice when they spoke. Jaime's mom. Brent, her soulmate. And Addy's fractured life.

She bowed her head and prayed for her soul. For freedom from the guilt that still lingered. *Dear God, if only I could feel free—washed clean.*

Meghan slipped into the pew next to her, clutching her hand. Shade turned and smiled. Addy's face smiled back at her. So pure. Almost angelic. She squinted, trying to focus.

"Are you all right?" whispered Meghan.

"Yes," replied Shade, her face ashen. "For a minute, you reminded me of my daughter," she said, squeezing her hand.

The tender hymn coursed through her veins. The words swirling in her head as voices echoed in perfect harmony, pulling her away—drifting into illuminating radiance. White silence crept in—the sound of heavenly snowflakes melting into her upturned face. The light of full knowledge rained down as the stain of bloodguilt fell away…

"My sin—oh, the bliss of this glorious thought,
My sin, not in part but the whole,
Is nailed to the cross, and I bear it no more,
Praise the Lord, praise the Lord, O my soul,
It is well, it is well with my soul!"

EPILOGUE

He has made everything beautiful in its time. He has also set eternity in the human heart; yet no one can fathom what God has done from beginning to end.

— ECCLESIASTES 3:11

Year 2018

God's forgiveness is the sweet taste of nectar that fuels a man's soul. Shade felt redeemed, despite the unforgiving heart of Jaime's mother. If only she could make things right for Donna, but her sins were carved in stone. She'd spent five years contemplating her actions on that fateful night. It was the cross she would bear for the rest of her days.

She said her goodbyes to the many women inside who had become sisters in Christ. Tears shrouded her eyes as she considered the broken lives she would leave behind. She gathered her meager belongings from the prisoner release station and walked the long, musty hallway to life on the other side.

A flash of adrenaline fired, as she stepped into the light, surprised by the warmth of the sun's rays against her skin. It was a peculiar euphoric sensation, standing on the righteous side of the towering barbed wire fence. She breathed deeply, filling her lungs with freedom air.

She squinted against the sunlight, searching. She saw him, leaning against his car, arms folded across his chest. His face ignited when their eyes joined. He was the most beautiful man she'd ever laid eyes on. His thick wavy hair flecked with splashes of gray, fan-like lines at the corner of his eyes, a tad more prominent. And those blue eyes. She could drown in them.

His heart danced when he saw her walking toward him. He loved the way she walked, so tall, almost languishing. He took her in.

She fell into his arms, her body disappearing into his, tears washing their faces. They kissed with liberation. The curtain torn in two. Despite his weekly visits, he couldn't hold her. Not like this. It was manna feeding his soul.

"It feels so good to hold you," she sighed, her fingers stroking his back.

He held her face in his hands, drinking her in. "Every time I see you, I fall in love all over again."

"Are we going back to your place?" she asked, as they drove away, their hands clasped between them.

"We're going back to our place."

"Too bad Tyler couldn't make it home. I'm eager to see him."

"Yeah. It's spring training. He tried to get away, but you'll see him soon."

She offered a weak smile. "I'm so thankful he kept in touch every week. And for the times he came to visit."

Brent pulled into the driveway of the cottage.

"What are we doing here?"

"This is our house. I wanted to surprise you. Tyler couldn't get out as much as he wanted, so I bought it."

"Oh, Brent," she said, tears spilling down, as she wrapped her arms around him.

They stood together on the beach, her hand locked in his, her head on his shoulder. "I've missed this place. So many memories here." She took off her shoes, feeling the sand between her toes, as the water lapped at her feet. "It feels good to be home, with you by my side. I've been dreaming of this day for so long."

He took her face and kissed her before leading her up the steps and into the cottage. She strolled from room to room, images resurfacing. The framed needlepoint, the weaver's tapestry, hung on the wall. She stood before it. Mabel's words echoing in her mind. Her tangled life had been woven into a masterpiece by the hand of God. It was too overwhelming to comprehend.

Brent stood beside her, his arm around her shoulder. "Tyler was very specific. The needlepoint was not to be removed. He said it held special meaning for you both."

She smiled, trying to suppress a flood of tears. "Yes, it does. Thank you for keeping it."

He took her in his arms. "I have another surprise for you. We're going to Hawaii. Day after tomorrow. To get married. Like we talked about."

A wide grin spread across her face, her eyes shining like stars against a blackened sky. "Are you serious? Oh, Brent. I'm so excited, but I have nothing to wear."

"Do you need clothes?" he asked. He pulled her into him. "I've missed you so much. All these years of waiting, and now we'll finally be together."

"I love you, Brent. This is the happiest day of my life."

The plane touched down at Kahului Airport in Maui. Brent reserved the penthouse suite at the resort where they had stayed for Sally's wedding. They would marry on the beach tomorrow at sunset.

"Why don't you get dressed and we'll have dinner," said Brent after getting settled in their room. "I reserved a table on the beach."

Shade beamed, as she threw on a sundress and a pair of sandals, compliments of Victoria and Amanda. With her new haircut and a touch of makeup, she felt like a princess.

"You're gorgeous," said Brent, as his eyes drifted over her. "Soon you'll be my wife. I never thought this day would come."

"Where is everyone?" asked Shade, after being escorted to their table. "It looks like we have the whole place to ourselves."

"Oh, here comes a family. I hope they don't spoil our romantic evening."

She turned. Tyler stood with Leah and their new baby. Tyler rushed over and gathered Shade into his arms, clinging to her like a lost treasure. Tears streamed down their faces, as she pulled away, gazing up at him.

"I can't believe you're here," cried Shade.

"You don't think I'd miss the wedding, do you? After all those years of praying, God finally answered. I always knew He would."

Leah wrapped her arm around Shade, leaning into her. "Welcome home. Meet your great-grandson, Brent."

Her eyes glistened, as she took the child in her arms.

A crowd formed around them on the beach. "Hey mister," said a small boy. "Are you Tyler Lane?"

"Yes, I am."

"Oh, wow! You're my favorite baseball pitcher on the whole planet. I can't believe it's you. Can I have your autograph?"

"Sure," said Tyler, smiling, as he signed the young boy's ball. "What's your name, son?"

"Devon."

"Nice to meet you, Devon. Here you go," said Tyler, handing him the ball.

"Sorry, Grandma," said Tyler, turning to Shade. "Oh, look who's here," he said, pointing.

Brent went to her side as she turned. There stood Amanda, Sally and Chad with their two children, Victoria and Roger, Blanche and Harry, Mindy, Kevin, and Hannah, and Pastor Ralph.

Brent whispered in her ear. "They came for our long overdue wedding."

Sally ran toward her, throwing her arms around her. "Shade. I'm so happy to see you."

"Oh, Sally. You look great. Who's minding the shop?"

"Meghan. She's turned out to be the best employee I've ever had. Thanks to you."

"Hey, girlfriend," said Victoria, embracing Shade. "So, is it true? Is there something going on between you and Brent? I hear there's a wedding tomorrow."

"It's so good seeing you," said Shade, laughing. "And thanks for your generosity. I love all the new clothes you and Amanda picked out for me."

"Oh, honey," said Blanche, squeezing in between Victoria and Shade—her white hair peppered with blooms of yellow hibiscus flowers. "So, you finally snagged that handsome man."

Shade embraced Blanche. "It's so good of you to come. I only wish Mary could be here today. But we know she's resting in the arms of her Savior."

Mindy came over and embraced Shade. "Thank you for making my brother's life complete. I haven't seen Brent this content in years."

"Thank you, Mindy," said Shade. "I plan to spend the rest of my life making him happy."

Amanda took both of Shade's hands. "You look beautiful, honey. I'm so happy you're home."

"Me, too, Mom. Me too. We have a lot of catching up to do."

ACKNOWLEDGMENTS

My deepest gratitude to all the early readers who encouraged me on my pilgrimage into unfamiliar territory; Jackie Atchison (a two-time reader), Debi Harmount, my sisters—Karen Hill and Sherry O'Brien, my sister-in-law—Lisa Murrell, Ken Darish, Paula Ford, my 90-year-old mother—Evelyn Cioccio (still going strong), and my incredible husband, Bill Miller, whose undying patience and support kept me sane.

I would also like to thank my Copyeditor, Debra Viguie, for her depth of experience, sense of humor, and insightful guidance. Your suggestion to cut an entire chapter (ouch!) was brilliant advice.

Seeing my book cover come to life was an awe-inspiring experience. Thank you, Emilie Hendryx, for your astute creative vision and for gently steering me down the right path. It was a pleasure working with you.

And finally, a huge debt of gratitude to my brother, Gary Murrell—another two-time reader—who never stopped believing in me. What an endearing sight watching you pull into my driveway each week, balancing an armload of edited pages and two Starbucks coffees. Our time together was precious. I am eternally grateful for your sacrifice.

CPSIA information can be obtained
at www.ICGtesting.com
Printed in the USA
LVHW041804080819
626994LV00006B/753